Stephen King called Jeffery Deaver's
New York Times bestselling crime fiction
**"SCARY, SMART, AND COMPULSIVELY
READABLE."**

Deaver's new Kathryn Dance thriller, *XO*,
is no exception.

"Excellent. . . . Sure to please fans."
—*Publishers Weekly* (starred review)

"Written with Deaver's usual keen eye for dialogue and
character and featuring his customary right-angle plot twists,
the novel will be a sure-fire hit with not only his legion of fans
but also with readers who have yet to sample a Deaver novel."
—*Booklist*

*The world has changed and so has Bond,
James Bond.*

Jeffery Deaver brings superspy 007 into the
twenty-first century with his #1 bestseller

CARTE BLANCHE

Chosen as a Must-Read Summer Book by
Newsweek!

"Brilliantly captures Fleming's style . . . with Deaver's
trademark twists flying."
—*The Washington Post*

"Ian Fleming was a master. . . . Deaver too is a genius and this
publishing marriage was truly made in heaven."
—*The Sunday Express*

"The pairing is as smooth as vodka and vermouth."
—*Parade*

The "grand master of the ticking-clock thriller" (Kathy Reichs) puts special agent Kathryn Dance on a harrowing online manhunt

ROADSIDE CROSSES

Chosen as a Hot Summer Thriller on TheDailyBeast.com!

"Clever and twisted. . . . Don't miss this one."
—*Library Journal*

"The techno-savvy Deaver . . . has one of those puzzle-loving minds you just can't trust."
—Marilyn Stasio, *The New York Times*

"Deaver's got the world of social networking and blogs down cold. . . . That dose of realism adds a fresh, contemporary edge."
—David Montgomery, TheDailyBeast.com

And praise for all of the Lincoln Rhyme novels, "masterpieces of modern criminology" (*Philadelphia Daily News*)

"A thrill ride between covers."
—*Los Angeles Times*

"Devious and heart-stopping."
—*Ottawa Citizen*

"Dazzling."
—*The New York Times*

"Prime Deaver . . . prime entertainment."
—*Publishers Weekly* (starred review)

"Deaver must have been born with a special plot-twist gene."
—*Booklist*

"A mastermind of manipulation."
—*Library Journal*

"High-tension wired. . . . Deaver . . . fills every keystroke with suspense."
—*People*

Books by Jeffery Deaver

XO°°
Carte Blanche
Edge
The Burning Wire°
Best American Mystery Stories 2009 (Editor)
The Watch List (*The Copper Bracelet* and
The Chopin Manuscript) (Contributor)
Roadside Crosses°°
The Bodies Left Behind
The Broken Window°
The Sleeping Doll°°
More Twisted: Collected Stories, Volume Two
The Cold Moon°/°°
The Twelfth Card°
Garden of Beasts
Twisted: Collected Stories
The Vanished Man°
The Stone Monkey°
The Blue Nowhere
The Empty Chair°

°Featuring Lincoln Rhyme and Amelia Sachs
°°Featuring Kathryn Dance

JEFFERY DEAVER

XO

A KATHRYN DANCE NOVEL

Pocket Books

NEW YORK LONDON TORONTO SYDNEY NEW DELHI

Pocket Books
A Division of Simon & Schuster, Inc.
1230 Avenue of the Americas
New York, NY 10020

This Pocket Books export edition January 2013

POCKET and colophon are registered trademarks of Simon & Schuster, Inc.

For information about special discounts for bulk purchases, please contact Simon & Schuster Special Sales at 1-866-506-1949 or business@simonandschuster.com.

The Simon & Schuster Speakers Bureau can bring authors to your live event. For more information or to book an event, contact the Simon & Schuster Speakers Bureau at 1-866-248-3049 or visit our website at www.simonspeakers.com.

Manufactured in the United States of America

10 9 8 7 6 5 4 3 2 1

ISBN 978-1-4767-1755-5
ISBN 978-1-4391-5898-2 (ebook)

Author's Note

The lyrics to all the songs in *Your Shadow*, the country-music album at the heart of this novel, can be found at the back of the book. These tunes are referred to throughout and may just contain some clues about the events that unfold along the way. And if you'd like to listen to the actual title track itself, and other songs from the album, recently recorded in Nashville, go to www.jefferydeaver.com for information on downloads.

To most listeners, the title track, "Your Shadow," is simply a love song.

Some feel differently.

Subject: Re: You're the Best!!!
From: noreply@kayleightownemusic.com
To: EdwinSharp18474@anon.com
2 January 10:32 a.m.

Hey there,
Edwin—

Thanks for your email! I'm so glad you liked
my latest album! Your support means the
world to me. Be sure you go to my website and
sign up to get my newsletter and learn about
new releases and upcoming concerts, and don't
forget to follow me on Facebook and Twitter.

And keep an eye out for the mail. I sent you
that autographed photo you requested!

XO,

Kayleigh

* * *

Subject: Unbelievable!!!!!
From: EdwinSharp26535@anon.com
To: ktowne7788@compserve.com
3 September 5:10 a.m.

Hi, Kayleigh:

I am totally blown away. I'm rendered
speechless. And, you know me pretty good
by now—for me to be speechless, that's
something!! Anyway, here's the story: I

downloaded your new album last night and
listened to "Your Shadow." Whoahhh! It's
without doubt the best song I have ever heard.
I mean of anything ever written. I even like
it better than "It's Going to Be Different This
Time." I've told you nobody's ever expressed
how I feel about loneliness and life and well
everything better than you. And that song does
that totally. But more important I can see what
you're saying, your plea for help. It's all clear
now. Don't worry. You're not alone, Kayleigh!!

I'll be *your* shadow. Forever.

XO, Edwin

                    * * *

Subject: Fwd: Unbelievable!!!!!
From: Samuel.King@CrowellSmithWendall.com
To: EdwinSharp26535@anon.com
3 September 10:34 a.m.

Mr. Sharp:

Ms. Alicia Sessions, personal assistant to
our clients Kayleigh Towne and her father,
Bishop Towne, forwarded us your email of this
morning. You have sent more than 50 emails
and letters since we contacted you two months
ago, urging you not to have any contact with
Ms. Towne or any of her friends and family. We
are extremely troubled that you have found
her private email address (which has been
changed, I should tell you), and are looking
into possible violations of state and federal
laws regarding how you obtained such address.

Once again, we must tell you that we feel
your behavior is completely inappropriate
and possibly actionable. We urge you in the

strongest terms possible to heed this warning. As we've said repeatedly, Ms. Towne's security staff and local law enforcement officials have been notified of your repeated, intrusive attempts to contact her and we are fully prepared to take whatever steps are necessary to put an end to this alarming behavior.

Samuel King, Esq.

Crowell, Smith & Wendall, Attorneys-at-Law

* * *

Subject: See you soon!!!
From: EdwinSharp26535@anon.com
To: KST33486@westerninternet.com
5 September 11:43 p.m.

Hi, Kayleigh—

Got your new email address. I know what they're up to but DON'T worry, it'll be all right.

I'm lying in bed, listening to you right now. I feel like I'm literally *your shadow* . . . And you're mine. You are so wonderful!

I don't know if you had a chance to think about it—you're sooooo busy, I know!—but I'll ask again—if you wanted to send me some of your hair that'd be so cool. I know you haven't cut it for ten years and four months (it's one of those things that makes you so beautiful!!!!) but maybe there's one from your brush. Or better yet your pillow. I'll treasure it forever.

Can't WAIT for the concert next Friday.
C U soon.

Yours forever,

XO, Edwin

Sunday

Chapter 1

THE HEART OF a concert hall is people.

And when the vast space is dim and empty, as this one was at the moment, a venue can bristle with impatience, indifference.

Even hostility.

Okay, rein in that imagination, Kayleigh Towne told herself. Stop acting like a kid. Standing on the wide, scuffed stage of the Fresno Conference Center's main hall, she surveyed the place once more, bringing her typically hypercritical eye to the task of preparing for Friday's concert, considering and reconsidering lighting and stage movements and where the members of the band should stand and sit. Where best to walk out near, though not into, the crowd and touch hands and blow kisses. Where best acoustically to place the foldback speakers—the monitors that were pointed toward the band so they could hear themselves without echoes or distortion. Many performers now used earbuds for this; Kayleigh liked the immediacy of traditional foldbacks.

There were a hundred other details to think about. She believed that every performance should be perfect, *more* than perfect. Every audience deserved the best. One hundred ten percent.

She had, after all, grown up in Bishop Towne's shadow.

An unfortunate choice of word, Kayleigh now reflected.

I'll be your shadow. Forever. . . .

Back to the planning. This show had to be different from the previous one here, about eight months ago. A retooled program was especially important since many of the fans would have regularly attended her hometown concerts and she wanted to make sure they got something unexpected. That was one thing about Kayleigh Towne's music; her audiences weren't as big as some but were loyal as golden retrievers. They knew her lyrics cold, knew her guitar licks, knew her moves onstage and laughed at her shtick before she finished the lines. They lived and breathed her performances, hung on her words, knew her bio and likes and dislikes.

And some wanted to know much more . . .

With that thought, her heart and gut clenched as if she'd stepped into Hensley Lake in January.

Thinking about *him,* of course.

Then she froze, gasping. Yes, someone was watching her from the far end of the hall! Where none of the crew would be.

Shadows were moving.

Or was it her imagination? Or maybe her eyesight? Kayleigh had been given perfect pitch and an angelic voice but God had decided enough was enough and skimped big-time on the vision. She squinted, adjusted her glasses. She was sure that someone was hiding, rocking back and forth in the doorway that led to the storage area for the concession stands.

Then the movement stopped.

She decided it wasn't movement at all and never had been. Just a hint of light, a suggestion of shading.

Though still, she heard a series of troubling clicks

and snaps and groans—from where, she couldn't tell—
and felt a chill of panic bubble up her spine.

Him . . .

The man who had written her hundreds of emails
and letters, intimate, delusional, speaking of the life
they could share together, asking for a strand of hair, a
fingernail clipping. The man who had somehow gotten
near enough at a dozen shows to take close-up pictures
of Kayleigh, without anyone ever seeing him. The man
who had possibly—though it had never been proven—
slipped into the band buses or motor homes on the road
and stolen articles of her clothing, underwear included.

The man who had sent her dozens of pictures of
himself: shaggy hair, fat, in clothing that looked un-
washed. Never obscene but, curiously, the images were
all the more disturbing for their familiarity. They were
the shots a boyfriend would text her from a trip.

Him . . .

Her father had recently hired a personal bodyguard,
a huge man with a round, bullet-shaped head and an occasional curly wire sprouting from his ear to make clear
what his job was. But Darthur Morgan was outside at
the moment, making the rounds and checking cars. His
security plan also included a nice touch: simply being
visible so that potential stalkers would turn around and
leave rather than risk a confrontation with a 250-pound
man who looked like a rapper with an attitude (which,
sure enough, he'd been in his teen years).

She scanned the recesses of the hall again—the best
place *he* might stand and watch her. Then gritting her
teeth in anger at her fear and mostly at her failure to
tame the uneasiness and distraction, she thought, Get.
Back. To. Work.

And what're you worried about? You're not alone.
The band wasn't in town yet—they were finishing some

studio work in Nashville—but Bobby was at the huge Midas XL8 mixing console dominating the control deck in the back of the hall, two hundred feet away. Alicia was getting the rehearsal rooms in order. A couple of the beefy guys in Bobby's road crew were unpacking the truck in the back, assembling and organizing the hundreds of cases and tools and props and plywood sheets and stands and wires and amps and instruments and computers and tuners—the tons of gear that even modest touring bands like Kayleigh's needed.

She supposed one of them could get to her in a hurry if the source of the shadow had been *him.*

Dammit, quit making *him* more than *he* is! *Him, him, him,* like you're even afraid to say his name. As if to utter it would conjure up his presence.

She'd had other obsessed fans, plenty of them— what gorgeous singer-songwriter with a voice from heaven wouldn't collect a few inappropriate admirers? She'd had twelve marriage proposals from men she'd never met, three from women. A dozen couples wanted to adopt her, thirty or so teen girls wanted to be her best friend, a thousand men wanted to buy her a drink or dinner at Bob Evans or the Mandarin Oriental . . . and there'd been plenty of invitations to enjoy a wedding night without the inconvenience of a wedding. *Hey Kayleigh think on it cause Ill show you a good time better than you ever had and by the by heres a picture of what you can expect yah its really me not bad huh???*

(Very stupid idea to send a picture like that to a seventeen-year-old, Kayleigh's age at the time. By the by.)

Usually she was cautiously amused by the attention. But not always and definitely not now. Kayleigh found herself snagging her denim jacket from a nearby chair and pulling it on to cover her T-shirt, providing another barrier to any prying eyes. This, despite the characteristic September heat in Fresno, which filled the murky venue like thin stew.

And more of those clicks and taps from nowhere.

"Kayleigh?"

She turned quickly, trying to hide her slight jump, even though she recognized the voice.

A solidly built woman of around thirty paused halfway across the stage. She had cropped red hair and some subdued inking on arms, shoulders and spine, partly visible thanks to her trim tank top and tight, hip-hugging black jeans. Fancy cowboy boots. "Didn't mean to scare you. You okay?"

"You didn't. What's up?" she asked Alicia Sessions.

A nod toward the iPad she carried. "These just came in. Proofs for the new posters? If we get them to the printer today we'll definitely have them by the show. They look okay to you?"

Kayleigh bent over the screen and examined them. Music nowadays is only partly about music, of course. Probably always has been, she supposed, but it seemed that as her popularity had grown, the business side of her career took up a lot more time than it used to. She didn't have much interest in these matters but she generally didn't need to. Her father was her manager, Alicia handled the day-to-day paperwork and scheduling, the lawyers read the contracts, the record company made arrangements with the recording studios and the CD production companies and the retail and download outlets; her longtime producer and friend at BHRC Records, Barry Zeigler, handled the technical side of arranging and production, and Bobby and the crew set up and ran the shows.

All so that Kayleigh Towne could do what she did best: write songs and sing them.

Still, one business matter of interest to her was making sure fans—many of them young or without much money—could buy cheap but decent memorabilia to make the night of the concert that much more special. Posters like this one, T-shirts, key chains, bracelets, charms, guitar chord books, headbands, backpacks . . . and mugs, for the moms and dads driving the youngsters to and from the shows and, of course, often buying the tickets, as well.

She studied the proofs. The image was of Kayleigh and her favorite Martin guitar—not a big dreadnought-size but a smaller, 000-18, ancient, with a crisp yellowing spruce top and a voice of its own. The photo was the inside picture from her latest album, *Your Shadow.*

Him . . .

No, don't.

Eyes scanning the doors again.

"You sure you're okay?" Alicia asked, voice buzzing with a faint Texas twang.

"Yeah." Kayleigh returned to the poster proofs, which all featured the same photo though with different type, messages and background. Her picture was a straight-on shot, depicting her much as she saw herself: at five-two, shorter than she would have liked, her face a bit long, but with stunning blue eyes, lashes that wouldn't quit and lips that had some reporters talking collagen. As *if* . . . Her trademark golden hair, four feet long—and no, not cut, only trimmed, in ten years and four months—flowed in the fake gentle breeze from the photographer's electric fan. Designer jeans and high-collared dark-red blouse. A small diamond crucifix.

"You gotta give the fans the package," Bishop Towne always said. "That's *visual* too, I'm talking. And the standards're different 'tween men and women. You get into trouble, you deny it." He meant that in the country music world a man could get away with a look like

Bishop's own: jutting belly, cigarette, a lined, craggy face riddled with stubble, wrinkled shirt, scuffed boots and faded jeans. A woman singer, he lectured—though he really intended to say "girl"—had to be put together for date night. And in Kayleigh's case that meant a church social, of course: the good girl next door was the image on which she'd built her career. Sure, the jeans could be a little tight, the blouses and sweaters could closely hug her round chest, but the necklines were high. The makeup was subtle and leaned toward pinks.

"Go with them."

"Great." Alicia shut off the device. A slight pause. "I haven't gotten your father's okay yet."

"They're good," the singer reassured her, nodding at the iPad.

"Sure. I'll just run it by him. You know."

Now Kayleigh paused. Then: "Okay."

"Acoustics good here?" asked Alicia, who had been a performer herself; she had quite a voice and a love of music, which was undoubtedly why she'd taken a job for someone like Kayleigh Towne, when the efficient, no-nonsense woman could have earned twice as much as a personal assistant for a corporate executive. She'd signed on last spring and had never heard the band perform here.

"Oh, the sound is great," Kayleigh said enthusiastically, glancing at the ugly concrete walls. "You wouldn't think it." She explained how the designers of the venue, back in the 1960s, had done their homework; too many concert halls—even sophisticated ones intended for classical music—had been built by people without confidence in the natural ability of musical instruments and voices to reach the farthest seats with "direct volume," that is, the sound emanating from the stage. Architects would add angular surfaces and free-standing shapes to boost the volume of the music, which did that but also sent the vibrations in a hundred different directions. This resulted in every performer's acoustic nightmare, reverberation: in effect, echoes upon echoes that yielded muddy, sometimes even off-key, sounds.

Here, in modest Fresno, Kayleigh explained to Alicia, as her father had to her, the designers had trusted in the power and purity of the voice and drum skin and sounding board and reed and string. She was about to ask the assistant to join her in a chorus of one of her songs to prove her point—Alicia did great harmonies—when she noticed her looking toward the back of the hall. She assumed the woman was bored with the scientific discussion. But the frowning gaze suggested something else was on her mind.

"What?" Kayleigh asked.

"Isn't it just us and Bobby?"

"What do you mean?"

"I thought I saw somebody." She lifted a finger tipped in a black-painted nail. "That doorway. There."

Just where Kayleigh herself had thought she'd seen the shadow ten minutes before.

Palms sweating, absently touching her phone, Kayleigh stared at the changing shapes in the back of the hall.

Yes . . . no. She just couldn't tell.

Then shrugging her broad shoulders, one of them sporting a tattoo of a snake in red and green, Alicia said, "Hm. Guess not. Whatever it was it's gone now. . . . Okay, see you later. The restaurant at one?"

"Yeah, sure."

Kayleigh listened absently to the thumping of boots as she left and continued to stare at the black doorways.

Angrily, she suddenly whispered, "Edwin Sharp."

There I've said *his* name.

"Edwin, Edwin, Edwin."

Now that I've conjured you up, listen here: Get the hell out of my concert hall! I've got work to do.

And she turned away from the shadowy, gaping doorway from which, of course, no one was leering at her at all. She stepped to center stage, looking over the masking tape on the dusty wood, blocking out where she would stand at different points during the concert.

It was then that she heard a man's voice crying from the back of the hall, "Kayleigh!" It was Bobby, now rising from behind the mixing console, knocking his chair over and ripping off his hard-shell earphones. He waved to her with one hand and pointed to a spot over her head with another. "Look out! . . . No, Kayleigh!"

She glanced up fast and saw one of the strip lights— a seven-foot Colortran unit—falling free of its mounting and swinging toward the stage by its thick electric cable.

Stepping back instinctively, she tripped over a guitar stand she hadn't remembered was behind her.

Tumbling, arms flailing, gasping . . .

The young woman hit the stage hard, on her tail-bone. The massive light plummeted toward her, a deadly pendulum, growing bigger and bigger. She tried desperately to rise but fell back, blinded as the searing beams from the thousand-watt bulbs turned her way.

Then everything went black.

Chapter 2

KATHRYN DANCE HAD several lives.

Widowed mother of two children approaching their teen years.

Agent with the California Bureau of Investigation, her specialty interrogation and kinesics—body language analysis.

Dutiful, if sometimes irreverent and exasperated, daughter to parents who lived nearby.

That was the order in which she placed these aspects of her life.

Then there was number four, which was nearly as vital to her psychic well-being as the first three: music. Like Alan Lomax in the middle of the last century, Dance was a folklorist, a song catcher. Occasionally she'd take time off, climb into her SUV, sometimes with kids and dogs, sometimes, like now, solo, and go in search of music, the way hunters take to the fields for deer or turkey.

Dance was now piloting her Pathfinder along Highway 152 from the Monterey Peninsula through a largely barren stretch of California to Fresno in the San Joaquin Valley, three hours away. This was the agricultural heart of the country and open double-trailer trucks, piled high with garlic, tomatoes, and other fruits and vegetables, rolled endlessly toward the massive food-processing plants in the hazy distance. The working fields were verdant or, if harvested already, rich black, but everything else was dry and dun as forgotten toast.

Dust swirled in the Nissan's wake and insects died splatty deaths on the windshield.

Dance's mission over the next few days was to record the homemade tunes of a local group of Mexican musicians, all of whom lived in or near Fresno. Most of them picked in the fields so they'd adopted the name Los Trabajadores, the Workers. Dance would record them on her digital TASCAM HD-P2, a bit more expensive than she could afford but superb, then edit and post the songs on her website, "American Tunes."

People could download them for a small fee, of which she would send most to the musicians, and would keep enough to cover the cost of the site and to take herself and the kids out to dinner occasionally. No one got rich from the downloads but some of the groups that she and her business partner in the venture, Martine Christensen, had discovered had come to regional and even national attention.

She'd just come off a tough case in Monterey, the CBI office she was assigned to, and decided to take some time off. The children were at their music and sports camps, spending the nights with their grandparents. Dance was free to roam Fresno, Yosemite, and environs, record Los Trabajadores and look for other talent in this musically rich area. Not only Latino but a unique strain of country could be found here (there's a reason, of course, the genre is often called country-*western*). In fact the Bakersfield sound, originating in that city a few hours south of Fresno, had been a major country music movement; it had arisen in reaction to what some people thought was the overly slick productions of Nashville in the fifties. Performers like Buck Owens and Merle Haggard began the movement and it had enjoyed a recent resurgence, in the music of such artists as Dwight Yoakam and Gary Allan.

Dance sipped a Sprite and juggled radio stations. She'd considered making this trip a romantic getaway and inviting Jon Boling to come with her. But he'd just gotten a consulting assignment for a computer start-up and would be tied up for several days. And for some reason, Dance had decided she preferred to make the trip solo. The kidnapping case she'd just closed had been tough; two days ago she'd attended the funeral of the one victim they couldn't save, in the company of the two they had.

She turned up the AC. This time of year the Monterey Peninsula was comfortable, even chilly occasionally, and she'd dressed according to her port of embarkation. In a long-sleeved gray cotton shirt and blue jeans, she was hot. She slipped off her pink-rimmed glasses and wiped them on a napkin, steering with her knees. Somehow sweat had managed to crawl down one lens. The Pathfinder's thermometer reported 96 degrees outside.

September. Right.

Dance was looking forward to the trip for another reason—to see her only celebrity friend, Kayleigh Towne, the now famous singer-songwriter. Kayleigh had been a longtime supporter of Dance's website and the indigenous musicians she and Martine championed. The singer had invited Dance to her big concert Friday night in Fresno. Though a dozen years younger than Dance, Kayleigh had been a performer since she was nine or ten years old and a pro since her late teens. Funny, sophisticated and one hell of a writer and entertainer, with no ego whatsoever, the woman was mature beyond her years, and Dance enjoyed her company very much.

She was also the daughter of country music legend Bishop Towne.

On the two or three occasions when Dance had come to Kayleigh's performances, or visited her in Fresno, bearlike Bishop had lumbered into the room with his thousand-pound ego and the intensity of somebody as addicted to recovery as he had been to cocaine and liquor. He'd rambled on about people in the Industry—spoken with an inflected capital *I*: musicians he knew intimately (hundreds), musicians he'd learned from (only the greats), musicians he'd mentored (most of the present-day superstars) and musicians he'd gotten into fistfights with (plenty of those too).

He was brash, crude and overtly theatrical; Dance had been enthralled.

On the other hand, his latest album had tanked. His voice had deserted him, his energy too, and those were two things that even the most sophisticated digital massaging in the studio can't do much about. And nothing could rescue the trite songwriting, so different from the brilliant words and tunes that had made him a hit years ago.

Still, he had his faithful entourage and he was in bold control of Kayleigh's career; woe to any producer or record company or music venue that didn't treat her right.

Dance now entered Fresno proper. Salinas Valley, one hundred miles to the west, was known as the nation's Lettuce Bowl. But the San Joaquin was bigger and produced more and Fresno was its heart. The place was a nondescript working town of about a half million. It had some gang activity and the same domestic, robbery, homicide and even terrorist threats that you saw in every small urban area nowadays, with the rate a bit higher than the national average for all crimes. That inflation, she surmised, was a reflection of unemployment—hovering here around 18 percent. She noticed a number of young men, living evidence of this statistic, hanging out on hazy street corners. Dressed in sleeveless T-shirts and baggy shorts or jeans, they watched her and other cars pass by or talked and laughed and drank from bottles swathed in paper bags.

Dust and heat waves rose from baking surfaces. Dogs sat on porches and gazed through her car at distant nothingness and she caught glimpses of children in backyards jumping happily over trickling sprinklers, a questionable if not illegal activity in perpetually drought-plagued California.

The satellite got her easily to the Mountain View Motel off Highway 41. It had no such vista, though that might be due to the haze. At best, she deduced, squinting east and north, were some timid foothills that would eventually lead to majestic Yosemite.

Stepping into the brittle heat, Dance actually felt light-headed. Breakfast with the kids and dogs had been a long time ago.

The hotel room wasn't ready yet but that didn't matter, since she was meeting Kayleigh and some friends in a half hour, at one. She checked her bags with the front desk and jumped back into the Pathfinder, which was already the temperature of a hotplate.

She punched another address into the GPS and dutifully headed where directed, wondering why most of the programmed voices in sat-nav were women's.

At a stoplight she picked up her phone and glanced at the incoming call and text list.

Empty.

Good that no one at the office or the children's camps had contacted her.

But odd that there was nothing from Kayleigh, who was going to call that morning to confirm their get-together. And one thing about the performer that had always impressed Dance: despite her fame, she never neglected the little things. In fact, in life, and performances, she seemed to be utterly responsible.

Another call to Kayleigh.

Straight to voicemail.

KATHRYN DANCE HAD to laugh.

The owners of the Cowboy Saloon had a sense of humor. The dark, woody place, giddily cool, had not a single cowboy artifact. But life in the saddle was well represented—by the *women* who rode the range, roped, branded and punched cattle . . . and did some fancy six-gun work, if you could believe the poster showing an Old West version of Rosie the Riveter shooting bottles off a fence rail.

According to the movie art, blown-up book jackets, lunch boxes, toys, paintings and photos, the era must have been saturated with flip-haired, excessively busty gals in five-gallon hats, cute neckerchiefs, suede skirts and embroidered blouses, as well as some of the finest boots ever made. Kathryn Dance loved footwear and owned two pairs of elaborately tooled Noconas. But neither came close to the ones worn by Dale Evans, Roy Rogers's partner, from the 1950s TV show, on impressive display in a faded poster.

At the bar she ordered an iced tea, drank it down fast and got another, then sat at one of the round tables, overvarnished and nicked, looking at the clientele. Two elderly couples; a trio of tired, jumpsuited utility workers, who'd probably been on the job at dawn; a slim young man in jeans and plaid shirt, studying the old-fashioned jukebox; several businessmen in white shirts and dark ties, minus jackets.

She was looking forward to seeing Kayleigh, to recording the songs of the Workers; looking forward to lunch too. She was starving.

And concerned.

It was now one-twenty. Where was her friend?

Music from the jukebox filled the place. Dance gave a faint laugh. It was a Kayleigh Towne song—a particularly good choice too, considering this venue: "Me, I'm Not a Cowgirl."

The song was about a suburban soccer mom, who seems to live a life very different from that of a cowgirl but in the end realizes that maybe she's one in spirit. Typical of Kayleigh's songs, it was lighthearted and yet spoke meaningfully to people.

It was then that the front door opened and a slab of powerful sunlight fell onto the scuffed linoleum floor, on which danced geometric shapes, the shadows of the people entering.

Dance rose. "Kayleigh!"

Surrounded by four others, the young singer stepped into the restaurant, smiling but also looking around quickly. She was troubled, Dance noted immediately. No, more than that, Kayleigh Towne was scared.

But whatever she'd been concerned about finding here was absent and she relaxed, then stepped forward, hugging Dance firmly. "Kathryn, hey. This is so great!"

"I couldn't wait to get here."

The singer was in jeans and, oddly, a thick denim jacket, despite the heat. Her lovely hair flowed free, nearly as long as she was tall.

Dance added, "I called a couple of times."

"There was . . . well, there was a little problem at the concert hall. It's all right. Hey, everybody, this's my bud, Kathryn Dance."

Dance greeted Bobby Prescott, whom she'd met a few years ago: thirtyish, an actor's looks belied by a shy smile, curly brown hair. There was also pudgy and terminally shy Tye Slocum, with long reddish hair in need of

a trim. He was the band's guitar technician and repair-
man. Unsmiling, athletic Alicia Sessions, who looked
to Dance like she belonged in a downtown Manhattan
punk-rock club, was Kayleigh's personal assistant.

And someone else was in the entourage. An African-
American man, over six feet tall, well into the 250-pound
range.

Security.

The fact that Kayleigh had a bodyguard wasn't surprising, though Dance was troubled to note that he was
intently on the job, even here. He carefully examined
everyone in the bar—the young man at the jukebox, the
workers, the businessmen and even the elderly couples
and the bartender, clearly running their faces through a
mental database of potential threats.

What had prompted this?

Whatever threat he was here to guard against wasn't
present and he turned his attention back to Kayleigh.
He didn't relax, though. People like him never did—
that's what made them so good. He went into a waiting
state. "Looks okay to me."

His name was Darthur Morgan and when he shook
Dance's hand he examined her closely and his eyes gave
a flicker of recognition. Dance, as an expert in kinesics
and body language, knew that she gave off "cop" vibrations, even when not intending to.

"Join us for lunch," Kayleigh said to the big man.

"No, thank you, ma'am. I'll be outside."

"No, it's too hot."

"Better there."

"Well, get an iced tea or soda. And come in if you
need to."

But without ordering a beverage, he steamed slowly
through the dim restaurant and, with one glance at a
wax museum cowgirl twirling a lasso, stepped outside.

The skinny bartender came around, carrying menus and a fierce admiration for Kayleigh Towne, who smiled at the young man in a maternal way, though they were about the same age.

Kayleigh glanced at the jukebox, embarrassed that it was her voice serenading them.

"So," Dance asked, "what happened?"

"Okay, I'll tell you." She explained that as she was doing some prep work for the Friday-night concert a strip light—one of the long ones above the stage—came loose and fell.

"My God. You're all right?"

"Yeah, fine. Aside from a sore butt."

Bobby, sitting next to Kayleigh, gripped her arm. He looked at her protectively. "I don't know how it happened," he said in a low voice. "I mean, it was a strip light, a cyc light. You don't mount or dismount it for a show. It was there permanently."

Eyes avoiding everyone's, big Tye Slocum offered, "And you checked it, Bobby. I saw you. Twice. All the lights. Bobby's the best roadie around. Never had an accident like that before."

"If it'd hit her," Alicia said, anger in her voice, "man, that would have been it. It could've killed her."

Bobby added, "It's a thousand watts. Could also've set the whole place on fire, if the lamps had shattered. I cut the main power switch in case they did. I'm going to check it out better when I'm back tonight. I've got to go to Bakersfield and pick up a new amplifier and speaker bank."

Then the incident was tucked away and they ordered lunch. Dance was in fighting trim after the two-week-long kidnapping case—she'd shed nine pounds—and decided to splurge with an order of fries with her grilled chicken sandwich. Kayleigh and Tye ordered salads. Alicia and Bobby had tostadas and opted for coffee, despite the heat. The conversation turned to Dance's musical website and she talked a bit about her own failed attempts at being a singer in San Francisco.

"Kathryn has a great voice," Kayleigh said, displaying five or six kinesic deception clues. Dance smiled.

A man's voice interrupted. "Excuse me, folks. Hey, there, Kayleigh."

It was the young man from the jukebox. Smiling, he nodded at Dance and the table and then looked down at Kayleigh.

"Hello." The singer's tone had gone suddenly into a different mode, bright but guarded.

"Didn't mean to be eavesdropping. I heard there was some problem. You all right?"

"Just fine, thanks."

Silence for a moment, the sort that means, Appreciate your interest but you can head off now.

Kayleigh said, "You're a fan?"

"Sure am."

"Well, thanks for your support. And your concern. You going to the concert on Friday?"

"Oh, you bet. I'll be there. Wouldn't miss it for the world. You sure you're okay?"

A pause, bordering on the awkward. Maybe Kayleigh was digesting the last sentence.

"Sure am."

Bobby said, "Okay, friend. You take care now. We're going to get back to lunch."

As if the roadie hadn't even spoken, the man said with a breathy laugh, "You don't recognize me, do you?"

"Sorry," the singer offered.

Alicia said firmly, "Ms. Towne'd like some privacy, you don't mind."

"Hey, Alicia," the young man said to her.

The personal assistant blinked. Obviously she hadn't recognized the man and would be wondering how he knew her name.

Then he ignored her too and laughed again, his voice high, eerie. "It's me, Kayleigh! Edwin Sharp. Your shadow."

Chapter 3

A LOUD BANG echoed in the restaurant as Kayleigh's iced tea glass slipped from her grip and slammed into the floor.

The big glass landed at just the right angle to produce a sound so like a gunshot that Dance found her hand moving to the place where her Glock pistol—presently locked away in her bedside safe at home—normally rested.

Eyes wide, breath rasping in and out of her lungs, Kayleigh said, "You're . . . you're . . . Edwin."

Her reaction was one approaching panic but, with a brow furrowed in sympathy, the man said, "Hey, there, Kayleigh, it's okay. Don't you worry."

"But . . ." Her eyes were zipping to the door, on the other side of which was Darthur Morgan and, if Dance was right, his own pistol.

Dance tried to piece it together. Couldn't be a former boyfriend; she'd have recognized him earlier. Must be an inappropriate fan. Kayleigh was just the sort of performer—beautiful, single, talented—to have stalker problems.

"No embarrassment you didn't recognize me," Edwin said, bizarrely reassuring her and oblivious to her distress. "Since I sent you that last picture of me I lost a bit of weight. Yep, seventy-three pounds." He tapped his belly. "I didn't write you about it. Wanted it to be a surprise. I read *Country Week* and *EW,* see the pictures of you with some of those boys. I know you like the slimmer builds. Didn't think you'd appreciate a chubby. And got myself a twenty-five-dollar haircut. You know how men are always talking about changing but they never do. Like your song. I wasn't going to give you a Mr. Tomorrow. I'm a Mr. Today."

Kayleigh was speechless. Nearly hyperventilating.

From some angles Edwin would be good-looking: full head of black hair trimmed conservatively like a politician's and sprayed firmly into place, keen, deep brown eyes, smooth complexion, if a bit pale. But that face was also very long, angular, with heavy, protruding eyebrows, like soot. He was trim, yes, but big—larger than she'd noticed at first, easily six-two or -three, and despite the weight loss he was probably two hundred pounds. His rangy arms were long, and his hands massive but curiously—and unsettlingly—pink.

Instantly Bobby Prescott was on his feet and stepping in front of the man. Bobby was large too but wide, not tall, and Edwin towered over him. "Hey," Edwin said cheerfully, "Bobby. The roadie. Excuse me, chief of the road crew."

And then his eyes returned to Kayleigh, staring at her adoringly. "I'd be honored if you'd have some iced tea with me. Just over there in the corner. I've got a few things to show you."

"How did you—"

"Know you'd be here? Hell, everybody knows that this is your favorite place. Just look at the blogs. It's where you wrote 'Me, I'm Not a Cowgirl.'" He nodded at the jukebox, from which that very song was playing—now for the second time, Dance noted.

The suburbs and the cities, that's what I'm about.
Me, I'm not a cowgirl, unless maybe you count:
Looking people in the eye and talking to them
*   straight.*
Not putting up with bigots or cheaters or with hate.
Remembering everything my mom and daddy said
About how to treat my family, my country and my
*   friends.*
Didn't think I was a cowgirl, but I guess that all
*   depends.*

"Love that song," he gushed. "Just *love* it. Well, you know that. I told you must be a hundred times."

"I really . . ." Kayleigh was a deer in the middle of the road.

Bobby put his hand on Edwin's shoulder. Not quite hostile, not quite friendly. Dance wondered if this would be the start of a fight and she reached for the only weapon she had—her mobile—to dial 911 if need be. But Edwin simply stepped back a few inches, ignoring Bobby. "Come on, let's get that iced tea. I know you think theirs here is the best in town. I'll treat. Mr. Today, remember? Hey, your hair's really beautiful. Ten years, four months."

Dance had no idea what that meant but the comment clearly upset Kayleigh even more. Her jaw trembled.

"Kayleigh'd like to be left alone," Alicia said firmly. The woman seemed to be just as strong as Bobby Prescott and her glare was more fierce.

"You enjoying working for the band, Alicia?" he asked her as if making conversation at a cocktail party. "You've been with 'em about, what? Five, six months, right? You're talented too. I've seen you on YouTube. You surely can sing. Wow."

Alicia leaned forward ominously. "What the hell is this? How do you know me?"

"Listen, friend," Bobby said. "Time for you to leave."

Then Tye Slocum slowly pushed back in his chair and strode to the door. Edwin's eyes followed and on his face was welded the same smile that had been there from the moment he'd stepped to the table. But something had changed; it was as if he actually expected Kayleigh to join him for tea and was perplexed she wasn't. Tye's mission to summon the security guard seemed to irritate him. "Kayleigh. Please. I didn't want to bother you here but you never got back to me on email. I just want to visit for a bit. We've got a lot to talk about."

"I really can't."

Bobby took Edwin's arm once more before Dance could intervene. But again the man simply stood back. He didn't seem to have any interest in a confrontation, much less a physical fight.

There was a blinding flash and the table was immersed in light as the door opened, then the illumination was blocked. Removing his aviator shades, Darthur Morgan moved in fast. He looked at Edwin's face and Dance could see the muscles around his mouth tighten, a sign of displeasure at himself for missing the slimmed-down stalker.

"You're Edwin Sharp?"

"That's right, Mr. Morgan."

It wasn't hard to get information about people nowadays, especially those connected with a very public person like Kayleigh Towne. But learning the name of her security guard?

"I'm going to ask you to leave Ms. Towne alone now. She wants you to leave. You're becoming a security threat."

"Well, under *Giles versus Lohan,* I'm really not, Mr.

Morgan. There's not even an implied threat. Anyway, the last thing that I want is to hurt or threaten anybody. I'm just here offering my friend some sympathy over something that happened to her, something traumatic. And seeing if she'd like some tea. Happy to buy you some too."

"I think that's about it now," Morgan said in a low, insistent baritone.

Edwin continued calmly, "You're private, of course. You can make a citizen's arrest but only if you see me committing a crime. And I haven't done that. You were a police officer, that'd be different, but you're—"

Well, it's come to that, Dance thought. Guess I knew it would. And she rose, displaying her CBI identification card.

"Ah." Edwin stared for what seemed to be an inordinately long time as if memorizing it. "Had a feeling you were law."

"Could I see some ID?"

"You bet." He handed over his driver's license, issued by Washington state. Edwin Stanton Sharp. Address in Seattle. The picture was of somebody who was indeed much heavier and with long, stringy hair.

"Where are you staying in Fresno?" Dance asked.

"A house by Woodward Park. One of those new developments. It's not bad." A smile. "Sure gets hot in Fresno."

"You moved here?" Alicia asked in a surprised whisper.

Kayleigh's eyes widened at this and her shoulders rose.

"Nope, just renting. For the time being. I'm in town for the concert. It's going to be the best of the year. I can't wait."

Why would he rent a house to attend a single concert?

"No, you wanted to stalk Kayleigh," Bobby blurted. "The lawyers warned you about that."

Lawyers? Dance wondered.

Edwin looked around the table. The smile dimmed. "I think all of you . . . how you're acting is upsetting Kayleigh." He said to her, "I'm sorry about that. I know what you're up against. But don't worry, it'll all work out." He walked to the door, paused and turned back. "And good-bye to you too, Agent Dance. God bless you for the sacrifices you make for the people of this state."

Chapter 4

WHEN DANCE SAID, "Tell me," they did. All of them.

At once.

And only after she reined in the intersecting narratives did she begin to grasp the whole picture. Last winter a fan had become convinced that Kayleigh's automated form letters and emails, signed "XO, Kayleigh," hugs and kisses, were to be taken personally. Because the songs had meant so much to him, perfectly expressing how he felt about life, he'd told himself that they were soul mates. He began a barrage of correspondence—email, Facebook and Twitter posts, handwritten letters—and he'd sent her presents.

Advised to ignore him, Kayleigh and her assistants stopped responding, except to send back any gifts, unopened, but Edwin Sharp nonetheless persisted, apparently believing that her father and handlers felt threatened by the connection between him and Kayleigh and wanted to keep them apart.

He was told to stop, dozens of times. The law firm representing Kayleigh and her father threatened him with civil action and referral to the police if he didn't cease and desist.

But he hadn't.

"It's been so creepy," Kayleigh now said, her voice breaking. She took a sip of tea from a new glass the bartender had brought her when he'd come to mop up the spill. "He'd want a strand of hair, a fingernail clipping, a piece of paper I'd kissed, with my lipstick on it. He'd take pictures of me in places where I'd never seen him. Backstage or in parking lots."

Dance said, "That's the thing about a crime like this. You never quite know where the stalker is. Maybe miles away. Maybe outside your window."

Kayleigh continued, "And the mail! Hundreds of letters and email messages. I'd change my email address and a few hours later he'd have the new one."

"Do you think he had anything to do with the light that fell?" Dance asked.

Kayleigh said she thought she'd seen some "weird" things that morning at the convention center, maybe shadows moving, maybe not. She hadn't seen an actual person.

Alicia Sessions was more certain. "I saw something too, I'm sure." She shrugged her broad shoulders, offering hints of tattoos largely hidden under the cloth. "Nothing specific, though. No face or body."

The band wasn't in town yet and the rest of the crew had been outside when they thought they'd seen the shadowy figure. Bobby hadn't seen anything other than the strip light starting to fall.

Dance asked, "Do the local deputies know about him?"

The singer answered, "Oh, yeah, they do. They knew he was planning to come to the concert on Friday—even though the lawyers threatened to get a restraining order. They didn't really think he'd done anything bad enough for us to get one, though. But the sheriff was going to keep an eye on him if he showed up. Make sure he knew they were watching him."

"I'll call the sheriff's office," Alicia said, "and tell them he's here. And where he's staying." She gave a surprised laugh. "He sure didn't hide it."

Kayleigh looked around, troubled. "This used to be

my favorite restaurant in town. Now, it's all spoiled. . . .
I'm not hungry anymore. I'd like to leave. I'm sorry."

She waved for and settled up the check.

"Hold on a second." Bobby walked to the front door
and opened it a crack. He spoke to Darthur Morgan.
The roadie returned to the table. "He's gone. Darthur
saw him get in his car and drive off."

"Let's go out the back, just the same," Alicia suggested. Tye asked Morgan to drive around to that lot
and Dance accompanied the small entourage through
a beer-pungent storeroom, past a grim toilet. They
stepped into a parking lot of bleached weeds and dusty
cars and crumbling asphalt.

Dance noticed Kayleigh glance to her right and
gasp. She followed the singer's gaze.

Twenty feet away a car was parked in the lot behind
the restaurant. It was a huge old model, dull red. Sitting in the driver's seat was Edwin Sharp. Through the
open window, he called, "Hey, Kayleigh! Check out my
wheels! It's not a Cadillac, just a Buick. Like it?" He
didn't seem to expect an answer. He added, "Don't worry, I'll never put my car ahead of you!"

"My Red Cadillac" was one of Kayleigh's smash hits.
It was about a girl who loves her old car . . . and dumps
any man who doesn't care for the big, battered vehicle.

Bobby Prescott stormed forward and raged, "Get
the fuck out of here, you son of a bitch! And don't even
think about following us to find out where Kayleigh
lives. You try that and I'm calling the cops."

Edwin nodded, smiling, and drove off.

With the sun's glare and the unsure kinesics of
someone she'd just met, Dance couldn't be certain but
her impression was that the stalker's face had registered
a hint of confusion when Bobby spoke—as if of *course*
he knew where Kayleigh lived. Why wouldn't he?

Chapter 5

NO SURPRISE, CALIFORNIA has always been home to Latino music, some Salvadoran, Honduran and Nicaraguan, but the bulk of the sounds are *mexicana:* traditional mariachi, *banda,* ranchera, *norteño* and *sones.* Plenty of pop and rock too and even South of the Border's own brand of ska and hip-hop.

These sounds flowed from the many Spanish-language stations up and down the Central Valley into the homes, businesses and fields here, taking up half the airwaves—the rest of the bandwidth split between Anglo music and check-seeking religious stations spouting incoherent theology.

It was close to 9:00 P.M. and Dance was now getting a firsthand taste of this musical sound in the sweltering garage of Jose Villalobos, on the outskirts of Fresno. The family's two Toyotas had been banished from the small, detached structure, which was usually a rehearsal hall. Tonight, though, it was a recording studio. The six musicians of Los Trabajadores were just finishing up the last number for Dance's digital recorder. The men, ranging in age from twenty-five to sixty, had been playing together for some years, both traditional Mexican folk music and their own material.

The recording had gone well, though the men hadn't been too focused at first—largely because of whom Dance had brought with her: Kayleigh Towne, hair looped in an elaborately braided bun atop her head, in faded jeans, T-shirt and denim vest.

The musicians had been awed and two had scurried into the house to return with wives and children for autographs. One of the women had tearfully said, "You know, your song 'Leaving Home'—we all love it. God bless you for writing it."

This was a ballad about an older woman who's packing up her belongings and leaving the house where she and her husband raised their children. The listener wonders if she's just become a widow or if the house has been foreclosed on by the bank.

> Now I'm starting over, starting over once again,
> To try to make a new life, without family or friends.
> In all my years on earth, there's one thing that I
>   know:
> Nothing can be harder than to leave behind your
>   home.

Only at the end is it revealed that she's undocumented and is being deported, though she's spent her whole life in the United States. Just after the woman is dropped off alone at a bus station in Mexico, she sings the coda: "America the Beautiful" in Spanish. It was Kayleigh's most controversial song, earning her the anger of those taking a hard line on immigration reform. But it was also hugely popular and had become an anthem among Latino workers and those preaching a more open border policy.

As they were packing up, Dance explained how the songs would be uploaded onto her and Martine's website. She couldn't guarantee what might happen but given that the band was so good they'd probably sell a fair number of downloads. And it was possible, with the growth of Latino radio throughout the United States and independent record labels specializing in that sound, that they might draw some producers' or ad agencies' attention.

Curiously, becoming successful didn't interest them in the least. Oh, they wouldn't mind making some money with their music but with the downloads only. Villalobos said, "Yeah, we don't want that kind of life—on the road. We won't travel. We have jobs, families, *bebés.* Jesus has twins—he got to go change diapers now." A glance toward the grinning, handsome young man who was packing away his old battered Gibson Hummingbird guitar.

They said good-bye and Dance and Kayleigh climbed into her dark green Suburban. Dance had left her Pathfinder at the Mountain View and had ridden here with Kayleigh in her SUV. Darthur Morgan began the drive back to Dance's motel. He'd stayed out in the SUV to keep an eye on the street. Six or seven small hardcover books, leather bound, were in the front seat. The titles were stamped in gold, on the spine only. Classics, Dance guessed. He didn't seem to read them when he was on guard duty itself. Maybe they were his pleasure when he was in his room at night. A portal to take him away from the persistence of threat.

Kayleigh was looking out the window at the dimly lit or black landscape. "I envy them," she said.

"How's that?"

"It's like a lot of the musicians on your website. They play at night and on weekends for their friends and families. It's not for the money. Sometimes I wish I wasn't so good. Ha, modesty alert . . . But you know what I mean. I never really wanted to be a star. I wanted to have a husband and"—she nodded back toward Villalobos's— "babies and sing to *them* and friends. . . . It just all got away from me."

She was silent and Dance supposed she was thinking: If I wasn't famous I wouldn't have Edwin Sharp in my life.

Dance could see Kayleigh's reflection and noted her jaw was set and there were possibly tears in her eyes. Then Kayleigh turned back, shoving her troubled thoughts away, it seemed, and said with a sly grin, "So. Tell me. Dish."

"Men?"

"Like yeah!" Kayleigh said. "You mentioned Jon somebody?"

"The greatest guy in the world," Dance said. "Brilliant. Used to be in Silicon Valley, now he teaches and does consulting. The most important thing is that Wes and Maggie like him." She added that her son had had a very difficult time with his mother's dating. He hadn't liked anybody until Boling.

"Of course it didn't help that one guy I introduced them to turned out to be a killer."

"No!"

"Oh, we weren't in any danger. He was after the same perp I was. It's just that I wanted to put him in jail. My friend wanted to kill him."

"I don't know," Kayleigh said ominously. "There's something to be said for that."

Thinking again, probably, of Edwin Sharp.

"But the kids love Jon. It's working out well."

"And?" the singer asked.

"And what?"

"You going to tell me or not?"

And here, I'm the kinesics pro. Dance debated but in the end demurred. "Oh, nothing . . . just who knows what's going to happen? I've only been a widow a few years. I'm in no hurry."

"Sure," Kayleigh said, not exactly believing the lame explanation.

And Dance reflected: Yes, she liked Jon Boling a lot. Hey, she probably loved him and on more than one occasion, lying in bed together during one of the few nights they'd spent out of town, she'd come close to saying so. And she'd sensed that he had too.

He was kind, easygoing, good-looking, with a great sense of humor.

But then there was Michael.

Michael O'Neil was a detective with the Monterey County Office of the Sheriff. He and Dance had worked together for years and, if she was instinctively on anyone's wavelength, it was O'Neil's. They worked in timepiece harmony, they laughed, they loved the same foods and wines, they argued like the dickens and never took a word of it personally. Dance believed that he was as perfect for her as anyone could be.

Aside from that little glitch: a wife.

Who had finally left him and their children—naturally, just *after* Dance started going out with Jon Boling. O'Neil and his wife, Anne, were still married, though she was living in San Francisco now. O'Neil had mentioned divorce papers being prepared but timetables and plans seemed vague.

This would be a topic for another evening with Kayleigh Towne, though.

In ten minutes they'd arrived at the Mountain View, and Darthur Morgan steered the Suburban to the front of the motel. Dance said good night to them both.

It was then that Kayleigh's phone buzzed and she looked down at the screen, frowning. She hit ANSWER. "Hello? . . . Hello?" She listened for a moment and then said firmly, "Who is this?"

Hand on the door lever, Dance paused and looked back at the singer.

Kayleigh disconnected, regarding the screen once more. "Weird."

"What?"

"Somebody just played a verse from 'Your Shadow.'"

The title track of her latest album and already a huge hit.

"They didn't say anything, whoever it was. They just played the first verse."

Dance had downloaded the track and she recalled the words.

> *You walk out onstage and sing folks your songs.*
> *You make them all smile. What could go wrong?*
> *But soon you discover the job takes its toll,*
> *And everyone's wanting a piece of your soul.*

"The thing is. . . . it was a recording from a concert."

"You don't do live albums," Dance said, recalling that Kayleigh preferred the control of the studio.

She was still staring at the screen. "Right. It'd be a bootleg. But it was really high quality—almost like a real voice, not a recording. . . . But who was playing it, why?"

"You recognize the phone number?"

"No. Not a local area code. You think it was Edwin?" she asked, her voice going tense with stress, looking up at Darthur Morgan, whose dark, still eyes were visible in the rearview mirror. "But, wait, only my friends and family have this number. How could he get it?" She grimaced. "Maybe the same way he got my email."

"Could it be somebody in the band?" Dance asked. "A practical joke?"

"I don't know. Nobody's done anything like that before."

"Give me the number. I'll make some calls. And I'll check out Edwin too. What's his last name?"

"Sharp. No *e*. Would you, Kathryn?"

"You bet."

Dance wrote down the number of the call and climbed out of the Suburban.

They said good night.

"I guess we better get home now, Darthur."

As the vehicle pulled away, Kayleigh was looking around the empty parking lot as if Edwin Sharp were lurking nearby.

Dance headed inside, aware that she was humming one line to "Your Shadow" as it looped through her thoughts, unstoppable.

What could go wrong . . . what could go wrong . . . what could go wrong?

Chapter 6

DANCE STOPPED AT the Mountain View bar and got a glass of Pinot Noir then walked to her room and stepped inside. She'd hung the DO NOT DISTURB sign on the knob earlier and she left it there now, looking forward to that mother's rarity—sleeping late.

She showered, pulled on a robe and, sipping the wine, plopped down on the bed. She hit speed dial button three.

"Hey, Boss," TJ Scanlon said cheerfully, answering on a half ring. Odd noises emanated from the background. Ringing, shouts, calliope music, though Dance realized that she didn't know exactly what a calliope was.

"Are you in an arcade or something?"

"Carnival. Date. We're in line for the roller coaster but I'll go around again for you." His voice faded as he spoke away from the phone. "It's my boss. . . . Right. You better finish that Slurpee before we get on. . . . No, I'm telling you. Really. Does the word 'inverted' mean anything?"

TJ was the most alternative of the agents in the Monterey office of the CBI, who were in general a conservative lot. He was the go-to man when it came to long, demanding assignments, undercover work and any trivia regarding the sixties, Bob Dylan, tie-dye and lava lamps.

Quirky, yes. But who was Dance to judge? Here she

was taking a week off in Fresno and sitting in a stiflingly hot garage to record obscure songs by a group of cheerful and likely undocumented farmworkers.

"Need you to check out something, TJ."

She gave him what she knew on Edwin Sharp. She then recited the number of the caller who'd played the song for Kayleigh not long ago.

TJ asked, "Anything in particular? On Sharp?"

"The usual. But civil too. Stalking, lawsuits, restraining orders. Here and Washington state. Throw in Oregon for good measure."

"Will do. Pine trees, Pinot Noir, cheese. No, that's Wisconsin."

"Have fun."

"We are. I won Sadie a panda. . . . No, I'm serious. Lose the Slurpee. Centrifugal force will not do it. . . . So long, Boss."

Dance disconnected. She tried Jon Boling but his phone went to voicemail. Another sip of wine and then she decided it was time for bed. She rose and walked to the window, drawing the drapes shut. Then brushed her teeth, ditched the robe and pulled on boxers and a faded pink T-shirt, way too big; Kathryn Dance was a nightgown girl only on special occasions.

She rolled toward the light, groping for the switch.

And froze.

The window!

Before leaving for Villalobos's Dance had closed the gauze curtain and the heavy drapes; the first-floor room overlooked the parking lot, a four-lane street and, across it, a small park.

The same drapes she'd just closed once again.

Only she'd never opened them earlier. Someone else had been inside her room and pulled them apart.

Who had breached the DO NOT DISTURB barrier?

It hadn't been Housekeeping—the room wasn't straightened up, the bed still mussed from where she'd plopped down to call the children that afternoon.

Nothing seemed to have been disturbed. Her dark green suitcases were where she'd left them. The clothes still in the closet as before, carelessly dangling on theft-proof hangers, and the five pairs of shoes were exactly where she'd set them in a row near the dresser. Her computer bag didn't seem tampered with and the computer itself was password protected anyway, so no one could have read her files or emails.

Shutting the light off, she walked to the window and looked out. It was eleven-thirty and the park across the road was empty . . . wait, no. Someone was in the shadows. She couldn't make out a specific person but she saw the tiny orange glow of a cigarette moving slowly as the smoker would lift it for a drag.

She remembered Edwin Sharp's slow, patient scan of her face and body in the restaurant that day. How he'd carefully read all the information on her ID card. Stalkers, she knew, were experts at getting information on people—both the objects of their obsession and those who threatened to impede their access. Edwin certainly had shown he was good at such research, knowing what he did about Kayleigh's associates.

But maybe it was a coincidence. There might have been some electrical or plumbing issue and workers had had to come into the room, despite the sign on the door. She called the front desk but the clerk didn't know if anyone had been inside.

She made sure all the windows were locked and the chain securely fixed to the door and she conducted one more examination of the park, through a crack in the drapes. The moon had emerged but it was still too dark and hazy to see much.

The orange glow of the cigarette flared as the smoker inhaled deeply. Then the dot dropped to the ground and vanished under a shoe or boot.

She saw no other motion. Had he left because she'd shut the light out and presumably gone to sleep?

Dance waited a moment more then climbed into bed. She closed her eyes.

And wondered why she bothered. Sleep, she knew, would be a long, long time coming.

Chapter 7

REELING THROUGH HIS mind was Jackson Browne's "The Load-Out" from the seventies album *Running on Empty*, the tune an homage to roadies.

A sort-of homage. You got the impression the singer came first.

But don't they always?

Still, nobody else ever wrote a song dedicated to Bobby Prescott's profession and he hummed it often.

Now, close to midnight, he parked near the convention center and climbed out of the band's Quest van, stretching after the marathon drive to and from Bakersfield to pick up the custom-built amp. Kayleigh Towne preferred that her musicians use amps with tubes—like old-time TVs and radios. There'd been a huge debate about which was a better sound: solid-state amps versus the tube models, with the tube purists contending that that older technology produced an indescribable "clipping sound" when played in overdrive, which digital amps had never been able to duplicate. Not surprisingly this had been Bishop Towne's philosophy and when the Old Man, as his own roadies called him, was performing, the stage was filled with Marshall JCM2000 TSL602s, Fender Deluxe Reverb IIs, Traynor Custom Valve YCV20WRs and Vox AC30s.

Bobby was a guitarist as well (there weren't many

roadies, techs or personal assistants in the music world who couldn't sit in at a show if they absolutely had to). He himself thought the richness of tubes was noticeable but only when playing blues.

He now unlocked the stage door at the convention center and wheeled the big unit inside. He also had a box of light mounts and safety cables.

Thinking again of the strip light falling that morning. *Jesus . . .*

Performing could be a dangerous business. His father had been a recording engineer in London in the sixties and seventies. Back then, the serious-minded professionals Robert Senior worked with—the Beatles and Stones, for instance—were outnumbered by crazy, self-destructive musicians who managed to kill themselves pretty frequently with drugs, liquor, cars and aggressively poor judgment. But even taking bad behavior out of the picture, performing could be dangerous. Electricity was the biggest risk—he'd known of three performers electrocuted onstage and two singers and a guitarist hit by lightning. One roadie had fallen from a high stage and broken his neck. A half dozen had died in traffic accidents, often because they fell asleep, and several had been crushed to death when gear trucks' brakes failed and the vehicles jumped the chocks.

But a light coming unfixed? That was weird and had never happened in his years as a roadie.

And endangering Kayleigh?

He actually shivered, thinking about that.

Tonight the cavernous hall was filled with shadows cast by the exit lights. But rather than the ill ease Kayleigh had described that morning, Bobby felt a low twist of pleasure being here. He and Kayleigh had always been in near-total harmony, except for one thing. To her music was a business, a task, a profession. And concert halls were about acoustics only. For Bobby, the romantic, these places were special, almost sacred. He believed that halls like this continued to echo with the sounds of all the musicians who'd performed there. And this ugly, concrete venue in Fresno had one hell of a history. A local boy himself, Bobby had seen Dylan here and Paul Simon and U2 and Vince Gill and Union Station and Arlo Guthrie and Richard Thompson and Rosanne Cash and Sting and Garth Brooks and James Taylor and Shania and, well, the list was endless. . . . And their voices and the ringing sound of their guitars and horn sections and reeds and drums changed the very fiber of the place, he believed.

As he approached the strip light that had fallen he noticed that someone had moved it. He had left instructions that the heavy black light fixture shouldn't be touched, after he'd lowered it to the stage. But now it sat on the very edge, above the orchestra pit, a good thirty feet from where it had stopped swinging after it fell.

He'd ream somebody for that. He'd wanted to see exactly what had happened. Crouching down, Bobby examined the unit. What the hell had gone wrong?

Could it be that asshole, Edwin Sharp?

Maybe—

Bobby Prescott never heard the footsteps of whoever came up behind him. He simply felt the hands slam into his back and he went forward, barking a brief scream as the concrete floor of the orchestra pit, twenty feet below, raced up to break his jaw and arm.

Oh, Jesus, Jesus . . .

He lay on his belly, staring at the bone, starkly white and flecked with blood, that poked through his forearm skin.

Bobby moaned and screamed and cried out for help. Who? Who did it?

Edwin? . . . He might've heard me tell Kayleigh in the café that I was going to be here late.

"Help me!"

Silence.

Bobby tried to reach into his pocket for his mobile. The pain was too great. He nearly fainted. Well, try again! You're going to bleed to death!

Then, over his gasping breath, he heard a faint sound above him, a scraping. He twisted his head and looked up.

No . . . God no!

He watched the strip light, directly above him, easing toward the edge of the stage.

"No! Who is that? No!"

Bobby struggled to crawl away, clawing at the concrete floor with the fingers of his unbroken arm. But his legs weren't working either.

One inch, two . . .

Move, roll aside!

But too late.

The light slammed into his back, going a hundred miles an hour. He felt another snap high in his body and all the pain went away.

My back . . . my back . . .

His vision crinkled.

Bobby Prescott came to sometime later—seconds, minutes, hours . . . he didn't know. All he knew was that the room was bathed in astonishing light; the spotlight sitting on his back had been turned on.

All thousand watts, pouring from the massive lamps.

He then saw on the wall the flicker of shadows, cast by flames. At first he didn't know what was on fire—he felt no heat whatsoever. But then the repulsive scent of burning hair, burning flesh filled the small space.

And he understood.

Monday

Chapter 8

AT THE BRAYING of the phone Kathryn Dance awoke, her first thought: the children.

Then her parents.

Then Michael O'Neil, maybe on assignment, one of the gang- or terrorist-related cases he'd been working on lately.

As she fumbled for her mobile, dropped it, then fumbled some more, she ran through a number of scenarios as to why anyone would call at the crack of dawn when she was on vacation.

And Jon Boling . . . was he all right?

She righted the phone but without her glasses she couldn't see the number. She hit the green button. "Yes?"

"Woke you up, Boss."

"What?"

"Sorry."

"Sorry what do you mean sorry is everyone all right there?" One sentence made of many. Dance was remembering, as she did all too often, the call from the state trooper about Bill—a brief, sympathetic but emotionless call explaining to her that the life she'd planned on with her husband, the life she'd believed would forever be her rock, would not happen.

"Not here, there."

Was it just that she was exhausted? She blinked. What time was it? Five A.M.? Four?

TJ Scanlon said, "I didn't know if you needed me."

Struggling upright, tugging down the T-shirt that had become a noose during an apparently restless night. "Start at the beginning."

"Oh, you didn't hear?"

"No, I didn't hear."

Sorry what do you mean . . .

"Okay. Got a notice on the wire about a homicide in Fresno. Happened late last night, early this morning."

More awake now. Or less unawake.

"Tell me."

"Somebody connected with Kayleigh Towne's band."

Lord . . . "Who?" Brushing her dark blond hair from her face. The worse the news, the calmer Kathryn Dance became. Partly training, partly nature, partly mother. Though as a kinesics expert she was quite aware of her own bobbing foot. She stalled it.

"Somebody named Robert Prescott."

She wondered: Bobby? Yes, that was his last name, Prescott. This was bad. She'd noted from their interaction yesterday that he and Kayleigh were close friends, in addition to being work associates.

"Details?"

"Nothing yet."

Dance also thought back to Edwin's unnatural smile, his leering eyes, his icily calm demeanor, which she believed might conceal bundled rage.

TJ said, "It was just a one-paragraph notice on the wire. Information only, not a request for assistance."

The CBI was available to help out local California public safety offices with major crime investigations, but with a few exceptions the Bureau agents waited until they were contacted. The CBI had a limited number of bodies to go around. California was a big state and a lot of bad things happened there.

The younger agent continued, "The vic died at the convention center."

Where the concert was going to be held on Friday.

"Go on."

"It's being handled by the Fresno-Madera Consolidated Sheriff's Office. The sheriff is Anita Gonzalez. The head detective is P. K. Madigan. Been on the force a long time, forever. Don't know anything else about him."

"I'll get over there now. You have anything on Sharp yet? The stalker?"

"No warrants or court orders came up here. Nothing in California at all. Still waiting for the locals from Washington and Oregon. The phone number you gave me? That somebody called Kayleigh on? It was a prepaid, bought with cash, from a drugstore in Burlingame."

South of San Francisco, where the airport was located.

"No video and no other record of the transaction. The clerks have no idea who it was. It was three days ago. No other details yet."

"Keep on it. Email Sharp's full bio. Anything you can get."

"Your command is what I wish for, Boss."

They disconnected.

What time *was* it? The room was still dark but light showed behind the drapes.

Glasses on. Oh, eight-thirty. The crack of mid-morning.

She walked into the bathroom for a brief, hot shower. In twenty minutes she was dressed in black jeans, a black T-shirt and a silk business jacket, navy blue, conservative, matter-of-fact. The heat would be challenging with these clothes but the possibility of duty loomed. She'd learned long ago that a woman officer had to be a length ahead of men when it came to appearing professional. Sad but the way of the world.

She took her laptop with her, just in case the intruder returned, if in fact she *had* been intruded upon yesterday.

Then she was out the door, slipping the DO NOT DISTURB sign onto the L-shaped knob of the hotel room.

Wondering briefly if the prohibition would have any effect.

Outside, under an uncompromising sun, her temples, face and armpits bristled as sweat flowed. Dance fished for the Pathfinder key in her Coach purse and absently slapped her hip, where her Glock normally resided.

A weapon that was, today, conspicuously absent.

Chapter 9

HAD THERE REALLY been just one victim?

Pulling into the convention center lot, aiming for the stage door, Dance noted more emergency and public safety personnel than seemed necessary. Two dozen, easily, walking slowly, speaking on phones or radios, carrying battered equipment, green and red and yellow—the colors of stoplights, colors of children's toys.

Four fire trucks, two ambulances, eight police cruisers and several unmarked.

She wondered again if TJ's information was flawed. Had others died?

She drove forward to a Dodge, unmarked but obvious, parked and climbed out. A woman in a deputy's uniform glanced Dance's way, C. STANNING stamped on a plate above her taut breast. Her hair was equally tight and it ended in pert, incongruous pigtails, tipped in blue rubber bands.

"Help you?"

Dance displayed her CBI card and the woman didn't seem to know what to make of it. "You . . . is Sacramento involved?"

Dance nearly said she was just here on vacation and believed she knew the victim. But law enforcement is a world in which instinct counts—when dealing both with suspects and with allies. She said, "Not yet. I happened to be nearby."

Stanning juggled these words, perhaps factoring in her own instructions from on high, and said, "Okay."

Dance continued on toward the bland concrete convention center. A slash of glaring light hit her in the face brutally as she approached. She slipped into the shade but this route was just as unpleasant; the air between two tall walls leading to the front doors was dead and stifling.

She stepped inside and in a half second the relief of the air-conditioning was utterly negated by the stench.

Kathryn Dance had been a law enforcer for some years and had attended hundreds of crime scenes. Being an investigator with CBI, she was rarely a first responder and didn't do forensics; much of the horror had been tamed by the time she arrived. Blood staunched, bodies covered with washable tarps, body parts recovered and cataloged.

So the scent of burned flesh and hair was unexpected; it hit like a fist in her belly.

She didn't hesitate but she did steel herself and pushed past the assault, somehow keeping the nausea under control. She walked into the massive arena, which would hold thirty thousand, she guessed. All the overheads were on, revealing the tired and shabby décor. It was as if a play or concert had ended and the promoters were eager to prod the audience into the lobby to buy CDs and souvenirs.

On the stage and main floor were a dozen people in the varied uniforms of law enforcement, fire and EMS.

Climbing to the stage, she joined a cluster at the edge, looking down into the orchestra pit. It was from there that a faint trail of fetid smoke rose. Slowing, she struggled not to gag, then continued on.

What had happened? she wondered. She recalled the falling light from yesterday.

Dance noted immediately, from their posture and the sweep of their eyes, that two of the law officers, who all wore tan uniforms, were senior to the others. One was a woman hovering in her fifties with long hair and a pocked face. With Latina features, she was stocky and stood in a pose that suggested she disliked the uniform—the tight slacks and the close-fitting blouse, which blossomed outward at the waist, painted on rolls of fat.

The man she was speaking to was Caucasian, though sporting a dark tan. He also was stocky but his was targeted weight, situated in his gut, which rode above thin hips and legs. A large, round face crisscrossed with sun wrinkles. His posture—leaning forward, shoulders up—and still, squinting gray eyes suggested an arrogant and difficult man. His head hair was black and thick. He wore a revolver, a long-barreled Colt, while on the hips of everyone else here were the semi-auto Glocks that were de rigueur among law enforcers in California.

Ah, yes, she was right in her guess; he was P. K. Madigan, the head of detectives.

Conversation slowed as they turned to see the slim woman in jeans and sport coat stride toward them.

Madigan asked brusquely, "And you are . . . ?" in a way that didn't mean what the words said at all. He looked over her shoulder darkly toward who might have let her breach his outer perimeter.

Dance noted the woman was named Gonzalez, the sheriff, and so she addressed her and displayed her ID, which both of the in-charge duo examined carefully.

"I'm Sheriff Gonzalez. This is Chief Detective Madigan." The decision not to offer first names in an introduction is often an attempt to assert power. Dance merely noted the choice now. She wasn't here to flex muscles.

"My office called me about a homicide. I happened to be in the area on another matter."

Could be official, might not be. Let the sheriff and chief detective guess.

Dance added, "I'm also a friend of Kayleigh Towne's. When I heard the vic was in her crew I came right over here."

"Well, thanks, Kathryn," Madigan said.

And the *use* of first names is an attempt to disempower.

The flicker in Gonzalez's eyes at this faint affront—but absence of any look Madigan's way—told Dance reams about the chief detective. He'd carved out a major fiefdom at the FMCSO.

The detective continued, "But we don't need any CBI involvement at this point. Wouldn't you say, Sheriff?"

"I'd think not," Gonzalez said, staring Dance in the eyes. It was a magnetic look and based not—as in the case of Madigan—on gender or jurisdictional power but on the woman's determination not to glance at a figure perhaps four sizes smaller than hers. Whatever our rank or profession, we're frail human beings first.

Madigan continued, "You said you were here on another matter? I look over the interagencies pretty good every morning. Didn't see any Bureau activity here. They—you—don't always tell us, of course."

He'd called her bluff. "A personal matter." Dance steamed ahead. "The victim was Bobby Prescott, the head of the road crew?"

"That's right."

"Anyone else hurt?"

Madigan wasn't inclined to answer and used a nearby deputy as an excuse to turn away and have a very quiet conversation with him, leaving his boss to respond to the interloper as she liked.

Sheriff Gonzalez offered, "Only Bobby."

"And what happened?"

Madigan rejoined the conversation. "We're in the preliminary stage. Not sure at this point." He definitely didn't want her here but since she was with a senior agency he had at least to act deferential. Dance was a large dog wandering into a picnic—unwanted but possibly too dangerous to shoo away.

"COD?"

A pause then Gonzalez said, "He was doing some work on the stage last night. It seems he slipped and fell, a spotlight landed on him. It was on. He caught fire. Cause was blood loss and the burns."

Lord, what a terrible way to die.

"Must've burned for a while. The alarms didn't go off?"

"The smoke detectors down there, in the pit, weren't working. We don't know why."

The first thing in her mind was the image of Edwin Sharp, glancing toward Bobby Prescott, with that fake smile and with eyes that could easily reflect a desire to turn the roadie into a bag of dust.

"You ought to be aware—"

"'Bout Mr. Sharp, our stalker?" Madigan asked.

"Well, yes."

"One of the boys with the crew, Tye Slocum, told me that there was an incident yesterday at the Cowboy Saloon."

Dance described what she had seen and heard. "Bobby confronted him a couple of times. And Edwin probably overheard Bobby say he was going to come back here later last night and check out some equipment malfunction. It would be late because he had to go to Bakersfield to pick something up."

Madigan added absently, "Edwin's on our radar. We know he's renting a house near Woodward Park, north part of town. For a month."

Dance recalled that Edwin had been quite forthcoming about his residence. She was still curious why he'd rented for that time length.

Dance noted too that both Madigan and she herself tended to refer to the stalker by his first name; this often happened when dealing with suspects who were potentially ED, emotionally disturbed. Dance reminded herself that whatever name they used, not to sell the young man short.

The chief detective took a phone call. Then he was back with Dance, though only for the briefest of times. And with the briefest of smiles—just as phony as Edwin's, she reflected. "Appreciate you stopping by. We'll give CBI a call if there's anything we need."

Dance looked over the stage, the misty air above the pit.

Gonzalez offered, "So long now."

Despite the double-barreled good-bye, Dance didn't feel like leaving just yet. "How did the light fall on him?"

The sheriff said, "Maybe tugged it after him when he fell. The cord, you know."

"Was it a strip light?" Dance asked.

Madigan muttered, "Dunno what that is. Take a look." The last sentence was delivered with a bit of challenge.

Dance did. It was indeed a hard thing to see: the scorched body. And, yes, the unit was a four-lamp strip.

"That might've been the one that fell yesterday."

"Tye mentioned that," Madigan said. "We're looking into it." He was clearly growing weary of her. "Well, all righty then." He began to turn away.

"How did it come undone?"

"Wing nuts worked loose?" He nodded up to the scaffolding.

Dance said, "And I wonder why Bobby *fell*. Not like it isn't marked." Yellow warning tape clearly indicated the edge of the stage.

Over his shoulder Madigan offered a dismissive, "Lot of questions, you betcha."

Then a woman's loud, haunting voice from the back of the hall: "No . . . no, *no!*" The last time that word was repeated it became a scream. Despite the hot, dank atmosphere of the hall Dance felt a stinging chill slither down her back.

Kayleigh Towne sprinted down the aisle to the stage where her friend had so horribly died.

Chapter 10

DANCE HAD SEEN the young singer a half dozen times and she'd always been carefully, if not perfectly, assembled.

But today she was the most disheveled Dance had ever seen. No makeup, long hair askew, eyes puffy from crying, not lack of sleep (there's a difference, Dance knew). Instead of her ubiquitous contact lenses, she wore thin black-framed glasses. She was breathless.

Detective P. K. Madigan instantly became a different person. His fake smile of irritation at Dance became a frown of genuine sympathy for Kayleigh. He stepped down the stairs and intercepted the young woman on the floor before she could get to the stage. "Kayleigh, dear. No, no, you shouldn't be here. There's no reason for you to be."

"Bobby?"

"I'm afraid it is."

"They told me . . . but I was praying it was a mistake."

Then Sheriff Gonzalez joined them on the main floor and put her arm around the girl's shoulders. Dance wondered if all friends and next of kin got this treatment, or only celebrities, and then decided the cynical thought was unkind. Kayleigh Towne was the city's star, yes, but she was at the moment a woman in terrible distress.

"I'm sorry, Kayleigh," Gonzalez said. "I'm so sorry."

"It was him! Edwin. I know it! Go arrest him. He's parked in front of my house. Right now!"

"He's *what*?" Madigan asked.

"He's parked in the lot of the nature preserve across the street. He's just sitting there in that goddamn red car of his."

Frowning, Madigan made a call and told a deputy to check it out.

"Arrest him!"

"We'll have to see, Kayleigh. May not be as easy as that."

Dance noticed Darthur Morgan standing, arms crossed, in the back of the theater, looking around carefully.

"The hell's that?" Madigan grumbled, catching sight of the man.

"My bodyguard," Kayleigh said, gasping from the crying.

"Oh."

Dance returned to the edge of the stage and looked down. The nausea rose again from the smell, here concentrated, but she ignored it and studied the scene carefully: the strip light, six feet long or so, lay atop the scorched remains of Bobby Prescott. Dance knew the messages the body gave off—in life and in death. She now assessed the broken bones, the claw shape of the hands, partly due to the typical fire victim's contractions, the pugilistic attitude, but also because he'd been trying to drag his broken body out from underneath the edge of the stage. He was headed away from the stairs—not the logical direction one would crawl if he was just seeking help.

"He fell first," Dance said to the deputy standing next to her, softly, so Kayleigh would not hear. "A few minutes *before* the lamp hit him."

"What's that, ma'am?" The man, in his midthirties, of rectangular build, with a luxurious black mustache, stepped closer. He too was tanned, like Madigan, though perhaps he also had a naturally dark complexion. His tag said DET. D. HARUTYUN.

She nodded down into the hole as the crime scene men, or women, in jumpsuits, moved the light away and began processing the body. She said, "His legs, the way they're angled, his hands. He fell first. He tried to get out of the way. Then the light fell."

The deputy examined the scene silently. Then: "The light teetered and fell. He knew it was coming 'cause he tugged on the cord."

But the wire was plugged into an outlet on the stage, not in the pit. Both she and the detective noticed this simultaneously. Bobby couldn't have pulled it down on himself. She asked, "And why's it plugged into the wall there? A light like that's mounted on the rigging *above* the stage. That's where the power is. . . . And why's it plugged in at all? That'd be worth mentioning too."

"I'll do that."

Which he now did, walking down the stairs, offering some words to Kayleigh and then pulling Madigan aside, whispering to him. The detective nodded. His face folded into a frown. "Okay," he called, "we're treating the stage as a crime scene. And the scaffolding where the light fell from yesterday. Clear everybody off. And get Charlie's folks searching there. Hell, we've already contaminated the damn place bad enough."

Dance wondered if Harutyun had taken credit for the observations. Probably had. But that didn't matter to her. As long as they got all the helpful evidence they could, that's what was important.

Gonzalez was fielding calls on her iPhone, concentrating. Dance now joined Kayleigh, standing alone, in a frantic state. Looking in many different directions, she began talking rapidly, gesturing. Dance was reminded of her own unhinged behavior in the few hours after she learned of the death of her husband, an FBI agent—not a victim of criminal activity but of a careless driver on Highway 1.

Dance hugged her hard and asked how she could help, phone calls to be made, rides to be arranged. Kayleigh thanked her and said no, she'd make the calls herself. "Oh, Kathryn, can you believe it? I . . . I can't believe it. Bobby." Her eyes strayed to the orchestra pit and Dance prepared to stop her physically from looking at the body if she needed to. But the singer turned instead to Madigan and Gonzalez and said that she thought somebody had been watching her yesterday here. No, been *sure* of it.

"Where?"

Pointing. "In those corridors there. Alicia—my assistant—saw something too. But we didn't see anyone clearly."

Dance said, "Tell them about the phone call last night."

This contribution from the interloper, at least, got Madigan's attention.

In a trembling voice, Kayleigh said to Dance, "God, you think that has something to do with this?"

"What?" Gonzalez asked.

Kayleigh explained about the call she'd received in the car, someone playing part of the title song from the band's most recent album, *Your Shadow*. Kayleigh added, "For what it's worth, the recording was very high quality—true fidelity. With your eyes closed, you couldn't tell the difference between someone really singing or the digital replay. Only a pro would have a recorder like that."

"Or a fanatical fan," Dance suggested. She then mentioned what she'd learned from TJ about the mobile phone. Madigan didn't seem pleased that a law enforcer from another jurisdiction had already started to investigate his case, though he wrote down the details.

At that moment another person joined them, Deputy C. Stanning, from out front.

"First names . . . Crystal," Madigan said coolly.

She said, "Reporters're starting to show up, Chief. They'll want a press—"

"You keeping people out of the crime scene, Deputy?"

He didn't look toward Dance but he didn't need to. Stanning did the job for him.

Her oblique apology: "Big area to keep track of. Lot of onlookers, you know, curious folks. I'm keeping them back, best I can."

"I'm hopin' you do. Let the reporters cool their heels." This time the glance was at the large bodyguard in the back of the hall.

The sheriff asked, "Kayleigh, tell me again—what exactly did you hear on the phone?"

"Just a verse from my song."

"He didn't say anything, the caller? Or she?"

"No. Just the song."

Sheriff Gonzalez took another call herself, had a brief conversation then disconnected. "Congressman Davis's here. I've got to meet him and his security detail. . . . I'm sorry for your loss, Kayleigh." This was offered sincerely and accompanied by two firm hands on the girl's shoulders. "Anything I can do, let me know."

A look passed from the older woman to her chief of detectives, meaning: Do what you need to on this case. This is big news here and Kayleigh's our own. Nothing is going to happen to her. Nothing.

The sheriff scanned Dance and said good-bye. She left, along with two of the other deputies.

Dance said to Madigan, "My specialty's interrogation and interviewing, Detective. If you have a suspect or witness you'd like me to talk to, just give me a call." She handed him her card.

"I do a bit of that myself," Madigan offered. "Well, all righty then, Kathryn." He pocketed the card like a used tissue.

"Oh, wait, that seminar," Harutyun said, frowning. "In Salinas. Body language, right? Kinetics. That was you."

"Kinesics, yes."

He turned to Madigan. "Alberto and I went last year. It was helpful. You were funny too."

"Seminar," Madigan repeated. "Funny. Well, that's good to know. Here's a thought. . . . Kayleigh, you saw somebody here yesterday?"

"Just a shadow," the girl said.

He smiled. "Shadows're left by somethin'. Or someone. Why don't you talk to people in the crew who were here, Kathryn. Any convention center workers too. See what they have to say."

"I could do that, Detective. But that's more along the lines of canvassing. I'm sure the people with the crew and anybody else here would cooperate. I'm usually involved if there's reason for a witness or suspect to be deceptive or if they can't remember important facts."

"And I sure hope we get somebody you can use those seminar skills of yours on, Kathryn. But until then, it'd be a big help if you'd see what the others have to say. Of course, don't feel you have to."

Seminar skills . . ,

She'd been outmaneuvered. Given a necessary, but minor task to keep her out of their hair. The dog had been sniffing around for juicy scraps at the picnic and got tossed a dry bone instead.

"Be glad to," Dance said. She pulled out her iPhone and got from Kayleigh the names of the people with the crew and convention center employees who were here yesterday, inputting them one by one.

The medical examiner arrived and approached the senior detective. They had a quiet conversation.

Dance called to Kayleigh, "I'll see you later." The young woman's eyes looked so mournful it was hard to keep contact. Dance started up the aisle when the thought slammed her.

Jesus.

She turned back. "Kayleigh, last night? The caller only played one verse, right?"

"The first verse. And the chorus."

"And it's about a concert hall," Dance said.

"Well, yeah, sort of. It's kind of about being a public person. But it mentions a venue."

"I don't know who's behind this," Dance said, "but if it's a stalker, like Edwin, I think he's going to keep killing."

"Oh, Kathryn," Kayleigh whispered. "Again? He might hurt somebody else?"

Committing murder was rare among stalkers but in her years as a reporter, a jury consultant and a cop, Dance had learned that when it came to violent crime, an outlier could kill you just as dead as a perp who fell smack in the middle of the bell curve. "The basis for stalking is repetitive, obsessive behavior. I think we should assume he's going to make more calls and more people will be at risk. I'd get a wire on Kayleigh's phone. And let's look at the other verses of that song and find out who or where he might attack again."

Madigan asked, "But why would the perp do that? What's in it for him?"

Dance replied, "I don't know. Some stalkers are simply psychotic."

"Sounds kinda far-fetched," Madigan said. Mostly he seemed irritated that Dance had upset Kayleigh.

"I think it's important."

"Seems you do." The chief detective took a call, listened and said to Kayleigh, "That was one of the patrols. They cruised past your house and didn't see him or his car."

"Where *is* he, where did he *go*?" Kayleigh sounded panicked.

"They don't know."

Madigan looked at his watch. He told Harutyun to go outside and make a statement to the reporters. "Don't give 'em anything specific, only Bobby's name. Being investigated. Apparent accident. You know the drill. And keep people *outa* here." Madigan apparently didn't think Deputy Stanning was up to the task.

He dismissed Dance too, in a stony voice, impatient: "And now, if you could get to that interviewing, I'd sure appreciate it, Kathryn."

Dance hugged Kayleigh once more. She then accompanied Harutyun toward the exit.

"Thanks for talking to him about the light, Detective Harutyun."

"Made some sense. Call me Dennis."

"Kathryn."

"I heard." Deadpan delivery.

They both nodded at a somber Darthur Morgan as they passed. His eyes left Kayleigh for a mere portion of a second.

In a few minutes the two were pushing out the front door of the facility. Dance was grateful to be in scorch-free air again, even if it was searing hot. Harutyun's square face, though, registered distress. The line of his shoulders had changed too. He was looking at the clutch of reporters and TV vans. Dance understood he'd rather be chasing down a perp in a dark alley than handling this duty. Public speaking, perhaps. A major and universal fear.

Dance slowed, typing an email into her phone. She sent it on its way. "Detective?"

The columnar man stopped, wary but seemingly grateful for any delay in confronting the media.

She continued, "I just downloaded a set of the lyrics—Kayleigh's song, the one she heard on her phone last night."

He seemed unsure of where this was going. "And I've forwarded a copy to the Detective Division. To your attention."

"Me?"

"I'd really appreciate it if you'd look over the second verse—well, all of them, but the second verse right away—and let me know if you can think of any places it could mean, where a perp might decide to kill somebody else, based on the words. Like the concert hall in the first verse. It might be impossible to guess the scene in particular but if we can just narrow it down a little we'd have a head start if he calls again."

A hesitation. "I could check with Chief Madigan about that."

Dance said slowly, "You *could,* sure."

Harutyun, not looking her way, surveying the reporters: "The Chief's got the best forensic outfit in the Valley, better than Bakersfield's. And his arrest and conviction rate's in the top ten percent in the state."

"I can tell he's good," she said.

Eyes still on the voracious journalists. "I know he'd

appreciate you getting him statements from those witnesses."

Dance said firmly, "Look over the lyrics. Please."

Swallowing, the big detective didn't respond but stepped forward reluctantly to meet the pack of hungry wolves.

Chapter 11

BOBBY PRESCOTT'S TRAILER was an impressive double-wide. A Buccaneer company Cole model, about fifty feet by twenty-five or so, Kathryn Dance guessed. Tan exterior, white trim.

It was, yes, a *mobile* home but a crumbling cinder-block foundation certified that it wasn't very. The dry ground around it was cracked and beige, the grass losing the battle but some hydrangeas and boxwood putting up a good fight.

The scene wasn't crowded. Only law enforcers, some curious children with bicycles or skateboards and a few older spectators were present. Most adults were either not interested or didn't want to draw attention to themselves. It was that sort of neighborhood. There were no other residents in the trailer; TJ had reported that Bobby Prescott was unmarried and had lived here alone.

It was 1:00 P.M., the sun at a September angle, but the air was still hot as July.

Two FMCSO cruisers were parked in the front and Dance nosed past them to the carport and climbed out of the Pathfinder. Chief Detective Madigan and Dennis Harutyun were standing together, talking to the kids. Well, they *had* been doing so. Now they were focused on her.

The mustachioed detective nodded noncommittally.

His boss said, "Ah, Kathryn." Not even a faux smile from Madigan. Beneath the leaf-thin veneer was anger—at her and probably at himself for having to play the politics game and not being able to simply kick the CBI agent out altogether. Her impression was that he was surprised she hadn't done as he'd hoped—got bored playing small-town cop and just gone away.

No such luck.

Dennis Harutyun regarded her solemnly and she wondered if he'd bothered to download and review the lyrics to "Your Shadow." Probably not. He brushed his mustache with the back of a finger and returned to interviewing locals. He moved with the same calm demeanor she recalled from earlier. His personal baseline. But he was also cautious, looking around frequently as if Edwin lurked nearby, armed with a handgun.

Which she couldn't be sure wasn't the case. Voyeuristic perps, like stalkers, always set you on edge, while the spying gives *them* comfort.

P. K. Madigan continued, "So. You didn't have a chance to talk to those witnesses."

"I did, yes. But I'm afraid it wasn't very productive. I talked to Alicia, Kayleigh's PA, and Tye Slocum and the rest of the crew. Darthur Morgan—"

"Who?"

"Her security guard."

"That . . . the big guy was there earlier?"

"That's right. The facility had a security guard and two other people, one was a gaffer—an electrician— and a carpenter to help out the band. They had to be present because of the union rules. I interviewed them too. Their security man said three of the doors were unlocked. But that wasn't unusual. During the day, if there's no show, it's a pain to keep finding him and unlocking the doors in front, the side and back, so they usually just leave them open. Nobody spotted anyone inside they didn't recognize, on the scaffolding or anywhere else."

"You got all that in three hours?"

Eighty minutes, actually. The rest had been devoted to learning where Bobby spent time—hiking in a state park nearby (no leads there), hanging out in a guitar store and a radio station with friends (nothing helpful) and sitting in a particular diner in the Tower District, where he drank copious amounts of coffee and nothing stronger, suggesting he was in recovery (ditto, the lack of leads).

And finally discovering where he lived.

Hence, her presence here.

She chose not to mention this, though. "How'd your crime scene team do at the convention center?"

A pause. "Collected a lot of stuff. Don't know the results yet."

Another Fresno-Madera Consolidated cruiser arrived—Crystal Stanning was at the wheel. She parked behind Dance's Nissan, climbed out and joined the others. She too looked around uneasily.

That's the thing about a crime like this. You never quite know where the stalker is. Maybe miles away. Maybe outside your window.

Stanning, it seemed, wanted to report to her boss about whatever her mission had been but would say nothing until Dance was elsewhere or she had the okay. The sweating Madigan was impatient. He snapped, "The phone?"

"Service Plus Drugs in Burlingame. Cash. They don't have any videos. Maybe that's why he went there."

Dance had told them all of this information.

But then Stanning continued, "And you were

right, Chief, he bought three other phones at the same time."

A question Dance had *not* thought to have TJ Scanlon ask.

Madigan sighed. "So this boy *may* have more on his plate."

Which was, she guessed, a backhanded acknowledgment of her "far-fetched" concern.

Four verses in "Your Shadow," Dance reflected. Four victims? And that song might not be the only template for murder; Kayleigh had written lots of tunes.

"I got the numbers and the ESNs."

You needed both the phone number and the electronic serial number of a mobile in order to trace it.

"We should get 'em shut off," Madigan said. "So Edwin'll have to buy one here. Easier to trace."

We don't know it's Edwin, Dance observed, but said nothing.

"Sure." Detective Stanning had three studs in one ear and a single silver dangling spiral in the other lobe. A dot in her nose too, marking where a ball might perch on off hours.

But Dance said, "I'd keep them active, like we haven't figured out what he's up to. And then put a locator notice on them. If the perp calls again we can triangulate."

Madigan paused, then glanced at Crystal Stanning. "Do that."

"Who should I—?"

"Call Redman in Communications. He can do it."

Motion from across the street, where a more modest trailer squatted in sad grass. A round woman stood on the concrete stoop, smoking a cigarette. Sunburned shoulders, freckles. She wore a tight white strapless sundress with purple and red stains at toddler level. She eyed everyone cautiously.

Madigan told Stanning to help Harutyun canvass. He walked to the shoulder and after two pickups had passed he crossed the road, making for the heavyset woman, Dance following.

The detective glanced back at her but she didn't slow down.

The neighbor walked forward uncertainly to greet them. They met halfway from her mailbox. In a rasping voice she said, "I heard the news. I mean, about Bobby. I couldn't believe it." She repeated fast, "It was on the news. That's how I heard." She took a drag.

The innocent usually act as guilty as the guilty.

"Yes, ma'am. I'm Deputy Madigan, this is Officer Dancer."

She didn't correct him.

"Your name?"

"Tabby Nysmith. Tabatha. Bobby never caused any trouble. No drugs or drinking. He was just into music. Only complaint was a party one time. Kinda loud. Can't believe he's dead. What happened? The news didn't say."

"We aren't sure what happened, ma'am. Not yet."

"Was it gangs?"

"Like I say, we aren't sure."

"The nicest guy, really. He'd show Tony, he's my oldest, these fancy guitars he had. He had one that Mick Jagger played years ago, he said. Bobby's daddy worked with them and the Beatles too. Or that's what he said. We didn't know, how would you know? But Tony was in heaven."

"Did you see anybody here recent you never saw before?"

"No, sir."

"Anybody he had a fight with, loud voices, drug activity?"

"Nope. Didn't see anybody here last night or this morning. Didn't see anything."

"You're sure?"

"Yessir." She pressed out her cigarette and lit another one. Dance noted from the butts by the door that she at least had the decency to step outside to smoke, to keep from infecting the children. She continued, "It's hard for me to see his place." She gestured at the windows in the front of her trailer, obscured by bushes. "I'm after Tony Senior to trim the bushes but he never gets around to it."

A look toward Dance, a smile.

Men . . .

"Would your *husband* have seen anything?"

"He's on the road. Truck driver. Been away for three days. No, four."

"All right then, ma'am. Thank you for your time."

"Sure, Officer. Will there be a funeral or anything?"

"Couldn't say. Good day to you." Madigan was loping back toward the trailer but Dance turned the other way, followed the woman back to her trailer and her brood.

"Excuse me."

"Uh-huh?"

"If I could ask a few more things?"

"I'm sorry. I really have to get back to the kids."

"How many?"

"What?"

"Children?"

"Oh. Four."

"I have two."

Tabatha smiled. "I heard this, like, expression. Diminishing returns. I don't exactly know what it means but I think of it having two kids sets the stage, you know? You can have ten more and it's not a whole lot worser."

"Diminishing returns" probably wasn't what the woman meant but Dance grinned understandingly. "Two is fine for me."

"But you work."

The tiny sentence carried a lot. Then Tabatha said, "I really don't know much else than what I told that man." She looked at Dance's trim figure, pressed jeans and her sunglasses, whose frames were the color of canned cranberry sauce.

A whole different world.

And I work.

"I left Sheryl and Annette watching the little one."

The woman kept walking, fast for her bulky frame. She drew hard on the cigarette, then paused to crush it out carefully. Smokers did that in California, the land of brushfires.

"Just one or two questions."

"If the baby starts crying—"

"I'll help you change him."

"Her."

"What's her name?"

"Caitlyn."

"Pretty. Mine's Maggie."

Then they were at the screen door of her trailer. Tabatha peered through the dusty, rusted mesh. Dance couldn't see much other than toys: plastic tricycles, castles, doll houses, pirate chests. The house was dim inside but exuded still heat. The TV was on. One of the last remaining soap operas.

Tabatha lifted an eyebrow.

"Just a few more details about Bobby."

Dance was continuing the discussion with Tabatha because of an important rule in kinesic analysis: the volunteering principle. When someone answers a question, then immediately offers what he or she anticipates will be the next question, that person is often trying to deflect or diffuse a line of inquiry.

Dance had noted that Tabatha said she hadn't seen anybody here last night—or *this morning*.

Why had she felt it important to mention that? It made no sense unless she was covering up something.

Dance removed her sunglasses.

"I really need to get in to the children."

"Tabatha, what did you see this morning at Bobby's trailer?"

"Nothing," she said quickly.

Effective kinesic analysis of witnesses and suspects involves conversing with the individual for a long period of time—days or, ideally, weeks. Initially nothing is said about the crime at all; the interviewer asks questions and makes comments that relate to the subject's life, all topics about which the truth is known. This establishes the suspect's baseline behavior—how he or she speaks and acts when responding honestly. It's then that the interviewer segues into inquiries about the crime and compares the subject's behavior when answering *those* questions to the baseline. Any variation suggests stress and therefore possible deception.

However, even without establishing a baseline, there are a few mannerisms that suggest lying, at least to an experienced investigator like Kathryn Dance. Tabatha's voice was now slightly higher in pitch than earlier—a sign of stress.

A glance toward Bobby's trailer, in front of which Madigan and his deputies were staring back at Dance. She ignored them and said calmly, "It would be good for everybody if you could give us a little more information."

Everybody . . .

You too.

At least she wasn't a crier. Often at this stage, when Dance tipped witnesses or suspects into admitting they'd been lying, many women, and a surprising number of men, began to cry. It could take upward of an hour to convince them that they were not subhuman for being deceptive; they were simply scared or concerned about their families or had other reasons. Tabatha gave no reaction, other than a thoughtful furrowing of her thick eyebrows as she probably considered the risk to her children if she was honest.

Dance assessed she was on the borderline.

"We'll make sure you're looked out for. But this is pretty serious."

A low voice, woman to woman, adult to adult. "You can say that. It's easy to say that."

"I give you my word."

One mother to another.

A very long ten seconds passed. "There *was* somebody in the trailer this morning."

"Could you describe them?"

"I couldn't see the face. 'Causa the angle, you know. Just the body, chest and shoulders, through the window. Like a, you know, silhouette. Not even clothes. That's all I could see. I swear."

Often a deceptive flag, that last sentence can also mean exactly what it says, as Dance now believed. "Which window?"

"That one there, in the front?" She pointed. It was horizontal, two feet high, three wide.

"You came out for a smoke and saw this person?"

"I'm aiming to quit. I will. Worried about the weight, you know. That always happens when you quit smoking. I try. Don't really want to gain any more pounds. Tony Senior's commented on it. And he should talk. Mr. Budweiser."

"What time?"

"Eleven, eleven-thirty."

"Did you see a car? Or when the person left?"

"No."

Then she noticed to her alarm that Madigan had given up shooting hate rays at her, had turned and was nearly to the front door of Bobby's trailer.

"Thank you, Tabatha. Go be with your children."

"Will I have to testify?"

As Dance sprinted toward the trailer she called over her shoulder, "We'll look after you, promise!" Then shouting: "Detective! Stop!"

Chapter 12

P. K. MADIGAN'S hand was nearly to the doorknob.

His eyes slid Dance's way and she saw his face cloud with the irritation he mustered so well.

But he also seemed to understand instantly that she had a point about not wanting him to go inside.

Or, she deduced from his hand dipping toward his pistol, maybe some risk awaited.

He stepped back. So did Dennis Harutyun.

Dance hurried across the street and joined them.

"Anybody inside?" the chief detective asked sharply.

Dance steadied her breathing. "Don't think so. But I don't know. The thing is the perp—or somebody—was here this morning. Eleven, eleven-thirty. You don't want to contaminate anything."

"In *here*?"

"I think we should assume it was the killer."

"She know that for sure? The time?" A glance toward Tabatha's trailer.

"Probably. The TV was on and it would've been all morning. Her husband's away a lot and she'd keep it on for comfort. She'd know the time according to the show she was watching."

"Who'd she see? Can she ID 'em?"

"No. And I believe her. She didn't see a face or vehicle."

A deep sigh. He muttered to Harutyun, "Get CSU over here. And tape off the property. As much as you can. All of the trailer."

The careful deputy made a call.

Madigan and Dance both stepped away from the trailer and stood on the crumbling walk.

"What'd Edwin, or whoever, be doing here? Afterward?"

"I don't know."

"Could've been a friend, one of the crew."

"A friend maybe. I talked to the crew. They would've said something about being here or acted deceptive. And none of them did."

Silence for a moment as he stared at the door, wanting to go in. He rocked on his feet. He asked her suddenly, "You like to fish?"

"No."

"Hm." He studied the crisp, jaundiced grass. "You don't fish? Or you don't like to?"

"Neither. But I've got a friend who'd live on his boat in Monterey Bay if he could."

Michael O'Neil was always out in the choppy water. Often with Dance's son, Wes, and his own children. Sometimes Dance's father, a retired marine biologist, went along.

"Monterey Bay. Hm. Salmon." Madigan looked around. "I like to fish."

"You catch and release?"

"No. Seems crueler to me. I catch and eat."

"Michael does that too."

"Michael?"

"My friend."

More silence, dense as the growing heat, as they watched Harutyun and Stanning string the yellow tape.

"I told her, Tabatha, that we'd have somebody keep an eye on her."

"We can do that."

"It's important."

"We can do that," he repeated, with a bit of edge. To Harutyun: "Get a car over here. Some rookie. Keep an eye on the place. That trailer across the street too."

"Thanks," Dance said.

He didn't respond.

She sensed Old Spice or something clove-oriented rising from his large body. He actually wore a gun belt with single spare cartridges stuck into loops, pointing downward, like a cowboy's. No speed loaders, those accessories that contained a disk of six or eight rounds to be dropped quickly into an open cylinder of a revolver. Detectives in Fresno probably didn't have much cause to shoot people, much less reload quickly.

Madigan stepped closer to the door, examined the lock. "Could've been jimmied."

They waited in more silence for the Crime Scene Unit to arrive and when they did, Dance was again impressed at the efficiency of the operation. The team dressed fast, in full jumpsuits, masks and booties, and—she was surprised—two of them with weapons drawn cleared the interior of the trailer, making sure there were no threats. Most police outfits have SWAT or regular officers—unswathed in evidence-protective clothing—handle this job, resulting in contamination of the scene.

CSU proceeded to process the trailer, dusting and using alternative light source wands for prints, taking trace evidence samples, electrostatic footprints on the front stoop and inside, looking for tire treads and anything else the perp might have discarded or shed.

Dance's friend, Lincoln Rhyme, was perhaps the country's leading expert in forensic evidence and crime scene work. She herself was a bit skeptical of the extreme reliance on the art; one case she knew of had

nearly resulted in the execution of an innocent man because certain clues had been planted by the real perp.
On the other hand, Rhyme and his partner, Amelia
Sachs, had worked miracles in identifying and convict-
ing suspects on the basis of nearly nonexistent evidence.

She noted that Madigan's eyes grew animated for the
first time since she'd arrived as he watched the team scour
the grounds and move in and out of the trailer. He likes his
forensics, she thought; he's a *thing* cop, not a *people* cop.

An hour later they'd finished and carted out some
boxes and bags, both paper and plastic, and announced
that they were releasing the scene.

Dance had a feeling she wasn't going to be welcome
much longer, despite the angling conversation she and
Madigan had had. She made quickly for the trailer. Stepping inside the place, which smelled of hot, plastic fur-
nishings, she froze. It was a museum. She'd never seen
anything like this, not in a residence. Posters, record
jackets, guitars, statuettes of musicians, a Hammond
B-3 organ, parts of wind and string instruments, ancient
amplifiers and hundreds of vinyl records—33⅓ LPs, 45
singles and ancient 78s, reels of tape. She found a collection of turntables and an old Nagra reel-to-reel, made
by the Kudelski Group, the best portable tape recorder
ever manufactured. Looking at all of these items, it was
like seeing beautiful but antiquated cars. These analog
devices had long ago lost the battle to digital.

Still, they were to Dance, as apparently they had
been to Bobby, works of art.

She found hundreds of concert souvenirs, mostly
from the sixties through the eighties. Mugs, T-shirts,
caps, even pens—an item, not surprisingly, commemo-
rating that most intellectual of singer-songwriters, Paul
Simon, whose "American Tune" had inspired the name
of her music website.

The majority of these artifacts, though, involved the country world. Photos covering nearly every square foot of wall space revealed the history of the genre, which, Dance believed, had reimagined itself more than any other musical form in America over the years. She spotted photos of musicians from the traditional era—the Grand Ole Opry and rockabilly styles—in the 1950s. And from the era of country rock a decade later, followed by outlaw with the likes of Waylon Jennings, Hank Williams, Jr., and Willie Nelson. Here were photos and autographs of Dolly Parton, Kenny Rogers and Eddie Rabbit, who were part of the country pop trend in the late seventies and eighties. The neotraditionalist movement in the eighties was a move back to the early era and brought superstar status to Randy Travis, George Strait, the Judds, Travis Tritt and dozens of others—all of whom were represented here.

In the nineties country became international, with artists like Clint Black, Vince Gill, Garth Brooks, Shania Twain, Mindy McCready and Faith Hill, on the one hand, and a strong alternative movement that rejected slick Nashville production values on the other. Pictures of Lyle Lovett and Steve Earl, who were part of the latter, stared down from one wall.

The present day was on display too. Here was a picture of Carrie Underwood (yes, of *American Idol* fame) and an autographed copy of the sheet music for Taylor Swift's "Fifteen," which spoke not about truck driving or God or patriotism or other traditional country themes but about high school angst.

Kayleigh Towne's career was, of course, well documented.

Dance knew there were many historians of the music scene in the past fifty years but she doubted they had as many artifacts as Bobby did. No death is worse than any other but Dance felt a deep pang that Bobby Prescott's devotion to archiving all aspects of country music in the twentieth century had died with him. It was the entire world's loss.

Dance pulled herself away from the archives and walked carefully through the place. What she was looking for, she didn't know.

Then she noted something out of the ordinary.

She stepped to a bookshelf, containing a number of binders and manila folders of legal and other official documents like tax bills and boxes of cassettes and reel-to-reel tapes, including some labeled "Master Tapes."

Dance was studying this portion of the trailer carefully when she happened to pass the window where Tabatha had said she'd seen the intruder that morning. Dance blinked in surprise as she found herself staring eye-to-eye at a very unhappy P. K. Madigan, a foot away on the other side of the glass.

His expression was: Come on out here to the woodshed.

But she summoned him first, calling loudly, "I've found something."

He grimaced and hesitated, then reluctantly joined her.

"Actually I've found something *missing.*"

He looked around. "Body language of the trailer tell you that?"

Madigan was being snide. But Dance said, "You could put it that way. People have patterns in their gestures and speech and expressions. They also have patterns in their living spaces. Bobby's a highly organized person. People who are organized don't happen to be that way accidentally. It's a psychological drive. Look at those shelves." She pointed.

"They're messy but so? I got a teenage boy."

"None of the others are. And your Crime Scene Unit marked where they'd taken things. Somebody else went through those boxes. Probably the intruder. It's near the window where Tabatha saw somebody."

"Why do you say something's missing?"

"I'm not sure it's missing. I'm making the deduction that if only those shelves were disturbed, the intruder was looking for something and he found it so he stopped."

Madigan reluctantly walked over to the shelves and, pulling on latex gloves, poked through the tapes, the papers, the pictures, the tchotchkes. He said, "Some of these snaps of Kayleigh, they're not souvenirs. They're personal."

That was one thing Dance hadn't noticed.

Madigan continued, "The sort of thing a son-of-a-bitch stalker'd want for a souvenir."

"That could be it, yes."

Madigan ran a finger over the shelf and examined it. The coat of dust was thick. Bobby was organized but not particularly concerned about cleaning. "Cement plant right up the road here. Looks like dust from there. I know it. We got a conviction in this trailer park 'cause of it, placing the perp here. That could be helpful." A cool glance her way. "You find anything else?"

"No."

Without a word he left the trailer, Dance after him. He called to Harutyun, "You guys find anything? Witnesses?"

"Nothing."

Stanning shook her head too.

"Where's Lopez?"

"Just finishing up at the convention center."

Madigan pulled a phone off his thick shiny belt and placed a call. He stepped away from the others and had a brief conversation. Dance couldn't hear what was said.

His eyes swiveled around the yard as he spoke, absently examining the deceased's residence. Dance was included in his gaze.

As he disconnected, Madigan said to Harutyun, "I want you to find Edwin. Bring him in. I don't care where he is or what he's doing. I need to talk to him. Now."

"Arrest him?"

"No. Make it seem like it'd be good for him to come in. In his interest, you know."

Dance heard a harsh exhalation as Madigan regarded her expression. "What? You don't think that's a good idea?"

She said, "No, I don't. I'd vote for surveillance."

Madigan squinted toward Harutyun. "Do it."

"Sure, Chief." Harutyun climbed into his cruiser and left, without a word to Dance.

No, she decided; the deputy *hadn't* looked at the verses to Kayleigh's song.

Madigan strode back to his car, his round belly swaying, as he looked over the scene. He grunted, "Crystal. Listen, I need you to come with me. Have a talk about something in my cruiser. We'll pick yours up later."

The woman dutifully climbed into the passenger seat of Madigan's cruiser. A moment later they were headed out onto the highway, without a word of farewell to Dance.

No matter.

She fished for her keys and turned toward her SUV. She stopped, closed her eyes briefly in frustration and gave a sharp, bitter laugh. Crystal Stanning's squad car was tight on the rear bumper of Dance's Pathfinder. In front was a carport full of junk. A V-8 engine block, weighing in at half a ton, she guessed, sat six inches in front of her SUV.

She wasn't going anywhere.

Chapter 13

AT THE FRESNO-MADERA Consolidated Sheriff's Office complex, P. K. Madigan stopped by the Crime Scene Unit, a block away, after returning from Bobby Prescott's trailer.

He wanted to urge the unit to make this case a priority, which of course they'd do. Anything for Kayleigh Towne, the girl who'd helped put Fresno on the map.

And anything for Chief Madigan too.

But he was only half thinking about pep rallies. He also pictured Kathryn Dance.

Thinking about her beached car. Some people you needed to hit over the head to deliver a message. He'd send Crystal back in an hour or two, spring the gal from her automotive jail. Oh, sorry Kathryn; I didn't know you'd be stuck between a rock and hard place—ha!

But he'd simply had it with people using Kayleigh like Dance was.

If Kayleigh hadn't been involved, the likes of Kathryn Dance would never have come to Fresno, never have taken the time to even say howdy-do to a soul here. Where was Ms. Agent Dance and the CBI when some MS-13 wannabes took an Uzi and sprayed it into the pizza place on Herndon, killing two children and missing the rival drug dealer altogether?

Sorry, *they* weren't celebrities.

He expected better from the CBI, thought they'd be above that publicity-grabbing shit. But Madigan had done his homework. He'd checked out Dance's boss, Charlie Overby, on YouTube and the archives. Man was faster with a press conference than Wild Bill Hickok with a six-gun.

Dance worked for him, which meant she'd surely be just the same.

Just happened to be in the area and a friend of Kayleigh's? My ass.

You don't mind if I take over your investigation, do you, P.K.?

Yeah, she'd come up with a few helpful things. But she was in the case for the wrong reasons and that just wasn't acceptable to P. K. Madigan. Besides, he didn't believe much in that fishy mumbo jumbo of hers. Kinesics? Crap. That'd be like learning about a trout from books and the Discovery Channel—as opposed to catching, cleaning and cooking one up in Crisco.

No, his approach was different. Cases were made nowadays on forensics, not voodoo. They'd have evidence from the convention center, they'd have forensics from Bobby's trailer—that cement dust, about as unique as trace could be, was a godsend.

Armed with that, Madigan would wear down the son of a bitch and get a confession in an hour or two.

He and Crystal walked into the CSU lab. He enjoyed the smell of the chemicals and the after-effects of the gas chromatograph, which reminded him of the Bunsen burner smell from high school, a good time in his life—football, his brother healthy, a girlfriend who ran the yearbook.

"Charlie," he called.

The pudgy, rosy-cheeked director of the CSU, Charlie Shean, looked up from a computer in his office—the only four-walled space in the large room. The rest of the place had cubicles and workstations and the up-to-date forensic *stuff* that Madigan had fought hard to get for his people.

"Hey, Chief." Shean's accent grounded him somewhere along the Massachusetts coast, just north or south of Bean Town.

Madigan thought Shean was the best forensic tech his budget could afford and he was one of the few employees on the force the detective was deferential to, though, of course, he'd get in a few good ones about the CSU man's name from time to time despite the different spelling.

"Need you to push everything through on this Towne case."

The round man shook his head. "Poor thing. She's got to be shook up. And that big concert this weekend. I got tickets, the wife and me. You going?"

"I am," Stanning said.

Madigan wasn't. He liked music but he liked music you could shut off with a switch when you wanted to. "What've we got?"

Shean nodded toward several techs in goggles, gloves and white jackets, working with quiet intensity at several stations not far away.

"Nothing yet. Three scenes. Convention center, Bobby's trailer and Sharp's rental. We're processing about two hundred unknown prints. We have what we *think* are Sharp's from his rental but he's not in AIFIS."

The FBI's Automated Integrated Fingerprint Identification System was, in Madigan's opinion, one of the few things the federal government was good for.

"But we aren't sure they're his."

"I'm going to talk to Sharp. I'll get 'em with the water bottle trick."

"Who's Agent Dance, CBI?"

Madigan snapped, "Why you asking?"

"She called—"

"Called *you*? Here? Direct?"

"Yeah. She talked to Kayleigh's assistant, Alicia Sessions, and found out where she thought somebody was spying on Kayleigh yesterday at the convention center. We dusted the area. Didn't find anything. CBI's involved?"

"No. CBI is *not* involved."

"Oh." When Madigan explained no further Shean continued, "You were right, that's the cement dust at Bobby's trailer, same stuff with the Baniero convictions. It's unique to that area."

"Have you got a match from Edwin's place? Lopez said there was plenty of dust on the Kayleigh pictures and memorabilia in his house."

"Lots of trace, yeah, but no results yet. Should know soon. And one more thing? The team found something in the orchestra pit. Some boxes had been moved—the manager said they usually kept stacks of them there to break somebody's fall in an accident, you know? They're special cartons. Stunt men use them. Whoever moved them, looked like he was wearing latex gloves. And similar marks on the smoke detectors; they had the batteries taken out."

Bingo!

Miguel Lopez, who'd searched Edwin's rental, had found a box of the gloves.

"The same as we got from Edwin's place?"

"We don't know that yet either. Wrinkle marks and manufacturer's trace'll tell us."

"Good, Charlie. Interrupt me, there're any break-throughs."

Madigan and Stanning left and walked to the sheriff's office proper, then inside and down a long corridor. Passersby going in the opposite direction nodded to him, a bit cautious, some downright intimidated.

He thought again about Kathryn Dance. She hadn't been the least intimidated by him. Thinking of her baking in the heat, he felt just a moment's bad. She could always put the AC on in that fancy Pathfinder of hers. Besides, soccer moms like her always toted round tons of bottled water. Tap wasn't good enough for them.

Madigan pushed through a swinging door on which was painted a fading sign: DETECTIVE DIVISION.

Detective Gabriel Fuentes, a bulldog of a man who sweated furiously, even in the winter, stood near the reception desk. Unlike deputies in the department who were former military, which was a lot of them, Fuentes had cast aside all trappings of the army and wore his black, shiny hair as long as he could get away with.

Edwin Sharp was here too. Madigan recognized the gangling man from the photos Kayleigh's lawyers had sent them, though he'd lost a lot of weight. He was standing over Fuentes, who, at five-eight or so, was six inches shorter than Edwin. The stalker also had long arms and massive hands. His eyes were sunken below thick brows, which gave him an ominous look though he was pretty normal otherwise. Those eyes were curious, Madigan thought. They weren't the least troubled. Hell, children on class field trips to the department looked guiltier than this boy.

His smile was the oddest Madigan had ever seen, a faint upward curving of the thin lips but mostly at the very ends.

Those underpass eyes now turned to him. "Detective Madigan, hi. How you doing? I'm Edwin Sharp."

I've got a name badge but this fellow hasn't once looked at it. What's this about?

"I'll just be a second, son. Thanks for coming in."

"Just for the record, I'm not under arrest. You've asked me here and I've come voluntarily. I can leave at any time. Is that correct?"

"That's right. You want some ice cream?"

"I . . . what?"

"Ice cream?"

"No, thanks. I'll pass. What's this all about?"

"You go by Ed, Eddie?"

The smile. It was damn eerie. "No. I like Edwin, Pike."

Madigan paused. The fuck is he using my first name for? And how the hell did he know it? A lot of *deputies* here don't know what it is.

"Well, then, Edwin it is. Be back in a second." He nodded for Fuentes to join him up the hall.

"Any problem?" Madigan whispered.

"No. Just asked him to come in and he didn't hesitate." Fuentes continued, "And I heard Miguel and a crime scene team found some good evidence at his place, after he left."

"Looks that way."

"Good," Fuentes said. "How's Kayleigh holding up?"

"Doing the best she can, I'd say. Not great."

"Son of a bitch," Fuentes muttered. And they looked back to see Edwin watching the men. He couldn't hear what they said; they were too far away. But it gave Madigan a chill to see those eyes crinkle with amusement as if he could sense every word.

He sent Fuentes back to the division and stepped into the lunchroom, opened the fridge and scooped himself some ice cream, dropped it into a paper cup. He loved ice cream. No taste for liquor other than a beer at a barbecue, no chew or smokes but he loved ice cream. Not yogurt or sherbet or low-fat. Real, honest-to-God ice cream. He carried an extra ten pounds due exclusively to the stuff but that was ten pounds he was willing to sacrifice for the cause.

People thought he ate ice cream to intimidate suspects, or to win them over if he offered a scoop or two. But fact was he just liked ice cream.

Today he was having mint chocolate chip.

He returned to the Detective Division. "Okay, Edwin. Just like to have a conversation with you, you'd be so kind."

A couple of big bites from the cup with a metal spoon. He always used metal. Hated plastic. Paper and foam cups were okay but you needed to eat your ice cream with a real spoon.

They'd just started toward the interview room when the door to the division swung open once again and someone else entered the lobby.

Oh, Jesus Christ.

It was Kathryn Dance.

Chapter 14

SHE'D TAKEN A cab.

Did they think she wouldn't?

The chief detective and Crystal Stanning had been gone from Bobby's trailer for ten minutes when she gave up her futile back-and-forth attempt to free the wide-wheelbase Nissan.

She'd pulled out her mobile, found a business search app and got a cab to pick her up and take her straight to the sheriff's office.

The stalker seemed the more amused of the two men she now walked up to. "Agent Dance, hope you're well," Edwin said, getting her title right—name too—and offering a modicum of respect.

Madigan's expression said: So much for the improvised detention center at Bobby's trailer.

She said firmly, "I'd like to talk to you, Deputy," now using the less impressive of his job titles, because she was really pissed off.

Madigan replied, "I'm pretty busy now, Kathryn. Come on, Edwin. That way. Say, you want a bottle of nice cold water?" He said to the assistant, "We'll be in number three."

And they vanished down the hall.

After a frustrating five minutes, Dance noticed Detective Dennis Harutyun, of the solid shoulders, rich complexion and supple mustache, walking up the corridor toward her. He'd left before Madigan's little game with the cars and might not know she was persona non grata. She made a decision, taking her ID card from her purse, wedging the holder into her belt, shield on display, something she never did, even on duty.

She approached Harutyun.

He didn't seem to smile any more than his boss but nothing suspicious glimmered in his eyes. If he seemed awkward it was probably because he hadn't bothered to drop everything and analyze Kayleigh's song "Your Shadow" for potential crime scenes.

"Dennis."

"Hello, Kathryn."

She remembered how Madigan was referred to by intimates. "The Chief's interviewing Edwin now. Where's observation for Interview Room Three? I got lost."

The bluff worked. Without any reaction, assuming that she was sanctioned to be here, Harutyun guided her up the corridor and even held the door open politely. He flicked the light on in the small, close chamber. There was no worry that Edwin or Madigan might see a flash; observation rooms were invariably light- and sound-proof, even if everyone who owned a TV knew the mirror was fake and there were cameras, cops and witnesses on the other side.

She felt a little bad, using Harutyun like this. But Dance was determined to keep Kayleigh Towne safe, and while she didn't doubt Madigan's devotion to that same goal, she wasn't at all sure of his competence when it came to a perp like Edwin.

And, oh, yeah, she was still pissed off.

She examined the interrogation room. It was austere. In the center were a large fiberboard table, a half dozen chairs and a smaller utility table on which sat bottles of water and pads of paper. No decorations on the walls.

No pencils or pens.

Madigan, she observed, took a professional approach. He sat forward, in a focused but unthreatening manner. He was confident but dropped the authoritarian, imperious attitude she'd seen earlier (apparently reserved for interloping law enforcers). He didn't engage in overt hand gestures, which can distract the suspect. He was respectful of Edwin, asking if he was comfortable, was the temperature too hot, too cold.

Dance supposed the ice cream had to be a prop of some sort. Every single word or gesture by an interrogator tells the subject something more about the questioner. You should never say or do anything that doesn't further the session. Sipping coffee, scratching your head, frowning. . . . But apparently the confection wasn't part of the detective's plan. He finished it with relish and tossed the cup away. Edwin's eyes followed every motion.

Madigan made a few mistakes, though. One was that he directed Edwin to sit across from him at the table. Better would have been to sit facing each other without any furniture between them. Tables, other chairs, *any* prop gives the suspect a sense of security.

He made a clumsy show of offering the suspect water. Dance noted that Madigan pointed at the Clear Spring, rather than simply picking up a bottle and handing it to Edwin. It was probably an attempt to lift Edwin's friction ridge prints—fingerprints—from the bottle and it seemed that Edwin deduced this; he didn't touch it. The problem was that Madigan's offer gave away something of the interviewer's strategy and intelligence.

But the big mistake, in Dance's opinion, came next:

"Can I ask what this is all about, Pike?"

"Robert Prescott."

Wouldn't've done that, she thought.

"Oh, Kayleigh's road manager," Edwin said, nodding and rubbing his prominent eyebrow.

"Where were you last night at the time he died."

Oh, no.

Dance realized she must have said this aloud because Harutyun tilted his head her way.

"What? No, he's dead?" Edwin looked alarmed.

"And you didn't know that?"

"No, no. That's terrible. He and Kayleigh were real close. What happened?"

"Got himself burned up. So, you're telling me you weren't at the convention center last night?" He now leaned toward Edwin ominously.

Dance understood Madigan's approach. It was referred to as a blunt-force attack—a term borrowed from hackers who used massive supercomputers to run through all possible passwords to break encrypted messages. With blunt force, officers would inundate suspects with information about them and about the case, suggesting knowledge they didn't actually possess and connections that were tenuous at best. When delivered with confidence, as Madigan clearly had, the details sometimes got suspects to confess quickly.

Yes, blunt force could be effective. But if it didn't work right away, you ended up with a subject who stonewalled; any chance of getting helpful information would be ruined. Accordingly, Dance herself never used this technique. Her belief was that information was the most valuable thing an interrogator has. It could be a steel trap, it could be a weapon but to be effective it had to be fed out slowly to lure the suspect into revealing details that could later be used to trip him up. Madigan had just given away the most important key facts—that Bobby was dead, where the crime occurred and how it happened. Had she been conducting the interview, she would have kept those details secret for the time being.

Edwin looked over the deputy somberly. "Well, I'm very sorry to hear that about Bobby. That's sad for Kayleigh."

Madigan didn't respond. He said quickly, "Could you tell me where you were when Prescott died? Midnight last night?"

"Well, I'm sure you know I don't have to tell you anything but I'm a little surprised at this. Really, Detective. You clearly think I hurt Bobby. Why on earth would I do that? I'd never hurt anybody close to Kayleigh. But the answer to your question is, I was home in my rental."

"Any witnesses?"

"Maybe somebody driving by saw me, I don't know. I was in the living room, listening to music most of the night. I don't have curtains up yet."

"I see. Okay." Then he sprung the trap. Madigan leaned closer and said firmly, "But what do you say to the fact that we've got two witnesses that place you at the convention center around the time he died and then at Bobby's house this morning?"

Chapter 15

WHAT EDWIN SHARP said in reply was probably not what Madigan expected.

With a frown, further blending his dense eyebrows, he asked simply, "Did they have clear views?"

Don't answer, Dance thought to Madigan.

"They sure did. The house right across the road from the convention center stage door. And directly across from Bobby's house."

Hell, Dance thought. Edwin could now figure out exactly who the witnesses were.

He said, shrugging, "Well, they're mistaken. I was home."

Dance said to Harutyun, "Tabatha didn't ID anybody. She couldn't. Was there somebody else there?"

A pause. "Not that I know of."

"And is there really a witness by the convention center?"

"Apparently," Harutyun explained. Then decided to tell her. "Some woman lived nearby saw somebody around midnight."

"She positively ID'd Edwin?"

"I don't . . . I don't think so."

The hesitation meant she *hadn't*, Dance decided. She recalled the layout. The house would have been across the parking lot, two hundred yards from the stage door. At night, she wouldn't have been able to make out more than a vague silhouette.

"Well, Madigan just told a possible homicide suspect about two witnesses and it wouldn't be that hard to find out their identities. They need looking after. He said he'd get some protection for Tabatha. Do you know if he did?"

"Tabatha, yes. The other one, I don't know."

"We need to."

"Okay."

And in the interrogation room, the one-on-one continued. Madigan was probably brilliant at getting confessions from the typical perp you saw in the Central Valley. But Edwin Sharp was not a typical perp.

Well, under Giles versus Lohan . . .

The stalker listened patiently, analytically as Madigan said, "And we've just been through your house, Edwin. We found a lot of interesting things, including latex gloves, the same sort that were used in the murder. And trace evidence."

Edwin said calmly, "I see. My house, hm? Did you get a warrant?"

"We didn't need one. My deputy noticed some things in plain sight."

"Even from the sidewalk?" the stalker asked. "Tough to see anything inside unless you entered on the property. Well, I don't really think you had the right to take anything. I want it returned."

Dance turned to Harutyun. "Did he get a warrant?"

"No, after we saw things were missing from Bobby's, the Chief sent a deputy over there—Miguel Lopez—and he saw things from the trailer through Edwin's window, in plain sight. . . . What's the matter?"

Dance didn't reply.

Inside the interrogation room Edwin was saying, "Well, I haven't been in Bobby's trailer, so . . ."

"Oh, how did you know it was a trailer?" Madigan demanded triumphantly.

"That's right, you called it a 'house' earlier. I thought that was odd. I know where he lived because of Kayleigh's song two years ago. 'Bobby's Double-Wide.' All about the history of country music. Sort of like Don McLean's 'American Pie.' Surprised you don't know it. Being all gung-ho for Kayleigh, I mean."

Madigan's smile deflated and he seemed to be wrestling down his anger. "Just confess, Edwin. You want to, I know you do."

A textbook line from blunt-force interrogation. This is the moment when the perp might start to cry and, indeed, confess.

But Edwin said, "Can I collect my things now? Where are they? In the Crime Scene Unit? That's in the building south of here, right?"

The detective blinked. Then he said, "Look, let's be realistic here. Work with me. I'll talk to the prosecutor. I'm sure he'll cut a deal. Maybe you were arguing with Bobby. You know, that chest bumping that started at the Cowboy Saloon that afternoon? It escalated. These things happen. We could be talking reduced counts. And maybe he'll cut out the stalking charge altogether."

"Stalking?" Edwin seemed perplexed. "I'm not a stalker. Kayleigh's a friend. I know it and she knows it."

"Friend? That's not the story according to her lawyers."

"Oh, she's afraid of them. They're controlled by her father. They've all been telling her lies about me."

"That's not the way it is," Madigan said. "You're in town to stalk her. And you killed her friend because he threw you out of the Cowboy Saloon yesterday."

Edwin remained completely placid. "No, Detective. I came to Fresno to get out of the Seattle rain for a time, to come to a public concert . . . and to pay respect to a performer I like, a woman who's been nice and frankly shown some interest in me. One of the best musicians of our era, by the way. You accuse me of stalking but I'm sorry, *I'm* the victim here. You never did anything about *my* call."

Madigan's face revealed confusion. "What do you mean?"

"I thought that was why your deputy Fuentes asked me here. *My* complaint."

"Complaint?"

"You don't know? I have to say that doesn't surprise me. Saturday night, I called nine-one-one and reported a Peeping Tom, a trespasser, behind my house. But nobody did anything about it. You've got, what? Twelve hundred deputies? I just needed one to come out and see where this guy was standing, talk to the neighbors. But did they? No. Not for an out-of-towner."

With a grim laugh, Madigan responded, "We have *four* hundred deputies in Fresno and sixty in Madera. They cover over six thousand square miles of territory from the Valley all the way up to the mountains. I'm afraid a Peeping Tom, if there really was one, isn't going to be all-hands-on-deck."

Dance noted that if the stalker was on a fishing expedition to get information about the limitations of the sheriff's office, he'd certainly succeeded.

Edwin kept up the offensive, easy as a June day. "Your hometown girl is, quote, 'stalked' and you think it's the end of the world. I'm a newcomer and nobody cares that somebody's casing out my house. If Bobby Prescott was murdered and witnesses place me at his house, or *trailer*, then I'm being set up. Somebody had another reason to kill him and they're using me as a fall guy. You really have to understand, Detective, I love her. I'd never hurt anybody close to her."

"You don't love her, Edwin. You're obsessed with a celebrity who doesn't know you from Adam."

"I think love has to have *some* obsession to it, don't you, Pike? Aren't you obsessed with your wife some? Or *weren't* you, at one point?" Edwin had spotted the wedding ring.

"You will not talk about my family!" Madigan sputtered.

"I'm sorry," Edwin said, frowning. His eyes were enigmatic but belied contrition.

Madigan said, "Kayleigh doesn't love you at all. You're way off base."

Efforts to get suspects to admit they were wrong, or that their beliefs were based on errors, were usually useless, especially in the case of fanatic- or obsession-based crimes like stalking.

Edwin shrugged. "You say that but you know she sent me emails and letters. She practically said she loved me."

With some difficulty Madigan controlled his anger. He said, "Son, you have to get real here. She sent you the same emails she sent to ten thousand fans. A hundred thousand. We've been briefed by her lawyers. You got a half dozen form emails and a couple of form letters."

"That's what they're telling you. Doesn't mean it's true."

"Edwin, a lot of fans feel that way about performers. I sent a fan letter to a star once. He sent me back an autographed picture and—"

"*He*?" Edwin asked quickly.

Madigan hesitated a moment. "We got you dead to rights, son. Tell me the truth. Tell me you killed Robert Prescott and we'll work something out. Tell me and you'll feel better. Believe me."

Edwin said, "You know, Pike, I think I don't want to say anything more. I'd like to leave. And I'd like to pick up my things now. *People versus Williams*. You have to arrest me or let me go."

Dance asked Harutyun, "The evidence? It places Edwin at the scene?"

She didn't even bother to wait for a reply. Harutyun's shift of eye away from her was all she needed. "He doesn't have any forensics, does he?"

"We think it'll probably match. . . . But no, he doesn't have any yet."

"Dennis, ask the Chief to come in here."

"What?"

"I need to talk to him. It's very important."

Harutyun examined her, glancing down at the ID on her belt. His mouth tightened beneath the mustache. He realized that she had deceived her way inside.

"I'm sorry," Dance said. "I had to do it."

He grimaced and sighed. Then snatched up a phone and dialed a number. They could hear it buzz inside. Madigan looked at it with surprise and irritation. Edwin didn't pay attention but instead turned and looked into the reflective glass. Since he couldn't see the occupants of the room he wasn't focused on either Dance or Harutyun but the mere transit of his eyes in their direction was unsettling.

And his smile was wax. That damn smile.

"Yes?" Madigan said casually into the phone, though Dance noted a white thumb where he gripped the handset.

"Detective?"

"What?"

"I'm here with Agent Dance. She'd . . . like to have a word with you? If possible."

His incredulous eyes started to swivel toward the mirrored window too, then he restrained himself.

"At this moment?"

"That's correct. It seems important."

"Wonder how she ended up in there."

Did the stalker know what was going on? Dance couldn't tell but he continued to look at the mirror.

"I'm busy."

Dance grabbed the phone. "Detective, let him go. Don't arrest him."

After a moment, Madigan dropped the phone into the cradle. "Edwin, have some water."

"I want to leave," he repeated, the essence of calm.

Madigan ignored him and stepped outside. It seemed like a matter of seconds before the door flew open in the observation room and he was storming up to Dance.

"What the hell do you think you're doing?"

"You've got to let him go. If you don't have probable cause—"

"This's my case, not yours."

She knew she'd embarrassed him in front of his people. But she couldn't help herself. "You have to let him go."

"Just 'cause you figured out somebody dropped that light on Bobby Prescott doesn't mean I want or need any more of your opinions."

So, she reflected. Dennis Harutyun *had* given her credit for that deduction, back at the convention center.

"He has to be released."

A jagged edge in his voice, Madigan said, "So you're on his side now?"

Dance found she was quite angry. "It's not a question of sides. It's a question of proving a case. Edwin may very well've killed Bobby. But if he goes to trial and gets off, that's double jeopardy. He's gotten away with murder."

"I answer to Sheriff Gonzalez, not you."

"Let him go and monitor him. It's the only way to make a case."

"And what if he gives the deputy the slip and decides it's time to kill Kayleigh. Like Rebecca Schaeffer."

The actress who was murdered in Los Angeles some years ago. Her tragic death at the hands of a stalker had led to California's enacting the first anti-stalking law in the nation.

"Well, you saw his—what do you call it, kinesics? That's your expertise, you were pretty quick to tell me. Was he lying when he said he was being set up? You'd trespassed into the observation room by then, hadn'tcha?"

"I couldn't tell under those circumstances. I didn't have time."

"Ah."

"He's asked to leave and you haven't let him. That's a problem."

Madigan looked at Edwin in the room. The young man had pulled out a pen and pad of paper and was jotting notes. A lot of them.

Madigan called to Harutyun, "Book him. Cuff him and get him to detention. Breaking and entering at Bobby's only at this point. I *know* there's evidence for that." He turned to Dance. "Crystal'll take you to your car and you better go now. You being in here's trespass and, as you can probably tell, I'm in an arresting mood at the moment."

Chapter 16

AFTER FIFTEEN MINUTES of silent driving, Crystal Stanning said to Kathryn Dance, "I didn't block you in on purpose. I just parked there."

"I know that."

In Stanning's personal car, a sun-faded Toyota, they were just pulling into the drive of Bobby's trailer. The young detective stopped, brakes squealing. A belt needed replacing pretty soon too. The grass here, pale and thin, looked dustier and more spiky than before. Heat ripples undulated like sheets of flowing water above the Pathfinder.

Stanning fished another set of keys from her purse and said, "Yours'll be hot. You'll be wanting to mind the wheel. People've gotten burns." They climbed out.

"I'll take care."

"And here it is September. I don't know 'bout glaciers melting but I'll tell you it's hotter now than when I was a girl."

"I hear you."

"You can buy those windshield shades at Rite Aid. They work pretty good. Though I imagine you won't be staying around."

Dance wondered if Madigan had asked his deputy to drop that into the conversation to see where it went.

She said only, "Thanks."

"Just 'tween us?"

"Sure."

"Kayleigh Towne's a big deal here. Fresno's not the

glitziest place on earth. We come in real low on nice-places-to-live surveys and Kayleigh's made us famous. I don't know, maybe the Chief thinks you're here to boost yourself up, you and the CBI, I mean. Take her away from us, you might say, with this investigation. And if that happens, the sheriff's office'll lose out on the money. Maybe a lot of it."

"Money?"

"Yeah, if we can't handle the case, he's thinking that'll go into the hopper when it's budget time. See, he fights hard for us in the department, the Chief. One time, he was convinced we couldn't find this girl got herself kidnapped and killed because CSU couldn't analyze some dirt trace at the scene. He still feels bad about that. So he's always fighting for more pennies."

"I see."

"He got his dirt machine, whatever it is. Don't know that it gets used much but that's the way he is."

Without another word, the deputy drove off.

Dance walked to her vehicle.

So what do I do? Even if she wanted to take on the case, which would mean working with a wholly uncooperative local team, she didn't think her boss or Sacramento would go for it. Whatever Madigan felt, the CBI was the least political law enforcement organization she'd ever had contact with. Even if the suspect had been after a much more famous star, a stalking case wasn't the sort the bureau would take on. Yet, Kayleigh was a good friend, other people were in danger, she was convinced, and Madigan was outgunned by Edwin Sharp.

That odd smile, the calculation, the calm demeanor, the research. They were armor and they were weapons.

And what was beneath that smile? What was in his heart and mind? To a degree unlike any other suspect she'd known, Edwin Sharp was a mystery. She simply couldn't read him.

She got into the Pathfinder.

Got out again immediately. It had to be 130 degrees inside. She leaned in, started the engine and rolled down the windows. Then turned the AC on full blast.

As she waited for the interior to moderate, she walked closer to Bobby Prescott's trailer, now marked with crime scene tape. She thought again about the astonishing collection of music history inside.

Brush and grass waved in the breeze and dust ghosts rose and vanished. She realized it was completely deserted here now, aside from the squad car in which a young Asian-American deputy sat in front on the shoulder, with a view of both Bobby's and Tabatha's trailers.

Despite the absorbing heat, Dance felt another chill of unease. She'd thought of another implication of Madigan's arresting Edwin Sharp. If someone else was the killer, and he was using "Your Shadow" as a template, then he'd have free rein to carry out the next murder without fear the police were searching for him.

Finally the Pathfinder was cool enough to drive. She put the vehicle in gear and drove away from the scene, the yellow police tape fluttering cheerfully in the breeze behind her.

Debating.

I don't want to do this. It'll be a nightmare.

But ten seconds later she made the decision and was on her phone to the CBI office in Monterey, on her boss's voicemail.

"Charles. It's Kathryn. I need to take over an investigation in Fresno. Call me for the details." She debated about explaining what kind of nuclear detonation this would provoke and the political nightmare that would ensue.

But she decided that was a conversation best had in real time.

Chapter 17

KAYLEIGH TOWNE'S TWO-STORY Victorian squatted on a twenty-acre plot north of Fresno.

The house wasn't large—twenty-five hundred square feet or so—but had been constructed by artisan builders, with one instruction: make it comfortable and comforting. She was a nester—tough for a performer who traveled seven months out of the year—and she wanted a home that cried cozy, cried family.

When she was twelve, Bishop Towne had sold the house she and her sister had grown up in, a ramshackle place north of Fresno, in the mountains. He said it was hard to get to in the winter, though the real reasons were that, one, his father had built it and Bishop would do anything he could to separate himself from his old man. And two, the rustic family manse hadn't fit the image of the lifestyle he'd wanted to lead: that of the high-powered country superstar. He'd built a ten-million-dollar working ranch on fifty acres in the Valley and populated it with cattle and sheep he had no interest in or knowledge about raising.

The move had been horrifying enough to Kayleigh but worse was that he'd sold the beloved family house and land to a mining company that owned the adjacent property and they'd bulldozed the structure, planning to expand, though the company'd gone bankrupt; the unnecessary destruction was all the more traumatic to the girl.

She'd written a song about the place, which became a huge hit.

> *I've lived in LA, I've lived in Maine,*
> *New York City and the Midwest Plains,*
> *But there's only one place I consider home.*
> *When I was a kid—the house we owned.*
> *Life was perfect and all was fine,*
> *In that big old house . . . near the silver mine.*
>
> *The silver mine . . . the silver mine.*
> *I can't remember a happier time,*
> *In that big old house . . . near the silver mine.*

Now, the man responsible for this displacement walked inside Kayleigh's spacious living room and bent down and hugged her.

Bishop's fourth wife, Sheri, accompanied him. She too embraced Kayleigh, then sat, after an awkward moment of debate about which piece of furniture to choose. Ash blond hair sprayed persuasively in place, the petite yet busty woman was a dozen years older than Kayleigh, unlike Wife Number Three, who could have attended the same high school as Bishop's daughter—in the class behind her, no less.

Kayleigh, like Bishop, couldn't remember much about Number Two.

Hulking Bishop Towne then maneuvered his massive frame onto a couch, moving slow—slower than a lot of people even older than he was. "The joints're catching up," he'd complained recently and at first Kayleigh thought he meant the dives he'd played in his early, drinking, fighting years, but then she realized he meant hips, knees, shoulders.

He was in cheap jeans and his ubiquitous black shirt, the belly rolling over his impressive belt, leaving the more impressive silver buckle only partly visible.

"Was he still there, across the road?" Kayleigh asked, looking out, noting Darthur Morgan, vigilant as ever, in the front seat of the SUV, pointed outward.

"Who?" Bishop growled.

"Edwin." Who did he think?

"Didn't see anybody," he said. Sheri shook her head.

Edwin—the first damn thing she saw this morning, looking out the window of her second-story bedroom. Well, his *car*, the big red car. That's what she saw. Which didn't make the sense of violation any less.

Kayleigh lived on the way to Yosemite and Sierra National Park, just where the area started to get interesting geographically. Across the two-lane road in front of her property was a public recreation area and arboretum, filled with rolling hills, jogging paths, groves of trees and gardens. The lot allowed twenty-four-hour parking, just the place for a sick stalker to perch.

She said, "He was there a while ago. Just sitting, staring at the house." She closed her eyes briefly, shivering.

"Oh, my," Sheri said.

"Well, nobody's there now," Bishop repeated distractedly, noticing a wad of tissues on the coffee table where Kayleigh'd been sitting with her iced tea and mobile, on which she'd called friends and family about Bobby's death.

"Hey, sorry about Bobby, KT. I know you . . . I mean, I'm sorry."

Sheri offered, "It's terrible, honey. I feel so bad for you. For everyone."

Kayleigh stepped into the kitchen, got a milk for her father and an iced tea for Sheri, another for herself too. She returned to the living room.

"Thank you, honey," the woman offered tentatively.

Her father lifted the milk as if toasting.

"Daddy." Her eyes avoiding his, Kayleigh said quickly, "I'm thinking of canceling." It was easier to stare toward where a murderous stalker had been spying on her than to make eye contact with Bishop Towne.

"The concert?" The big man grunted. His ragged vocal style was not a function of any emotion, of course, but was simply because that's the way he talked. No lilting tones, never a whisper, just a guttural rasp. It hadn't always been that way; his voice—like his joints and liver—had been a victim of his lifestyle.

"I'm thinking of it."

"Sure. Course. I see."

Sheri tried to deflect what might be an uncomfortable moment. "If there's anything I can do? . . . I'll bring some dinners by. Tell me what you'd like. I'll make you something special."

Food and death had always been linked, Kayleigh now thought.

"I'll think on it. Thanks, Sheri."

The word "Mom" had, of course, never been on the table. Kayleigh didn't hate her stepmother. Either you were a woman of steel, like Margaret, her mother, and you fought with and—at times—corralled a man like Bishop Towne, or you took the residual prestige and the undeniable charisma and you surrendered. That was Sheri.

Though Kayleigh couldn't blame her. Nor could she her father either. Margaret had been his first choice and, despite the others along the way, they'd still be together if not for fate. There was no one who could take his first wife's place so why even try? Yet it was impossible to imagine Bishop Towne surviving without a woman in his life.

He grumbled, "You tell Barry?"

She nodded toward her mobile. "He was the first one I called. He's in Carmel with Neil."

Tall, fidgeting Barry Zeigler, her producer, was full of nervous energy. He was a genius in the studio. He'd produced some of the biggest hits of the nineties, when country got itself branded with the adjective "crossover" and began to transcend its Nashville and Dallas and Bakersfield roots to spread to mainstream TV and overseas.

If anybody had created a Kayleigh Towne sound it was Barry Zeigler. And that sound had made her a huge success.

Zeigler and the label hadn't escaped the shadow of Edwin Sharp either, though. The stalker had inundated the company with emails criticizing instrumentation choices and pacing and production techniques. He never dissed Kayleigh's voice or the songs themselves but argued that Zeigler, the recording techs and backup musicians weren't "doing her justice." That was a favorite phrase of his.

Kayleigh'd seen several of the emails and, though she never told anyone, she thought Edwin had a point on a few of the issues.

Finally Sheri said, "Just one thing. I mean—" A glance toward Bishop, sipping the milk he drank as religiously as he had once drunk bourbon. When he didn't object to her getting this far, she continued, "That luncheon tomorrow—for the fan of the month. You think we can still do that?"

It was a promotion Alicia Sessions had put together on Facebook and on Kayleigh's website. Bishop had more or less shoehorned Sheri into working on various marketing projects for the Kayleigh Towne operation. The woman had been in retail all her life and had made some valuable contributions.

"It's all scheduled, right?" Bishop asked.

"We've rented the room at the country club. It'd mean a lot to him. He's a big fan."

Not as big as someone I know, Kayleigh thought.

"And there'll be some publicity too."

"No reporters," Kayleigh said. "I don't want to talk about Bobby. That's what they'll want to ask me." Alicia had been deflecting the press—and there'd been plenty of them. But when the steely-eyed personal assistant said no, there wasn't room for debate.

Bishop said, "We'll control it. Set the ground rules. Make sure they don't ask questions about what happened at the convention center."

"I can do that," Sheri said, with an uncertain glance toward Bishop. "I'll coordinate with Alicia."

Kayleigh finally said, "Sure, I guess." She pictured the last time she had lunch alone with Bobby, a week ago. She wanted to cry again.

"Good," Bishop said. "But we'll keep it short. Tell that fan it'll have to be short."

Having conceded one issue, Kayleigh said, "But I really want to think about the concert, Daddy."

"Hey, baby doll, whatever you're happiest doing."

Bishop leaned forward and snagged one of the guitars his daughter kept in her living room, an old Guild, with a thin neck and golden spruce top, producing a ringing tenor. He played Elizabeth Cotten's version of "Freight Train."

He was a talented, syncopated fingerpicker, in the style of Arty and Happy Traum and Leo Kottke (and damn if he couldn't also flat-pick as well as Doc Watson, a skill Kayleigh could never master). His massive hands totally controlled the fret board. In pop music, guitar was originally for rhythm accompaniment—like a drum or maracas—and only in the past eighty years or so had it taken on the job of melody. Kayleigh used her Martin for its original purpose, strumming, to accompany her main instrument—a four-octave voice.

Kayleigh remembered Bishop's rich baritone of her youth and she cringed to hear what he'd become. Bob Dylan never had a smooth voice but it was filled with expression and passion and he could hit the notes. When, at a party or occasionally at concerts, Kayleigh and Bishop sang a duet together, she modulated to a key he could pull off and covered the notes that would give him trouble.

"We'll make sure it's short," he announced again.

What? Kayleigh wondered. The concert? Then recalled: the luncheon with the fan. Was it tomorrow, or the next day?

Oh, Bobby . . .

"And we'll talk about it, the concert. See how you feel in a day or so. Want you to be in good form. Happy too. That's what matters," he repeated.

She was looking out the window again into the grove of trees separating the house from the road, a hundred yards away. She'd done the plantings for seclusion and quiet but now all she thought was it would provide great cover so that Edwin could get close to the house.

More arpeggios—chords broken into individual notes—rang out. Kayleigh thought automatically: diminished, minor sixth, major. The guitar did everything Bishop wanted it to do. He could get music out of a tree branch.

She reflected: Bishop Towne had missed concerts because he was unconscious or in jail. But he'd never chosen to cancel one.

He racked the guitar and said to Sheri, "Got that meeting."

The woman, who seemed to have a different perfume for every day of the week, rose instantly and started to reach for Bishop's arm, then thought better; she tried to be discreet in his daughter's presence. She *did* work at it, Kayleigh reflected.

I don't hate you.

I just don't like you.

Kayleigh wafted a smile her way.

"You still got that present I got you a coupla years ago?" Bishop asked his daughter.

"I have all your presents, Daddy."

She saw them to the door, amused that Darthur Morgan seemed to regard them with some suspicion. The couple piled into a dusty SUV and left, petite Sheri behind the wheel of the massive vehicle. Bishop gave up driving eight years ago.

She thought about making more calls about Bobby but couldn't bring herself to. She strode to the kitchen, pulling on work gloves, and stepped outside into her garden. She loved it here, growing flowers and herbs and vegetables too—what else, in this part of California? She lived in the most productive agricultural county in America.

The appeal of gardening had nothing to do with the miracle of life, the environment, being one with the earth. Kayleigh Towne just liked to get her hands dirty and concentrate on something other than the Industry.

And here she could dream about her life in the future, puttering around in gardens like this with her children. Making sauces and baked goods and casseroles from things she herself had grown.

> *I remember autumn, pies in the oven,*
> *Sitting on the porch, a little teenage lovin',*
> *Riding the pony and walking the dogs,*
> *Helping daddy outside, splitting logs.*

Life was simple and life was fine,
In that big old house, near the silver mine.

I'm canceling the fucking concert, she thought.

She stuffed her hair up under a silly canvas sun hat and examined her crops. The air was hot but comforting; insects buzzed around her face and even their persistent presence was reassuring, as if reminding that there was more to life than musical performances.

More than the *Industry*.

But suddenly she froze: a flash of light.

No, not Edwin. There was no brilliant red color from his car.

What was it? The light was coming from the south, to the left as you faced the garden, about one hundred yards away. Not from Edwin's hunter's blind at the arboretum or main road in front. It was from a small access road, running perpendicular to the highway. A developer had bought the adjacent land a year ago but gone bankrupt before the residential construction had started. Was this a survey team? Last year, she'd been glad the deal fell through; she'd wanted her privacy. Now, perversely, she was happy there might be crews around—and eventually neighbors—to discourage Edwin and others like him.

But what exactly was the light?

On off, on off. Flashing.

She decided to find out.

Kayleigh made her way through the brush toward the stuttering illumination.

Bright, dark.

Light, shadow.

Chapter 18

KATHRYN DANCE WAS in south Fresno, trying to find a restaurant that Crystal Stanning had recommended.

Her thoughts, though, were on how to handle the explosion when Charles Overby or, more likely, the CBI director in Sacramento told Sheriff Anita Gonzalez that Dance was going to be running the Bobby Prescott homicide.

She actually jumped when her phone buzzed.

Ah, Charles, hope I didn't disrupt one of your leisurely lunches. . . .

But the number on caller ID was a local one.

"Hello?"

"Kathryn?"

"Yes."

"It's Pike Madigan."

She said nothing.

"Talk for a minute?"

She thought she heard scraping of a spoon. A smack of lips. Was he eating lunch, the phone tucked between shoulder and ear? More ice cream? "Go ahead."

"What're you up to?"

She said, "Going for chicken mole at Julio's."

"Good choice. Only don't do the tamales. Lard city."

A pause on his part now. "I got a call from the

head of our Crime Scene Unit, Charlie Shean. Spelled *S-H-E-A-N*. Not like the actor. Takes some grief for that. Good man."

She recalled the efficient team at the convention center and at the trailer, on a par with a big-city CSU.

"All the forensics were negative. None of the dust or other trace on the pictures and memorabilia in Edwin's rental matched what was in Bobby's trailer. And one of our people ran Edwin's credit card data? He bought everything we found in his house on eBay. And we got his prints when we booked him. None of the ones at Bobby's or the convention center match. No footprints, no nothin'. Tire treads for his car, zip. Was a washout."

"You let him go."

"Yeah, an hour ago. And released everything we took."

This was, Dance supposed, the best someone like Madigan could do for a contrition.

But she was wrong.

"I wanted to say I'm sorry."

And the apology wasn't over yet.

"You were right, I was wrong. I got outgunned by that fellow. It was like the only reason he came in was to find out information about the investigation."

"If he's the perp, then, yes, I think that's a possibility."

"This guy's pretty different from what I've been used to. You have a handle on him better than me. If you're still game would you be willing to help us out? We sure could use you."

Without hesitation: "I am, yes."

She'd be sure to call Overby and withdraw her prior request.

"That's much appreciated."

Dance thought back to what Stanning had said about Madigan's concerns. "One thing I wanted to say, Detective. This is your case. I'm a consultant only."

In other words, the glory and the press conferences are all yours. By the way, I hate them as much as your associate Dennis Harutyun does.

"Well, thank you for that. Now get yourself back here, if you would. Oh, and welcome to the FMCSO, Deputy Dance. Hey, that's got a nice ring to it, don'tcha think?"

BUT IT WAS *him*, after all.

The reason she hadn't seen any red was that the light was glare off the windshield, which shot her way like a theater spot. The crimson of the Buick was below eye level from the house.

Edwin Sharp was fifty feet from her. He'd found a new vantage point. His car was parked on the shoulder and he sat on the hood, legs dangling, as he stared directly toward her house, that sick smile curving his mouth. His rocking, back and forth, had created the intermittent flashing.

She dropped to her knees. He gave no reaction, though, and she knew he hadn't seen her.

Moving a few dozen feet to the side, Kayleigh looked out again, through the brush. He was wearing earbuds and tapped his hand on his thigh in time to the music. It would be one of her songs. Which one?

Occasionally his head would swivel, scanning the property as if he were admiring a work of art.

Or . . . wait. There was something about his face. What was that expression?

And then she sensed it was pleasure. Almost ecstasy. And not in a religious sense. His eyelids would droop from time to time and his smile would deepen.

He seemed to be breathing hard too, his chest rising.

It was like he was making love.

Was he tapping his thigh to keep time to the music? Or, my God, was he doing something *else* with his hand? She couldn't see clearly.

No, he couldn't be doing *that*!

But the look on his face.

Oh, disgusting!

His half-open mouth, the lowered lids beneath the outcropping of eyebrows . . . it was too much for her.

She stepped back fast and stumbled. But the tree she'd grabbed to keep from falling was a small pine sapling and bent sideways under her weight.

And caught Edwin's eye.

The motion stopped and he gazed toward where a horrified Kayleigh now crouched on the ground.

Did he see her? Was he coming toward her now, his pants unzipped?

Panicked, Kayleigh turned and fled, sprinting all out.

Dodging trees, brush, not daring to look behind her . . . Then the fence surrounding her precious garden loomed. She slowed but didn't bother with the gate. She stretched her hands out and vaulted the fence like she used to do the horse in gymnastics class—always game to take on the challenge but often, like now, landing in a sprawl on the other side.

Heart drumming, she was on her feet and scrabbling into the house, slamming the door shut and wheeling about.

She looked over her garden. It was *ruined*! Ruined forever. She could never step into it again without thinking of *him* and what *he* had been doing.

She pressed her face against the window.

The flashing continued for a moment.

Then it began to move toward the main road. She

caught a glimpse of red as the car proceeded slowly to the intersection, turned right and vanished.

Kayleigh jumped as her phone rang, a steel guitar ring tone and a hum of vibration. She approached slowly. Was it Edwin, or someone else, calling with the second verse to "Your Shadow"? Announcing another killing?

She picked up the mobile. Looked down at the screen. After a moment's hesitation, she hit ANSWER.

Chapter 19

LAW ENFORCEMENT BRIEFING rooms are the same the world over: scraped, scuffed, dented, repaired with tape, filled with mismatched furniture and cryptic signage, grimy windows.

The Fresno-Madera Consolidated Sheriff's Office was about average, though the smell of sour garlic was a unique addition, maybe from a late-shift Chinese dinner. Dance stood in front of the green-lit room with P. K. Madigan and Dennis Harutyun, whose taciturn face had offered a faint quasi-smile beneath his opulent mustache at the announcement that Dance was joining the team.

Her ruse at using him to slip into the observation room earlier was apparently forgiven.

Detectives Crystal Stanning and Miguel Lopez were here too. They, along with Detective Gabriel Fuentes, presently in the field, would be the Prescott homicide/ Kayleigh Towne stalker task force, backed up by TJ Scanlon in Monterey ("You have a very bizarre idea of taking a vacation, Boss").

Two civilians were in the room, as well. Dance had called Kayleigh Towne thirty minutes ago and asked her to join them. The woman had reluctantly agreed and Alicia Sessions had come along for moral support. Kayleigh was bleary-eyed and sallow, her impressive honey hair tied back in a taut ponytail and protruding from a burgundy sports cap without a logo as if she were trying to disguise herself.

She also, Dance noted, wore baggy jeans, not the usual closer-fitting numbers from her album covers and concerts, and a thick, long-sleeved knit shirt, which would be merciless in the heat.

The concealment would be futile, though, if that was the purpose, Dance could have told her. To Edwin Sharp she was the sexiest, most beautiful woman in the world, whatever clothes she wore and however makeup-free her face.

Kayleigh reported that Edwin had been spying on her again, forty minutes ago, parked at a new vantage point; apparently he'd gotten tired of the police driving past and staring at him in the parking lot of the nature preserve across the road from her house. So, right after he'd been released from the lockup, he'd headed to this new observation post for his high like an addict looking for meth.

The singer's voice wavered as she told the story, suggesting to Dance that there was more to it than her just spotting him. She wondered if there'd been an actual confrontation between the two. But whatever might have happened, it was clear Kayleigh didn't want to talk about it.

Alicia Sessions was dressed the opposite of her boss, almost pick-a-fight defiant: tight jeans, light blue cowboy boots, a green tank top with bright orange bra straps showing. Significant muscles too. Dance wondered what the rest of the tattoo, disappearing down her back, might be. Her face was grim and angry, some of that directed, it seemed, toward the deputies themselves as if they weren't doing enough to protect her boss.

Dance said, "Chief Madigan's been kind enough

to invite the CBI to assist in the Prescott murder case and we're going to be focusing on the possibility that it's linked to the stalker who's been troubling Kayleigh. I'm not here to step on toes and if you think there's a conflict between your department and mine, you can come to me or Chief Madigan at any time. I'm helping because I've got some experience with stalkers."

"Personally?" Lopez said.

Everyone laughed.

"They're discouraged when they see a Glock Twenty-three on your hip."

Kayleigh was among those laughing but it was too loud. Poor thing's terrified, Dance assessed. Alicia watched warily.

"First of all, my associate in Monterey's found out that there are no warrants or court orders on Edwin—nothing federal or in California, Washington or Oregon. A few traffic violations, that's it. Which is a little unusual for a stalker; normally there's a history of complaints. But, on the other hand, he could simply be very careful. And we know he's smart.

"Now, I'm going to tell you a little about stalking and where I think Edwin fits into the diagnosis. There are several types of stalkers. The first type is known as simple obsessional. These are usually domestic situations. The stalker and his object have had some prior contact, usually romantic or sexual. Relationships, marriages or even one-night stands that go bad. Think of *Fatal Attraction*."

"Now *that* was a movie to keep husbands on the straight and narrow," Lopez said, engendering uneasy laughter.

Dance continued, "Then there are erotomanic stalkers."

"Like sex perverts?" Madigan wondered aloud.

"No, it's more about love than sex. Traditionally erotomanic stalkers were women who fell in love with powerful men in higher economic or social classes. Like secretaries or shop clerks fawning over their bosses. But now, as many men fall into the category as women. The profile is that there's been some minor, completely innocuous contact that the stalker misreads. They become convinced the subject of their obsession is in love with them but is too shy or reluctant to reciprocate.

"The third type is called love obsessional. These are the ones who go after celebrities, people they've worshiped from afar and come to believe they're soul mates with. I think Edwin is a mix of erotomania and love obsessional. He honestly believes that you're the woman for him. He wants a relationship with you and he believes that you feel the same about him."

"That damn 'XO,'" Kayleigh muttered. "It was just a form letter."

Alicia said, "We send out thousands of them a week. It didn't have anything personal about him except a name—and we've got an automail program that inserts that."

"Well, you have to understand: all stalkers are more or less delusional. They range from serious neurosis to borderline personalities to truly psychotic: schizophrenic or severely bipolar. We have to assume that Edwin has a reality problem. And he doesn't want to fix that because he gets a high out of contact with you—it's as powerful as a drug to him."

Crystal Stanning asked, "But what's his motive for killing Bobby Prescott—if he's the one who did?"

Dance said, "That's a good question, Detective. It's the one thing that doesn't quite fit. Erotomanic and love obsessional stalkers are the least dangerous, statistically much less so than domestic stalkers. But they can certainly kill."

Madigan added, "I think we should remember too that Bobby could just have been at the wrong place at the wrong time. If that song *was* an announcement it was just about the concert hall. Maybe had nothing to do with Bobby. The perp might just've been waiting for anybody to show up."

"Good point, yes," Dance said. "But what we should do is look into Bobby's life a little more, see what he was up to, anything illegal, for instance."

"He wasn't," Kayleigh said firmly. "He had a problem a few years ago, drugs and drinking, but he was clean recently."

Skepticism is part of being an officer but Dance wasn't going to contest the girl. It was important to her to preserve the memory of her friend and they could learn independently if Bobby had been engaged in any risky activity. From the comments by his neighbor, Tabatha, it seemed that he wasn't.

"But that doesn't mean somebody still wouldn't want him dead," Dance said. "And we have to remember some intruder—likely the killer—took some things from his trailer the morning after he was killed."

"I could look into his personal life, his background," Harutyun offered in his low, easy voice, silken mustache bobbing.

Dance glanced at Madigan, who nodded his agreement. "Dennis's our librarian. Mean that in a good way. He does his homework. He knew what Google was when I thought it was a character on the Cartoon Network."

"Good."

"Can't you interrogate him?" Alicia asked Dance, who didn't offer that the first interview had not been particularly successful.

"Possibly. But I'm not sure how helpful it would be."

In her lectures, Dance talked about the difficulty of kinesically analyzing suspects like Edwin: *People on the borderline of psychosis, like stalkers, might tell you facts that can be helpful in running a case and can lead to your uncovering their deception. But such people are often impossible to analyze kinesically. They don't feel any stress when lying—because their goal of getting close to the object of their obsession trumps everything.*

She explained this now and added that they also had no leverage to bring him in.

Alicia grimaced in frustration, then asked, "Isn't there a stalking law here?"

"That's right—California's was first in the country," Madigan said.

Dance paraphrased the statute: "You're guilty of stalking if you willfully, maliciously and repeatedly follow or harass the victim and make a credible threat with the intent to place that person in reasonable fear for his or her safety, or the safety of the immediate family." She added, "It doesn't have a lot of teeth, though. Some jail time and a fine."

"Well, it's something; arrest him anyway," Kayleigh said.

"It may not be that easy. Tell me about his stalking."

"I mean, my lawyers'd know more, I left it pretty much up to them. But I know he sent me about a hundred and fifty emails and thirty or so regular letters. He'd ask me out, hint about a life together, write about what he'd done that day."

Not nearly as bad as some, Dance noted.

"And he sent me some presents. Pictures he'd drawn, miniature instruments, old LPs. We sent everything back."

"You said he showed up at concerts but you never saw him."

"Right."

Lopez asked, "Disguises, maybe?"

"Could be," Dance said. "Stalkers have a whole arsenal they use to get close to their objects and keep them under control. They steal mail to find out who the victims know and where they might be. They threaten witnesses into lying that they've never been around the victims' houses. They get to be good at hacking phones and computers and some even go to locksmith school to learn how to break and enter. These're really desperate people. Their whole worth is tied up in their love for their object; they're nothing without that person in their life."

Alicia said, "We threatened him with restraining orders and everything but . . . he just ignored the letters and the lawyers said he was never quite across the line of legality."

"They talked to the FBI about hacking into our computers," Kayleigh said, "and hired a private computer security firm. But there was never any proof he did it."

Madigan then asked the key question, "In all those letters was there any threat at all? Under the statute there has to be a credible threat."

"Isn't Bobby's death enough of a threat?" Alicia asked harshly.

"We don't have proof he did it," Harutyun said.

"Please. Of course he did."

Dance continued, "When we're talking about an arrest for stalking under the statute, Detective Madigan is right; you need a threat against you or a family member. It can be implied, but if that's the case there has to be a reasonable belief that you're actually in danger of harm."

"Not, you know, mental or psychic harm?" Crystal Stanning asked.

"No. Physical."

Kayleigh was staring at a poster, a cartoon of a police officer and a contrite teenage boy.

SCHOOL PATROL DETAIL: IF IT'S ONLY POT, TALK TO THEM . . . A LOT.

She turned back and reluctantly said, "No, no threats. It's just the opposite, really. He was always telling me how he wanted to protect me. How he'd be there for me—just like in that song, 'Your Shadow.'"

It was then that Dance's phone sang out with an incoming message. It was from TJ Scanlon. She read quickly then looked up.

"You want to hear a bio of our stalker?"

But the question, of course, needed no answer.

Chapter 20

DENNIS HARUTYUN HELPED Dance log on to her email from a terminal in the corner of the room and she printed out TJ's document.

Scanning, disappointed.

"There isn't much, I'm afraid." Edwin Stanton Sharp had been born in Yakima, a town in eastern Washington state. His father was a traveling salesman, his mother worked in retail. "To judge from her income, she must have had several jobs. This could mean that the boy spent a lot of time alone. Psychologists think stalking begins from attachment issues. He was desperate to spend time with his parents, mother particularly, but she wasn't available.

"Now, his grades were very good. But he was held back a year in the seventh grade, which is pretty old for that, and his marks weren't too bad so that suggests emotional problems in school. But there's no record of disciplinary action, other than for a few fights on the school yard. No weapons were involved. He also had no extracurricular activities, no sports, no clubs.

"When he was sixteen his parents split up and he went to live with his mother outside of Seattle. He went to the University of Washington for two years. Again, he did fairly well. But for some reason he dropped out just after the start of his third year. No record of why. Again, no interest in other activities. That too is typical—stalking takes a lot of time. He started working at jobs stalkers sometimes gravitate toward: security guard, landscaping, part-time retail sales, offering samples of food at grocery stores, door-to-door selling. They're good professions for those with voyeuristic or stalking tendencies because you get to see a lot of people and are largely unsupervised. And invisible."

"Good ponds for fishin'," Madigan said.

Well put, Dance reflected.

"His mother died in July of last year, cancer. His father's off the grid. Hasn't filed a tax return in six years and the IRS can't find him. Edwin does no international travel, according to the State Department. TJ, my associate in Monterey, has checked out his online activity. His Facebook page is filled with pictures and information about Kayleigh. He doesn't have many friends—at least not under his own username. He might have a page under another one."

"I sure didn't friend him," Kayleigh muttered.

"TJ's found four different screen names he uses—'nics,' they're called, like nickname. Edwin's pretty active online but no more so than millions of other young men. He posts to a lot of music blogs and is in a few chat rooms. Some sexual but they're pretty tame. And special interests—music mostly but movies and books too." Dance shook her head. "Typically a stalker is more engaged in online activities than Edwin is—and a lot darker ones too."

She continued to read. "Ah, may have something here. Looks like he went through a breakup last year. TJ found a reference to someone named Sally in one of the blogs. He was talking about your song, 'You and Me.'"

"That's right," Kayleigh said. "It's about a breakup."

"The posting was in December." Dance asked Kayleigh, "Not long before the stalking started, right?"

"Yes. January."

"Trauma often precipitates stalking. Getting fired, a physical injury, death in the family. Or the end of a romantic relationship." Dance nodded toward TJ's email. "He said the song really meant a lot to him. It was a hard time in his life and he talked about the trouble he was having with Sally. He said it's like you knew exactly what he was going through. Then a few days later he posted about a single you'd just released, 'Near the Silver Mine.' He said he'd been feeling bad because he'd lost his house when he was about that age too but his girlfriend told him to get over it."

Kayleigh's lips tightened. "He knew about my house?" She explained about how she'd loved the old house she'd grown up in, north of Fresno, but her father had sold it to a mining company when she was young. "I probably mentioned in an interview that I wished he hadn't."

She'd be thinking: Isn't there anything private about my life anymore?

Dance flipped through TJ's homework. "Again, though, nothing threatening or troubling in any way." She read some more. "One thing to keep in mind. He's smart. For instance, he wrote, 'Happy or sad, you speak the truth.' The sentence is a bit of a dangler but look at how he set off the modifier 'Happy or sad' with a comma, which is correct, but a lot of people wouldn't do that. His spelling and grammar are very good. Which tells me he's in control. Very in control."

"Is that bad?" Crystal Stanning asked.

"It means that if he's the one who killed Bobby, he's going to be covering up his tracks and planning out the stalking very carefully. He's not likely to slip up."

Madigan finished his ice cream and surveyed the paper cup to see if he should scrape the sides, Dance supposed. He pitched it away. "What're you thinking about where we go from here?"

"First, we've got to keep him under surveillance."

"Deputy Fuentes is doing that."

"Where is Edwin now?"

"Seeing a movie. In the Rialto."

Harutyun explained that this was an old movie theater in Fresno's Tower District, an eclectic area of galleries, restaurants, tattoo parlors and shops.

His being at a movie didn't surprise her. "Stalkers spend a lot of time in theaters and watching movies at home—the link between voyeurism and stalking is strong."

"What about those prepaid mobiles from the drugstore in Burlingame?"

Madigan said, "Not traceable. They might've been destroyed or the perp's taken the batteries out. Or who knows, maybe he just bought a bunch to keep us busy and he's got another one here to make more calls."

Dance then turned to Kayleigh. "Now, some basic stalker rules. You probably know them from Darthur Morgan and your lawyers but remember you have to have no contact with him at all. Nothing. Even threatening him or telling him to leave you alone gives him a high—any contact at all is positive to him. If he approaches don't say anything, just walk away."

"Okay. Fine with me."

"And I want to know more about him. We need to find this former girlfriend. Sally."

"Lopez, you handle that. Have her call Agent Dance."

"Sure, Chief."

The head detective then added, "We should identify other possible victims, don't you think? Keep an eye on them. Who'd be at particular risk?"

Dance said, "Probably first is anybody he sees as a romantic rival." To Kayleigh: "You and Bobby dated?"

Apparently this wasn't public knowledge. Kayleigh blushed and Alicia turned to her with a hint of frown. Dance wasn't much interested in the delicacies of disclosure. She lifted an eyebrow, tacitly repeating the question.

"Well, yes, a while ago. Just casually. It wasn't a big deal. How'd you know? I wasn't even performing then. It didn't make the press."

Because, Dance thought, when I saw you with Bobby yesterday I noticed a decrease in the angle of your shoulders when you were speaking, signifying relaxation and comfort. Bobby's leaning forward slightly when he spoke to you, indicating that what he was saying was meant for you and you alone. A faint smile at the reference to the word "amplifier," which had become a code word for some private joke between the two of you. The way his eyes dwelt on your face, the message abundantly clear that whatever had gone on between you two was not, to him, completely over.

Kinesics, in other words.

But what she said to Kayleigh was, "A hunch."

Crystal Stanning said, "So anyone that Kayleigh ever dated or men she was real friendly with are at risk?"

"Yes, possibly, though women too. Stalkers are extremely jealous. Remember, they have a very skewed sense of reality—even casual friends could be perceived as threats." Then she eyed the young singer again. "But you're not seeing anyone now?"

"No."

"Also, a stalker's likely to target anybody who's a threat to you, or even offended you. He's taking real seriously his role as a protector; I could see that yesterday. Can you think of any enemies you might have that he'd know about?"

Kayleigh looked around. "Not really."

Alicia said, "She's a good girl. She doesn't get into cat fights with other artists."

Dance continued, "Well, keep in mind, he could also consider going after critics who'd dissed you. Or fans who were critical of your work. Then, next, he could target anyone he saw as keeping you two apart."

"Like Darthur?"

"Yes, him. But it could also be your lawyers." She glanced at Alicia. "Or you. You seem very protective of her."

The broad-shouldered woman shrugged. "*Somebody's* got to be."

A sentence with many possible implications.

"And it could also be us. The police. Truly obsessive stalkers have a different sense of right and wrong. In extreme obsession cases, the stalker's murdering a policeman is no worse than killing a fly."

"My family? The crew?"

"Generally, family and nonromantic friends are only at risk if they try to protect the object from the stalker, though we're not dealing with hard-and-fast rules. Stalkers're unpredictable. I talked to some of the crew about what they'd seen yesterday but I think I should interview all of them. Assess if they're at risk."

Or potential perps, Dance thought, but didn't say aloud.

"The crew's at the convention center now," Kayleigh said, then added, "The band's in Nashville still, finishing up some studio work for our new album. They won't be here till Thursday or Friday."

That was good news. Fewer potential victims to worry about. Fewer suspects too.

Dance added, "Finally, there's the Hinckley scenario. Killing someone of some notoriety to impress Kayleigh."

She reminded them that John Hinckley, Jr., was obsessed with Jodie Foster. "He figured that by assassinating Ronald Reagan he'd be linked forever to the actress."

"And they are," Harutyun observed. "In a sick way, he accomplished his goal."

Madigan said, "I've talked to Edwin. You have too. He doesn't seem like a psycho. How could he possibly think killing people is going to get him closer to Kayleigh?"

"Oh, he *doesn't* think about it. Not on a conscious level. Even if Edwin seems functional on the surface, there's more at work. Remember, it's *his* reality, not ours."

Madigan: "I've ordered a box on Kayleigh's phone and the service provider's security unit is on standby. And we're still on those numbers of the other mobiles he bought in Burlingame. So if he calls again from any of those phones or even powers 'em up we can get a car there fast."

"Good."

Harutyun said to Kayleigh, "Kathryn asked me to look into the verses of the song, the one that was played to you the other night." He passed out copies to everyone in the room. "I've been trying to think of where he might be planning an attack but can't come up with much."

So he *had* taken her request seriously. She nodded her thanks.

Your Shadow

*1. You walk out onstage and sing folks your
      songs.*
You make them all smile. What could go wrong?
But soon you discover the job takes its toll,
And everyone's wanting a piece of your soul.

Chorus:
When life is too much, just remember,
When you're down on your luck, just remember,
I'm as close as a shadow, wherever you go.
As bad as things get, you've got to know,
That I'm with you . . . always with you.
Your shadow.

*2. You sit by the river, wondering what you got
      wrong,*
How many chances you've missed all along.
*Like your troubles had somehow turned you to
      stone*
*and the water was whispering, why don't you come
      home?*

Chorus.

*3. One night there's a call, and at first you don't
      know*
*What the troopers are saying from the side of the
      road,*
*Then you see in an instant that your whole life has
      changed.*
Everything gone, all the plans rearranged.

Chorus.

4. You can't keep down smiles; happiness floats.
But trouble can find us in the heart of our homes.

Life never seems to go quite right,
You can't watch your back from morning to night.

Chorus.

Repeat Chorus.

"I don't know if he's going to keep going with that song or find a different one. Or give up on the idea altogether."

Kayleigh took her glasses off and cleaned them on her sweatshirt. "I'll bet he'd use 'Your Shadow.' He thought it was the best song ever written."

Miguel Lopez looked over the lyrics. "You read it one way, it's a love song, looking out for somebody. Could be a lover or even a parent or friend. But from a stalker's point of view, it's pretty creepy."

Dance focused on the second verse. "A river."

Madigan gave a brief laugh. "We got plenty of those around here."

Harutyun pointed out, "Some dry beds, some with water. Could be anywhere."

Dance summarized, "I'll be talking to the crew at the hall. Detective Harutyun is getting information about Bobby's past and Detective Lopez is tracking down Edwin's former girlfriend, Sally."

Madigan regarded the song lyrics. "And I'll tell patrol officers to pay special attention to riversides, the public areas primarily, and ones out of view of any roads."

"Good."

Alicia gave the first smile Dance could recall seeing on the tough woman's face. "But I guess the good news is that Kayleigh's not at risk, if he's that much in love with her."

"That's true. But only for a time. Remember his

separation from reality? He's been in the courting stage for a while." She turned to Kayleigh. "Probably since he heard the first song that drew him to you, or saw you in concert or on TV. To him that was your first date and you've been going out ever since."

"Date?" Crystal Stanning asked.

"At the moment he's still under the illusion that you care for him. You've been brainwashed, he thinks. At some point, though, he'll see your behavior as if you're breaking up with him.

"And when that happens, he'll become simple obsessional. Like spurned husbands or lovers. They're the dangerous stalkers. It could happen in án instant. He'll snap. He'll want revenge." Dance debated but decided there was no point in sugarcoating her assessment. "Or he'll just want to kill you so nobody else can have you."

Chapter 21

THE CONVENTION CENTER had been sanitized.

Kathryn Dance wasn't cynical about the world of business—she'd been a consultant and journalist. And music at Kayleigh Towne's level was a very serious business indeed, so she wasn't surprised that the crime scene had been cleaned as quickly as possible, all traces of the death removed, to make sure the concert could proceed as planned.

Dance had prepared herself for the smell; nothing lingers like the odor of burned hair and flesh, but whatever commercial forensic cleaning operation Madigan or Charlie Shean used had done a bang-up job. The perfume was of Lysol and, of all things, cinnamon.

Kayleigh was blocking out stage directions for the show—what she'd been doing when the light fell. Tye Slocum, the guitar technician, was temporarily chief roadie, until Alicia could fill the job with a pro; they needed someone who not only knew equipment but could mix sound at the console, as complicated as an airplane's cockpit. The quiet, heavyset young man was distracted and not particularly confident but trying to rise to the occasion. There were, of course, hundreds of decisions to be made. Sweating, he kept glancing at Kayleigh for direction, which she provided, along with smiles and nods of encouragement, though she was clearly distracted to be near the place where her friend had died.

With Kayleigh's okay, Dance called Tye over and explained what she needed—to speak to all of the crew. He rounded them up—ranging from their early twenties to forties and physically fit, thanks probably to the demanding nature of their jobs. Dance spoke to them in the scuffed, black-painted wings of the hall.

She noted great camaraderie among them and Kayleigh—the whole operation was like a big family—but no one stood out as approaching Bobby's level of closeness to Kayleigh, and therefore an obvious threat to Edwin. Of any of them, Tye was the one who seemed to know Kayleigh best but she felt merely a brotherly kind of affection, she'd deduced from the singer's body language when speaking to him.

Nor did Dance sense that any of them might have a motive to kill Bobby Prescott—another reason for her mission here, though she hadn't stressed that to Kayleigh.

The only one Dance didn't interview was Alicia. She'd been here at the convention center earlier when Dance arrived, standing outside beside a Ford F150 pickup with a trailer hitch on the back and a bumper sticker that announced: I ♥ MY QUARTER HORSE

A cigarette had dangled from her lips and she'd looked more like a local Teamster than a personal assistant—considering her muscular arms, inkings and attitudinal visage. Of anyone on the staff, Alicia was probably the most at risk; she'd defied Edwin the most at the Cowboy Saloon on Sunday and would present an obstacle to the stalker's getting close to Kayleigh.

Dance, however, couldn't impart this warning in person, only via a phone message. The assistant had left the convention center by the time Dance went to find her.

As she looked over her notes, movement at the corner of her eye caught her attention. Dance's gaze swept to the confusion of shadows throughout the concert hall. She'd counted two dozen doors and emergency exits. Recalled too the casual attitude of locking doors when there was no event in progress.

Was he here now, observing from the shadows? Was there a faint movement from that window? That doorway?

Her eyes were tricking her.

Had to be.

A moment later Dance noticed Kayleigh freeze and pull her mobile from her pocket. The look on the young woman's face left little doubt. It would be a call she didn't recognize.

She stared for a moment and then lifted the unit to her ear.

The woman gasped, a wrenching sound clearly audible, thanks to the acoustics of the center.

Her head swiveled toward Dance and she said, "It's another call, Kathryn. It's the second verse!"

Chapter 22

IN A QUARTER hour, Dance was at the sheriff's office, hurrying inside. Harutyun met her at the door.

She asked, "Could the mobile providers triangulate on his phone?"

Harutyun said evenly, "It wasn't one of Edwin's prepaids. Or any mobile at all. The call was from a pay phone, on the Fresno College campus. School's not in session yet. It's pretty deserted there. Nobody saw the caller."

"Well, where's Edwin?"

"That's the curious thing. Still in the Rialto—the theater. It must be somebody else."

They stepped into Madigan's office, where both the chief detective and Stanning, next to her boss, were on their phones.

Madigan looked up. He disconnected his mobile and ignored his desk phone when it rang, after a glance at caller ID. He looked too at a half-empty ice cream cup and pitched it. Rocky Road.

"Where's Kayleigh?" Harutyun asked.

Dance said, "She and the crew are at the convention center. Darthur Morgan's with her, and the deputy you sent is outside. Alicia's the only one not accounted for. I called her on the way here and left a message. I haven't heard back."

The detective glanced toward his phone. "That was Fuentes. Edwin's still watching his movie."

Harutyun asked, "Any way he could've called from the theater, either the landline or another mobile, and routed the call through the phone at the college?"

Good question. But Madigan had a good answer: "No, we checked with the Bell folks, or whoever the hell they are nowadays. The call was made from the phone at the school, direct to Kayleigh's."

Dance had to ask, "And there's no way he could've gotten out of the theater?"

"No. Fuentes is in a restaurant on Olive. He's watching the front entrance. The back doors're alarmed. He checked."

Dance supposed that Edwin was just what he seemed to be: a sad lump of a young man without a life, drawn to a woman who existed in an entirely different universe from his.

A common and boring story, once you took the violence out of the equation.

And yet she couldn't help but recall his icy demeanor, his calm attitude, his laser-like focus on Kayleigh, that phony smile.

And his intelligence.

Which prompted her to ask, "Basements?"

"What?" Madigan asked.

"In that block are there connecting basements?"

"I don't know." Madigan said this slowly and hit a button on the landline. A tone filled the room, then the rapid eleven digits of a phone number being dialed.

"Fuentes."

Without identifying himself, Madigan barked, "We're thinking he might've snuck out through the basement. The hardware store next door? They share a basement?"

A pause. "Let me check. I'll get right back."

Three minutes later they got the news that Dance suspected they would. "Yep, Chief. I went down there. There's a door. It's unlocked."

"Evacuate the theater," Dance said. "We need to be sure."

"Evacuate?" Fuentes asked.

Madigan was staring at her. Then he said firmly, "You heard Agent Dance, Gabe. Get the lights on and evacuate."

"The theater isn't really going to want to . . ." His voice faded and he realized this wasn't the time to be worried about business relations in economically challenged Fresno. "I'll get on it."

Ten minutes later, Fuentes came back on the line. Dance knew from the first word, "Chief," what the story was going to be.

Madigan sighed. "You're sure he's gone?"

"There weren't that many people inside, it being early. Yeah, I'm sure."

"Damn," Stanning muttered.

But the limp in Fuentes's voice came from another source as well. "And I have to tell you. . . . While I was keeping an eye on the theater? I was in the restaurant?"

"I know, you told me. What?" Madigan growled.

"Somebody broke into my cruiser."

"Go on."

"I wasn't thinking, I had a Glock in the backseat. It was in a box and under my jacket. I don't know how anybody could've seen it or thought it was there."

Dance knew from the way he volunteered the information that the gun hadn't been hidden at all.

"Goddamn it!" Madigan shouted.

"I'm sorry. It should've been in the trunk. But it was completely hid."

"It shoulda been *home*. That's your personal weapon. It shoulda been at home."

"I was going to the range tonight," the deputy said miserably.

"You know what I gotta do, Gabe. Don't have any options."

"I know. You want my service piece and shield?"

"Need 'em. Yeah. I'll get the paperwork done today. We'll have the inquiry as fast as we can but it'll be three or four days. You're out of commission till then."

"I'm sorry."

"Bring your stuff in." He stabbed the speakerphone button.

Harutyun said in his low, stress-free voice, "It could be one of the gangs."

"It's not one of the gangs," Madigan snapped. "It's our fucking stalker. At least if we find it on him, he'll go to jail for a long, long time. Hell, this's one clever son of a bitch. He got Fuentes suspended and a nice big gun, to boot."

Dance looked at the lyric sheet they had pinned up on a badly mounted corkboard.

"Where's he going to strike? A river . . . a river."

"And," Crystal Stanning added, "who's he got in mind for the next victim?"

Chapter 23

"MARY-GORDON, STAY OFF that. See the sign?"

"It's not moving, Mommy," the six-year-old pointed out. Suellyn Sanchez reflected what perfect logic that was. The warning sign on the baggage carousel: STAY OFF THE MOVING BELT.

"It could start at any minute."

"But when the light comes on I can get off."

How they tested the limits.

The mother and daughter were at the arrivals area in Fresno–Yosemite airport, their flight from Portland having arrived twenty minutes early. Suellyn looked around for their ride. Saw no one yet and turned back to the girl. "And it's filthy. You'll get your dress stained."

That risk apparently didn't carry much weight either. But all it took was one "Mary-Gordon," uttered in a certain tone, that very special tone, and the cute blonde stepped back immediately. Funny, Suellyn thought, she and her husband never laid a hand on the girl, never even threatened spanking, and their daughter was far better behaved than the children of neighbors who did wallop their kids—all in the name of raising them right.

Sadists, she thought.

And then reminded herself to chill. Bobby Prescott's death had cast a pall over everything. And how was Kayleigh holding up? She and Bobby had quite a history, of course, and Suellyn knew that her kid sister would be reeling from the loss.

The poor thing . . .

And the possibility that he'd been murdered?

Maybe by that gross stalker who'd been bothering Kayleigh for the past few months. Terrible.

She remembered Bishop's call that morning, after she'd learned the sad news from Kayleigh. The conversation with her father had been conducted in the clumsy way he bobbled nearly everything personal. Suellyn was thinking it was odd that he'd called in the first place, much less to ask if she'd come to Fresno to support her sister during this tough time . . . until Suellyn realized: Bishop would want to share the bereavement duty with someone else. *Anyone* else. Well, no, he'd want to hand off the job completely if he could.

But who knew his real motive? Their father was both transparent and unreadable.

And where was the luggage? She was impatient.

Suellyn resembled her younger sister in a vague way. She had a wholly unsupported theory that the greater the distance in age, the less siblings looked like each other. Eight years separated the two, and Suellyn was taller, of broader build and fuller face, which couldn't be traced to the fifteen pounds she had on her sister. Her nose was longer and her chin stronger, she felt, though her light brown hair was of the same fine, flowing texture, light as air. Today she was prepared for the assault of a late Fresno summer, in a burgundy sundress, cut low in front and back, and Brighton sandals, whose silver hearts covering the first two toes fascinated Mary-Gordon.

Even in this outfit, though, she was uncomfortably hot. Portland had clocked in at 62 degrees that morning.

"Where's Aunt Kayleigh?"

"She's getting ready to sing a show. The one we're going to on Friday."

Maybe. Her sister hadn't actually invited her to the concert.

"Good. I like it when she sings."

With a blare of a horn and a flashing orange light, the baggage belt started to move.

"See, you wouldn't have had time to get off."

"Yes, I could. And then I could ride around and see what's behind that curtain."

"They wouldn't like that."

"Who?"

Suellyn was not going to talk about TSA and terrorists.

"They," she repeated firmly and Mary-Gordon forgot about the question as she spotted the first suitcase and gleefully charged toward it, her white Keds squeaking on the linoleum, her pink dress, accented with a red bow, fluttering around her.

The luggage was retrieved and they both walked away from the belt and the crowds and paused in front of one of the doors.

Her mobile rang. She glanced down. "Hey, Daddy."

"You're in," the man growled.

And hello and nice day to you too.

"Ritchie's on his way to pick you up."

Or you could've come to collect your daughter and granddaughter in person. Bishop Towne didn't drive but he had plenty in his crew to play chauffeur—if he'd wanted to come.

Suellyn found a bogus smile on her face as often happened when she was talking to her father, even though he was miles away. Bishop Towne intimidated Suellyn less than he did his younger daughter but it was still plenty.

"I can take a cab."

"No, you won't. You got in early. Ritchie'll be there."

Then as if he remembered he should be saying something—or possibly had been prodded by Wife Number Four Sheri—he asked, "How's Mary-Gordon?"

"She can't wait to see you," Suellyn told him.

Is that passive-aggressive? A little.

"Me too." And he disconnected.

I'm taking a damn cab, she thought. I'm not hanging around. "Do you need to use the girls' room?"

"No."

"Are you sure? It'll be a while before we get to Aunt Kayleigh's house."

"No. Can I get some Jelly Bears?"

"There'll be treats at your aunt's house."

"Okay."

"Excuse me, Suellyn?"

She turned to see Bishop's minion, Ritchie, a young man looking every inch the member of a country musician's entourage. "I'm your chauffeur. Nice to meet you." He shook her hand and smiled toward Mary-Gordon. "Hello."

"Hello," she said.

"Welcome to Fresno. You're Mary-Gordon, I'll bet."

"He said my name right." She beamed.

Hers wasn't Mary with Gordon as a middle name. It was a good, double-barreled Southern name and the girl wasn't shy about correcting anyone who got it wrong.

"Let me get those for you," he said and took both suitcases.

Mary-Gordon yielded up the bag without protest to the Man Who Knew Her Name.

"Get ready for the heat, a lot different from Oregon. You going to your father's or Kayleigh's?"

"Kayleigh's. We're going to surprise her."

"That'll be fun."

Suellyn hoped so. Bishop had been adamant that Suellyn not call Kayleigh and tell her of the visit—because the younger of the sisters would probably have told her not to come. She wouldn't want any sympathy because of Bobby's death, Bishop said. But family had to stick together.

Father knows best . . . Uh-huh.

"Kayleigh's got a great swimming pool," Ritchie said to Mary-Gordon. "You going to go swimming?"

"I have two suits so one can dry and I can still swim in the other."

"Isn't that smart?" Bishop's associate said. "What kind of suits are they? Hello Kitty?"

Mary-Gordon wrinkled her nose. "I'm too old for Hello Kitty and SpongeBob. One has flowers on it and the other is plain blue. I can swim without floaties."

They stepped outside and the heat was as fierce as promised.

He turned around and glanced down at the girl with a smile. "You know, you're cute as a button."

Mary-Gordon asked, "What does that mean?"

The young man looked at Suellyn and they both laughed. He said, "I don't have any idea."

They waited for traffic then crossed into the lot. He whispered, "It's good you're here. Kayleigh's pretty upset about Bobby."

"I can imagine. Do they know what happened?"

"Not yet. It's been terrible for everybody." He lifted his voice and said to Mary-Gordon, "Hey, before we go to your aunt's, you want to see something fun?"

"Yeah!"

"It's really neat and you'll like it." He glanced at Suellyn. "Little detour? There's this park practically on the way."

"Please, Mommy!"

"All right. But we don't want to be too late, Ritchie."

He blinked. "Oh, I'm not Ritchie. I came to fetch you instead." They arrived at his car. He took the suitcases and her computer bag and stashed them in the trunk of the big old Buick. It was bright red—a color you didn't see much nowadays.

Chapter 24

AT KAYLEIGH'S HOUSE Kathryn Dance was talking to Darthur Morgan, who was holding but, being on duty, not reading, one of his old books.

"You've got an unusual name," she said.

"Means 'morning' in German. Spelled different." The huge man's still face didn't break character.

"That's funny," Dance told him. She'd been referring to his given name.

"Used it before."

They were sitting in the living room, all the shades drawn, while Kayleigh was upstairs, changing clothes, as if being in the place where Bobby Prescott had died had somehow tainted what she'd worn.

The security man continued, "You know people think, being black, I was named Darthur because my parents didn't know how to spell Arthur, or got confused. You hear that sometimes."

"You do, true."

"Fact is, they were both teachers and they like the classics." He lifted his leather-bound book. Dickens. He added, "Malory's *Morte d'Arthur* was one of their favorites."

"The King Arthur stories."

He lifted an eyebrow. "Not a lot of cops know that. But then, you're not just a cop."

"Not any more than you're just a bodyguard." She

didn't add that she was also a mother who helped her children with their homework. She eyed the book in his hand.

"Great Expectations."

She asked, "Is Kayleigh handling this okay?"

"Borderline, I'd say. I don't go way back with her. Her lawyers and her father hired me when that fellow started popping up. She's the best of the celebrities I've ever worked with. Nicest. Polite. I could tell you some stories about clients I've had."

Though he wouldn't. He was a pro through and through. When this assignment was over, Darthur Morgan would instantly forget everything he knew about Kayleigh Towne, even the fact that he'd worked for her.

"You're armed?"

"Yes."

Dance had been pretty sure but she was glad to hear the confirmation. And glad to hear too that Morgan didn't continue to chat about his weapon or how proficient he was, much less whether he'd ever used it.

Professional . . .

"It could be that Edwin's stolen a Glock."

"I know. I talked to Chief Madigan."

The big man retired to the front door, sat down in a chair challenged by his weight.

Dance sipped the iced tea that Kayleigh had brought her. She looked around the room at the many awards and gold and platinum records hanging on the walls. There was a framed picture from the cover of *Country Times* and Dance had to laugh. It was a picture of Kayleigh holding the Country Music Association's Singer of the Year award. As she'd been accepting it, a young man, a country singer with a self-polished reputation for being a bad boy, had leapt onto the stage and taken the microphone away, berating her for being too young to win and not true to traditional country roots. He railed that another singer should have won.

Kayleigh had let him finish and then pulled the microphone out of his hand and said if he was such a supporter of traditional country, then name the top-five lifetime hits of George Jones, Loretta Lynn and Patsy Cline. "Or name *any* five of them," Kayleigh had challenged.

He did a deer in the headlights thing for a long ten seconds, in front of a live TV audience of millions, and then slunk off the stage, his arm raised, for some reason, like a heavy metal rocker's. Kayleigh finished her acceptance speech and, to a standing ovation, concluded by naming all the hits she'd asked him to recite.

Kayleigh now joined them, wearing blue jeans and a thick dark gray blouse, untucked and concealing as if Edwin were observing her from the distance through high-powered binoculars.

And who's to say he wasn't?

The singer sighed and sat on a floral sofa in the middle of the spacious room.

Dance said, "I just talked to the deputy at the convention center. All of the crew are accounted for except Tye and Alicia."

"Oh, she called ten minutes ago. I told her about the second verse and made sure she was looking out for herself." Kayleigh smiled. "She almost sounded like she was hoping Edwin'd try something with her. She's pretty tough. And's got a temper." She called Tye Slocum and left a message. "I don't know why he left."

And all the while Darthur Morgan said nothing and didn't even seem to hear the conversation. He simply scanned the house, the windows. He took a phone call and put the mobile away. Then stiffened.

The big man was on his feet, looking out the front window. "Visitors." He paused. "Hm. Whole entourage. And it looks official."

Chapter 25

"ENTOURAGE" DESCRIBED IT pretty well, Kayleigh Towne decided.

Two SUVs—one dusty white Lexus, Bishop's, and a big black Lincoln Navigator.

Bishop and Sheri climbed out and turned to the other vehicle.

Four passengers. First was security, it was easy to tell. A solid, sunglassed man, well over six feet, a pale complexion. He looked around and then leaned into the SUV and whispered something. The next to climb out was a slim, thoughtful-looking man with thinning hair. The third, also in a dark suit, white shirt and tie, was much taller and had a politician's head of hair.

Which made sense, because, Kayleigh realized, that's exactly who he was: one of California's star congressmen, William Davis, a two-term Democrat.

Kayleigh glanced at Dance, who observed this all with a careful gaze.

A woman was the last to climb out of the Navigator, dressed also in a conservative matching navy jacket and skirt, flesh-colored stockings.

The guard stayed with the SUV and the others followed Bishop and his wife into the house.

Inside, Bishop hugged his daughter and as if in an afterthought asked how she was holding up. Kayleigh thought it was the way he'd ask a gaffer whose name he didn't know how he was weathering the loss of an elderly parent. He also didn't seem to remember that he'd been here just a few hours ago.

What on earth were they doing here, anyway?

Bishop examined Dance as if he'd never met her and he ignored Darthur Morgan completely.

He said to his daughter, "This here's Congressman Davis. And his aides, Peter Simesky. And . . ."

"Myra Babbage." The slim, unsmiling woman, with square-cut, brunette hair, nodded formally. She seemed a bit star-struck to be in Kayleigh's presence.

"Ms. Towne, it's an honor," the congressman said.

"Hey, call me Kayleigh. You're making me older than I want to be."

Davis laughed. "And I'm Bill. It's easy to remember. I've sponsored a few of them in Congress."

Kayleigh gave a brief smile. And she introduced Dance and Morgan.

"We just flew into San Francisco a few days ago and have been making our way south. I was in touch with your father, asking about getting to your concert. Oh, I'm paying for tickets, don't you worry. I'm afraid we just need a little extra security."

Bishop said, "We've got it all taken care of."

"I was hoping for a chance to meet you and to say hi in person. Your father suggested bringing me along today, before the concert."

So, that was it. Kayleigh understood. Dammit. Her father had said they'd think about canceling the show and yet he was going to do whatever he needed to make sure it went forward. Anything to edge her career in the right direction. He'd be thinking that her knowing that the congressman—and accordingly more reporters—would be in the audience would pressure her not to cancel.

Kayleigh fumed but smiled pleasantly, or tried to, as Davis rambled like a schoolboy, talking about songs of hers he particularly loved. He really was quite a fan. He knew every word of every tune, it seemed.

Myra Babbage said, "I can't thank you enough for letting us use 'Leaving Home' on the website. It's really become an anthem for Bill's campaign."

Kathryn Dance said, "I heard you on the radio, Congressman. On the drive over here—that debate on immigration issues. That was some heated discussion."

"Oh, it sure was."

"I think you won, by the way. You drove 'em into the ground."

"Thanks. It was a lot of fun," Davis said with a gleam in his eye. "I love debates. That was my, quote, 'sport' at school. Less painful to talk than getting run into on the football field. Not necessarily safer, though."

Kayleigh didn't follow politics much. Some of her fellow performers were active in campaigns and causes but she'd known them before they'd hit it big and they hadn't seemed particularly interested in animal rights or hunger before they started drawing the public limelight. She suspected that a number had been tapped by their public relations firms or their record company publicity departments to take up a cause because it would look good in the press.

She knew, though, about U.S. Congressman Bill Davis. He was a politico with an electric mix of positions, liberal and conservative, the most controversial of which was relaxing border controls to let in more foreigners, subject to requirements like an absence of criminal conviction, an English-language test and guarantees of employment prospects. He was one of the front-runners for the next presidential campaign and had already started stumping.

Peter Simesky, the aide, said, "I'll confirm he's a fan. On the campaign buses, you're right up there with Taylor Swift, Randy Travis, James Taylor and the Stones for our listening pleasure. Hope you're okay with that company."

"I'll take it, you bet."

Then the congressman grew serious. "Your father said there's a bit of a problem at the moment, somebody who might be stalking you?" This was half directed to Dance, as well. Kayleigh's father must have mentioned that she was an agent.

"Afraid that's true," Dance said.

"You're . . . with Fresno?" Myra Babbage asked. "We've been working with a few people there on security."

"No, CBI." That she was here would normally mean the case was a major one. But she added, "I'm based in Monterey. Happened to be here unofficially and heard about the incident. I volunteered to help."

"We were just in Monterey too," Davis said. "Campaigning at Cannery Row."

"That's why the traffic was so bad back at home before I left," Dance joked.

"I wish it had been worse. It was good turnout, not a great turnout.".

Kayleigh supposed Monterey and particularly Carmel were bastions of conservative voters, who would not be particularly happy about a pro-immigration candidate.

The congressman nodded toward the agent. "I'm sure the CBI and the local authorities are doing everything they can but if you need any help from me, just let me know. Stalking can be a federal crime too."

Kayleigh thanked him, Dance did too and Simesky gave the agent his card. "You need any help, seriously," the slim young man said earnestly, "give me a call. Any time."

"I'll do that," Dance replied and glanced down to her hip as her phone buzzed. "It's a text from Detective Harutyun." She looked up. She sighed. "They've found the next crime scene. It's another killing, another fire. But it was worse than at the concert hall. He says there might be more than one victim. They just can't tell."

Chapter 26

"THE FIRE'S STILL going," Harutyun told her over the phone. "He must've used five gallons of accelerant. It's in a shed beside the San Joaquin River."

> *You sit by the river, wondering what you got*
> > *wrong,*
> *How many chances you'd missed all along.*
> *Like your troubles had somehow turned you to*
> > *stone*
> *and the water was whispering, why don't you come*
> > *home?*

Everyone in the room was staring at Dance. She ignored them and concentrated on her conversation with Harutyun. "Any witnesses?"

"No."

"How do you know it's related to the stalking?"

"Well, I don't know how to put it but out front we found a little shrine to Kayleigh."

"What?"

"Yes'm. Pretty sick. A mound of rocks and a couple of her CDs next to them in front of the shed. And, you know what was weird?"

More than that? Dance couldn't begin to guess.

"A twenty-dollar bill under a rock. Like an offering."

"And no idea of the victim?"

"Or victims," he reminded. "The team got a look inside and saw a couple of legs. That's about all that was left. Then the roof came down. It was part of an old gas station so they're being careful, thinking there could be a buried tank nearby. Charlie Shean has his CS people running the scene outside, as close as they can. It's hot as Hades out there. One of the techs fainted from the heat, the jumpsuit. No tire treads or footprints. We've found two shell casings. Nine-millimeter." A click of the detective's tongue. "Same as Fuentes's gun, got stolen. But that could be a coincidence. At least—I pray this happened—he shot 'em before he set 'em on fire."

"We can hope."

"No bloodstains but looks like he swept over the dirt with a branch or something. They're taking samples. DNA could be the only way to find out who he killed."

An altar to Kayleigh. Well, it was in keeping with stalker behavior.

"Charlie's folks also ran the scene of the phone booth where he called Kayleigh. They got some trace but the fingerprints—close to forty—don't match anything else and they're not in AIFIS."

"Any spotting of Edwin?"

"Nope. I've got to go. I'll call you when I know more, Kathryn."

"Thanks."

She disconnected, turned to Kayleigh, her father and the others and gave them a report.

Bishop closed his eyes and muttered what might've been a prayer. Dance recalled he'd gone through a phase where he released a Christian album—after rehab. It hadn't sold well.

"Who's the victim?" Kayleigh asked breathlessly.

"We don't know. It could be more than one. But

because of the fire they couldn't get a good look inside."

"But where's Alicia? And Tye?" Kayleigh called and got through to both of them. All the rest of the crew were accounted for too, Kayleigh reported after speaking to Tye Slocum. "Jesus. Alicia was out riding her horse. And Tye? He was picking up extra guitar strings. We've got a thousand in the truck. Why did he need to do that? Drives me crazy."

The congressman and his entourage looked uneasy and Davis seemed to be thinking that a visit at this moment had not been a good idea. He said, "We've got some campaigning to do. Sorry to have bothered you."

"Not at all." It was Bishop, not Kayleigh, who made this comment.

Davis reiterated that he'd help out however he could. He'd see her at the concert.

"I'm not—" She fell silent, looking at her father, who gave no reaction. "Hey, thanks for your support."

"Hope I can say the same to you on Election Day."

Peter Simesky, the aide, stepped up to Dance once more. He shook her hand. "You have my card. If there's anything else you need, please, just let me know."

Kinesics is a skill that doesn't shut off when you leave the office. The instant he'd made eye contact with her earlier, she knew that Simesky wanted to get to know her better, if circumstances allowed. She gave him credit: He wore no wedding ring and his first glance had been at her left hand; he might very well be one of those men who was not interested in an extramarital affair.

He also exuded a comfortable but not blunt self-confidence. He wasn't put off by the two inches of height she had on him or abashed about his small frame and thinning hair (ironically her present romantic partner, Jon Boling, shared those attributes). But with Kathryn Dance's complicated personal life, there was no room or inclination for expansion.

She nodded politely to Simesky and made sure the handshake was brief and professional. She couldn't tell if he got the message.

Then Davis, followed by Simesky and Myra Babbage, left the house and made their way to the SUV. The security man opened the doors for them. In a minute they were speeding down the dirt and gravel driveway.

Then Kayleigh's eyes flashed in shock and she began to cry. "Wait, he burned them?" she whispered.

"That's right."

"No, no! *This*'s my fault too!" Her shoulders rose, jaw tight. She angrily wiped away tears. "My song! He's using another one of my songs."

Dance pointed out, "The crime scene's by the river, just like the second verse."

"No, the fire! First Bobby and now these other people. Edwin sent me an email, well, a bunch of them, saying how much he liked my song 'Fire and Flame.'"

She picked up the CD of *Your Shadow* and showed Dance the liner notes.

Love is fire, love is flame
It warms your heart, it lights the way.
It burns forever just like the sun.
It welds two souls and makes them one.
Love is fire, love is flame.

Bishop said to his daughter, "Hey, KT, don't go blaming yourself. You can't take into account all the damn crazies out there. That boy's a sicko and nothing but. If it wasn't you it'd be somebody else." The sentences were wooden. He wasn't adept at offering solace.

"He *burned* those people to death, Daddy!"

Bishop didn't know what to say and he walked to the kitchen and got himself a glass of milk. Sheri stood uneasily beside one of the guitars. Dance called Harutyun again but there'd been no new developments.

When Bishop returned he looked at the watch on his big, ruddy wrist. "Hey, you heard from your sister?"

"Well, I talked to her this morning. I called her about Bobby. Why?"

"They shoulda been here by now. Or maybe—"

Kayleigh's mouth actually dropped. "What do you mean, Daddy?"

"Maybe she's headed to our place."

"No, what are you talking about? 'Been here'? Why would she be here?"

Bishop looked down. "I thought it'd be good for her to come. Moral support, with Bobby. Called her this morning. They flew up, landed an hour ago."

This would be how he delivered important news. Tossed out casually like a softball.

"Oh, Christ. Why didn't you tell me? She has no business . . . Wait, you said 'them.' Is the whole family coming?"

"Uh-uhn. Roberto's working. It's just Suellyn and Mary-Gordon."

Kayleigh raged, "Why on earth would you do that? With this madman around. A little girl?"

"Moral support," he growled back, flustered. "Like I said."

"Oh, Jesus. Oh, Jesus." Kayleigh sat down. "That's not why you asked them. . . ." But then her voice rose to a high pitch. "The fire . . . the attack. Oh, you don't think . . . it's not *them*?"

"Settle there, KT. How would this Sharp fella even know they were at the airport?" Bishop asked. "And what flight they were coming in on?"

Kayleigh grabbed her phone and dialed. She slammed the disconnect button. "Voicemail. Who was going to pick them up? Why didn't you tell me, why didn't *you* go?"

"Had that meeting with the congressman. I sent Ritchie. All right, I'll give him a call." Bishop found his mobile and placed a call. "Hey. Me. What's the story? Where are they? . . . *Who?* Who d'you think I mean? Suellyn and her kid, that's who . . . *What?*"

Every eye in the room was locked on him.

"When? . . . Oh, fuck." He disconnected. "Okay, well, what happened was he got a call from a friend of yours." A glance at his daughter. "*He* was going to give them a ride here."

"Who?" Kayleigh cried. "Who the hell was it?"

"Ritchie doesn't remember the name. But whoever it was knew the flight number, knew their names. Said you'd rather he picked them up."

Sheri said, "But if it was him, Edwin, how'd he know Ritchie was going to pick them up?"

Bishop's eyes bored into the carpet at his feet. "Well . . . shit."

"What, Daddy? What!"

"This morning, we had breakfast at the Herndon Café, Sheri and me. We were pretty much alone in the place, pretty much had it to ourselves. Except there was somebody else, sitting nearby, his back to us. Tall fellow, black hair. Couldn't see him. He coulda overheard me talking to Suellyn and calling Ritchie, giving him the information. I doubt it but coulda happened."

"What time?" Dance asked.

"I don't know. Nine-thirty, ten."

Dance reflected: Edwin was at the movie theater about eleven. The timing could work.

Sheri Towne stepped up to Kayleigh and touched

her shoulder tentatively. Dance noticed the singer's lips tighten. Sheri stepped back.

"But how would he know Ritchie?" Kayleigh asked. "To get his number and call him?"

"Could he be connected to you on your site or in the press?" Dance asked.

"Maybe. He's listed on the last albums, he was one of my assistants and drivers. In the acknowledgments."

Dance said, "With all the research Edwin does, sure, he could've found out."

Kayleigh began to cry. "What're we going to do?"

Dance called Harutyun and told him their concern. He said he was going to check something.

As she waited her eyes were on Bishop. He was fuming; Sheri kept a bit of distance. Dance wondered who the anger was directed at. She guessed it would be Ritchie. Bishop seemed the sort to blame everyone but himself for the problems in life.

Harutyun came back on after an interminable five minutes. "Video at the airport. A woman in her thirties and little girl got into Edwin's Buick. About thirty minutes after the flight from Portland landed."

Dance looked at the expectant faces. She told them what the deputy had said.

"No!" Kayleigh screamed. "No!"

"And. Agent Dance . . . Kathryn," Harutyun was saying on the line. "Just heard from the fire team. There's only one body inside." He hesitated. "Not too big. Could be a teenager—boy or girl—or a woman. Can't tell; body's burned down to the bone. At least, if it is the sister, the little girl's still alive. But that also means he's got her. And that, I don't even want to think about."

Chapter 27

KAYLEIGH PLACED YET another frantic call.

"Answer, answer, answer," she whispered. She grimaced. "Suellyn, it's me. Call me right away. I mean *immediately*. There's a problem." She looked at the screen. "How do I mark it urgent?" Her voice broke. "I don't know how! How do I mark it urgent?"

Dance took her phone, examined the screen and hit a button.

And Dance had given her opinion that stalkers tended not to target family members.

What was going on in Edwin's mind, if he had in fact kidnapped the two? Had he been so incensed about the arrest that he'd snapped? Had he started stalking Bishop that morning to learn what he could and found out about the arrival of Kayleigh's sister and niece? In the car maybe he'd confessed his love for Kayleigh and enlisted Suellyn's aid to win her over. When the woman refused, he'd killed her and taken the girl. Maybe he intended to raise her, treating her like a young Kayleigh of his own. Dance was a tough policewoman, yes, but she was a mother too and she simply didn't want to face that scenario.

"Please," Kayleigh begged once more. "Isn't there anything you can do? Track her phone or something?"

"That can be done. It takes time. But sure. I'll order it."

Not sharing with anyone, least of all Kayleigh, that if the body in the shed was Suellyn there would be no phone left to track.

Dance was speaking to TJ Scanlon about contacting the woman's provider, when Darthur Morgan called from the entryway, "Another car coming. Well, what on earth's this?"

Dance wondered what that cryptic comment might mean.

A moment later there was the clunk of car doors closing and the sound of a vehicle accelerating away on the gravel drive.

Then the front door opened and in walked a woman in her thirties and an adorable little golden-haired girl of about six, in a pink dress. She held a stuffed plush toy. She ignored everyone in the room except the singer, whom she ran to and hugged. "Aunt Kayleigh, look! We went to this neat museum and we brought you a stuffed redwood tree!"

Chapter 28

KATHRYN DANCE SMILED a greeting to the woman she'd been introduced to—Suellyn Sanchez, Kayleigh's sister—and walked to the door. She noted the big red Buick speeding away.

"It was him," Kayleigh whispered, also looking out the window and struggling to put on a calm facade so as not to worry the little girl.

Suellyn embraced her father—a seemingly pro forma gesture. She greeted Sheri too, more affectionately than Kayleigh had. "What's with the police? Is this about Bobby?"

Kayleigh, however, glanced icily toward her father and turned her attention to Mary-Gordon. "Honey, let me show you some new games I got for the next time you visited. Just for you."

"Yay! . . . Where's Freddie?"

"He's in the stable at Grandpa's house. You and your mommy are going to be staying there."

"I like Freddie but I want to stay with you," the girl announced.

"Oh, I'm not going to be here much. I'll come see you at Grandpa's."

"Okay."

"Come on."

Her arm around the girl, Kayleigh steered her to the

bodyguard. "And this is Mr. Morgan. He's a friend of mine. He hangs out with us."

He delicately shook the girl's hand. "My name's Darthur. You can call me that."

The girl looked at the security man with curiosity. "That's a funny name."

"You bet it is," the man said, looking uncertainly at Kayleigh, but following gamely.

"My name's Mary-Gordon but it's not two names, it's one. Mary and Gordon, with a line in between. They call the line a hyphen."

"It's a very pretty name."

"Thank you. I like you."

Dance called Harutyun and told him that the sister and niece were safe. He reported they still had no ID on the victim but the fire was out and the CSU and medical examiners were about to go inside, process the body and run the scene.

Kaleigh and the girl vanished into the den and Kayleigh returned a moment later, steamed up to her sister and said, "What *were* you thinking?"

"What?"

"Do you know who gave you that ride?"

"That friend of yours. Said his name was Stan."

Dance pointed out, "Stanton. Middle name."

"Jesus Christ." Kayleigh's voice dropped. "It's my goddamn *stalker*. Did you think to call? He's the one who murdered Bobby."

"What? Oh, my God. But you said he was fat, disgusting. . . ."

"Well, he made himself unfat," Kayleigh snapped, looking angrily into her sister's brown eyes. She shook her head and relented. "Sorry. It's not your fault. You just . . . you shouldn't be here." A cold glance toward Bishop.

Dance said, "We aren't sure who's behind it. Edwin Sharp is a possible suspect. But you should avoid any more contact with him."

"Where did you go?" Kayleigh asked.

"He asked if we wanted to see something Mary-Gordon might like. He said it was on the way. We went to the tree museum near Forty-one and the Bluffs. He said he knew you liked to spend time hiking in the forest."

Kayleigh closed her eyes. "He knew that too?" Her hands were shaking. "I was so scared! Why didn't you pick up when I called?"

"The phone was in my computer bag. He put that in the trunk. I was going to keep it with me but he took it. I mean, I'm sorry, K, but he knew *everything* about you. He said you'd written a song about trees but it got co-opted by Greenpeace or some eco movement and you stopped performing it. I didn't even know that. He knew about everybody in the band, he knew about Sheri. I thought he was a good friend."

Morgan said, "So the other killing, just now? By the river? That couldn't have been him?"

Dance considered the timing again. She decided that Edwin could have abducted and shot the victim, set fire to the body and made it to the airport in time to pick up Suellyn and her daughter.

"Oh, Jesus. We were in the car with somebody who'd just killed a man?" Suellyn whispered.

Bishop said, "Well, you're safe now. That's all that matters. But that fucker. He's going down."

Kayleigh wiped more tears.

Suellyn said, "This is just so strange. I almost got the idea he was your boyfriend. He said he was worried about you; you looked so tired. There was a lot of pressure on you. He wasn't even sure it was a good idea to give the concert. He thought you should reschedule."

Kayleigh's eyes swiveled to her father once more but that topic remained buried.

"He said . . ." Suellyn struggled to get it just right. "He said sometimes Kayleigh needed to think more about what's good for *her*. Too many people wanted a piece of her soul."

Your shadow . . .

Bishop turned to his older daughter, asking casually, "How was the flight?"

"Jesus, Dad. Really." Suellyn looked exasperated.

Kayleigh said she didn't want Mary-Gordon here any longer. She was afraid Edwin would come back again to spy and might try to approach the girl. They should go with Bishop and Sheri to their house, outside town. And they should leave now.

Kayleigh blinked and then looked down, realizing she was still holding the goofy stuffed redwood tree. She started to throw it out angrily but changed her mind and set it aside, on a shelf.

Suellyn went into the den to get her daughter and the toys Kayleigh had bought her.

At that moment Dance's phone rang; Dennis Harutyun was calling. She asked, "So you've identified the vic?"

"That's right."

"Is there any connection with Kayleigh?" she asked.

"Yes and no. You better come see."

Chapter 29

THE STENCH WAS bad, but so much rubber and plastic and oil had burned that at least the smell of human flesh and hair was largely obscured. The wind helped too.

Not that Dance didn't need all her willpower to keep from gagging, if not worse.

Love is fire, love is flame . . .

The scene was a broad dusty field, a cracked and crumbling parking lot, a long-closed gas station collapsed in on itself and the burned shed, of which there wasn't much left. The smoke was still rising in furious plumes. The heat you could feel from the shoulder of the road. Not far away was the gray-brown strip of low river that had inspired this location for the killing.

The CSU team was still at work, though the firefighters outnumbered the police. Fire was a much greater risk to the population of Fresno than a single crazed stalker.

Harutyun, the senior detective on the scene, explained what they'd found, which wasn't much. The shell casings, the CDs, the money—the altar to Kayleigh. But even the twenty-dollar bill seemed to have been washed—literally laundered. And the fire had been such a serious threat that the men and women had charged onto the grounds with hoses to contain the flames, surely contaminating the scene worse.

Besides, Dance guessed, if Edwin was behind the killing he wouldn't have left much evidence. He was too clever for that.

Harutyun continued the explanation he'd begun over the phone.

The victim had indeed known Kayleigh—and about a thousand other performers.

His name was Frederick Blanton. "He's a crook," Harutyun summarized. "*Was* a crook."

Dance thought of the CDs, the altar . . . and what she knew of the music business. "Into illegal file sharing?"

"That's very good, Kathryn. Yes."

"What's the story?"

"There were close to ten thousand computers on the network. People would download songs, music videos too. Kayleigh's were among the most popular."

"How'd you ID him?" Dance glanced inside. "Obviously, no prints."

"Weren't hardly even any hands or feet. One hand must've burned down to ash, gone completely. We'll have to confirm with DNA but we found his wallet in a part of the shed that didn't burn so bad. We checked his address—he lived in the Tower District, about seven, eight miles from here. A team's going through his house now. They found his door kicked and it was a mess—all his computers were wrecked. We figured the perp probably forced him to destroy the file-sharing servers then made him get into the trunk of his car. If it's Edwin he's got plenty of room in that Buick of his. Drove him here, shot him and set the fire."

Dance mused, "How easy would it have been for Edwin to find him?"

"Google 'torrent' and 'Kayleigh Towne' and 'download,' and his site"—a nod toward the shed—"was in the top ten. Some basic research and he'd've come up with the address, I'd guess. Our boy seems good at that."

"And he left the altar as a warning not to steal from Kayleigh."

A stalker's likely to target anybody who's a threat to you, or even offended you. He's taking real seriously his role as a protector. . . .

"And the crime scene at his house? Evidence?"

"Nothing. No prints, foot or finger. Some trace but . . ." He shrugged, an indication of its marginal usefulness. "They *did* find he had a partner."

"Who's feeling a little uneasy at the moment," Dance speculated.

"Well, he's not in the area."

"Guess you don't need to be next-door neighbors with your co-conspirator if you're doing computer crimes. You could be in South America or Serbia. Where's he based?"

"Salinas."

Hm. Monterey County.

"You have the guy's name—and physical or computer address?"

"CSU'd have it." The detective made a call and asked that the information be sent to her phone. She noted that he'd memorized her number.

The unit chimed a moment later with the incoming message.

"I'll send it to some people I know there. They can follow up with him." She composed an email and sent it off.

Harutyun then said, "I'm trying to keep an open mind. I know it seems to be Edwin but I'm still looking into motives anybody else would have had to kill Bobby. I've been getting a lot of information about him but so far nothing jumps out. And now I guess I better add this guy into the mix. But, well, there've gotta be a lot of people who'd like to murder a file sharer. Half the record companies and movie studios."

Another squad car arrived, crunching over the gravel, dirt and bleached twigs that bordered the site of the blackened earth. It parked near a faded Conoco sign depicting a pale green dinosaur. Dance's daughter, Maggie, was presently in a Jurassic phase. Her room was littered with plastic versions of the reptiles. Dance tamped down a pang, missing her children.

P. K. Madigan climbed out, surveyed the scene with hands on his slim hips overshadowed by his belly. Then he joined Dance and Harutyun. "So, he was stealing her songs?"

"That's right."

Madigan grumbled, "Never thought he'd switch to landlines. Should have."

"We all should have."

"And where the hell is he? He's got a car as big as my boat and it's bright red, to boot. I don't see how he keeps losing my folks." His phone rang and he regarded the screen. "'Lo? . . . You don't say. . . . Naw, I'll go myself." He disconnected. "Well, all righty then. I can't tell you where Edwin was when this fella died but I can tell you where he is now. He's parked in front of Kayleigh's house again. In the arboretum lot across the road."

"What's he doing?"

"Sitting on the hood of his car, happy as a clam, having himself a picnic. I want to have a talk with him. Well, actually, I'd like *you* to have a talk with him, Kathryn. You up for that?"

"You bet I am."

Chapter 30

THAT CONVERSATION DID not, however, occur.

Driving in tandem, they were at Kayleigh's house fast, in twenty-five minutes, but Edwin Sharp had left by then.

He has a sixth sense, Dance thought, though she did not believe in sixth senses.

Was it her imagination or did she see a cloud of dust hanging over the spot from which he might have just sped off? Hard to tell. There was a lot of dust in Fresno. The sky was clear but wind rose occasionally and a near-by vortex of beige powder swirled into a tiny funnel and then melted away.

Dance and Madigan both parked across the road from Kayleigh's house and climbed out. This side of the road was lush, thanks to the park. Kayleigh's yard too was thickly landscaped. In the distance, south and west, was a vista of low fields, now just dark dirt. Whatever was grown there had been harvested.

The detective gave a knowing glance toward her—acknowledging frustration at their missing quarry—and leaned against his car to make a call. From the brief conversation Dance deduced it was to the deputy at Kayleigh's house—provided to supplement Darthur Morgan when the manpower allowed. He disconnected. "Was Jose, at the house." A nod.

"Edwin was here ten minutes ago. They didn't see which way he went."

Dance could understand why. From here you could see only the second story of the house, which was about three hundred feet away, down the gravel driveway. She wondered if the windows visible from here—the ones Edwin had just presumably been staring at while he had his meal—were Kayleigh's bedroom.

Silence for a time. The sun was low and Dance could feel the day shedding heat in layers.

Madigan said, "Had a snake in my backyard a couple, three years ago. Big rattler. I mean, a big one. Saw him once and never again for the rest of that summer. Was he under the barbecue, the house, had he left altogether? Walked around with my sidearm all the time, which I never do."

"Because of the kids," Dance said.

"Because of the kids. We took to calling him the 'invisible snake.' But it wasn't funny. Ruined the backyard for the whole season. And saw him one time only. All right." He stood with hands on his hips again, looking over the park. "You're in town all alone. You want to come over for dinner? My wife, she's a pretty good cook."

"I'll probably just get something back at the motel. Get some sleep."

"We got good desserts."

"Ice cream?"

A laugh. "Naw. Judy bakes. Well, ice cream ends up being involved."

"Think I'll pass, thanks."

"Good evening to you, Kathryn."

"You too, Chief."

Dance returned to the Mountain View. The locks on her suitcases were intact and nothing seemed to be disturbed. Dance glanced out the window at the park, saw no surveillance and closed the blinds.

As soon as she did, the hotel phone rang.

"Agent Dance?" A pleasant male voice.

"That's right."

"It's Peter Simesky? Congressman Davis's aide?" he asked as if she'd have no clue who he was.

"Yes, hi."

"Hi. Actually I'm in the lobby . . . of your motel. The congressman was speaking at a farm nearby. Could I talk to you? Am I interrupting anything?"

She could find no credible excuse and said she'd be out in a minute.

In the lobby she found the man on his phone and he politely ended the call when he spotted her. They shook hands and he grinned, though the smile soon morphed into a frown.

"I heard they confirmed another attack."

"That's right. Homicide."

"Anyone connected to Kayleigh?"

"Not directly."

"Is there anything we can do?"

"So far, no. But appreciate that."

"It's this stalker?"

"Pointing to him but we don't know for sure."

Simesky tilted his head in a certain way and Dance knew a related story would be forthcoming. "The congressman's had a few problems himself. A couple of campaign workers and interns. Two women and a gay man too. They got infatuated, I guess you could say."

Dance explained about erotomania. "Fits the classic profile. A powerful man and somebody in a lower professional position. Any physical threats?"

"No, no, just got awkward."

Simesky had a large bottle of water and he drank it thirstily. She noticed his white shirt was sweat stained.

He followed her glance and laughed. "The congress-man's been delivering his ecofriendly speech at farms from Watsonville to Fresno. The temperature was a lot more pleasant in your neighborhood."

Watsonville, just north of where Dance lived, was near the coast. And, she agreed, a lot more pleasant, weather-wise, than the San Joaquin Valley.

"You got a good turnout, I'll bet."

"At the farms, because of his immigrant position, you mean? Oh, you bet. We considered it a success—and there were only forty protesters. Maybe fifty. And no one threw anything. We get tomatoes sometimes. Brussels sprouts too. Kind of ironic, a candidate in sup-port of farmworkers getting pelted by vegetables from the anti-farmworker contingent."

Dance smiled.

Simesky looked toward the motel's bar. "How 'bout a glass of wine?"

She hesitated.

"This won't take long. It's important."

Dance remembered his look her way at Kayleigh's house and his slightly overlong handshake. Was she the object of a stalker herself? She said, "Just to set the rec-ord straight, I'm seeing somebody."

He gave a wistful, embarrassed smile. "You caught that, hm?"

"I do this for a living."

"I've heard about you." A grin. "I better watch my body language. . . . Well, Agent Dance—"

"Kathryn."

"Yeah, I was flirting a bit—then and just a few sec-onds ago. And I'm disappointed to hear about your friend. Never hurts to ask."

"Never does." Edwin Sharp should take some les-sons from Peter Simesky.

"But there was another point to this too. Completely innocent."

"Okay, let's get that wine."

In the dim, tacky bar she ordered a Merlot and Simesky a Chardonnay. "What a case you've got yourself, that stalker," he said.

"He's persistent and smart. And obsessed. The most dangerous kind of perp."

"But you were saying you're not sure it's him."

"We're never sure until we get a confession or the evidence proves the case."

"I guess not. I'm a lawyer but I never did criminal work. Well, now, my agenda."

The wine arrived and they sipped without tapping glasses.

"About Kayleigh Towne?"

"No, it's about you."

"Me?"

"Bill Davis likes you. Oh, wait . . . not that way," the aide added quickly. "The only person he's ever flirted with since college is his wife. They've been together twenty-eight years. No, this is a professional interest. Do you follow politics much?"

"Some. I try to keep informed. Davis is somebody I'd vote for if I was in his district."

Simesky seemed to take this as very good news. He continued, "He's pretty liberal then, you know. And some people in the party are afraid that as a presidential candidate he's going to be perceived as soft on law and order. It'd go a long way if—yes, you can see this coming—a long way if somebody like you were aligned with him. You're smart, attractive—sorry, can't help myself—and have a great record with the CBI."

"And I'm a woman."

"That doesn't count the way it used to."

"What does 'aligned' mean?"

"What he'd like, if you were interested, is to discuss a Justice Department appointment. Something pretty senior. We'd just like to broach it at this point. No commitments on anybody's side."

Dance had to laugh. "Washington?"

"That's right."

Her initial reaction was to dismiss the idea as absurd, thinking that uprooting the children might be difficult. Also, she'd miss the fieldwork. But then she realized that she'd have the chance to spread word of her kinesic analysis techniques of investigation and interrogation around the country. She was adamantly opposed to extreme interrogation techniques as both immoral and ineffective, and she was intrigued by the idea that she might have influence in changing those practices at a very high level.

And, reconsidering, as for the kids, what was wrong with exposing them to a different city, especially the nation's capital, for a few years? Maybe she could commute between the two coasts.

Peter Simesky had to laugh. "I don't have your expertise but if I'm reading your face right, you're considering it."

And then she wondered: What would Michael O'Neil think of this?

Oh, and Jon Boling too? Though as a consultant, he could live anywhere. She wouldn't do anything without talking to him first, though.

"This is completely out of left field. I never in a million years thought about anything like it."

Simesky continued, "There're too many career politicians messing up government. We need people who've lived in the trenches. They'll work for a while and go home to the back forty, take up farmin' again." A smile. "Or being cops. Is it okay to say 'cop'?"

"Not the least offensive."

Simesky slid off the bar stool, paid the check. "I've given you a lot to think about and you don't need to decide now, not with this investigation going on. Just let it sit." He stood up and shook her hand. At the doorway he paused. "That guy you mentioned? Pretty serious, huh?"

"Yep."

"Tell him he's a lucky man and, by the way, I hate him." A cherubic smile and then he was gone.

Dance finished her wine—this would be it for the evening, she decided—and returned to her room, laughing to herself. Deputy Director of the Federal Bureau of Investigation, Kathryn Dance.

Maybe, just maybe she could get used to that.

It was now nine-thirty, hardly late, but she was exhausted. Time for yet another shower and sleep.

But that too was interrupted. Her phone rang once more and she didn't recognize the caller ID number. Let it go?

But the investigator within her decided to answer.

Just as well. It turned out that the caller was Edwin Sharp's former girlfriend.

Chapter 31

SALLY DOCKING WAS her name.

Deputy Miguel Lopez had tracked her down in Seattle and left a message to contact Dance, who now thanked her for calling.

A hesitant, melodious voice. "Like, sure."

"I'd like to talk to you about Edwin Sharp."

"Oh, Edwin? Is he okay?"

Odd question.

"Yes, he is. I wonder if you could answer a few questions for me."

"I guess. But, like, what's this about?"

"You were in a relationship with him, correct?"

"Yeah, for a while. We met in February a year ago. We worked in the same mall. We started going out and moved in for a few months. It didn't work out. We broke up around Christmas. What's . . . I mean, I'm kind of curious why you're asking."

Sometimes you can be too evasive and the subjects clam up. "He's been showing some inappropriate interest in someone here in California."

"He has? Really? What's that mean?"

"We're looking into whether or not he's guilty of stalking."

"Edwin?" She sounded genuinely surprised.

Dance jotted this impression in her notebook.

"Have you heard from him lately?"

"No. It's been months and months."

"Sally, tell me: Did he ever threaten you?"

"Threaten? No, never."

"Did he ever threaten or show excessive interest in other women that you know about?"

"No. I can't even picture it."

"Did you ever see him engage in any obsessive behavior?"

"Well, like, I don't know what you mean exactly. He got pretty intense, maybe you'd call it obsessive. He'd get into something, like totally get excited about a Wii game or some fantasy author and he'd buy all their books."

"How about people, stars, musicians?"

"He liked movies. Yeah, he went a lot. In theaters, not on TV so much. But his big thing was music, yeah. He really liked Cassie McGuire and Kayleigh Towne and Charlie Holmes and Mike Norman—you know them?"

"Yes, I do." The latter two, Dance noted, were men.

"And then this band from Seattle, the Pointless Bricks. I know it's a stupid name but they're really, really good. Edwin totally loved them. If he was going to see somebody in concert he'd get tickets way ahead of time and make sure that his schedule let him get away. He'd be at the concert hall like three hours early, even if he had reserved seats, and he'd stand in line afterwards, hoping to get an autograph. And he'd get their souvenirs on eBay. It was a waste of money. I mean, to me, that's pretty obsessive."

"After you left him, did you have a problem with him calling you, following you? Harassing you?"

"No. I mean he'd call sometimes about something he'd left at my apartment, and we'd taken out a loan together and we had to talk about that, sign some papers.

But, stalking, no, nothing like that. Only one thing? You said when I left him. That's not what happened. He left me."

Dance could have kicked herself. And earlier she'd been mentally chastising P. K. Madigan for leading Edwin during the interview; here she was doing exactly the same.

"Tell me what happened."

"He just said the relationship wasn't working. I was pretty bummed. He wasn't, you know, real ambitious. He never wanted to be more than a security guard or work retail. But he was romantic and he was dependable. He didn't drink and he'd pretty much given up smoking when I was with him."

"So he used to smoke," Dance said, thinking of her own voyeur in the park near the motel.

"Yeah, but only when he was stressed. So, he left and I was pretty bummed out for a couple of months."

"Did he go out with anybody else?"

"Not really. He dated a few girls. I don't know who. We fell out of touch."

"One last question. Did you ever see him get violent or lose control?"

A pause. "Yeah, I did."

"Tell me."

Sally explained, "Okay, once me and my girlfriend and Edwin were walking down the street and this drunk guy came up, I mean, way, way drunk. And he called us sluts. And Edwin goes up to him and shouts, 'Apologize right now, you asshole.' And the guy did."

Dance waited. "That was it? He never hit this man?"

"Oh, no. Edwin'd never do that. I mean, he's scary-*looking*, sure. Those eyebrows, you know. And he's big. But he'd never hurt anybody. Look, there's a lot Edwin doesn't get, you know what I mean? He's kind of like a kid. That's part of what makes him so charming, though."

Hardly a word Dance would use. But she'd given up trying to figure out what made couples click.

Dance thanked the young woman and disconnected. She jotted a summary of the conversation into her notebook. So, what do I make of this? A relatively normal relationship with one woman didn't mean he couldn't stalk another. But stalking was habitual. For Sally to be involved for a year and to live with him for part of that time yet not see any danger signs was significant.

On the other hand, he'd exhibited *some* obsessive interest in music and performers.

But then, Dance admitted, so did she. Hence, her trip to *casa de Villalobos* with her tape recorder here in beautiful downtown Fresno during the dog days of September.

After a furtive examination of the park revealed no cigarette-smoking surveillance, Dance took a shower. She dried off and slipped into the Mountain View bathrobe, which the sign announced ironically she was *free* to take with her for $89.95.

Dance curled up in the sumptuous bed. Who needed views of snowy peaks when the furniture was so opulent?

She now wished Jon Boling were here with her. She was thinking of the recent overnight trip they'd taken to Ventana, the beautiful, surreal resort in the cliffs near Big Sur, south of Carmel. The trip had been a milestone—it was the first time she'd told the children that she and Boling were going away overnight.

She offered nothing more about the trip and the news was greeted with no interest whatsoever by either Wes or Maggie. At their ages, though, the broader implications had probably been lost on them. But their bored response was a huge victory for Dance, who'd stressed about their reaction to the fact Mom was traveling with another man. (Wes worried her most; Maggie wanted her mother to get married again so she could be "best woman.")

The weekend away had been wonderful and Dance had been pleased that the last holdout of widowhood—the discomfort with intimacy—was finally vanishing.

She wanted Boling here now.

And was thinking it curious that they hadn't spoken for two days. They'd traded messages but voicemail had reared its head at every instance. She was involved in a murder investigation so she had an excuse, she reflected. But Boling was a computer consultant. She wasn't quite sure why he was so inaccessible.

Dance called her parents, chatted with her father for a few minutes then asked to speak to the children.

It was a pure comfort, pure joy, hearing their voices. Dance found she was smiling to herself as they rambled on enthusiastically about their days at camp. She laughed when they signed off with a "Loveyoumom" (Maggie) and "Gottagoseeya" (Wes), verbal signals perfectly defining the differing parent-child relationships at the moment.

Then her mother came on the phone. Edie reported that Dance's father was finishing up some work at her house in Pacific Grove to get it ready for the party she was hosting this weekend; house guests would be staying for a few days, after driving down from San Jose on Saturday.

And then there was a pause.

Dance tried not to practice her profession in her personal life. Nothing ruins a date faster than a man saying he's divorced as he leans forward and looks her in the eye—a complete deviation from his earlier baseline behavior. (One of her favorite Kayleigh Towne songs, "The Truth About Men," was a hilarious look at how that gender tends to be, well, less than forthright.)

But now she noted that something was up.

"How's it going there?" Edie Dance offered some clumsy verbal padding.

"Good. Fresno's actually kind of interesting. Parts of it are. There's a real-estate development built around a runway. You get a hangar for your plane, instead of a garage. Well, maybe you get a garage too. I didn't look."

Throughout Kathryn Dance's life, her mother had been kind and fair but also resolute, opinionated, unyielding and at times exasperating. Get to the point, Dance thought.

"There's something I found out. I wasn't sure what to do. If it weren't for the kids . . ."

Of course, those words are like gasoline on the candle of motherhood and Dance now said bluntly, "What? Tell me." The tone was unmistakable: Don't screw around. I'm your daughter but I'm an adult. I want to know and I want to know now.

"Jon brought some computer games over for the kids. And he got a phone call . . . Honey, he was talking to a broker about property. I heard him say he'd gotten a job and wanted to take a look at a house."

This was interesting. But why the concern in her mother's voice? "And?"

"It's in San Diego. He's moving in a couple of weeks." Oh.

Weeks?

Dance now understood what Edie meant about the children. They were still vulnerable from the death of their father. For them to lose the new man in their life would be very hurtful, if not devastating.

And then there's me.

What the hell was he thinking of, not telling me anything? Here I was just offered a job in D.C. and the first thing I think of is talking to him about it.

Weeks?

So that's why he hadn't picked up the phone but used the coward's hideout of voicemail.

But the first rule of law enforcement was not to make assumptions. "Are you sure? You couldn't have misunderstood?"

"No, no. He was alone, in the back by the pool. He thought I couldn't hear. And when Wes stepped out, he changed the subject completely. He basically hung up on the broker."

Dance could say nothing for a moment.

"I'm sorry, honey."

"Yeah. Thanks, Mom. Just need to think about this a little."

"You get some sleep now. The kids are happy. We had a fun dinner. They love camp." She tried to be light. "And more important, can you believe it? They're looking forward to school. We're going book bag shopping tomorrow."

"Thanks. 'Night."

"I'm sorry, Katie. 'Night."

A moment later Dance found she was still holding her phone, disconnected, in front of her face. She lowered it.

The loss of her husband was like a digital event to Kathryn Dance, as Jon Boling the computer genius would describe it. On or off. Yes or no. Alive or dead.

But Jon Boling's leaving? It was analog. It was maybe. It was partly. Was he now in her life or not?

The big problem, though, was that he'd made this decision without her. It didn't matter that the job had probably happened quickly and he'd had to move fast.

Dammit, she was a part of his life. He should have said something.

She recalled that Edwin Sharp had referred to a song of Kayleigh's at the restaurant yesterday. "Mr. Tomorrow." It was about an abusive, straying man who swears he'll get his act together and mend his ways. He promises he'll change. Of course, the listener knows he never will.

As Dance lay in bed now, the lights out, she stared at the ceiling and that song looped through her mind until she fell asleep.

You know me by now, you've got to believe
You're the number-one girl in the world for me.
I've sent her the papers and she's promised to sign
It'll just be a while, these things take some time. . . .

And his words are so smooth and his eyes look so
*   sad.*
Can't she be patient, it won't be so bad?
But sometimes she thinks, falling under his sway,
She got Mr. Tomorrow; she wants Mr. Today.

Tuesday

Chapter 32

DANCE WAS IN the sheriff's office with P. K. Madigan and Dennis Harutyun.

There was another law enforcement jurisdiction present too: Monterey County.

Via Skype, Michael O'Neil's calm eyes looked back at them from 150 miles away. He was the person she'd tapped to look into the Salinas partner of Frederick Blanton, the murdered file sharer. She might have sent the request to TJ Scanlon in her own office. But on a whim she'd decided to contact O'Neil instead.

Madigan was briefing the Monterey deputy. "Edwin never went home last night. Kayleigh said that about ten-thirty she heard a car start somewhere in the park out in front of her house. Her bodyguard said he thought he heard it too."

The invisible snake . . .

"Kathryn and I want to interview him but he's not answering his phone. We don't even know where he is. This morning a deputy spotted his car on Forty-one, a pretty major road here. He tried to follow but Edwin must've seen him and wove around in traffic and got away."

O'Neil said, "Tough to follow with just one car."

"And I haven't got a lot of people to spare, what with

protecting witnesses and Kayleigh," Madigan muttered. "We cover more than six thousand square miles. Grand total of about four hundred and sixty patrol deputies."

O'Neil winced. Monterey wasn't small but that county didn't embrace nearly as much territory with such little manpower. He asked, "Kathryn told me he'd picked up Kayleigh's sister and niece at the airport. Any charges possible there?"

"Kathryn's going to interview them some more," Madigan said, "but doesn't look like it. Edwin was the boy-next-door, didn't do a thing wrong. The little girl loved him and the sister thought he was—get this—the nicest of Kayleigh's *boyfriends* in recent years."

Dance regarded the man on the screen—strong and solid but not heavy. O'Neil was wearing his typical outfit. Light blue shirt, no tie and a dark sport coat. Most detectives in the Monterey County Sheriff's Office, like here, wore uniforms but O'Neil didn't. He thought casual clothing got you further in investigations than khaki and pointed metal stars.

Dance briefed them about the interview with Sally Docking, Edwin's former girlfriend. "I have to tell you that his behavior with her doesn't fall into a stalker's profile." She explained that it had actually been Edwin who broke up with the woman.

"Still don't trust him," Madigan said.

"No. It's just odd."

O'Neil continued, "I paid a visit to Josh Eberhardt."

The file-sharing partner in Salinas.

"How polite a visit?" Dance asked.

"I talked Amy into going with me."

Amy Grabe, the FBI's special agent in charge in San Francisco.

"They decided there'd been enough federal copyright violations to justify a raid. Joint task force."

Which meant it wasn't very polite. "Feet apart, spread 'em" had probably been involved. Dance and O'Neil shared a smile. It was hard to say, given the optical mechanics of Skype, but it seemed to Dance that he winked at her.

Of course, he hadn't.

Then she admonished herself again: Concentrate.

"Good job, sir," Madigan said and enjoyed a bite of what Dance believed to be pistachio ice cream. She'd missed breakfast and was thinking of asking for a cup of her own.

The Monterey detective continued, "They did find some file sharing going on out of his house but Eberhardt was more of a researcher. He keeps track of hundreds of above- and underground fan sites for musicians. Looks like he'd comb through them and get potential customers for illegal downloads. It really wasn't all file sharing—it was file *stealing* and *selling* too. They charged a fee for the songs. They'd ripped off albums of about a thousand artists.

"There's this really . . . dark underground of websites out there. They have to do with cultural things, mostly: books, movies, TV shows, music. A lot of them are about stealing the artists' work—bootlegs, for instance. But most of them are about the celebrities themselves: Stephen King, Lindsay Lohan, George Clooney, Carrie Underwood, Justin Bieber . . . and Kayleigh Towne.

"And it's all off the radar. The people posting use proxies and portals . . . and anonymous accounts. None of this shows up on Google. They've worked around that." O'Neil gave them the list of websites whose addresses were only numbers or letters: 299ek333.com was typical. Once inside them, there were various pages that seemed nonsensical—"The Seventh Level," for instance. Or "Lessons Learned."

But navigating through the links, he explained, you got to the true substance of the sites: the world of celebrities. TJ Scanlon had found none of these.

O'Neil said, "It looks like that's where Edwin's getting a lot of his information. In fact, he posted plenty about the file sharer who got killed—the vic in Fresno."

Madigan asked, "Anything that'd implicate Edwin in the killing?"

"No. He just urged people not to use file sharing."

Of course, he wouldn't slip up. Not clever Mr. Edwin Sharp.

O'Neil turned away for a moment and typed. Dance received an email containing several URLs. Harutyun took her phone when she offered it to him and he set to work typing them into a computer nearby.

O'Neil asked the room, "You're monitoring all her calls?"

"That's right but we're trying to buy some time, make it harder for him to contact her with another verse," Harutyun said. "We've given her and her family new phones, all unlisted. He'll probably find the numbers eventually but by then we hope we'll nail him on the evidence or witnesses."

"I'd dig through those sites," O'Neil advised. "You should be able to get some good information about him. Looks like he spends a lot of time online."

O'Neil took a brief call and turned back to the screen. He said he had to leave, an interrogation was on the schedule. His eyes crinkled with a smile and though Skype didn't allow for a clear image of where he cast his gaze, Dance believed it was to her. "You need anything else, just let me know."

Madigan thanked him and the screen went dark.

They turned to the second monitor, on which

Miguel Lopez had called up one of the underground sites O'Neil had found.

"Lookit that," Crystal Stanning said.

The site, which boasted more than 125,000 fans, was a stalker's paradise. It had pages for several hundred celebrities in all areas of entertainment and politics. Kayleigh's was one of the most popular, it seemed. Within her pages was one headed "Kayleigh Spotting," and was a real-time hotline bulletin board about where she was at the moment. "She Can't Fool Us!" contained pictures of Kayleigh in various outfits—disguises, almost—so fans could recognize her when she was trying to remain anonymous. Other pages contained extensive bios of the crew and band members, fans' stories about concerts they'd attended, discussions of which venues were good and bad acoustically, who'd tried to scalp tickets.

Other pages gave details of Kayleigh's personal life, down to her preferences about food and clothing.

The page "WWLK, We Who Love Kayleigh" offered information about famous fans—people who had commented in the press about their affection for her music. As Dance scrolled through she found Congressman Davis's name mentioned. He'd been quoted at a campaign rally about how much he appreciated Kayleigh's talent, and her stance on immigration in her song "Leaving Home." Dance followed a hyperlink to his own page and noted that he had reproduced the lyrics in full—with Kayleigh's permission. Dance remembered he'd thanked Kayleigh for this earlier at her house.

"In the Know" offered press information, thousands of photographs, announcements from Kayleigh's record company and Barry Zeigler, her producer. There was also a feed from her official site, giving updates—for instance, about upcoming events, like Friday's concert and the luncheon today at a local country club for the Fan of the Month. Dance read the press release, written by Kayleigh's stepmother, Sheri, noting to her relief that Edwin was not the winner.

Other links led to even more troubling pages, which offered bootleg albums, recorded illegally at concerts, and links to file sharing services. One page gave gossip about disputes within celebrities' families, Kayleigh's included, though aside from tepid public spats with Bishop, Sheri and a few musicians, like the man who'd interrupted the award ceremony, her gossip page was pretty sparse.

She's a good girl . . .

Another page offered for sale items of Kayleigh's clothing, including undergarments, undoubtedly not really hers. There were risqué pictures of her too, though it was obvious they'd been manipulated with Photoshop.

This explained Edwin's innocuous and infrequent online activity that TJ Scanlon had found earlier. That was the public side of Edwin Sharp; *this* was the stalker's real Internet life. Though they couldn't tell for certain, a number of the posts with initials ES or ESS in the username were probably his. Dance assessed that the grammar, syntax and construction of many of these posts were reminiscent of the ones they knew he had done.

Dance hoped they could find even a hint of a threat to Kayleigh Towne, so they could invoke the stalking statute. But, no, this trove of Edwin-related activity wasn't much more helpful than the other. As with the more public sites, most of the posts that were or might be his didn't appear threatening in the least; if anything, he staunchly defended Kayleigh. Nor were they able to identify particular potential victims. Other fans were far more insulting than he was, some viciously so. Edwin came across as nothing more than a loyal, if strident, fan. Dance reflected that it was likely Edwin Sharp was not the only obsessed fan Kayleigh Towne had. Indeed, reading the posts suggested that he might be among the more innocuous.

There wasn't a single aspect of these celebrities' lives that was private. Kathryn Dance leaned away from the computer screen. She actually felt unclean from the imperious, invasive attitude of the posters—as if the entertainers and celebrities that were the objects of their interest were simply fodder for amusement and self-gratification.

It was as if the more successful you were at pleasing the populace, the more they felt entitled to suck your soul from your body.

Crystal Stanning took a phone call. Dance paid no attention to her until she noticed the deputy's shoulders rise and her brow furrow—a configuration often signaling bad, or at least perplexing, news. "You sure?" she asked.

By now the others in the room were watching her.

She disconnected, grimacing. "That was my husband. He took Taylor, that's our son, to football practice, the early one before school starts? And, it was weird. I told him about the song the perp's playing, Kayleigh's song? And he said somebody got into the PA system at the high school field and rigged the tape player so the third verse played over and over."

"Oh, hell," Madigan muttered. "He's not using the phones."

Thinking ahead of them once again.

And what were the clues in the lyrics? Dance looked over the sheet that Harutyun had printed.

> *One night there's a call, and at first you don't know*
> *What the troopers are saying from the side of the*
> *road.*

> *Then you see in an instant that your whole life has changed.*
> *Everything gone, all the plans rearranged.*

Dance did a double take at the verse, which spoke to her personally—thinking about the death of her husband. A trooper's call was how she'd learned of the accident.

Then she forced the thought away.

Where did the perp have in mind for attacking next? Somewhere by a roadside?

A glance at the map of the Madera-Fresno area revealed what had to be a thousand miles of roads.

Another thought occurred to her: the assault on Bobby Prescott and on the file sharer followed closely on the calls to Kayleigh; they had perhaps an hour or so to identify and save the next victim.

Chapter 33

MADIGAN SAID, "REMEMBER, 'road' could mean more than just a highway."

Dance nodded. "Road crew. Like Bobby. Let's call them. I told them to be careful but we ought to let them know he's played another song. And Alicia Sessions. At the Cowboy Saloon I could see Edwin didn't like her any more than he did Bobby."

She opened her notebook and displayed the numbers she had for everyone in the crew. Dance, Harutyun and Stanning notified them all. Half of the crew were at the convention center; the other half at the luncheon venue, being held at a nice country club in the northern part of town. Kayleigh would be singing a few songs so they'd set up a small performing space. Tye Slocum was en route to the venue, but Dance alerted him about the danger. Alicia, it seemed, had run out of gas on the way to Kayleigh's luncheon but was safe. She was waiting in a coffee shop for a service truck.

Dance bent toward the screen and was reading through one of Kayleigh's unofficial sites, which gave details of the luncheon. A lot of posters wished they could have gotten tickets but they'd sold out quickly.

Madigan was speaking into his phone, "Come on, how hard is it? The fucking car is a mile long! And goddamn bright red." He glanced at the others with a shrug, meaning the snake remained invisible.

Dance called Kayleigh, who'd just arrived at the luncheon, on the singer's new mobile number and told her of the possible threat.

"No! Not again. Are you sure?"

"Afraid we are. We haven't said anything to the press about using the song verses as announcements so we have to assume it's really a threat. Where are your sister and niece?"

"They're at home with Daddy and Sheri."

"Darthur's with you?"

"Yes. And there're about a dozen people here now. We're expecting a hundred or so. There's lots of security. You need a ticket to get in."

Dance continued to read the screen; an idea occurred to her. "Kayleigh, this fan of the month. Who is it?"

"I think his name's . . . hold on. Sam Gerber. Do you think he's in danger? Oh, Kathryn, what are we going to do?"

"So he's not there?"

"No, we don't get started for another forty-five minutes or so. I came early for a sound check. Should we call him?"

"Do you have his number?"

"I'll find it."

As she waited, Dance looked down and her eyes caught a series of posts on the fan site. They'd been made just that morning.

Who is this Gerber? Is he worthy of our wonderful Kayleigh? He hasn't posted much about her, hardly anything. Doesn't seem fair to some of us that he's going.

—ESKayleighfan

Just chill Edwin. there's room for more than
one fan.

—Musiqueman3468

yeah come on, he won a contest, whats the
big deal? I'm happy for him. he gets to have
LUNCH with Kayleigh!!!!!

—Suzi09091

He doesn't deserve it. Other people do. That's
my point.

—ESKayleighfan

Kayleigh came back on the line with Gerber's number. Dance jotted it down. "Thanks. We're doing everything we can. I'll call you back."

She called Sam Gerber and got voicemail. It was a local area code and exchange so maybe not a mobile. She left an urgent message.

"He lives in Madera," Madigan said. "I'll get a car to his house. If we're lucky he may not have left yet."

"The road," Dance mused. "Let's assume Edwin's going to try something on the route from Madera here."

She realized that, despite Sally Docking's report and the ambiguous evidence otherwise, she was making the assumption that Edwin was the killer. Still, she couldn't help herself and she continued to scroll through the fan site, trying to put herself into the young man's troubled mind.

WHAT SHE WANTED most was for Kayleigh to love her.

Sheri Towne knew she started from a disadvantage,

of course. No, she wasn't like Wife Number Three—the Child, as Sheri cattily thought of her, or Number Two, the Tarot Card Reader.

Yet Sheri *was* a lot younger than Bishop and in her own opinion didn't bring a lot to the table. She was insecure and knew she was worlds away from Margaret, the strong woman who was Kayleigh's and Suellyn's mother. Sheri knew about her not because anyone in the Towne family talked about Margaret in front of her, least of all Bishop, but because she'd listened to and memorized all of Kayleigh's songs; many of the early ones were about her mother.

Despite the tension, though, Sheri liked Kayleigh a lot, independent of being her stepmother, and she liked Suellyn and her husband, Roberto, and Mary-Gordon too. Oh, what a cute kid! Just the sort of child she wished she'd had, whom she *would* have had, if life had gone just a bit differently.

Sheri wanted badly to fit in. She loved Bishop, loved the odd mix of his power and his neediness, loved his talent—brilliant in the past and still glimmering now. (And maybe it would blossom again in the future; he talked sometimes about returning to performing. This was a secret that he'd shared with no one but her.)

Still, her connection with her new husband wouldn't be complete if she couldn't form a real relationship with Kayleigh. And not that superficial cordiality.

Hey there, Sheri, how ya doing? You have a good day now. Take care.

Hell. To Kayleigh, I'm like the most anonymous fan she sees at a concert.

She finally turned off the long drive from their house on the route to the highway. The car bounded along; the road, though paved, wasn't much better than gravel.

And yet, maybe, just maybe, things could change.

There'd been crumbs of hope. Kayleigh's sending Sheri the occasional greeting card. A present on her birthday. And then a half hour ago she'd gotten an email from Kayleigh saying when she came to the luncheon, could she bring a couple of dozen of her CDs from Bishop's house as giveaways to fans? Kayleigh'd forgotten them.

Thanks, Sheri. You're a star!

The woman had been hurt that Kayleigh hadn't even asked her to the event, which she herself had helped put together. But she'd noted the word *"when"* she came to the luncheon. So the girl hadn't snubbed her at all. Maybe she'd assumed Alicia had asked her. Or maybe Kayleigh had just assumed all along Sheri would be attending.

Or was the invitation a backhanded apology, reflecting the girl's cooling anger? The two had had an embarrassing fight at the show in Bakersfield not long ago. It had been minor, stupid, really. But some asshole had recorded a minute or two of their harsh words and the video had gone viral. Sheri had been mortified—even if, in her opinion, Kayleigh had started the fight.

All might be forgiven, though. Maybe Sheri wasn't doomed to be the Evil Stepmother forever.

The condition of the road improved and she pressed the accelerator of the Mercedes down further, speeding along the deserted highway, groves of trees on either side.

Maybe she should get Kayleigh a present, thanking her. She—

The flat happened so fast she couldn't respond before the car was careening along the shoulder. Sheri gave a faint scream and struggled to control the heavy vehicle, swerving perilously close to the trees, streaking by at seventy miles an hour.

But Sheri Marshal Towne had grown up in the Midwest and started driving at fourteen. Snow and powerful engines conspired to teach her how to handle skids. She now steered into the swerve, easing off the gas but never touching the brake.

Slower, slower . . . the car fishtailed, went straight, fishtailed some more, spewing gravel and leaves and twigs from the tires. But she managed to keep it from flying over the thirty-foot cliff to the right or slamming into the row of pines close by the opposite side.

Fifty miles an hour, forty . . .

In the end, though, the ground was too slippery—gravel and pebbles on hardpack—and she couldn't quite prevent the crash as the big Merc slid off the road toward the trees, wedging itself into a ditch, and shuddered to a stop.

Her hands sweaty, her heart thudding, Sheri rested her head against the steering wheel.

"Lord, Lord, Lord," she whispered, thankful she'd been to church that Sunday.

God had looked out for her.

She was thinking about Him when there was a loud crack and the windshield spiderwebbed; fragments of glass hit her in the head.

She blinked, more startled than hurt, and touched the small wound.

How would a rock—

Then again, a crack and flying glass—and this time she heard a loud bang outside.

Oh, God, no . . . Somebody was shooting at her! These were *bullets*!

She saw motion from the shadows between a tall stand of trees. Another flash. And the car resounded with a ringing thud. He'd missed the windshield this time.

Hunters?

Or was it that crazy man obsessed with Kayleigh?

Sheri popped the seat belt and slithered down to the floor as best she could, searching for her phone. Where, where, where?

One more shot. This wasn't aimed for the windows either, but, like the other, for the rear of the car. A resonating bang as it hit.

Why would somebody shoot there? Sheri wondered manically.

And then realized: Shit. He was aiming for the gas tank! The stalker, Edwin Sharp—it had to be him! Why was he doing this? She hadn't done anything!

She tried to roll down the side window of the passenger seat but the power was off. And the doors were wedged closed by the ditch.

Then the sweet, rich smell of gasoline grew thicker, reminding her of spending hot hours at the wannabe NASCAR track where her first husband raced every Saturday.

And as she sobbed, kicking futilely at the windshield, another thought occurred to her: the email about the luncheon hadn't been from Kayleigh after all. It was Edwin Sharp who'd created an email address with Kayleigh's name in it and sent the message to Sheri through the girl's website, to lure her here.

Kayleigh hadn't wanted her at the luncheon after all.

Chapter 34

KATHRYN DANCE HAD left the sheriff's office fifteen minutes earlier.

After word that "Your Shadow" had been played at the football stadium during practice, the task force had split into three groups: one was trying to intercept Sam Gerber. Others were at the luncheon at the country club in northern Fresno, thinking that Edwin might try to find Gerber or maybe another victim there. And yet others were trying to find Edwin and his car, coordinating with Highway Patrol. Harutyun had also alerted medical teams that there might be an assault in progress. A burns center had been put on notice too; fire seemed to be one of the perp's preferred weapons—inspired, perhaps, by Kayleigh herself.

Love is fire, love is flame
It warms your heart, it lights the way.
It burns forever just like the sun.
It welds two souls and makes them one.
Love is fire, love is flame.

Kathryn Dance was en route to the luncheon too; she didn't know the roads in the area so it would have made little sense for her to participate in the manhunt. She thought it was best simply to be the point person at the country club and to reassure Kayleigh with her presence.

But as she piloted the SUV quickly through traffic, a thought occurred.

This happened sometimes, a little tapping, a hiccup in her mind, something she just couldn't explain. A jump from Thought A to Thought B to . . . Thought Z. (Michael O'Neil had recently described it as her brain doing "one of its little *dances*.")

No, no, this isn't right. Edwin would be aware of the logistical difficulties of targeting a victim at the luncheon. But the event *would* provide a good distraction and draw off the police. And was Sam Gerber really a likely target? No. Edwin wouldn't go after somebody he'd commented on in a posting. It was too obvious. Besides, why kill Gerber, one of fifty thousand harmless fans? He didn't fit the profile of a stalker's victim.

The crew was safe. Alicia was among people.

So who else might the target be?

Dance asked herself again the basic question: If Edwin was the stalker, what was his goal? Killing someone who threatened to keep them apart, whom Edwin was jealous of, who was perceived as Kayleigh's enemy or whose death would bind them together forever.

Dance had recalled the gossip pages in the underground websites O'Neil had found, involving sensational stories reported by fans. A hot topic—since there weren't many of them—was the tension between Kayleigh and her stepmother. There was even an embarrassing mobile phone video about a recent argument in Bakersfield.

This wasn't a full-blown feud; Kayleigh seemed incapable of either the pettiness or the mean spirit that would involve. And from what Dance read, Sheri Towne seemed like a decent woman, solid, loyal to her new husband and even helpful in Kayleigh's career. But Sheri was the most recent in a long line of stepmothers and she and Kayleigh never seemed to get along. The young woman hadn't even invited Sheri to the luncheon she herself had helped with.

Thought Z . . .

Dance now called Bishop Towne and identified herself.

"Sure, Officer Dance," the man grumbled. "What's going on with that asshole? Heard he's played another song."

"Where's your wife?"

"Gone off to that luncheon thing. Kayleigh invited her, after all."

An alarm pinged within Dance, though she'd half expected that answer.

"When did she leave?"

"'Bout twenty minutes ago."

"Did Kayleigh call her?"

"No, she emailed. Wanted her to bring some CDs to the lunch. Giveaways. Also said it'd be better if her sister and Mary-Gordon didn't come 'cause that asshole Sharp."

"So she's alone?"

"Right."

"Bishop, I think Sheri might be in danger. Edwin might've sent that email."

"No!"

"Maybe. Which way would she go?"

"Oh, no, no . . ."

"Which way?"

"From the house, have to be Los Banos Road to Forty-one. You've got to do something! Please! Don't let anything happen to her."

It was unnerving to hear the gruff man sounding so desperate, so vulnerable.

"Give me her number."

Dance memorized it. Then told him, "I'll call you when I know something. What's she driving?"

"I think she's in . . . yeah, it's the Mercedes. Silver."

Dance first tried Sheri but the woman didn't answer. She then called Kayleigh and learned, after a brief, awkward pause, that, no, Kayleigh hadn't really wanted Sheri at the luncheon and hadn't emailed her. Dance hit DISCONNECT with her thumb and the brake with her foot, skidding to a stop on the shoulder. She punched Los Banos Road into her GPS, and raced back onto the highway.

Los Banos was a narrow, winding line leading into the foothills toward Yosemite. It would be the only place where Edwin could attack Sheri. If she'd gotten to Forty-one, a wide, multilane road, then she would probably be okay.

But Dance knew Edwin wouldn't let her get that far. He would have planned out the perfect site for the attack.

She tried Sheri's number again. No answer.

In two minutes she was speeding through the forests on Los Banos.

It was then she saw the smoke, maybe a half mile ahead.

She gripped the phone and started to dial Madigan, jamming the accelerator down even harder as she took a curve. Nissan makes a great SUV but it doesn't corner like a sports car and she nearly went off the shoulder and into a ravine forty feet below.

You're a bad driver to start with, she told herself. Don't be stupid.

She brought the skid under control and slowed a bit. She called Madigan and left a message, telling him where she was and to get cars there immediately, fire trucks too. Soon she was speeding along a straightaway toward the smoke, which had gone from gray to black.

Burning tires? she wondered. Oil? A car wreck?

Dance skidded around this turn too and saw the horrific scene before her—the silver Mercedes had gone off the road and was in a ditch near the asphalt. The back end of the car was burning, though the front, not yet. The angle of the accident—with the car's hood in the air—meant the gasoline from the ruptured tank was flowing backward. Still, the flames were spreading toward the passenger compartment.

There seemed to be movement from inside the car. Dance couldn't see clearly but knew it would be Sheri, whose feet were kicking desperately against the windshield.

No, Dance thought. You'll never break through a windshield! The side windows!

Dance brought the Pathfinder to a skidding stop on the shoulder and leapt out, opening the back door and reaching behind the seat to snag the small fire extinguisher. She pulled it out and turned toward the Merc but dropped the heavy canister. She bent to pick it up.

Which is what saved her from a bullet.

No, as it turned out, two or three of them.

"Jesus," she gasped, dropping to the ground, earning a scraped elbow.

The bullets slammed, loud, into the sheet steel of the Pathfinder a foot or so from her head and shoulders. Where was the shooter?

She couldn't tell. He was somewhere in the pine forest.

In shadows, of course.

Reaching for her phone, which sat on the passenger seat, to call 911, she rose. The shooter fired again and a slug snapped over her head, then another. Dance flattened herself on the ground as another bullet loudly punctured the side of the driver's seat.

A cry echoed from the Mercedes.

Move, move, move!

Crawling fast, cradling the extinguisher, Dance made it to a fallen tree, about forty feet from the Mercedes.

She risked a look. The flames were rising faster now.

And from the gap in the dense pine forest she saw a ragged flash of gunshot. A bullet snapped over her head before she could duck.

The attacker would have gotten a look at her and if it was Edwin, he would recognize her as a CBI agent, which meant he might assume she was armed. If it wasn't Edwin, or if he decided she didn't have a weapon, the assailant could casually stroll a hundred feet in her direction and shoot her.

Dance then heard another wailing scream from the Mercedes.

A flash bloomed from the woods, and six inches from her face a bullet blew a handful of dry rotting wood into the air.

Chapter 35

"I SHOULD CHECK in with my people," P. K. Madigan said angrily, nodding toward his office. "We've got an operation going here. Possible homicide. It's urgent." The bewildered chief was feeling panic—which was not a sensation he was used to.

Two California Department of Justice officers stood in front of him in the lobby of the detective division, back a bit, out of deference. Maybe. One was redheaded and one had black hair. They otherwise looked similar, trim, in suits. Polite. Very polite. Madigan was so shaken he'd forgotten their names. The redhead said, "Yessir, I'm afraid calls'll have to wait. Same procedure you have in an arrest, I'm sure."

FMCSO sheriff Anita Gonzalez stood nearby, her face too a mask of dismay more than anger. "This is nonsense, gentlemen. Utter nonsense. I've got a call in to the Sacramento office."

Which had not, Madigan noted, returned that call.

The two officers obviously didn't consider their present assignment as nonsense, utter or otherwise.

Their two suspects didn't either: Detectives Madigan and Miguel Lopez, who were being arrested for breaking and entering, false imprisonment, misuse of legal authority, criminal trespass.

Madigan said, "Look, this is part of a plan by a perp

we're investigating. He's trying to get some of us out of commission." He explained to them what Kathryn Dance had said about how stalkers target people who are protecting the object they're obsessed with.

The state officers weren't much interested in that either.

The reason for the arrest was, Madigan knew before they'd even mentioned the charges, his decision to keep Edwin Sharp in the interrogation room longer than he should have. And to have Miguel Lopez go to Edwin's house and gather evidence.

The dark-haired agent was saying, "Here's how it'll work, Detective. We'll take you in and I'm sure the magistrate'll expedite arraignment. Probably recognizance. Can't imagine he'll go for bail. You'll be out in a few hours."

"I don't care when I'll be out. The problem is I'll be suspended until it's resolved. That's procedure." Like Gabriel Fuentes, the detective so careless with his gun.

Gonzalez said to the officers, "We can't afford to have the chief down now—not with the perp on the streets."

The redhead said, "We know how you feel about this singer of yours. But . . ."

He didn't add, That's not enough to bend the law over.

Madigan wanted to hit him.

The panic swelled. Hell, this could be the end of his career—the only career he'd ever cared about. What would he tell his family?

And he'd bent the rules just a bit, done it for Kayleigh.

This singer of yours . . .

Goddamn Edwin Sharp!

The officers were debating but it was only the cuff issue.

"Oh, please," Madigan said, sounding as desperate as he felt. "You can't—"

"Look, gentlemen," Sheriff Gonzalez said. "This is a critical operation. We think a murder could be occurring at any moment."

Madigan looked back into his office again.

The redhead offered to Gonzalez, "You understand a warrant has been issued for his arrest? I'm sorry. We don't have any choice."

They took his Colt and ID and badge.

Madigan repeated, "At least let me check in with some of my people." He was growing more agitated.

They debated a moment but settled for, "You'll be out in an hour."

"Two, tops."

And they also decided yes on the cuffs.

Chapter 36

DANCE HUDDLED BEHIND the fallen pine tree.

There'd been no more shots; was the assailant still there? Waiting for her to show? It would make more sense for him to leave. He'd have to assume that Dance had called in reinforcements and would have fled. He couldn't risk staying any longer.

Or could he?

Clutching the fire extinguisher, she debated. If I don't do something now, Sheri'll die. She'll burn to death.

Dance looked up cautiously, then ducked down again. No gunshots.

She thought of her children, how she couldn't stand the idea of their being orphans. Thought too that she'd specifically gone into kinesic analysis and investigations to avoid tactical situations that might put her life in danger.

And here, I'm not even on duty, she thought.

Another cry from the car, but muted. Sheri Towne was losing the battle.

Now. It has to be now.

She leapt to her feet and began to sprint to the Mercedes, just as the flames were reaching into the passenger compartment.

Waiting for the bullets.

None came her way but still she dove into the ditch, out of the line of fire of the shooter in the woods, and crawled fast to the car. Inside, Sheri was pounding on the windshield with bloody hands. She was retching and coughing as the smoke roiled into the interior. Dance's skin prickled in the heat from a grass fire surrounding the car.

The woman inside turned desperate eyes to her and mouthed something.

Dance gestured for her to move back and she slammed the extinguisher base into the passenger-side window. It shattered easily. Dance tossed the extinguisher away—it wasn't going to do any good on a fire like this—and reached inside to yank the woman out. Sheri was convulsing in spasms and coughing hard, spittle flying from her mouth. Tears streamed down her sooty face.

The agent dragged her thirty feet from the car, crouching, in case the attacker was still there with his gun. They sprawled on the ground in a depression by the roadside.

The woman dropped to her knees and vomited hard and tried to stand.

"No, stay down," Dance said, starting for her SUV and her phone to see if Madigan had gotten her message and, if not, to call 911.

Which was when she heard a loud bang behind her and felt something slam into her lower back. She pitched forward onto the hard, sunbaked earth.

Chapter 37

DENNIS HARUTYUN WAS standing over the gurney Kathryn Dance lay on, face down.

The medic was on the opposite side from the deputy, laboring away on her back.

"No leads yet," the detective said.

With her perpendicular view of the scene, Dance could see the ever-efficient CSU team scouring the grounds where the attacker had nearly killed Sheri Towne . . . and Dance herself. But there wasn't much left; the fire had spread and taken out some of the trees and brush where he'd been standing.

"That hurt?" the med tech asked.

"A bit."

"Hm." He continued working on her, without otherwise acknowledging her answer.

After a few minutes: "You almost through there?" Dance asked, irritated that the doctor was taking so long and that he hadn't responded to her comment about the pain. She should have said, "Yeah, hurts like hell, butcher."

"I think that'll do it."

She pulled her shirt down.

"Just a scratch. Wasn't deep at all."

Dance was sure she'd been shot in the back—her immediate thought was of her friend, the crime scene expert, Lincoln Rhyme, who was a quadriplegic, paralyzed from the neck down. How can I be a good mother if I can't walk? she'd thought, tumbling over Sheri Towne from the impact. In fact, what had happened was that the fire extinguisher she'd tossed aside had landed in the burning grass and exploded, sending either a rock or a piece of its own casing flying into her back. She'd lain stunned for a moment then had turned to see on the ground a big disk of white foam or powder from the detonated extinguisher. And she'd understood, then crawled on to the SUV and retrieved her phone and—giving up on Madigan—called 911. A quarter hour later the police and fire and medical teams arrived.

The medic took his bad bedside manner and wandered off to tend to his other patient—Sheri Towne, who was sitting next to her husband. She was breathing oxygen and staring at her bandaged hand. Her long nails were, coincidentally, the color of fresh blood.

"It's a real mess," Harutyun said. He explained that Edwin had complained to the state DOJ about his detention and the illegal search. Madigan and Miguel Lopez had just been arrested, though released right away, no bail required, but they were no longer active-duty law enforcers.

"Oh, no," Dance said in a harsh whisper. "He's out of commission?"

"Sure is." Harutyun added bitterly, "The perp took out Gabriel Fuentes, stealing his gun. Now it's the Chief and Miguel. The whole team now's Crystal, me and you."

"Any sightings of Edwin?" Dance asked.

"No sign of him or that bull's-eye-red car of his. The luncheon went on as scheduled. Kayleigh didn't look too good, to hear the stories. She sang a few songs, had lunch with the fan and then left. People were saying she wasn't really there. Not mentally."

Dance nodded toward the smoldering Mercedes. "Pretty dangerous to be on Kayleigh's bad side."

"Still have trouble seeing that for a motive for murder."

"It's a *stalker*'s reality, not our reality," she reminded.

Harutyun looked toward Sheri and Bishop. "She nearly burned to death but what she took hardest was that Kayleigh didn't really ask her to the lunch."

"What's the story on the email he used to invite Sheri to the party?" Dance asked.

"Set up an anonymous account this morning. Something like 'KTowne' and some numbers. Sent from an Internet café in the Tower District. One of the deputies checked but nobody recognized Edwin's picture. 'Course, the baristas said they'd had about two hundred people in over the course of the morning."

"And sent it to Sheri's address that was what? On Bishop's website?"

"Kayleigh's own."

"Sure."

There was silence for a time.

"Hey, Charlie." Harutyun nodded to a round, pinkish man, approaching in a jumpsuit. "You know Kathryn Dance, CBI? This's Charlie Shean, head of our crime scene unit."

He nodded to her, then, frowning: "That true about P.K.? He's suspended? And Miguel too?"

"Afraid so."

"And this stalker fellow's the one orchestrated it?"

"We don't know."

"Bullshit and a half," Shean muttered. And Dance got the impression that he wasn't a man who cursed much.

"What'd your folks find, Charlie? Business cards? Phone bills with Edwin's name on it?" Dennis Harutyun, of the thick mustache and unflappable face, seemed to be loosening up a bit.

"He's good, whoever he—or she—is. No footprints, tire treads or trace other than the five million bits of trace you're going to find in a forest. Though we did get a little cigarette ash that's recent, just past the perimeter of the burn. Analysis'll take time."

Dance explained about seeing the person smoking outside her motel room window. "I didn't catch anything specific, though." She added, "Edwin did smoke. Still may, but I don't know for sure."

The crime scene chief said, "The gun was a nine—like Gabriel's Glock—but we don't have any casings or slugs from his so we don't know if there's a match. No immediate prints on the casings we found."

"And I didn't get any description here either," Dance muttered. "He was in the shade of the trees." Stalkers were not only good at disguises; they were good at camouflage too. Anything that helped them observe their target undisturbed and unobtrusively, for as long as possible. "Did Sheri see anything?"

"Haven't been able to interview her. Smoke inhalation was pretty bad."

It was then that a vehicle sped up to the scene. Dance instinctively reached for her absent Glock once again. But then saw it was Kayleigh Towne's dark green SUV, driven expertly by Darthur Morgan. They hadn't stopped completely before the singer was out of the Suburban and running toward Bishop and Sheri. She bypassed her father completely and bent down and threw her arms around her stepmother. Morgan didn't seem happy his charge had come to the site of a shoot-out but Dance supposed that, aside from relations with her father, Kayleigh could be pretty single-minded.

Dance was too far away to hear the conversation but

there was no doubt about the messages in the body language: apology, regret and humor.

A heartfelt reconciliation was under way.

Bishop Towne stood and embraced them both.

Family is about love and affection but about friction and separation, too. Yet, with work and luck, the distances—geographic and emotional—can be shrunk, even made to vanish. What struck Dance at the moment was not what she was witnessing in this reunion, but a very different thought: about her and Jon Boling and the children . . . and what her mother had learned about Boling's move to San Diego.

Once again, Kayleigh's lyrics echoed, from the very verse that had inspired the attempt on Sheri Towne's life.

> One night there's a call, and at first you don't know
> What the troopers are saying from the side of the
>   road,
> Then you see in an instant that your whole life has
>   changed.
> Everything gone, all the plans rearranged.

Is that what would happen to her? Was everything changed, the life she'd tacitly hoped for, for herself and her children, with Boling?

And where, she thought with some bitterness, is *my* shadow, someone looking out for me, someone to give me the answers?

Chapter 38

A PLEASANT, IF hot, September evening in Fresno.

It was a quiet time in the Tower District—featuring the famous Art Deco theater, at Olive and Wishon, which boasted an actual, if modest, tower (though the neighborhood had probably been named for *another* tower some distance away).

Tonight, locals were returning from early suppers at Mexican taquerias or boutiquey cafés or were visiting art galleries, tattoo parlors, discount stores, ethnic bakeries. Maybe headed for the movies or an improv comedy club or community theater. It wasn't San Francisco but you weren't in Fresno for art, music or literature. You were here to raise a family and work and you took what culture was offered.

Tonight, teenage boys had come to the District to cruise the streets in their pimped-out Subarus and Saturns, enjoying the last few evenings free from homework.

Tonight, girls had come here to gossip and sneak cigarettes and to look toward, but not at, boys and sit over sodas for hours and talk about clothes and looming classes.

And tonight Kayleigh Towne had come to the District to kill a man.

She'd formulated this plan because of one person:

Mary-Gordon Sanchez, the little girl Edwin Sharp had—whatever the police said—kidnapped.

Oh, God, she was furious.

Kayleigh had always looked forward to being a mother but those plans had been delayed by her own father, who felt that a career wasn't compatible with a home life.

"Hell, KT, you're a child yourself. Wait a few years. What's the hurry?"

Kayleigh had gone along but the maternal urge within her only grew.

And to think that Mary-Gordon had been in danger—and might be in the future—well, no, that wasn't acceptable.

Edwin Sharp was going down.

The sheriff's office wasn't going to do it. So Kayleigh would, all by herself.

I'd prefer together, I'd hoped for two not one.
You and me forever, with a daughter and a son.
It was tough that didn't work out, but now it's plain
*   to see*
When it comes to things that matter, all I really
*   need is me.*

With these lyrics, which she'd written years ago, rolling through her mind, Kayleigh Towne climbed out of the Suburban, which Darthur Morgan had parked on Olive Avenue. They were in front of a Victorian-style auditorium. It was Parker Hall, a small theater and lecture venue from the nineteenth century. She noted the brass plaque that read:

KAYLEIGH, OUR HOME "TOWNE" GIRL, GAVE HER FIRST CONCERT HERE.

She'd been thirteen. The "first concert" part was not

exactly true—she'd done churches and sporting events since she was nine or ten. But this was, yes, the first performance in a concert hall, though she'd shared the stage with a few other kids from the children's choir of George Washington Middle School.

"About a half hour," she told Morgan.

"I'll be here," he said. And began immediately to study the street for signs of Edwin Sharp or any other threat.

Kayleigh found the key to the hall and slipped inside the musty place. That afternoon she'd contacted the foundation that owned it and explained that she was thinking about giving a concert there. Could she borrow the key to check the place out? They'd been delighted and she'd had politely to decline the several invitations by the staff to give her a tour of the venue. Her time was so limited, she'd said, that she wasn't sure when she could get there.

Inside, the murky hall resonated with its own brand of creaks and snaps but this time, unlike at the convention center, she wasn't made the least uneasy by the atmosphere. She knew where the danger was.

And it wasn't in the shadows that surrounded her.

Kayleigh headed straight for the loading dock in the back, opened the door and stepped outside, looking over the street, which ran parallel to Olive. A few minutes later she saw the red Buick driven by the man who had killed Bobby and tried to kill Sheri and who had kidnapped Mary-Gordon and Suellyn. He cruised past the theater to the stoplight. One of the sheriff's deputies was following.

Hell, she hadn't counted on that.

She couldn't have the police near when Edwin died. What was she going to do? Give up? She was furious at the thought.

The Buick waited for a light, signaling left.

A block away the deputy, trying to be clever, slowed and turned left, apparently hoping to pick up the Buick after Edwin turned.

She nearly laughed to see Edwin floor the accelerator and speed right into a largely residential neighborhood. He'd eluded the deputy completely.

It was tough that didn't work out, but now it's plain to see
When it comes to things that matter, all I really need is me.

Stepping back inside, she opened her purse and slipped on leather gloves, then unfixed the twist ties securing the eight-inch filleting knife to the cardboard backing. She wrapped the blade in a tissue and slipped it into the inner pocket of her denim jacket.

And then she double—no, triple—checked the other thing she'd brought with her.

You still got that present I got you a coupla years ago?
I have all your presents, Daddy. . . .

Kayleigh was now thinking of the song Edwin Sharp had played on the jukebox at the Cowboy Saloon yesterday. "Me, I'm Not a Cowgirl."

I haven't got a cowgirl hat to shield me from the sun.
My boots they have high heels. I don't own a single gun.

For Kayleigh Towne that last sentence was not exactly true.

The present her father had given her was a Colt revolver. He'd bought it for her for protection when she was in her teens. Suellyn was away at college, their mother dead, and he was spending insane amounts of time on the road, trying futilely to salvage his career.

She'd fired it a few times but hadn't liked the recoil or the noise, even with the earmuffs, and she'd thought: What a joke.

The idea of taking a human life was impossible for her to imagine.

And yet two years ago she recalled spotting a coyote, twitchy and probably rabid, in her garden behind the house, hissing and baring yellow teeth.

Kayleigh had matter-of-factly blown the ragged thing away with a single shot to the head.

That's all Edwin Sharp was to her now.

Not human. A mad coyote.

She tore up and flushed the packaging materials for the knife and the receipt down the toilet in the staff bathroom.

Determined, yes. But nervous as hell.

And where is the fucker? Did he leave?

No, he wouldn't, of course. Because Kayleigh, the center of his universe, had called him a half hour ago—from a pay phone at the hospital where Sheri had been examined and released. She'd asked to meet him here. The stuffed redwood tree that Edwin and Mary-Gordon had bought for her at the museum had sported a label, on which Edwin had written a phone number. And the words, "Call me."

She'd nearly thrown it out yesterday but had decided not to—because this plan had begun brewing in her mind the moment she saw his number.

Standing at the grimy window in the service door to the dock, she now wiped her hands on her jeans. Then, finally, Edwin Sharp appeared, walking in that eerie gait of his, not a care in the world. As if the murders and kidnappings were nothing to him.

He made a beeline for the auditorium, carrying his

camera with him. He paused and began to take some pictures. If he snapped one of her she'd have to steal his camera and get rid of it.

Remember that.

Kayleigh took a deep breath. Through the thick denim of her jacket, she felt the knife in her inner pocket. Against her belly, the gun.

> *Not you, not him, not her, not them. In the end*
> *we're all alone*
> *Whatever's needing to get done, I can do it on my*
> *own.*
> *That's all I need, just me.*

Chapter 39

FROM THE WINDOW, she could see the flash from his camera as he took pictures of his shrine. Coming to Fresno, she realized, would be a pilgrimage to Edwin Sharp.

More sweat spreading on hands and forehead, heart pounding in vivace tempo.

Steady girl, you can do this. Think of everybody at risk.

Think of Mary-Gordon, think of Sheri.

He's a rabid coyote. That's all he is.

She paused. No, don't do it. Get the hell out of here! Before you fuck up your life forever.

But Kayleigh Towne decided:

I can do this, I can do this. For my sister, for Mary-Gordon, for anyone else who'd be at risk.

For me.

Your shadow . . .

She stepped out onto the loading dock and looked toward Edwin. He turned, that skewed smile contorting his face. She gave a cautious nod and looked down at the asphalt, crumbling and cracked and sprouting dry weeds. Another brief nod. As if shy, as if uncertain.

As if innocent.

"Well, lookit this." He glanced behind her and around. No Darthur Morgan. "You're alone?"

"Yeah. Only me."

"Where's Darthur?"

"Up the street. I gave him the slip."

He said, "Good." He looked up at the theater. "You know, I wish that concert of yours'd been recorded. . . . Thirteen years old and you had the whole house in your hand. Nobody cared about the other students. It was just you. Only you, Kayleigh."

The show had been written up in one of the tiny local papers. He must've read about it there.

Edwin followed her inside.

"We're thinking of filming a concert here."

"A video. Cool! Excellent. When?"

"We don't know yet."

"Like re-creating your first concert? That'd be so neat. You'll have to do 'Walking After Midnight.' Like you opened with back then."

Jesus. He knew that too?

Edwin studied her again. "Wow, you're looking spectacular today. Your hair . . . it's so beautiful. After your voice, your hair's probably my favorite part about you."

Kayleigh struggled to remain placid as she recalled his request to send him a lock of her hair. From her pillow would have been best. *Oh, Lord . . .*

"I don't have much time," she said.

"I know. They're always watching you."

They?

He put his hands on his hips and smiled. His jeans were tight. She thought about the incident outside her house, tapping out the music, or doing something else? He peered down at her adoringly from under those overhanging brows.

Kayleigh Towne wondered if she was going to be sick.

"Oh, my God," he whispered. "Hearing your voice

on the phone? It just made my whole day. My whole year! I was sitting at Earl and Marge's having dinner and feeling kind of bad. Then to hear you. After all these months, finally hearing you."

"That's a good diner."

"The pies looked nice. I like cherry pie, if there's milk with it. But I cut all that out." He patted his belly. "Staying trim, you know. Mr. Today. That's such a great song. I hope it becomes an anthem for women. Don't settle for abuse, don't settle for less than you deserve. You know what I mean?"

Of course she did. She'd written the song. It was odd, though, how many fans didn't get the meaning, as obvious as it was.

"Look at that. An old percolator." He nodded toward an ancient coffeemaker. "That's what my mother'd use."

Her eyes stayed on the canister as she said, "Listen, Edwin, what I wanted to talk to you about. I was pretty upset you picked up my sister and niece." She'd decided she couldn't make it sound like he was her new best friend. He'd be suspicious if she was too nice. She looked at him now sternly.

"Oh, that. Sorry. I didn't know what else to do. I was worried."

"Worried?"

"About Ritchie."

"Who's that?"

"Ritchie Hampton, the guy your father was going to send to pick up Suellyn and Mary-Gordon. You don't know about his record?"

Record? What was he talking about? "Well . . . no."

"Okay, what happened was, I was in a café. Your father and Sheri happened to be there—"

"Happened?" Kayleigh asked suspiciously.

The smile seemed to deepen slightly. "Okay, I'll admit. I followed them there. I thought they were going to meet you for breakfast. It's been hard to park out in front of your house. I keep getting hassled by the deputies."

Well, *yeah*. He was actually complaining, as if he honestly didn't get it that somebody might object to his spying? Still, her role required her to say nothing, but just nod sympathetically.

Edwin examined the coffee percolator. Lifted the lid, with a glass dome in the center, and replaced it. "I heard Bishop call Ritchie and ask him to pick up Suellyn and Mary-Gordon. I know your father doesn't drive anymore, but Sheri could've driven him to pick them up. Why couldn't her grandfather come to pick up that little girl?"

Kayleigh's very thought at the time. Bishop, though, had been too busy with Congressman Davis.

"But anyway, he asked Ritchie. You know, Ritchie's had three speeding tickets and one reckless in the last year. License's been suspended a couple of times. And even your father doesn't know he was pulled over at a DUI roadblock. He was let go but he'd been drinking."

Kayleigh stared. How on earth does he know these things?

"Your father was going to have your sister and that precious little niece of yours in the hands of a man who drives that badly? I'm sorry. I couldn't let that go by. And if I'd come to you or to him and said anything, you'd've called the cops, right? And ignored me. I wasn't going to let anything happen to the people most important to you in the world. I even used my middle name, in case the lawyers or your father had told them to look out for somebody named Edwin."

Lawyers or father. But not me. He was truly delusional.

"You know, you really come on too strong. Don't you see that?"

"I guess I get a little carried away." Was his smile genuine or a leer? She couldn't tell. Despite the dry heat, Kayleigh Towne shivered. He added, "You'll feel more comfortable when you get to know me." Another look at her hair. "I like you alone."

"What?"

"I mean, instead of at the Cowboy Saloon. All those other people around. Wasn't natural, you know."

No, she didn't know.

"Well," Kayleigh said uncertainly.

He grew somber. "I'm really sorry about Bobby. I know you guys were close. You went out, right?"

What an actor he was! Sorry? You killed him!

And then she reflected, Wait, how does he know Bobby and I were close?

"Yeah, thanks. He was a good friend."

"Friend. Yeah."

"It's pretty tough."

"Oh, it's gotta be." His face screwed up like a funeral director's. "I feel so bad for you."

"And all his other friends and family," Kayleigh reminded, trying to keep an edge from her voice.

"Sure. Do the police have any leads?"

You prick.

Pull out the gun and blow the motherfucker away. Put the knife in his hand later.

But, no. Be smart.

"I don't think so."

"You want to get that iced tea?" he asked. "Your fave?"

She said, "I really can't. I better get back."

"I love you, Kayleigh." He said this casually as if he were saying the earth is round, or the dollar is U.S. currency.

"Well—"

"It's okay. I know the situation. I'm amazed they let you out on the town by yourself."

"They?"

"You know who I mean. Everybody . . . from the song. *Everyone* wants a piece of your soul." He was exhaling hard, shaking his head. "I worry about you so much."

Insane. Pathetic and completely insane.

Now! If you wait any longer you won't be able to do it.

"Hey, let me give you something."

"You have something for me?" he asked, surprised.

She stepped forward, smiling, convinced that as she got close she'd be overwhelmed by a repulsive smell but all she could detect was faint deodorant or aftershave. Was it what her father used? Okay. *That's* weird.

Kayleigh reached into her jacket and, gripping the knife blade, wrapped in tissue, she slipped the handle into his palm quickly. He instinctively closed his fingers around it. She backed up fast.

"What's this, a pen?" he asked. Maybe thinking it was something for him to write her letters with.

Then he realized what it was.

Edwin's smile faded. And he looked up to see the girl of his dreams holding a large revolver pointed at his chest. She pulled the hammer back. It seated with a loud click.

Chapter 40

THE KNIFE DROOPED in his hand, his eyelids and shoulders sagged too. "Kayleigh . . . no."

"Don't move."

"Oh, Kayleigh." Smiling again but sorrowfully. "Do you know what kind of trouble you'll get into, you do this?"

She stayed strong.

"This'd be terrible. So terrible. Don't do this to yourself. Please! Think of your fans, think of your family." As if he was genuinely worried for her, not himself. "It's the first thing the police'll look for, setting me up. They won't want to believe you did it, they'll hope it isn't true, but the deputies have been there before. It happens all the time. Domestic, stalking . . . It happens all the time."

"You killed Bobby!"

Thick brows knit further, making him even more ominous. "I didn't do that, of course not. And I heard about the attack on Sheri. I'm sure they told you I was behind that too. But I'd never hurt anybody close to you. It's all lies."

Shoot him! she told herself. And yet her finger remained outside the trigger guard. The gun wavered for a minute then she thrust it forward. Edwin Sharp didn't even squint.

"And you *kidnapped* my sister and niece."

"Maybe I *saved* their lives. From Ritchie's driving, like I told you."

She looked around but held the gun steady.

"You're a smart woman, Kayleigh."

And she had a flashback of a recent conversation she'd had with her father, who'd called her a "smart girl."

"You called me from a pay phone but can anybody place you where you made that call? It'll be in my cell phone records. That'll be easy to find. . . . And, I'm sure you used gloves or a paper towel when you were handling this." A glance at the knife. "And you probably bought it at a store with a self-checkout. But they'll link it to you, Kayleigh. That's what they do for a living."

"Shut up! I'm going to kill you!"

He examined the knife. "It's new so they're going to check every store in town that sells this brand. There won't be that many of them. You'd pay cash but all they have to do is look at the data-mined records of anyone who bought this model knife in the past few days with cash. They'll figure out the exact store and register fast because you probably only bought this one thing, right? That's a giveaway. They'll get a warrant to collect the cash paid into the checkout machine. They'll fingerprint the bills. And they'll trace serial numbers of the bills you got from an ATM. That's all recorded, you know."

Of course it isn't!

Is it?

Don't listen to him. Scream for help then pull the trigger. . . .

"There could even be a video or still picture of the self-serve transaction. It'll take them all of five minutes to link you to this knife. And meanwhile there'll be rookies searching the trash around the area here to look for bags and packaging and the receipt." He glanced toward the toilet, which trickled as it continued to fill. "Or the sewer pipes here. They'll get you in an interrogation room and, Kayleigh, you're such a good, honest person, you won't hold up; they'll have a confession in ten minutes. Madigan won't want to but he won't have any choice." He glanced at her hand. "Can you even carry a concealed gun legally?"

I'll do it on my own.

Except I can't.

I'm a fucking coward.

The gun lowered.

"Oh, Kayleigh, they've brainwashed you so badly. *I'm* not the enemy. *They're* the enemy. Here, I'm going to set the knife down." He wiped it on his shirtsleeves, removing his own prints, and then he rested it on the floor. "That way there'll be no connection between us. You take it and use it or throw it out. This never happened."

He sounded so sincere. Kayleigh wished Kathryn Dance was here to look at the stalker and nod that he was telling the truth or shake her head that he was lying. He stepped back and she eased forward, picked the knife up and slipped it back into her jacket.

"Think about *this*, Kayleigh: Sure, you're being stalked. But not by me. Maybe it's the reporters and photographers. Maybe it's your *father*. He claims he wants what's best but does he? I'm not so sure. And what about the others? Maybe . . . I don't know—Alicia, Tye Slocum—oh, keep an eye on him. I've seen how he looks at you. And Barry Zeigler. He's holding on to you pretty tight. Who else does the label have as big as you? Neil Watson—but come on, he's like a bad tribute act to himself. And who *else* is out there watching you, stalking you? Fans and strangers. People who don't even know your music, but only that you're beautiful and famous and rich. And they figure, why should you have all those things and not them? They don't get how hard you work for them, how much you sacrifice."

She whispered, "Can't you just leave me alone? Please!"

"Oh, Kayleigh, you don't want me to leave you alone. You just don't know it yet."

Chapter 41

"LEAVING HOME . . ."

Her hit song about the middle-aged immigrant woman being deported back to Mexico. The lines kept running through Kayleigh's mind as she packed several suitcases and lugged them downstairs to the living room of her house, where Darthur Morgan took them from her and placed them in the SUV.

Alicia Sessions was there too, helping her with the temporary move in her Ford F150. Kayleigh hadn't wanted her to go to the trouble but the woman insisted on schlepping guitars, amps and boxes of provisions from Whole Foods—the store where organic-minded Kayleigh shopped, as opposed to Safeway, the source of the staples in the household where she was bound.

"I can really manage."

"No problem at all," Alicia said.

"Well, stay for dinner, at least."

"I'm seeing some friends in town."

As efficient as she was, as important to the operation, Alicia remained largely a mystery to Kayleigh, the band and crew. She was a loner, who'd lived on the periphery of the professional music scene for years, performing alternative and post-punk in New York and San Francisco, without much success. She'd get her job done for Kayleigh and the business and then disappear in the evenings and on weekends for horseback riding and listening to music. Who the friends she was meeting tonight might be, Kayleigh had no idea. She assumed Alicia was gay. While the singer didn't care one way or the other, aside from hoping she was in a loving relationship, in the country world the taboos were falling, but slowly; the genre was still the sound track of middle, conservative America. And Kayleigh guessed Alicia wasn't comfortable bringing up her preferences.

After the SUV and Alicia's pickup were loaded, Kayleigh turned and looked over the house, as if for the last time.

Leaving home . . .

She climbed into the driver's seat of the SUV, Morgan in the passenger for a change, and gunned the engine, then headed down the long drive, Alicia's truck following.

Expecting to see him, *him,* in the lot of the park, she rolled fast through the turn onto the road, skidding. Morgan grabbed the handhold and gave a rare smile. Kayleigh glanced around and into the rearview mirror but there were no red cars.

"It's for the best," he said.

"I suppose."

She realized that he was looking at her face closely. "Something happen at the theater?"

"What do you mean?" Kayleigh kept her eyes pointed fiercely straight ahead, avoiding his as if he'd think: Oh, I know. She lured Edwin into that hall to kill him. I recognize that look.

"Just checking to see if everything's all right," he said placidly. "You get an odd phone call or run into somebody there?"

"No, everything's fine."

Kayleigh reached for the radio but her hand paused

then returned to the wheel. They drove all the way to Bishop Towne's house in complete silence.

She parked in the drive and Morgan helped Alicia carry the boxes, musical equipment and suitcases to the porch, then the guard strode into the night to check out the perimeter. The two women went inside.

The small ground floor might have been an exhibit in a wing of the Grand Ole Opry. There were pictures and reviews and album covers—mostly of Bishop Towne and his band, of course. Some were photos of women singers whom Bishop had had affairs with long ago—and whose albums had been nailed up only after Wives Two through Four appeared. Unlike Margaret, they wouldn't have known about the earlier indiscretions and would have assumed the women were professional associates only.

But there were also a lot of pictures of Bishop and Margaret. He'd never taken those down, whatever the Later Wives' jealous concerns might have been.

Mary-Gordon came running up to Kayleigh and flew into her arms. "Aunt Kayleigh! Yay! You've gotta come look. We're doing a puzzle! I rode Freddie today. I wore my helmet, like you always say."

Kayleigh slipped to her knees for a proper hug, then rose and embraced her sister. Suellyn asked, "How you doing, K?"

The singer thought: Considering I could be in jail for murder, not bad. "Hanging in there."

Kayleigh introduced her and Mary-Gordon to Alicia, who smiled and shook their hands.

"Wow," the girl whispered, looking at Alicia's tattoos. "Those are neat!"

"Uh-oh," Suellyn said. "I see trouble." The women laughed.

Kayleigh greeted her father and Sheri, whose voice

was still ragged from the smoke. Oddly, she now sounded much like her husband. Her skin seemed pale, though that might have been only because she was wearing none of the makeup she usually applied in swaths.

Kayleigh's attitude toward her stepmother had changed 180 degrees since the attack, and she regretted her pettiness toward the woman. She now hugged Sheri, in whose eyes tears appeared at the display of affection.

Alicia gave Bishop and Sheri some details of the ad plans for the upcoming Canadian tour and then she glanced at her watch and headed off.

"Better you're here," Bishop said to Kayleigh. "I told you, you should've come. Right at the beginning, I told you. Sheri's got the room made up. For that guard too. Where is he?"

Kayleigh explained that Morgan had remained outside to check the property. He'd be in, in a moment.

"I did a picture for your room, Aunt Kayleigh. I'll show you."

Mary-Gordon gripped the handle of one of the wheelie suitcases and sped off down the hallway. Kayleigh and her sister smiled.

"In here! Here it is, Aunt Kayleigh!"

She'd seen this guest room before and it had been functional, stark. Now the bed had new blue gingham linens, frilly pillow cases, matching towels, candles, some cheap decorations from Michaels craft store, like geese in bonnets, and framed pictures of young Kayleigh and her family—photos that had been in shoe boxes when last seen, before Sheri. It was really a very comfortable space.

She'd be sure to thank her stepmother—who, of course, had done all this work while injured.

Kayleigh admired Mary-Gordon's picture of the

pony and set it prominently on the bedside table. "Can we go riding tomorrow?"

"We'll have to see, Mary-Gordon. It's a busy time. But we'll have breakfast together."

"Grandma Sheri and Mommy made pancakes. They were pretty good. Not the best but pretty good."

Kayleigh laughed and watched the little girl help unpack the suitcases and, with an expectant gaze toward Kayleigh, put away each article of clothing or toiletry where directed. As the girl made decisions about how to stow everything, she was absorbed and seemed to get huge pleasure from the simple tasks.

A tap in Kayleigh's mind, like a finger flicking a crystal glass. An idea for a song. "I Could Learn a Lot From You." A parent to a child. How the mother or father has gotten some things wrong in life and it's the child who rearranges the adult's perspective. It would have a twist. The first three verses would make listeners believe that the child was singing to the parent; only in the last would it be revealed that the parent was narrating the story. A melody came almost immediately. She sat down and wrote out the words and music on improvised staff paper.

"What're you doing, Aunt Kayleigh?"

"Writing a song. You inspired me."

"What's 'inspired'?"

"I wrote it for you."

"Oh, sing it to me!"

"It's not finished but here's part of it." She sang and the girl stared raptly at her.

"That's a very good song," Mary-Gordon announced with a furrowed brow as if she were the artists and repertoire director of a major label, passing judgment on a young songwriter's submission.

Kayleigh continued to unpack, pausing momentarily

to look at a picture of the family from fifteen or so years ago: Bishop, Margaret, Suellyn and Kayleigh on the porch of the old family house in the hills an hour north of here.

> *I've lived in LA, I've lived in Maine,*
> *New York City and the Midwest Plains,*
> *But there's only one place I consider home.*
> *When I was a kid—the house we owned.*

The girl turned her bright blue eyes toward the singer. "Are you crying, Aunt Kayleigh?"

The singer blinked. "Well, a little, Mary-Gordon, but you know sometimes people cry because they're happy."

"I didn't know that. I don't think I do."

"Not everybody."

"Where does this go?" she asked, picking up a pair of jeans. And placed them carefully in the drawer at which Kayleigh pointed.

"TIDE'S TURNED."

Dance heard the man's voice behind her in the lobby of her hotel. She wasn't alarmed. She knew his voice by now.

Though for a moment she didn't recognize P. K. Madigan. He was wearing civvies—blue jeans, a plaid shirt, cowboy boots and a tan cap embroidered on the crest with a hooked fish flying out of the water.

"Chief."

She was headed out—on her way to Bishop's house to continue the interviews of Kayleigh's family—but she diverted and walked up to him. She glanced into the bar. She almost asked, "You want some ice cream?" but decided: "Coffee? Soda?"

"Naw," the big man said. "See you're on your way out. Had to stop by and talk to you."

"Sure." Dance noted his slumped posture, very different from the in-your-face pose when she'd met him at the scene of Bobby's death.

"Here's the thing. Anita's playing it by the rules. Nobody in the division can talk to me—for their sake too. I'm cut out completely. And you're in charge now."

Ah, the meaning of the turned tide, she realized.

"Not exactly in charge."

"More than anybody else. Damn. Wish I'd listened to you back in that interrogation room and let that son of a bitch go then."

Her heart went out to the detective. He seemed lost.

"I asked the sheriff if I could consult or anything. But she said no. It'd look bad. Might prejudice the case." He gave a laugh, harsh and cold. "Didn't know whether she meant the case against the killer or the case against me. So, I'm sidelined."

"I'm sorry it worked out that way."

He waved his hand. "Nobody to blame but myself. I feel worse for Miguel. He's got a wife doesn't work and three kids. Won't have any savings." He was awkward now. "I've got to stay off the radar, Kathryn, but I'm just wondering, is there anything I can do?"

"I don't know, Chief. I'm interviewing, Charlie's working on the evidence, Dennis is still looking into if anybody else has a motive to kill Bobby and the others."

"Yeah, sure. I understand."

"You could just take some time off, get some fishing in."

"Funny about that," Madigan said. "Yeah, I like it. Been going out every weekend for years. But fact is I spend more time thinking about cases than I do about the fish."

"You get some good ideas, floating around?"

"Oh, you bet I do." A grim smile. "But the thing is, until now, I'd get outa the boat, put my uniform back on and do something about it."

"Sorry, Chief."

"Got it. That's okay. Just thought I'd ask."

He was halfway to the door, when Dance called, "Chief, wait."

Madigan turned and she said, "There is one thing, I'm thinking. Nobody'd have to know. But it's not the . . . well, most pleasant job in the world."

A fraction of a smile. "Well, all righty then. Let's get to it."

Chapter 42

IT WAS ABOUT eight-thirty in the evening when Kathryn Dance got to Bishop Towne's house.

She greeted Kayleigh and the family, who flocked around her and thanked her for saving Sheri's life. Damp-eyed, hoarse, the stepmother hugged Dance hard and bled gratitude.

Bishop offered his thanks too and then asked, "That sheriff, or deputy, Madigan? He got suspended?"

"That's right. Two other deputies too."

"That son of a bitch!"

"Daddy," Suellyn warned. But Mary-Gordon was in the kitchen and out of hearing.

"Well, he is. And M-G's going to learn words like that sooner or later."

"It's going to be later," Kayleigh snapped.

Dance now explained, "We're not making any progress putting together a case against Edwin. He's either innocent or very, very smart. We don't have any leads at all. I'd like to get a few more details from Sheri and"—with a glance at Suellyn—"from you and your daughter about when he picked you up at the airport."

She was hoping to find something that she could use to infer threatening behavior, which would, in turn, justify an arrest for stalking. That would give her access to

Edwin—with his lawyer's approval—and she hoped to conduct a full kinesic analysis.

"At the least it could help get a restraining order. To keep him at a distance."

"Oh, I'd love that," Kayleigh said.

Dance noted she'd been crying recently. Because of Bobby? Today's attack or some other reason?

Bishop escorted her to a small, dimly lit den, which smelled of pipe smoke and pine. Sheri and Mary-Gordon, her blue eyes sparkling, brought in cookies and a pot of coffee. The little girl's golden hair was tied back in a ponytail, the way Dance's daughter, Maggie, would often wear it, and for some reason Dance thought: How on earth am I going to tell Maggie and Wes that Jon Boling is moving?

But then Sheri ushered the girl from the room and sat down across from Dance, who forced aside her personal thoughts and began the interview.

Which, however, proved to be singularly unsuccessful. The woman could provide no more information about the attacker. She'd seen flashes of gunshots, and that was all. Not even an outline of the assailant.

Dance then met with Suellyn Sanchez. The matter-of-fact woman tried hard to recall something helpful but she confessed to Dance that she was still astonished that Edwin was the suspect. "He was just so nice and easygoing. And it sounded like he knew Kayleigh so well, they *had* to be friends."

"And there wasn't anything he said that could be taken in any way as threatening?"

When the sister hesitated, Dance said, "You'd have to testify to it. Under oath."

The woman got it, deciding not to tell the lie she'd been about to. "No, nothing at all. Just the opposite. He sounded so protective. I actually felt good that somebody was looking out for her."

Your shadow . . .

Strike one.

Next Mary-Gordon joined them. Dance showed her pictures of her own children and the dogs. The agent sipped her coffee and ate the cookies and chatted with the little girl, who meticulously set her place for her own cookie and milk and ate precisely.

With children, deception isn't uncommon, of course; kids lie about as frequently as adults but their motives are clearer: missing candy, broken lamps. But the main problem with children as witnesses is that they don't know how to characterize what they observe. Behaviors that seem suspicious to them might not be; and they'll often miss the most egregious crimes because they don't *know* they're crimes.

Dance slowly shifted the conversation to the drive from the airport. But this talk too was futile. All the little girl remembered was a nice man who told her lots of neat things about the area and really liked her aunt. Her bright blue eyes sparkled as she talked about "Stan," Edwin Sharp's pseudonym.

She liked it that he was so helpful in picking out a present for Kayleigh. "He wanted me to get something she'd like. It was really neat! A stuffed tree."

"Thank you, Mary-Gordon," Dance said.

"You're welcome. Will we see that man again, Mr. Stan? I liked him."

"I don't know, honey."

"You can take a cookie with you, if you want. Or two."

"I think I'll do that." Dance wrapped them up in a pink napkin. They were really good.

As they left the den, Suellyn said, "Not much to use, right?"

"Don't think so but appreciate the help."

After knocking and being waved in by Sheri, Dar-

thur Morgan walked inside, his own bag in one hand
and two books in the other. Mary-Gordon took his suitcase.

"No—"

"I'll show you your room, Mr. Morgan."

"You don't have to get—"

"I'll take it," the little girl said and charged off, drawing a look of amused confusion from the huge man.

Dance said goodnight to Bishop and Sheri and then
stepped outside. She found Kayleigh on the front porch
swing. The two women were alone. Dance sat on a
creaking rattan chair next to the swing. The singer lifted
her hands, indicating her father's house. "Look at this,"
she said with an edge to her voice. "Look what's happened. People're dead, lives're ruined. I'm hiding out
with my father, for God's sake. My life's a mess. And we
don't even know for sure he's behind it. He is, don't you
think?"

Dance sensed that something had happened recently, something Kayleigh did not want to share.
She knew Kayleigh's baseline behavior pretty well
and there were now deviations in her eye contact and
shoulder position. It would have to do with something
internal—thoughts she was having, memories that she
didn't want to share with Dance, something she'd done
wrong. And recently.

"I honestly don't know. We always build cases slowly
but generally there's some definite evidence or clear
witness testimony to tell us we're headed in the right
direction, at least. With Edwin, it's all ambiguous."

Kayleigh lowered her voice. "It's all too much, Kathryn. I'm really thinking of canceling the show on Friday.
My heart is totally not in it."

"And your father's okay with it?" Dance asked, because she'd noted the swivel of her eyes toward Bishop

Towne and the decrease in volume when she used the word "canceling."

"Yes," she said, but uncertainly. "He seems to agree but then he goes on like I never mentioned anything. 'Sure, I understand. But if you don't cancel, when you play "Drifting," I think you should modulate up to D for the third and fourth verses.'"

She waved her hand, indicating where they sat. "Remember what I was telling you after you recorded the group at Villalobos's? This is all the stage I'd like, my front porch. Cook big dinners, get fat. Play for the kids and family, have a bunch of Mary-Gordons and Henrys. Don't know why I picked that name. I don't know a single Henry in the world."

"You could have a family and still be a pro."

"I don't see how. That kind of life takes its toll."

"Loretta Lynn did it."

"Nobody's Loretta Lynn. She's one of a kind."

Dance had to agree.

And yet despite Kayleigh Towne's protests, she suddenly dug into her pocket and pulled out a pen and small pad of lined paper and jotted words and musical notes.

"A song?"

"'Just can't stop.'"

"You have to write your songs, you mean?"

Kayleigh laughed. "Well, that's true. But what I mean is, that's a line that just occurred to me. 'Just can't stop . . . spending hours . . . with you.' First it was 'spending time with you,' but it needed the other syllable in 'hours.' I'll write it up tonight."

"The whole song?"

"Hank Williams said any song that takes more than twenty minutes to write isn't going to be any good. Sometimes it takes me a day or two but for that one, it's pretty much done."

She hummed a very hummable few bars.

"You record it, I'll buy it," Dance said. "You . . ." Her voice faded as lights appeared through the trees. A car was approaching slowly.

Kayleigh stiffened. She whispered, "It can't be him. I mean, it can't. We weren't followed. I'm sure not. And when we left, Edwin wasn't at my place. He doesn't even know I'm not there."

Though Dance wasn't so sure about that. It made sense for her to come here largely so she wouldn't be alone—Bishop always had plenty of his crew around. And they could hope Edwin wouldn't figure it out but he'd proved persistent, to say the least, when it came to finding Kayleigh's whereabouts.

The lights seemed to stop, then continue on as if the driver wasn't sure of the route.

Or didn't want to be seen.

"Should we get Darthur?" Kayleigh asked.

Not a bad idea, Dance decided.

But before she rose to summon the guard, twin lights crested a hump in the drive and the car they were attached to stopped.

Kayleigh froze—literally in the headlights.

Dance eyed the vehicle carefully but it was impossible to see anything specific.

What was the driver doing?

Was it Edwin? Was he going to jam the accelerator to the floor and crash into the house, in a bid to kill Kayleigh and then take his own life?

Dance stood up and pulled Kayleigh to her feet.

Just as the car bucked and started forward.

Chapter 43

BUT THE VEHICLE turned out to be a very unthreatening—and slow moving—powder blue Ford Taurus.

And one did not need to be a kinesics expert to note the sea change in Kayleigh's body language when she saw the driver.

"Oh, it's Barry!" she cried, offering a smile.

A very tall man, lanky and long-faced handsome, was climbing out. He had a shock of black curly hair and round glasses. Kayleigh ran down the stairs and embraced him hard.

She said, "I didn't expect you for a couple of days."

Glancing once toward Dance, Zeigler said, "Really? I called Bishop earlier and told him I was driving in tonight."

"Oh, that man," Kayleigh muttered. "Never said a word."

"I was in Carmel seeing Neil. I got your message about Bobby. Terrible. I'm so sorry."

"It's the worst, Barry." Kayleigh turned to Dance and introduced them. Zeigler, Kayleigh's producer at her record label, was based in Los Angeles. Dance realized he looked familiar and recalled, at Kayleigh's house, seeing him in a half dozen framed pictures with the singer going back years. In one they both held a Recording Industry Association of America platinum record award, signifying that she'd sold more than a million of one of her songs or albums.

In jeans, a white T-shirt and dark jacket, Zeigler seemed a bit nineties to Dance but it was a reasonable look for a record producer from any decade. Except for a touch of gray and only at the temples, he didn't look any different from the man in those photographs.

"And Sheri was attacked too?"

"She was hurt but she'll be all right."

"Do you have any leads?" he asked Dance. "Is it that guy Sharp?"

Kayleigh nodded and explained, "Barry knows all about our friend. Edwin's sent plenty of letters to the label, complaining about production standards, orchestration, technical quality."

"Pain in the ass," Zeigler grumbled.

The law enforcement disclaimer: "We're just gathering information at this point. But tell me, did he ever threaten you or anyone?"

"Like physically?"

"Yes," Dance replied.

Zeigler shook his head. "He's been more insulting. I mean, BHRC's the third oldest record company in L.A. We've been producing Kayleigh for six years. She's had eight gold and four platinums. We must be doing something right. But not according to Sharp. Just last week he sent us a two-page email about the acoustic dynamics on the download of 'Your Shadow.' He said it was off in the high ranges. Why was Delmore playing Dobro and not pedal steel? . . . He said, 'Kayleigh deserves better than this.' And then he said we should issue her on vinyl. He's an analog hound."

But Dance didn't think comments about acoustic tonal quality, however harsh, rose to the level of threat under California Penal Code section 646.9.

Zeigler said to Kayleigh, "Bobby was the greatest guy in the world. I can't believe somebody'd hurt him on purpose. And to die that way. You must be . . ." Then he grew silent, apparently deciding he shouldn't be further revisiting the horror.

"Aaron and Steve said if there's anything anybody at the label can do, you let us know. You've got the whole company behind you."

"Barry, I think he's going to keep doing this. He picks verses of my songs and plays them and then kills somebody or tries to."

"That's what Bishop was telling me." The producer turned to Dance. "Can't you arrest him?"

She demurred but Kayleigh said, "He's too smart. They haven't been able to find anything he's done that quite breaks the law. Oh, this is just terrible." The anger was gone and her eyes welled with tears. Then she tamed the emotion and the same stillness came over her as it did onstage.

Control . . .

Zeigler's voice dimmed as he said to Kayleigh, "I want to say hi to Bishop and Sheri. But could I talk to you for a minute? Alone?"

"Sure." To Dance she said, "Be right back."

The two rose and walked into the living room, the producer ducking automatically as they approached the doorway arch. He had to be six feet, seven inches tall, Dance estimated.

She gave it a minute, then rose quietly and moved to the swing Kayleigh had just occupied, which was next to a half-opened window. From there she could hear their conversation. Whatever Zeigler was going to tell Kayleigh might have something to do with the case, even if neither of them realized it, provided she could make out the conversation.

As it turned out, their words were plenty loud enough to hear. Dance remembered that her children, when younger, believed that if they couldn't see their parents, they were invisible and produced no sound whatsoever.

"Look, this is a terrible time to bring this up. But I . . . I'm sorry, I have to ask."

"What, Barry? Tell me. Come on. I'll worm it out of you. You know I can."

"Are you talking to JBT Global?"

"What?"

"JBT Global Entertainment. The three-sixty outfit."

"I know who they are. And no, I'm not talking to them. Why are you asking?"

Zeigler was explaining how a friend of a friend of a friend in the complicated world that's entertainment had told him that Global really wanted to sign her.

"You were in discussions, I'd heard."

"Barry, we get calls all the time. Live Nation, Global . . . I don't pay attention to them. You know I'd never leave you guys. You're the ones who made me. Hey, what's this all about?"

It was odd to hear someone half the age of the producer talking to him as if he were a child with troubles at school.

"I told you I was in Carmel?"

"Seeing Neil, you said."

Neil Watson, one of the superstars of the pop music world of the past twenty years.

"Yeah, to get fired."

"No!"

"He's going with . . . get this, SAV-More. Yep, the big box store, like Target and Wal-Mart. They're producing him and backing his road shows."

"I'm sorry about that, Barry. But I'm *not* talking to Global. Really."

Dance's website flew below the radar of the big business of music but she was aware of what Barry Zeigler was talking about: a complete shift in how people got that most addictive of drugs, music.

Before the nineteenth century, music was something that one generally experienced live—at concerts, opera, dance halls, bars. In the 1800s, the powerhouses of the Industry became the publishers of sheet music, which people would buy and bring home to play themselves, on the piano mostly. Then, thank you, Mr. Edison, wax cylinders came about, played on phonographs. A needle in an etched groove of the cylinder vibrated and reproduced sound through a flower-petal-like speaker. You could actually listen to music in your home, anytime you wanted!

The cylinders became disks, to be played on various wind-up machines—phonographs, gramophones (originally an Edison phonograph competitor), Victor Talking Machines, Victrolas and others. Soon the devices were powered by electricity, and in the late 1930s the miracle substance of vinyl became the standard for the records, which were differentiated by the speed at which the turntable revolved: originally 78 rpms, then 45 for singles and 33⅓ for long-playing, or LPs.

Later in the twentieth century, tape became popular—sound-faithful but inconvenient reel-to-reel models, followed by cassettes, perpetually looping eight-tracks, and then CDs, optical compact discs.

And though the media changed over the years, people could be counted on to spend millions and millions of dollars to bring music into their homes and cars. Artists often performed, of course, but concerts were mostly a form of promotion to sell the albums. Some artists never set foot on a stage and still grew rich from their music.

But then something happened.

Computers.

On which you could download and listen to any song or piece of music ever recorded.

In the new world order, disks and tapes weren't needed and the record labels, which made fortunes—for themselves and artists—by producing, pressing and distributing albums weren't as important either.

No longer did you have to buy a whole album; if you liked only two or three songs on it (and wasn't that always the case?), you could pick what you wanted. It's a mixed-tape universe nowadays, thanks to dirt-cheap download and streaming companies like Napster, Amazon, iTunes and Rhapsody and other services—and satellite radio—that let you listen to millions of tunes for a few dollars a month.

And you could even have most of your heart's desires for free: with music, as with so many other creative arts in recent years, a sense of entitlement has grown pervasive. The little inconvenience of the copyright law shouldn't stop you from getting what you want. YouTube, the Pirate Bay, BitTorrent, LimeWire and dozens of illegal file-sharing arrangements make virtually any song available free as air.

Record companies used to sue file shares—winning judgments of hundreds of thousands of dollars against broke college kids and housewives, and earning a public relations black eye in the process. Now, they've largely given up their police work.

And presently many artists were giving up too—or, more cleverly, were recognizing the value of offering some content at no charge to the public under the open source model. The theory is that free music downloads can generate new fans who will buy future albums and attend concerts, where all the money is being made.

All of which renders the traditional record stores and labels relics of the past.

People like Barry Zeigler are still needed as producers but as for-fee technicians only. With revenues from downloads tumbling, it's hard for some of them even to make a living at their craft.

Dance had heard of JBT Global Entertainment—it was a competitor of Live Nation, which owned entertainment arenas and concert halls and Ticketmaster and had contracts with many rock, pop, rap and country superstars. These companies were typical of the 360 model, as in degrees. Global covered all aspects of a musician's professional life—producing the albums, pressing the few CDs that were still sold, cutting deals with download services and big corporations for exclusive promotions and—most important—booking musicians into live performances and arranging lucrative deals for movie sound tracks and advertising, known as synchronization.

Ironically, the music world has come full circle in a mere two hundred years: from live performances prior to the nineteenth century to live performances in the twenty-first.

Barry Zeigler's world was vanishing fast and Dance understood his desperate concern that Kayleigh might leave him.

The drama of the music Industry was, of course, important to Zeigler and the singer. But the subject had virtually vanished from Dance's mind now that she knew the private conversation had nothing to do with the Edwin Sharp case. Dance gave up her eavesdropping and collected her purse from inside, deciding she wanted to get back to the motel. As she waited on the porch for Kayleigh to return, she looked out over the darkening pine grove surrounding Bishop's house.

She was concentrating once more on how best to find a killer as invisible as a snake, who could be stalking them anywhere—even from the thousands of shadows surrounding the house at that very moment.

Chapter 44

AN HOUR LATER Kathryn Dance was doing some stalking herself.

She'd returned to the Mountain View, where she'd called her mother—the kids had gone to bed. Dance had dialed the number with some uneasiness, afraid she'd learn something more about Jon Boling's impending departure. But Edie Dance said nothing further on the subject, explaining that the children were doing well and Stuart, Dance's father, had her house ready for the guests and the party planned for this weekend.

After disconnecting, she debated calling Boling. Then decided not to.

Partly because she was a coward, she chided herself. But she also had work to do.

Stalking . . .

She turned on the TV, a commercial network with a lot of commercials, so the many random flickers from the screen on the window shade would suggest someone was inside. She pulled on the only night-op camouflage she had: a navy sport coat, black jeans and a burgundy T-shirt. The outfit would have to do. For shoes, Aldo pumps; she had no tactical boots.

Finally ready, Dance slipped outside and stepped into the parking lot.

Her mission was to find out who might be the person with the bad habits of nicotine and, possibly, espionage. She'd just seen the glow of the cigarette again, in nearly the same place that she'd seen it earlier, in the park across the road. The smoker was still there.

She glanced out from behind a Caravan filled with dog show paraphernalia and a bumper sticker bragging that the driver was the proud owner of a German shepherd smarter than your honor student.

Dance focused again on the tiny orange glow in a recess between two thick stands of pine.

Was the cigarette just a coincidence? Dance might have thought so except for the fact that Sheri Towne's attacker had possibly been smoking. And that Edwin might still have the habit.

In any event, she wanted to get a glimpse of the person. If it was a teenage boy sharing a cigarette—or a joint—with his buddies, that would be that. If it was Edwin Sharp—or someone else she might have come in contact with recently—that would be a different matter.

Dance waited until a car entered the lot and drove past her, parking at the entrance. Then she stepped out of the shadows and made her way to the four-lane road and hurried across.

Very aware of the lightness on her hip where her pistol normally was, she circled wide and entered the park through one of the half dozen gaps in a rusty chain link fence.

She stayed close to the trees—the path through the playground would have offered a good view of her approach in the cool moonlight. She waved away lethargic but persistent late summer insects, and bats dipped close, dining on them. Keeping her eyes down to spot noisy vegetation and food wrappers, she moved forward steadily but slowed as she approached the cul-de-sac where the spy, or an innocent citizen, was ruining his health.

Twenty feet farther on she smelled cigarette smoke.

And she slowed even more, crouching.

She couldn't see him yet but noted that the place where he was sitting seemed to be a picnic area; there were several tables nearby, all of them chained to thick concrete posts in the ground. Was table theft from public facilities a big problem in Fresno?

She moved closer yet, one careful step at a time.

The orange glow was evident but thick pine boughs completely obscured her view of the smoker, about twenty feet away.

She reached out and gripped the bough, moving it aside.

Squinting . . .

Oh, no! Dance gasped.

The lit cigarette was stuck into a fork of a sapling near a picnic table.

That meant only one thing: Edwin or whoever it might be had seen her leave the motel and drawn her into a trap.

She spun around but saw no attacker. She dropped to her knees fast, remembering that his weapon of choice was a pistol, probably Gabe Fuentes's stolen Glock. She wasn't much of a target in the moonlight but you can spray ten or twelve rounds very quickly with a weapon like that and all you needed to do was point in the general direction of your victim.

Still no sign of him.

Where could he be?

Or had he lured her here to get into her room, steal her computer and notes?

No. He'd be coming after her.

She couldn't wait any longer. She rose and turned,

feeling a painful tickle of panic on her back, as if he were actually rubbing the muzzle of the gun along her spine.

But instead of returning in the same direction she'd come, she decided to head directly for the motel. This route was closer, though it required her to vault the six-foot fence. Still, she felt she had no choice, and she headed that way now, turning away from the lone cigarette and moving as fast as she could, keeping low, toward the road.

Thinking about getting across those four lanes, which would expose her to—

It was then that he sprang the trap.

Or rather she sprang it herself, tripping over the fishing line—or maybe guitar string—he'd strung across the route he'd anticipated she would take back. She fell hard, slamming into the packed dirt; there were none of the many pine needle beds here, which would have broken her fall. She lay gasping, breath knocked from her lungs.

Damn, oh, goddamn. That hurts! Can't breathe. . . .

She heard footsteps, not far away, moving in.

Closer, closer.

She desperately tried to scramble toward the road, where at least a car might be driving past, discouraging him from shooting.

But the asphalt was at least forty or fifty feet away, through the woods.

She tried to rise but couldn't; there was no air in her chest.

Then through the still, humid night she heard behind her the double snap of an automatic pistol's slide, back and forward, chambering a round.

Chapter 45

KATHRYN DANCE TRIED once more to get to cover.

But there was no cover, nothing here but skinny pine trees and anemic brush.

Then a firm voice, a man's from not far away, called in a sharp whisper, "Kathryn!"

She glanced about but could see no one.

Then the speaker called, "You, by the gym set. I have a weapon. I'm a county deputy. Do not move!"

Dance tried to see who this was. She couldn't spot her attacker either.

There was an eternal pause and then from behind her she heard fleeing footsteps as the attacker escaped.

Then her rescuer was running too, in pursuit. Dance rose unsteadily, trying—still largely unsuccessfully—to breathe. Who was it? Harutyun?

She expected to hear gunshots but there was none, only the sounds of returning footfalls and a man saying in a whisper, "Kathryn, where are you?" The voice was familiar.

"Here."

He approached. Finally she sucked in a solid breath and wiped tears of pain from her eyes. She blinked in surprise.

Walking through the woods, holstering his weapon, was Michael O'Neil.

She barked a laugh, which contained part relief, part joy and a dash of hysteria.

THEY SAT IN the bar, drinking Sonoma Cabernets.

Dance asked, "That was your car? That I saw pulling in fifteen minutes ago?"

"Yeah. I saw you crossing the street. You looked . . . furtive."

"I was trying. Not furtive enough."

"So I followed."

She lowered her head to his broad shoulder. "Oh, Michael, I never thought it'd be a trap."

"Who was it, Edwin?"

"Probably. Yes, no. We just don't know. What did you see?"

"Nothing. A shadow."

She gave a faint laugh at the word, sipped her wine. "That's the theme of the case: shadows."

"He's still using that song you told me about?"

"Right."

She gave him an update of what had happened so far, including how the information on the website he'd found from the file sharer's partner in Salinas had let them save the life of Kayleigh's stepmother.

"So he's targeting family?" O'Neil, as a Major Crimes detective, had some experience with stalker cases too. "That's rare."

"Yes, it is." She added, "There's one verse of 'Your Shadow' left. But Kayleigh's written a lot of songs. She's convinced he's using fire because of her hit 'Fire and Flame.' Who knows what else he could decide to do? Each verse in 'Shadow' has a theme but they're also pretty vague so we can't figure out just who he's going to target next."

"How does the last verse go?"

Dance recited it.

You can't keep down smiles; happiness floats.
But trouble can find us in the heart of our homes.
Life never seems to go quite right,
You can't watch your back from morning to night.

"Maybe it's a love song but it's plenty creepy to me. And, right, it doesn't exactly give GPS coordinates about where he's going to attack."

"So," Dance asked, looking him over, "you just jumped in the car and drove three and a half hours after supper?"

O'Neil was not big on eye contact even with those close to him and he examined the bar and the ruby-colored ellipse of the light refracted through his wine-glass. "With that fellow in Salinas, there was a Monterey connection. It made sense I come on over here."

She wondered if he'd have made the journey because he'd learned Jon Boling wasn't here.

The detective continued, "And I figured I should bring you a present. The sort I couldn't send FedEx. TJ said you came here unarmed. I checked out a Glock for you from CBI. Does Overby always insist on filling out so many forms?"

Yes, the head of her office would be worried that protocol involving firearms might end up with bad publicity for the Bureau. Well, for *him*.

"Charles is a triplicate kind of guy," she said, smiling and adjusting her position on the seat as some pain from the tumble shot through her side.

He reached into his computer bag and handed her a black plastic gun case. "Fifty rounds. If you need more than that, well, we're all in trouble."

She took his arm, squeezed it. Wanted to rest her head against his shoulder again but refrained. "This was a vacation. That's all it was."

Just then Dennis Harutyun walked into the bar and Dance introduced them—though the local deputy remembered O'Neil from the Skype conference call. It was midnight but the detective looked as fresh as if it were the start of his daily tour, uniform shirt perfectly pressed. He said to Dance, "Charlie's folks've been through the park. Nothing other than the cigarette and the fishing line used as a trip wire. We'll send the cigarette in for DNA but there probably isn't any. If he was smart, which he seems to be, he just lit the end, probably wore gloves. The line is nylon, the sort you'd buy in any one of a hundred sports or big box stores."

O'Neil reported what he'd seen, which was very little. Dance had heard the weapon's receiver but neither of them had actually seen a gun, much less the attacker himself.

The Monterey detective said, "Could be the weapon he stole from that deputy of yours, the one who's out of commission now?"

"Yeah, could be. Oh, and it gets worse. You tell him?" Harutyun asked Dance, who said, "No."

"The head of the detectives here and another officer were a little casual in a search and seizure. Edwin filed DOJ complaint and they're suspended too."

"Hell," O'Neil muttered. "Pike Madigan?"

"That's right. You saw him in our Skype conference."

Dance glanced out the window and noted a few cars slowing as they drove past the now brightly lit park, filled with crime scene officers and uniformed deputies, flashing lights from cruisers. Dance wouldn't have been surprised to see the big red Buick. But of course she didn't.

"I think I better get some sleep." A glance toward O'Neil. "You must be tired too."

"Haven't checked in yet either."

No, he came to rescue *me*. . . .

As Dance signed the drinks to her room, her mobile dinged with an incoming text. She'd turned it back on after her disastrous mission into the park.

"What is it?" Michael O'Neil asked, noting she was frozen, staring at the screen.

"It's a text." She barked a laugh. "From Edwin Sharp."

"What?"

"He'd like to see me."

"Why?"

"To talk, he says. He wants to meet me at the sheriff's office." Her eyes rose and she glanced at O'Neil and then Harutyun. "He also asked if I had a pleasant night."

Harutyun exhaled in surprise. "That man is something else."

She texted back that she'd meet him at nine.

He replied: *Good. Look forward to spending some alone time with you, Agent Dance.*

Wednesday

Chapter 46

AT NINE ON the dot Kathryn Dance met with Edwin Sharp in an apparently little-used office in the FMCSO, not an interrogation room. No intimidating decor, no mirrors.

The location was Dance's idea; to put Edwin at ease, though it wasn't exactly comfy. The room was windowless and featured a gray battered desk, propped up by books where a leg was missing, a trio of dusty dead plants and stacks of boxes containing files. On the walls were a half dozen bleached pictures of a family vacation at a lake, circa 1980.

The imposing man entered ahead of her and sat, slumping in the chair and regarding her with amused, curious eyes. She noted again his outsized arms, hands and eyebrows. He was wearing a plaid shirt, tight jeans and a thick belt with a large silver buckle, an accessory that somehow had come to be a stereotypical element of cowboyness, though she wondered if anyone had ever really worn one on the plains of Kansas or West Texas in the 1800s.

His boots, with pointed toes tipped in metal, were scuffed but looked expensive.

"You mind if I take notes?" she asked.

"Not at all. You can even record this." He looked around the room as if he knew they were doing just that;

Dance wasn't obligated to tell him, since they'd gotten a magistrate's okay, given that he was a suspect in the murders.

Dance remained placid but was troubled by his perception, or intuition. And his utterly calm demeanor. That false wisp of a smile added to the eeriness.

"Any time you want to take a break for some coffee or a smoke, you just let me know."

"I stay away from coffee," he said and gave no reaction to the other offer. Was he being coy? Dance had been fishing to find out about his current smoking habit. But whether he'd outmaneuvered her or just hadn't thought to refer to the vice didn't matter; she'd raised the issue once and couldn't bring it up again without giving something away—as Madigan had done throughout the first interview.

He then surprised her further by asking casually, "How long've you been in law enforcement, Agent Dance?"

Just the sort of question she herself would ask early in an interview to establish a baseline for kinesic analysis.

"For some time now. But please call me Kathryn. Now, what can I do for you?"

He smiled knowingly as if he had expected such a deflecting answer. "'Some time.' Ah. You seem seasoned. That's good. Oh, and you can call me Edwin."

"All right, Edwin."

"You enjoying Fresno?"

"I am."

"Little different from Monterey, isn't it?"

Dance wasn't surprised that she herself had been the subject of Edwin's own investigation. Though she wondered how far his knowledge of her life extended.

He continued, "It's pretty there. I don't like the fog much. Do you live near the water?"

"So, what can I do for you, Edwin?"

"You're busy, I know. Let's get to the nut of it. That was an expression of my mother's. I thought it was about squirrels, hiding nuts. I never did find out what it meant. She had all sorts of great expressions. She was quite a woman." His eyes scanned her face, dipped to her chest and belly, though not in a lascivious way, then back to her eyes. "I wanted to talk to you because you're smart."

"Smart?"

"I wanted to talk to somebody involved in this situation who's smart."

"There're a lot of good people here, on the sheriff's office staff." She waved her arm, wondering if he'd follow the gesture. He didn't. He continued to study her intently, soaking up images.

And that smile . . .

"Nobody as smart as you. That's a fact and a half. And the other thing is you don't have an agenda." He grimaced and his brows furrowed even more. "Don't you hate phrases like that? 'Having an agenda.' 'Sending messages.' 'Drinking the Kool-Aid.' Clichés. I regret saying that about the agenda. Sorry. Put it another way: You'll stay focused on the truth. You won't let your . . . let's say 'patriotism' for Kayleigh mess up your judgment, like's happened with the deputies here."

She noted he was articulate, which she recalled was true of his emails as well. Most erotomanic or love-obsessional stalkers were above average in intelligence and education, though Edwin seemed smarter than most. Lord knew, if he was behind the killings, he was clever. This, of course, had nothing to do with a completely skewed sense of reality—like believing Kayleigh would actually be touched that he'd murdered her stepmother or a file sharer stealing her songs.

He continued, "Officers here, they won't listen to me. End. Of. Story."

"Well, I'll be happy to hear what you have to say."

"Thanks, Kathryn. Basically, it's real simple. I didn't kill Bobby Prescott. I don't believe in file sharing but I wouldn't kill anybody because they did it. And I didn't attack Sheri Towne."

He would have learned about the second and third attacks in the press. And she noted that he didn't say, "or anyone with her." The stories had *not* reported Dance's own presence at the incident involving Sheri.

"You tell me that, Edwin. But everyone I interview denies the crime, even when we have them dead to rights—"

"Hey! Another expression of my mother's."

"I don't really know you well enough to determine if you're capable or inclined to hurt anybody or not. Tell me a little about yourself."

Again, a knowing look, eerie. But he played along. And for five minutes or so he went through facts that she largely knew—his unfortunate, but not tortured, family history. His jobs in Seattle. His impatience with formal education. He said he often got bored in class; his teachers and professors were slower than he was— which might explain his checkered record at school.

He downplayed but didn't deny his skill at computers.

He didn't mention his romantic life, past or present.

"You have a girlfriend?"

That caught him a bit off guard as if he was thinking: Obviously, I do. Kayleigh Towne.

"Last year I dated somebody in Seattle. We lived together for a while. Sally was okay but she wasn't into doing anything fun. I couldn't get her to go to concerts or anything. I had to break up with her. Felt kind of bad about it. She really wanted to get married, but . . . it wouldn't've worked out. I mean, is it too much to ask to have fun with somebody, to laugh, to be on the same, you know, wavelength?"

Not at all, Dance reflected but gave no response. She asked, "When did you break up?"

"Around Christmas."

"I'm sorry about that. It must've been tough."

"It was. I hate hurting people. And Sally was real nice. Just . . . you know, with some people things click, some not."

She now had enough information and decided it was time to start her kinesic analysis. She asked him again what specifically she could do for him, noting his behavior closely.

"Okay, I'm not the brightest bulb on the tree. Another Mom expression, ha. And I'm not very ambitious. But I'm smart enough to figure out that I'm the victim here and I'm hoping you're smart enough to take that seriously. Somebody's setting me up— probably the same people who were spying on me last weekend. Behind the house, checking me out, my car, even my trash."

"I see."

"Look, I'm not the ogre everybody says I am. Deputy Madigan and Lopez? I'm sorry I had to have them arrested but I didn't start it. They broke the Fourth and Fourteenth Amendments and some other state statutes by detaining me and searching my house. Those souvenirs were important to me. If you break the law there have to be consequences. That's exactly what *your* job is all about. I read that article you wrote when you were a reporter a few years ago, about the justice system? In the paper in Sacramento. That was a good article. All about presumed innocence."

Again, Dance struggled to keep the surprise off her face.

"Did you get a look at who was watching you?"

"No. They stayed in the shadows."

Did his smile deepen at the word "shadows"? Just a faint reaction? She couldn't tell.

"Why didn't you call the police?"

"Why do you assume I didn't?"

She'd known that he had; he'd told Madigan about the incident when she'd been observing in the interrogation room when Edwin was detained. She'd wanted to see his consistency. "You did?"

His eyes narrowed. "Nine-one-one. And they asked me if the man was trespassing and I guess technically he wasn't."

"You're sure it was a man?"

A hesitation. "Well, no. I just assumed." His odd smile. "That's good, Kathryn. See, that's what I mean. You're being smart."

"Why would somebody make you a fall guy?"

"I don't know. It's not my job to prove my innocence. All I know is I haven't hurt anybody but someone's going to a lot of trouble to make it look like I have." His eyes scanned her face closely. "Now, here's where I need your help. I was by myself when Bobby was killed and the file sharer too. But when Sheri Towne was attacked, I have an alibi."

"Did you tell the deputies?"

"No. Because I don't trust them. That's why I wanted to talk to you now. I wasn't sure it was a good idea— because you're a friend of Kayleigh's—but after reading that article you wrote, after meeting you, I decided you wouldn't let your friendship interfere with your judgment. Maybe that comes from you being a mother." He dropped that sentence without adding anything further or even looking for a response. Dance wondered if her face ticked with the alarm she felt.

"Tell me about the alibi," she calmly asked.

"I was going to go to the luncheon, for the fan? I didn't think they'd let me in but I thought I could watch from a distance, I didn't know. Maybe hear Kayleigh sing. Anyway, I got lost. Around Cal State I stopped and I asked directions. It was twelve-thirty."

Yes, just around the time of the attack.

"Who'd you talk to?"

"I don't know her name. It was a residential area near the sports stadium. This woman was working in a garden. She went inside to get a map and I stayed at the door. The noon news was just finishing."

At the time I was dodging bullets and being hit by fire extinguisher shrapnel.

"The street name?"

"Don't know. But I can describe her house. It had a lot of plants hanging from baskets. The bright red little flowers. What're they called?"

"Geraniums?"

"I think so. Kayleigh likes to garden. Me, not so much."

As if he were talking about his wife.

"My mother did too. She had—cliché alert!—a real green thumb."

Dance smiled. "Anything more about the house?"

"Dark green. On the corner. Oh, and the house had a carport, not a garage. She was nice so I moved some bags of grass seed for her. She was in her seventies. White. That's all I remember. Oh, she had cats."

"All right, Edwin. We'll look into that." Dance jotted down the information. "Will you give us permission to search the yard where you saw that intruder?"

"Of course, sure."

She didn't look up but asked quickly, "And inside your house too?"

"Yes." A microsecond of hesitation? She couldn't tell. He added, "If Deputy Madigan had asked in the first place I would have let him."

Dance had called his bluff, which may not have been a bluff at all, and said she'd schedule a time for deputies to come by.

And she asked herself the big question: What did the kinesics reveal? Was Edwin Sharp telling the truth?

She frankly couldn't say. As she'd told Madigan and the others in the briefing on Monday, a stalker is usually psychotic, borderline or severely neurotic, with reality issues. That meant he might be reciting what he believed was the truth, even though it was completely false; therefore his kinesics when lying would be the same as his baseline.

Adding to the difficulty was Edwin's diminished affect—his ability to feel and display emotion, such as stress. Kinesic analysis works only when the stress of lying alters the subject's behavior.

Still, interviewing is a complex art and can reveal more than just deception. With most witnesses or suspects, the best information is gathered by observations of, first, body language, then, second, verbal quality—pitch of voice and how fast one talks, for instance.

The third way in which humans communicate can sometimes be helpful: verbal content—*what* we say, the words themselves. (Ironically, this is generally the least useful because it is the most easily manipulated and prone to misunderstanding.)

Yet with a troubled individual like Edwin, where kinesics weren't readily available, looking at his verbal content might be the only tool Dance had.

But what had he offered that could be helpful?

He shook his head as if answering her silent question, and the smile deepened. It was unprofessional but she wished he'd lose the grin. The expression was more unnerving to her than the worst glare from a murderer.

"You think I'm smart, Edwin. But do you think I'm straightforward?"

He considered this. "As much as you can be."

"You know, with everything that's been happening, don't you think it might make sense for you to get back to Seattle, forget about the concert. You could see Kayleigh some other time."

She said this to prime the pump, see if he'd offer facts about his life and plans—facts that she might use for content-based analysis.

She certainly didn't expect the laugh of disbelief and what he then said: "I can hardly do that, now, can I?"

"No?"

"You know that song of hers, 'Your Shadow'?"

There wasn't a single clue in his face that this song was a calling card for murder. She said casually, "Sure. Her big hit. You thought it was the best song she ever wrote."

Edwin's grin for once took on a patina of the genuine. "She told you that, did she?" He glowed; his lover had remembered something about him. "Well, it's about her, you know."

"About her, Kayleigh?"

"That's right. The first verse is about how people take advantage of her as a musician. And then there's a verse about that car crash—when her mother died. Kayleigh was fifteen. You know Bishop was driving, drunk."

No, Dance had not been aware of that.

"He spent eight months in jail. Never drove a car after that. Then that other verse, about the riverside?" At last the smile faded. "I think, I don't know, but I think something pretty bad happened to her when she was about sixteen. She disappeared for a while. I think she had a breakdown, tried to kill herself. Drowning, you know. That's the lyrics in the song."

Was that true? Dance had never heard of this either.

Now the uncomfortable smile faded. "How sad is that? Writing a song to comfort yourself, because nobody else is there for you? Awful. . . ." Eyes focused intently on his interviewer. "Kayleigh sent me a dozen emails and a few real letters, and you know what I read between the lines in every single one? She needs me, Agent Dance. She needs me bad. If I left, who else would look out for her?"

Chapter 47

DEPUTY CRYSTAL STANNING, Michael O'Neil and Kathryn Dance were in the briefing room of the FMCSO. Acting Chief Detective Dennis Harutyun too.

Dance was reporting about the interview with Edwin. "I'll have to be honest. He's very hard to read kinesically. He's coming off as completely nondeceptive, which either means he's telling the whole truth or he's completely delusional."

"The son of a bitch did it," Stanning grumbled.

It seemed the woman had grown more self-confident and edgier as the case had progressed. Or maybe it was just Madigan's absence.

A call to the Joint County Emergency Communications headquarters revealed that Edwin had in fact called 911 to report a Peeping Tom. It was Saturday night, 7:00 P.M. He was complaining about somebody watching him from the backyard. No details. The dispatcher said to call back if the perp actually trespassed or threatened him.

Charlie Shean's crime scene team had just gone out to the place and conducted a search for where the intruder might have been. He was due any moment with the results.

O'Neil asked, "Saturday—the night before Bobby was killed. Who could've been watching him, who knew he was in town?"

Harutyun said, "We got the notice about a week ago—from Kayleigh's lawyers—that he might be in Fresno and could be a problem."

But Dance pointed out, "Anybody could've found out where he was."

"How's that?" Harutyun asked.

The Monterey detective added that on the fan websites, Sharp had posted that he was going to Fresno "for a while."

Harutyun took a call, spoke for a few minutes and then disconnected. "Patrol's canvassing the area around Bulldog Stadium. Cal State. Lotta people. It's slow going."

This was to find the woman who'd given Edwin directions at the time of Sheri's attack. Dance was calling her Alibi Woman.

A moment later Charlie Shean walked into the office. He greeted them all and briefed them about the scene.

In his thick Boston accent, rare in these parts, he said, "We went through his house and collected some trace but it was clean. I wonder if he scrubbed it down, after he gave you permission to search." A glance toward Dance.

She recalled the faint hesitation before Edwin gave his okay.

"Cigarettes?" Dance had asked them to check.

"No. No lighters or matches or ashtrays. No odor of cigarettes either. . . . Now, I know from before that the latex gloves in Edwin's kitchen probably aren't the same as at the Bobby Prescott homicide. The wrinkle patterns are different. Outside, where the alleged perp was spying on him? Well, we found some shoe prints in the dust, cowboy boots, it looks like, not the sort that garbage men or workers back there would wear. They were distorted because of the wind but at least it hadn't rained and washed the damn prints away. Can't tell size, male, female or age. And we collected about thirty samples of trace but the preliminaries are pretty useless. Sorry, Dennis—if there's anything there, I don't know how it can help.

"Now, we confirmed that the cigarette from last night at your motel is a Marlboro. We have ash from the site of the Sheri Towne attack—cigarette ash, I mean—but we don't have the equipment to analyze it proper to tell what brand it is or how long ago it was left."

It was then that Dennis Harutyun's assistant came to the door and handed him a sheaf of papers. "These're those emails you were waiting for, about Bobby Prescott. They finally came in."

The deputy read them over, laughed. Subdued but for him a significant outpouring of emotion.

He said to the officers, "One of the things I was look-ing into was another motive for killing Bobby Prescott, by somebody other than Edwin?"

"Right," Dance said.

"Well, I may've found one."

"Go ahead."

He said, "You ever hear about these guys, John, Paul, George and Ringo?"

Chapter 48

DANCE AND O'NEIL conducted the search themselves.

It felt good, being with him again, working with him. Some of this was simply the comfort of being with a person you were close to, whose subtle looks and smiles and gestures communicated perfectly, without the need for words.

But part of the pleasure was their combined skills as law enforcers. A *Gestalt*—the whole greater than the sum of the parts. Policing's a tough business and can't be done alone. The job can be a nightmare when you aren't connected with your partner—and that not only makes for a tough working day but it also means the bad guys are less likely to get caught.

Police investigation can be an art form, like ballet, a choreography of technique, purpose, and she felt this in near perfection with Michael O'Neil.

The scene where they were practicing their harmonies was Bobby Prescott's trailer and what had inspired the search here was the revelation by Harutyun about the Fab Four.

Dance believed she now knew what had been stolen the morning after the roadie had been murdered—by the person Tabatha Nysmith had seen in Bobby's trailer. And the object of this theft wasn't Kayleigh

Towne memorabilia. Indeed, it had nothing to do with the singer at all or with the stalker—except to the extent that, yes, Edwin Sharp probably *was* a fall guy as he'd claimed all along.

"Well," she said, somewhat breathlessly, examining a binder from the shelves where she'd noted something missing several days ago, when she was here with P. K. Madigan.

O'Neil stepped closer and together they looked over a spiral notebook in which Bobby Prescott's father had jotted details about the recordings he'd helped engineer at Abbey Road Studios in London during the 1960s and '70s.

Dance recalled that Tabatha had mentioned Bobby's father's illustrious career.

It was a breathtaking list of talent from the era: Cliff Richard, Connie Francis, the Scorpions, the Hollies, Pink Floyd and of course the Beatles, who recorded *Yellow Submarine* and *Abbey Road* there. Much of the man's scribbling was cryptic—notes about synthesizers and amplifier dynamics and acoustic baffles and instruments.

But the most relevant was a carbon copy of a letter to Bobby's father.

> *June 13, 1969*
> *Bob Prescott:*
>
>   *Hey mate, thanks for the GREAT job,*
> *you're the best engineer, we mean it. Loved*
> *working with you. So, in appreciation for all*
> *those sleepless nights the tapes to those songs*
> *we did playing around after 'Abbey Road,'*
> *are yours, all the rights, everything. The list's*
> *below. Cheers!*

"Wait," O'Neil said. "Are those . . . ?"

Dance said in a whisper, "I think they are. My God, I think they are." At the bottom of the letter were the titles of four songs. None of them was a known Beatles song.

She explained that the composing and recording of the songs on the *Abbey Road* album began in the spring of 1969. It was the group's last studio album. *Let It Be* was released a year later, though that song was finished by January of '69.

Dennis Harutyun—the "librarian of the FMCSO," as Madigan dubbed him—had indeed done some impressive research into the life of Bobby Prescott and his family to see if anyone other than Edwin might have a motive to kill him. The deputy had found some rumors, buried on the Internet, that his father might have had some outtakes of Beatles songs he'd helped engineer in London years ago.

But these weren't outtakes; they were complete songs, original and unreleased, never heard in public.

"And the Beatles just gave them away?" O'Neil asked.

"The band was breaking up then. They were rich. Maybe they just didn't care about them. Or maybe they just didn't think they were any good."

"The letter's not signed by any of them."

Dance shrugged. "A handwriting expert could verify which of the four wrote it. But they talk about 'after "Abbey Road."' Who else could it be? They must've stayed around the studio afterward and just thrown a few songs together. Doesn't matter; they're still Beatles songs."

"Bobby got the tapes from his father."

"Right," Dance said, gesturing at the shelves. "The perp found out and has been waiting for a chance to kill him and steal them."

"Waiting for Edwin or somebody like him to show up as a fall guy."

"Exactly."

O'Neil said, "So it's somebody who knew Bobby and his archives and would have heard the rumors about the Beatles songs." He regarded the lyrics. "Could the perp sell them, though?"

"I'd think at the least he could work out a finder's fee in the millions. Or maybe he could sell them to a reclusive collector—like that Japanese businessman who got busted for spending fifty million for a stolen Van Gogh. He was going to keep it in his basement, never let anybody see it."

O'Neil pointed out, "Well, we know the motive. The second question is, who's the perp? You have any ideas? I don't know the cast of characters here."

Dance thought for a moment, looking round the trailer.

A to B to Z . . .

"I need you to do something."

"Sure," the detective said. "Evidence, crime scene? You're a better interrogator than I am but I'm game."

"No," she said. She took him by the shoulders and walked him backward five feet. She then stepped away and examined him closely. "Just stand right there and don't move."

As she walked out the door, O'Neil looked around and said, "I can do that."

A HALF HOUR later, Dance and O'Neil, along with a contingent of FMCSO deputies, sped through the hazy late-summer afternoon toward a motel off Highway 41.

It was a Red Roof Inn. Decent, clean but surely far below what the guest they were about to arrest had been used to at certain points in his life.

The four cars approached silently.

There were jurisdictional considerations, of course, but Dance and O'Neil weren't here to claim the trophy, merely to help out. They were happy to let the local constabulary handle the arrest. She had, after all, agreed to let Madigan take the collar and corner the publicity, though it would be FMCSO in general who'd get the credit, since he wasn't on active duty.

The three police cars and Dance's Nissan slipped silently up to the motel and parked. With a shared smile and tacit understanding, Dance and O'Neil glanced at each other and wandered to the back of the place, while Harutyun, Stanning and four other deputies sprinted through the halls to the room where surveillance had revealed the suspect was staying.

As they'd guessed, the nervous perp had been anticipating the visit; he'd seen the cars approach and he literally leapt out the window of his room onto an unpleasant patch of grass reserved for dogs doing their business. He righted himself fast, wrapped his computer bag strap around his chest and poised for a sprint, then wisely chose to stop as he glanced at the guns in the hands of Dance and O'Neil, both of the muzzles pointed steadily at his head.

Two other somber deputies, one Latino and one Anglo, joined them in the back. They were the ones who slapped the cuffs on Kayleigh's producer, Barry Zeigler, and led him toward the parking lot around front. It was Kathryn Dance who took possession of the computer bag that would contain the priceless songs that he'd stolen from Bobby Prescott's trailer, the morning after he'd killed the roadie.

Chapter 49

"YOUR HEIGHT," DANCE explained to him.

Zeigler sat, miserable, in the backseat of a sheriff's office cruiser. The door was open and he was facing outward, hands shackled behind him.

She continued to elaborate, answering his question about how she knew it was he. "The perp would know Bobby pretty well and had probably been in his trailer before. And he'd been somebody who was very familiar with everyone connected with the band."

The deciding factor was what she told him next: "And he was tall."

"Tall?"

She explained about her interview with Tabatha, across the street, several days ago. "She said she'd seen somebody inside that morning. Except, she couldn't see the intruder's head, only his chest."

This was why she'd put O'Neil in front of the window of the trailer a half hour ago. Recalling that she'd been eye-to-eye with P. K. Madigan, outside, when she'd searched the trailer, she'd positioned the Monterey detective about where Tabatha had seen the intruder. She'd then stepped outside and walked across the street. Looking back, she'd clearly seen O'Neil's face.

Which meant that the intruder Monday morning had been well over O'Neil's height of six feet. The only person she'd met recently with an interest in Kayleigh Towne who knew Bobby and who fit that stature was Barry Zeigler.

"Shit," the man muttered, utterly defeated. "I'm sorry. I don't know what to say. I'm sorry."

Dance heard that often as an interrogator.

Sorry . . .

Of course what it meant, ten times out of ten, was: I'm sorry I got caught.

"When I met you at Kayleigh's house you said you'd just driven there from Carmel. But we talked to the desk clerk here. You checked in the morning after Bobby was killed."

"I know, I know. I lied. I'm sorry."

That, again.

Dance said, "And then there was the recording of Kayleigh singing 'Your Shadow.' That you played to announce the attacks? It was done on a high-quality digital recorder. The sort that pros use—pros like you, producers and engineers."

"Recording?" he asked, frowning.

She glanced at Dennis Harutyun, who ran through the Miranda warning. He added, "You're under arrest for murder, for—"

"Murder? What do you mean?"

Dance and Harutyun exchanged glances.

"You're being arrested for the murder of Bobby Prescott, sir," the Fresno detective said. "And Frederick Blanton. And assault and battery on Sheri Towne and Agent Dance. Do you wish to—"

"No, no, I didn't kill anyone! I didn't attack anyone!" The producer's face was shocked. Dance had seen a lot of performances from suspects; this was one of the best. "I'd never do that! Why would I do that?"

"Yessir. You'll have your day in court. Do you understand your rights?"

"Bobby? You're thinking I killed Bobby? No! And I'd never hurt Sheri. This is—"

"Do you understand—?"

"Yes, yes. But—"

"Do you wish to waive your right to remain silent?"

"Sure, yes. This is ridiculous. This is a huge misunderstanding."

Harutyun asked, "Did you drive up here on Sunday and kill Bobby Prescott that night?"

"No, no. I drove in on Monday morning, about eleven. After I heard from Kayleigh that Bobby had died. Yes, I broke into Bobby's trailer but it was just to get some personal things."

"The songs," Harutyun said. "We know all about them."

"Songs?"

"The Beatles songs."

"What are you talking about?"

The quality of his confusion seemed genuine so she decided to add, "Bobby's father was a technician at Abbey Road in the sixties and seventies."

"Right. A pretty famous one. But what does that have to do with anything?"

"The Beatles gave him four original songs they wrote after they finished *Abbey Road*."

Barry Zeigler laughed. "No, no, no . . ."

O'Neil said, "You killed him and stole the songs. They're worth millions."

The producer continued, "It's an urban legend. All those rumors about outtakes and secret recordings. All that nonsense about Paul is dead. No rumor spreads faster in the music world than ones about the Beatles. But there's nothing to it. There are no undiscovered songs."

Dance was sizing up behaviors. Zeigler seemed more or less credible. She said, "What about this?" She showed him the plastic envelope containing the letter to Bobby's father.

Zeigler looked at it and shook his head. "Those

aren't Beatles songs. It was some local group from Camden Town in London, I don't even remember the name. They were nothing. After the Beatles wrapped *Abbey Road*, this group booked studio time. They laid down fifteen or sixteen tracks and used twelve or so for their album. I guess they liked Bobby's father so much they let him have the ones they didn't use. Nothing ever came of the group. Fact is, they wrote pretty sucky songs."

Dance looked at the language of the note again.

So, in appreciation for all those sleepless nights the tapes to those songs we did playing around after 'Abbey Road,' are yours, all the rights, everything. The list's below. Cheers!

Yes, it could simply refer to studio time after the Beatles had finished recording their album.

"But you just admitted you stole something from Bobby's trailer that morning."

Zeigler was debating. He looked to O'Neil and the other deputies. "Leave us alone, Agent Dance and me. I want to talk to her alone."

She considered this. "It's all right."

The others walked away from the squad car. Dance crossed her arms and said, "Okay, talk."

"You can't tell a soul."

"You know I can't agree to that."

The man's long face screwed into a disgusted knot. "All right. But take a look first and then decide. In the bag, there's a zipper liner. Some papers. *That's* what I took from Bobby's."

Dance opened the computer bag and found the compartment. She withdrew an envelope and opened it, reading through a four-page document.

"Oh my God," she whispered.

"Happy now?" Zeigler muttered.

Chapter 50

WHAT HE'D STOLEN was a letter from Bobby Prescott about how he wanted his property distributed in the event of his death.

Most of it would go to one person: the child who was his and Kayleigh Towne's, Mary-Gordon.

Apparently Kayleigh had had the child at sixteen and Suellyn and her husband, Roberto Sanchez, had adopted the little girl within weeks of her birth.

The envelope included a copy of the adoption papers and some personal messages to the girl, for her to read when she was older.

"He told me a few years ago that he'd written it," Zeigler said. "I couldn't let it become public."

Dance recalled the close relationship she'd sensed between Bobby and Kayleigh at the restaurant. And the other things she'd noted: Mary-Gordon's blond hair color, the girl's forthright demeanor. Her eyes were Kayleigh's bright blue, while Suellyn's—and presumably her Latino husband's—were brown.

She thought too about Edwin's comment in the recent interview.

I think something pretty bad happened to her when she was about sixteen. . . .

Dance asked, "But how come no one knew she was pregnant?"

"Oh, Kayleigh didn't start performing professionally until she was seventeen. She wasn't on the press radar before then but Bishop had big plans for her. He pulled her out of school when she was about two months pregnant, got a tutor for homeschooling. He kept it secret and spun the story pretty well to friends—Kayleigh was real upset her mother had died. She was depressed. Made sense for her to disappear for eight, nine months. He suggested to people she'd had a breakdown."

Dance was appalled. "And he forced her to give the baby up?"

Zeigler's long face moved up and down. "Bobby was twenty-two, she was six years younger. Okay, that's bad, no question. On the other hand, he was a really nice guy and if anybody would fall for a father figure, it'd be Kayleigh. Her mother had just died, she was living in a house she hated, with her father on the road most of the time. She was vulnerable. And it wasn't just a fling. They wanted to get married. They were in love. But when Bishop heard, he flew back to town right after a concert and said if they didn't agree to the adoption he was going to get Bobby arrested for statutory rape."

"He did *that*?"

"Sure did. Kayleigh agreed to the adoption—but only to placing the girl with her sister so she could still see her. And she insisted that Bobby stay with the band. Bishop figured that was the best he was going to get and he agreed."

. Dance recalled her own observations about Bobby and what Kayleigh had told her. "That's when Bobby started drinking and got into drugs, right?"

Zeigler lifted an eyebrow. "You caught that, hm? Yep, that was it. He was really upset it didn't work out between them."

"But why couldn't she keep the baby?" Dance asked. "I know she wants children."

"Oh, that wouldn't work," Zeigler said bitterly. "Bishop's own career was dying at that point. All he had left was Kayleigh."

"And he was convinced that she needed to build her career on a good-girl image to be successful."

"Exactly. He was ahead of the curve there. Like he usually was. Look at those *Twilight* vampire books my daughter loves. They're about kids being in love but not having sex. That's Kayleigh Towne. And parents—the ones with the credit cards—love that image. If word had gotten out that she was pregnant at sixteen, that could have been the end of her career."

Dance didn't know if that was true or not. She had a lot of faith in the intelligence and discernment of audiences. She said coolly, "But it was about you too, right? You can't afford to lose her. Not with the way record labels are headed nowadays."

Zeigler's shoulders, high above Dance, slumped. "Okay, okay. Kayleigh's my only major act left. Everybody else is gone. If I lose her it's all over with. I'm forty-five and all I've ever done is produce albums. I can't afford to be a freelancer. Besides, Kayleigh's an amazing talent. I love working with her. She's a genius. One of a kind."

Dance looked at the adoption paperwork, the letter.

"Mary-Gordon doesn't know?"

"No. Bishop forced Suellyn and her husband to sign a nondisclosure agreement. If they said a word they might lose custody."

Dance closed her eyes briefly and shook her head at this news about Bishop Towne, which disturbed but didn't surprise her one bit.

Zeigler gave a bitter laugh. "I'm not the only desperate person in this business."

She slipped the documents back into the envelope and put it into her purse. "I'll think about it. For now, you were looking for some personal papers at Bobby's. What you found and took had no value and had nothing to do with the case." She looked him over coolly. "But you're still a suspect in the murders."

"I was in Carmel, at a hotel, when Bobby died."

"Can anybody verify that?"

He thought for a moment. Then said, "I was by my-self. . . . I was really upset—I'd just been fired by my other major artist. The only contact I had with anybody was a message I left for my wife." He glanced up at Dance with miserable eyes. "Is that any good—a voice-mail where you're sobbing like a ten-year-old that your career is probably over?"

"It could be," Dance told him.

Chapter 51

"NO BEATLES?" DENNIS Harutyun asked, visibly disappointed the news wasn't true. This was the most emotional she'd seen him.

"Doesn't look that way."

Dance had phoned Martine, her website partner and a true musical historian, who made some calls and reported back about what Zeigler had said. Yes, there'd been rumors for years of undiscovered Fab Four songs but the consensus was just as the producer explained.

Dance, Harutyun and Crystal Stanning stood in a cluster in the parking lot of the Red Roof Inn. The lights of the patrol cars were flashing urgently. Maybe this was procedure but Dance wished they'd shut them off.

O'Neil was on the phone. Finally he ended the call and looked up. "His alibi? It's good."

The cell phone data and the voiceprint of the "sobbing ten-year-old" confirmed that at the moment Bobby Prescott was being murdered in the Fresno convention center, Barry Zeigler was over two hours away.

"Why'd he break into Bobby's trailer?" Harutyun asked. "What was he after?"

Dance shrugged. "Apparently it's personal. Nothing to do with the case. I believe him."

O'Neil's eyes swung toward her, amused. Was her

behavior deviating from her baseline? Which he, of all people, would know very well.

The Fresno deputy said, "Hardly seems worth the trouble, collaring him for that. But, I'll tell you, bad judgment ought to be a misdemeanor." He walked over to his car, got Zeigler out and uncuffed him. Dance didn't know what transpired between the two but she assumed it involved a stern talking-to. With a glance toward Dance, the producer collected his computer bag and returned to his room, rubbing his wrists.

Dance decided to give the documents to Kayleigh and let her decide how to handle the matter.

"So," Harutyun said, returning to them. "No leads. No suspect."

"We have the evidence," Crystal Stanning offered. "From the crime scenes and what we collected in Edwin's backyard."

"Evidence," Harutyun muttered, a sour tone that Dance counted as yet another shred of emotion from the reserved detective. "Life's not like *CSI*, I'm sorry. Charlie's folks are good but you need more than finding. You need figuring out."

Yet another dust devil whirled up nearby. Dance cocked her head as she stared at it.

"What?" O'Neil asked, perusing her face. He sensed something was up.

The miniature cyclone vanished.

Kathryn Dance pulled out her phone and made a call.

Chapter 52

TWO HOURS LATER this foursome reconvened in the sheriff's office—in the digs of ousted P. K. Madigan, specifically. It was the largest in the Detective Division, the only one with room for more than two or three people at one time.

Dance noted, with some sad poignancy, that the chief detective had been clipping coupons from Safeway. Maybe he did the family shopping. Only one coupon was for ice cream. Buy one pint, get another free.

She received a text, read it and then asked the deputies, "Can you show me your service door?"

Harutyun and Stanning regarded each other and she said, "Sure, I guess. Follow me."

Dance and others did and after a brief walk stopped at a wide doorway in a delivery area at the back of the main building, opening onto a ramp that led to the parking lot.

"Good. This'll do." She made a call and gave directions to this entrance. Dance disconnected and explained, "I'm having some houseguests this weekend. They've been in San Jose at a conference. I took the liberty of asking them here. I had our San Francisco office lend them a set of flashing lights. They made better time than I thought."

Just then a white van pulled up and stopped. The side

door opened and a disabled-passenger ramp extended to the ground. A moment later a handsome man with dark hair and a fleshy nose drove a red motorized wheelchair quickly down the ramp and through the doorway of the service area. Wearing tan slacks and a long-sleeved burgundy shirt, he was pale, as befits someone who does not get outside very much. Joining him was a tall, redheaded woman in jeans, black T-shirt and black jacket, and a slim, younger man with perfectly trimmed hair. He wore well-tailored slacks, a white shirt and a striped tie.

"Lincoln!" Dance bent down, pressing her cheek against that of the man in the wheelchair. "Amelia." She embraced the redhead, Amelia Sachs, Lincoln Rhyme's partner.

"Hello, Thom," she said to Rhyme's caregiver, who also hugged her warmly.

"Been way, way too long," the aide said.

"Kathryn . . . and Michael O'Neil," Rhyme said, casting his eyes quickly on the detective.

Surprised, O'Neil said, "That's right." He'd never met Rhyme. "How'd you know?"

"A few observations. You're carrying a weapon so you're public safety and those Fresno-Madera folks there"—a nod toward Harutyun and Stanning—"are in uniform but their name badges show they're detectives. So, the policy here is that even detectives wear uniforms. You're not, so you're probably from another jurisdiction. There's a car outside with a Monterey County wharf pass on it. You're tanned and pretty fit—the way somebody who boats or fishes in the ocean would be. I know you and Kathryn work together frequently. Therefore . . . you were Michael O'Neil. Or, maybe I could tell that from the body language between the two of you." This was delivered, like most of Lincoln Rhyme's wry comments, without a smile.

Rhyme made a slight movement of his neck and his right arm extended smoothly. He shook O'Neil's hand. Dance knew he'd recently had some surgery to improve his condition—he was quadriplegic, mostly paralyzed from the neck down; he'd been injured on the job as head of the NYPD Crime Scene Unit some years ago. The operation had been successful and he'd regained nearly all the use of his right arm and hand, which he controlled by subtle gestures of his neck, shoulder and head muscles.

He similarly greeted Harutyun and Stanning, and Sachs introduced Thom Reston, Rhyme's caregiver.

Harutyun continued, "Kathryn said she'd called in an expert but I never thought it'd be someone like you. Well, thanks for coming. You're based in New York, I heard. What brings you to California?"

"Came for a visit," the man said shortly. And let it go at that. He was not a conversationalist—even less of one than Michael O'Neil.

Sachs filled in, "He's been lecturing at a forensics conference in San Jose. Then we were going to spend a few days with Kathryn and her family in Pacific Grove."

Dance had known and worked with Rhyme for several years. She'd been after him and Sachs to come for a visit. Rhyme was disinclined to travel—certainly there were logistical issues and he was naturally a bit of a recluse—but he was in demand as a consultant in forensics and crime scene work and he decided to accept a lecture assignment on that subject in San Jose.

The preparations for her house that her father was taking care of in anticipation of the visit involved building a ramp to let Rhyme motor up to the front door and some modifications to a bathroom. Rhyme had told them not to bother, they'd stay at a motel but retired Stuart Dance loved any excuse to use his many woodworking tools.

Harutyun said, "Well, it's a true pleasure to meet you, Detective Rhyme."

A fast: "'Lincoln' is fine. I'm decommissioned." He revealed a hint of pleased irritation at the man's comment.

"Amelia drove, I assume," Dance said, with a wry glance at Thom. This was a reference to the timing. It was about 120 miles from San Jose to Fresno and they'd made the trip in an hour and a half—and in a disabled-accessible van, no less. Unlike Dance, the policewoman from New York was a car aficionado—she actually worked on them herself—and would take her muscle car out to the track to "relax" at 180 miles per hour.

Sachs smiled. "It was pretty much a straightaway. The flashing blue lights always help too."

Rhyme looked around the storage facility with a grimace as if he expected this to be the crime lab. "Now. You have some things you'd like me to look over?" The criminalist was never one for socializing, Dance recalled.

"We have a pretty good lab," Harutyun offered.

"Do you now?" There was cynicism in his voice. Dance had been to Rhyme's town house on Central Park West in Manhattan; he'd turned the parlor into a well-equipped forensics lab, where he, as a consultant, Sachs and other officers would run the crime scene side of major cases in the metro area.

Not picking up on the sardonic tone, Stanning said proudly, "Yes, sir. Sheriff Madigan's fought pretty hard to build up our CSU. Officers as far away as Bakersfield send samples here. And I don't mean just rape kits. Pretty complicated things."

"Bakersfield," Rhyme said, even more ironically, drawing a sharp glance from Thom, a reminder that condescension was not necessary. Dance guessed his attitude had nothing to do with a prejudice against small towns, though. Rhyme was a nondenominational curmudgeon. He gave the NYPD, Scotland Yard and the FBI a lot of crap too. The New York governor's and mayor's offices had not escaped his wrath either.

"Well, we better get to it, you don't mind."

"Let's go this way," Harutyun said and led them inside, then out the front door.

As they walked and wheeled toward the crime lab, Dance briefed them on the case, explaining that their main suspect had proved to be very slippery. "His name's Edwin Sharp. He could be the perp, he could be a fall guy, could be completely innocent."

Harutyun said, "The UNSUB announces the attacks by playing a verse from one of Kayleigh's songs."

This clearly intrigued Rhyme. "Interesting, good," he said, then decided he was exhibiting too much glee. "And he's smart, right? He started with phones, then switched to other ways to play the song, like radio call-in requests?"

"Very good, sir," Stanning said. "Not call-ins but most recent he played a song over a high-school-stadium PA system."

Rhyme frowned. "Didn't think of that one. Interesting, like I said."

Dance added, "We're tracking down a witness now, maybe an alibi. And he claims somebody's been conducting surveillance on *him,* presumably to set him up for the crimes. That's part of the evidence we need you to look at."

Sachs asked, "You've interviewed him?"

"Yes. But the kinesics were inconclusive. I can say, though, that he's got a stalker's personality: reduced affect, attachment issues, reality problems."

The woman from New York nodded. Kathryn Dance

glanced down; she loved shoes and she couldn't help but admire Amelia Sachs's black, high-heeled boots, which sent the tall woman—a former fashion model—even further into the stratosphere.

Rhyme asked, "Samples from Edwin's house or apartment?"

Dance said, "House. He gave us permission, though he might've scrubbed the place down before the team searched."

Harutyun added that an earlier search, without a warrant, had resulted in getting the chief of detectives and another deputy suspended. The perp had also stolen the gun of another detective, temporarily removing him from the force.

"Crazy like a fox," Rhyme commented and seemed oddly pleased at this news—maybe because he liked adversaries who were particularly smart and challenging. His number-one nemesis was boredom.

Then they were entering the lab and meeting Charlie Shean. If Harutyun was impressed that Rhyme was here, Shean was beside himself, having a crime scene legend in his "modest abode."

Rhyme, though, was visibly impressed at the sophistication of the operation, despite his apparent misgiving earlier. Some people, Dance knew, are easier to read than others and although his body language was obviously severely limited, Rhyme was, to her, an open book.

Charlie Shean now briefed the criminalist on where they needed his expertise. "We've searched and we've done the analysis. But most of the results're just raw data. We don't know what to make of it. If you could offer some thoughts it'd be much appreciated."

Rhyme was taking all this in as his eyes swept the ceiling. Then abruptly: "Sachs, let's get a chart going."

Rhyme used graphics in running his cases—having

someone write down the evidence that had been gathered—in front of which he would then wheel back and
forth, frowning and muttering to himself, as deductions
and conclusions came or didn't come. Shean explained
what they'd found and she wrote.

• Sunday. Robert Prescott homicide, convention center stage/
orchestra pit/scaffolding
—strip lamp
  —no matching friction ridge prints
  —no matching tool marks (unit removed by wing nuts)
—fifty-foot power cord
  —no matching fingerprints
—smoke detectors in pit, disabled
  —no matching fingerprints
  —smudges determined to be produced by latex gloves, brand
    unknown, not associated with gloves in Edwin Sharp's
    possession
—cardboard cartons moved from projected path of victim
  —no matching fingerprints
  —smudges determined to be produced by latex gloves, brand
    unknown, not associated with gloves in Edwin Sharp's
    possession
—unique trace from stage/orchestra pit/scaffolding
  —triglyceride fat (lard)
    —2700K color temperature (yellowish)
    —melting point: 40–55 degrees F
    —specific gravity: 0.91 at 40.0 C
—no footprints/vehicle tread marks

• Monday. Frederick Blanton homicide, gas station, near San
Joaquin River
—two 9 mm shell casings
  —weapon possibly Det. Gabriel Fuentes's, no casings for
    comparison
  —no friction ridge prints
  —extractor marks match those found at Sheri Towne scene
—one 9 mm slug recovered
  —lands and grooves match slugs from Sheri Towne scene
—accelerant
  —Shell gasoline, 89 octane
  —gasoline container destroyed
  —no footprints/vehicle tread marks

• Monday. Frederick Blanton's residence, Fresno
—no relevant friction ridge prints, footprints, vehicle tread
  marks

• Monday. Public phone in classroom building at Fresno College
—No relevant friction ridge prints

   —unique trace collected
      —calcium powder. Medical/dietary supplement?
      —chemicals: limonite, goethite and calcite
   —no footprints/vehicle tread marks

- Tuesday. Sheri Towne crime scene
   —cigarette ash
   —twenty-three 9 mm shell casings
      —weapon possibly Det. Gabriel Fuentes's, no casings for
         comparison
      —no friction ridge prints
      —extractor marks match those at gas station scene
   —seven 9 mm slugs
      —lands and grooves match those at Frederick Blanton scene
   —no friction ridge prints
   —no footprints/vehicle tread marks

- Tuesday. Emerson High School stadium, PA system facility
   —no friction ridge prints
   —no footprints/vehicle tread marks
   —unique trace recovered
      —calcium powder. Medical/dietary supplement?

- Tuesday. Park across from Mountain View Motel
   —Marlboro cigarette. DNA analysis requested
   —fishing line trip wire, generic brand
   —no friction ridge prints
   —no footprints/vehicle tread marks

- Wednesday. Edwin Sharp's house
   —outside:
      —boot print, probably cowboy-style, unable to determine
         size, male or female
      —no vehicle tread marks
      —unique trace materials
         —triglyceride fat (lard)
         —2700K color temperature (yellowish)
         —melting point: 40–55 degrees F
         —specific gravity: 0.91 at 40.0 C
         —fungus
         —chemicals: limonite, goethite and calcite
         —mineral oil, with lime sulfur
         —calcium powder. Medical/dietary supplement?
         —ammonium oxalate
   —inside:
      —latex gloves, not associated with those at Prescott homicide
      —household cleaning materials (to eliminate trace?)
      —no cigarettes, matches or lighters, odor of cigarettes

   Lincoln Rhyme regarded the chart closely. "Not good, not bad. Let's get to work."

Chapter 53

"**ENTRANCE AND EXIT** routes from the convention center?"

Shean explained, "There're twenty-nine of them, including the windows and infrastructure access doorways and loading docks. There were thousands of prints and samples of trace."

Lincoln Rhyme said, "Yes, yes, sometimes the problem is too *much* evidence, rather than not enough. . . . I'm glad you know the number of exits, Charlie. Good searching."

"Thank you, sir."

"Lincoln," he corrected absently, absorbing the chart.

Rhyme and Shean got to work. Dance had wondered if being a guest would temper Rhyme's edge but, clearly, no. When he learned that there were two different places behind Edwin's house where an intruder might have stood to spy, he asked which trace came from which area. The tags on the half dozen collection bags reported only: *Trace evidence from behind E. Sharp's house, Woodward Circle West.*

"Well, we didn't really differentiate them."

From Rhyme: "Oh." It was the same as a loud dressing-down. "Might want to think about that in the future."

Rhyme had once told Dance, "*Where* you find the clue is critical, vital. A crime scene is like real estate. It's all about location, location, location."

On the other hand, Shean had satisfied Rhyme's number-one requirement when it came to trace: isolating "unique" material that might have been shed by the perp. This was done by taking many samples from spots nearby: samplars, they were called. If certain materials differed from these indigenous ones they might have come from the perp.

Shean's officers had collected hundreds of samplars at all the scenes for comparison.

"That was competent," Rhyme said. One of his more enthusiastic compliments. He then said, "And now, the cigarette ash."

Stanning asked, "We'd like to know if the samples of ash match."

"Yes, well, they wouldn't *match,* of course." He turned to the young woman. "*Matching* is when two or more items are identical," Rhyme muttered. "Very few things actually match. Friction ridge—fingerprints *and* footprints, of course. DNA and—going out on a limb—the lands and grooves on slugs and extractor marks on the brass. Tool marks under rare circumstances. But as for trace? I could make the argument about some substances *matching* by analyzing half-life but that's on a nuclear level."

He turned his wheelchair and faced Stanning. "Let's say you find cocaine that's been cut with eighteen percent baking soda and two percent baby powder, and you have another sample that's cut with exactly the same substances in those proportions. They don't match but they're *associated,* and a jury can infer they came from the same source. Of course, in our case, it's possible that somebody could smoke the same cigarette at two different locations, miles apart on different days. But the odds of that are rather low. Wouldn't you say?"

"I would. Definitely." Stanning looked as if she'd decided not to make any more comments.

"You get a lot of convictions when you testify, I'd imagine," Shean offered.

"Nearly one hundred percent," Rhyme said, with only a veneer of modesty. "Of course, if the odds aren't good up front I recommend not going to trial. Though I'm not above bluffing somebody into a confession. Now, I need to run an inductively coupled plasma test."

Shean said, "Mass spectrometry. Well, we can do that."

"I'm so pleased."

"But—well, just curious—why that, if you're analyzing ash?"

"For the metals, of course," Amelia Sachs pointed out.

The CSU head tapped his forehead. "Trace metals in cigarette ash. Brilliant. I never thought of that."

Rhyme said absently, "It's the most definitive way to determine the brand and origin of cigarettes when all you have is ash. I vastly prefer a fleck of tobacco itself too, because then you can factor in desiccation and other absorbed trace substances. That can pinpoint location of storage and time." He added a caveat, "Up to a point."

Shean prepared the sample and ran the test and a short time later they had their answer.

Looking over the computer screen, Rhyme offered, "Zinc 351.18, iron 2785.74 and chromium 5.59. No arsenic. Yep, that's Marlboro."

"You *know* that?" Harutyun asked.

A shrug—one of the few gestures the criminalist was capable of—and one that he used with some frequency.

He announced, "I'll say it's likely that the same person was at both scenes. But remember, Person A could have been at the first site, smoking a Marlboro. Person B could have bummed one off him and set up the trap at the Mountain View Motel. Not likely but it could be. How long for the DNA?"

"Another few days."

A grimace. "But it's not any better in New York, of course. I don't think you'll find any, though. Your perp is smart. He probably lit it by blowing on the tip, not holding it in his lips. So, does this Edwin Sharp smoke?"

"He used to," Dance said. "Still may sometimes but we don't know."

They couldn't draw any conclusions from the boot print—really just the toe. Sachs studied the electrostatic print. "Agree that it's probably a cowboy boot. Pretty common in New York a few years ago—line dancing was all the rage." She added that Rhyme had compiled a footwear database but the electrostatic image was too fuzzy to give them a brand name.

"All right, the fishing line . . . nothing there, I'm afraid. 'Generic' is a word I dislike very much. Let's look at the shell casings."

Shean reiterated that he thought the gun at both the Blanton shooting and the Sheri Towne attack was probably the same.

"You can say 'match,'" Rhyme said. "Won't bite you, in this context. But where did the gun come from? Stolen from one of your officers, you were saying?"

"Possibly—Gabriel Fuentes. He's been suspended."

"I heard."

"I wish we could tell. It might help incriminate Sharp. He was near Gabe's car when the gun was stolen. But we don't know for sure."

"No? Let me have the close-ups of the extractor

marks and scratches," Rhyme said. "And the ones of the lands and grooves on the slugs."

Shean placed them on a table for Rhyme to examine. "But we don't have known samples from Gabe's Glock. I asked him and—"

"I know you don't."

"Oh, right, otherwise we would have identified the gun."

"Exactly." Rhyme's brow furrowed as he examined the pictures. "Sachs?"

Dance recalled that though they were both romantic and professional partners, they tended to refer to each other by their last names. Which she found rather charming.

Sachs studied the pictures too. Apparently she knew exactly what he was interested in. "I'd say four thousand."

"Good," Rhyme announced. Then: "I need the serial number of Fuentes's gun."

A fast computer search revealed it. Rhyme glanced at the number. "Okay, the gun was made four years ago by our talented friends in Austria. Call this Fuentes and ask him when he got it and how often he fired it."

Harutyun made this call. He jotted notes and looked up. "You need anything else from Gabriel, Lincoln?"

"No. Not now. Maybe later. Don't let him wander too far from his mobile."

The answer was that he'd bought the weapon new—three years ago—and took it to the range twice a month or so. He would typically fire fifty rounds.

Rhyme gazed into the air over the local officers. "Fifty rounds, every two weeks, for three years means it's been fired about thirty-nine hundred times. From the pictures of the shells and the slugs, Sachs estimated they came from a gun that had been fired about four thousand times. Good eye." He glanced at her.

Sachs explained to the others, "The distension of the brass, cracks around the neck and the spread of the lands and grooves are typical of a gun fired with that frequency."

Shean was nodding as if memorizing this. "So it *is* Gabe's weapon."

"Most likely," Sachs said.

Rhyme called, "Microscope! Charlie, I need a 'scope."

"Well, the scanning electron—"

"No, no, no. Obviously that's not what I need. We're not at the molecular level. Optics, optics!"

"Oh, sure."

The man had a tech wheel over two heavy compound microscopes—one a biological, which illuminated translucent samples from beneath, and a metallurgic model, which shone light down on opaque samples. Shean was setting it up when Rhyme shooed him away. Using his right hand he prepared several slides from the trace and examined them one by one, using both of the scopes.

"And good job with the analysis of the trace, Charlie. Let me see the original printouts."

Shean called them up and Rhyme studied the screen and then some of the samples visually. Peering through the eyepieces, he was muttering to himself. Dance couldn't hear everything he said but caught an occasional, "Good, good . . . What the hell is that? Oh, bullshit . . . Hm, interesting . . . Good."

Rhyme set slides out and pointed. "Fungi database on that one and I need a fast reagent test on those."

A tech ran the reagent tests. But Charlie Shean said, "We don't exactly have a fungus database."

"Really?" Rhyme said. And gave the man a website, user name and pass code. In five minutes Shean was browsing through Rhyme's own database on molds and fungi, jotting notes.

Eyes on the chart, Rhyme said, " 'Harutyun.' Armenian."

The detective nodded. "Big community here in Fresno."

"I know."

And how *did* Rhyme know that? Dance wondered. But speculating about the criminalist's encyclopedic mind was useless. Some facts that even children knew he was completely ignorant of. Others, far more esoteric, were stored front and center. The key, she knew, was whether they had helped him analyze evidence or might help him do so in the future. She wouldn't have been surprised to learn that he didn't know the earth revolved around the sun.

Finally the results from the new tests were compiled and Rhyme reviewed them, as well as the results from the earlier analysis that Shean's techs had run. It was raw data only but no one was better at turning raw data into something useful than Lincoln Rhyme. "Now, outside Edwin's house. The fungus is often used in place of traditional toxic chemical pesticides and the mineral oil is also found in alternative pesticides.

"Also, at his house and at the convention center, the triglycerides . . . With that color temperature and melting point, I'd say it's neatsfoot oil. That's used for treating baseball gloves and leather sports equipment, equestrian tack and gunslings. Snipers buy a lot of it. Used to be made from cattle bones—'neat' is an old word for oxen or cow—but now it's made mostly from lard. Hence the triglycerides." He consulted the chart, frowning. "I don't know about the ammonium oxalate.

That's going to take more digging. But the limonite, goethite and calcite? It's gangue."

"What's that, 'gangue'?" O'Neil asked.

"It's by-product—generally unused materials produced in industrial operations. Those particular substances are often found in ore collection and processing. I also found the same materials in the trace at the public phone at Fresno College, where he called Kayleigh to announce one of the attacks.

"And something else here," Rhyme said with some excitement in his voice. He glanced at the evidence bags. "From the PA system control room, the phone *and* from behind Edwin's house: calcium powder? But it's not what you suggested, Charlie—medical or dietary supplement. It's bone dust."

"Well, couldn't people still take it like a supplement?"

Rhyme frowned. "Don't think they'd want to. I forgot to mention: it's human."

Chapter 54

THE BONE MATERIAL was quite minimal and to confirm the source would require a confocal laser scanning microscope, Rhyme explained, looking around the room as if one of these magical devices were nearby.

Charlie Shean said that while he was aware of the machine and had wanted to acquire one, the FMCSO could not, in fact, afford it.

"Well, I'm ninety-nine percent sure. The morphology of the particles and the geometry of the dust almost guarantee it's human. I'd be very surprised if it wasn't."

What they could do with that information, though, Rhyme wasn't positive. "Can't quite see how it fits into the big picture," he admitted. "Anybody among the cast of characters here have a job that might involve bone? Surgeon, dentist?"

"No."

"Undertaker?" Harutyun suggested.

"They don't do much bone work. I could see medical examiners, pathologists. Wait, Fresno College—where he made the call—does it have a medical school?"

"Yes," Harutyun reported.

"Ah, that could be it. Human skeletons in the classrooms and then procedures too, involving bone saws. Until we get more information, I think we'll go on the assumption that he picked up the bone dust at the school and then continued his surveillance at Edwin's."

O'Neil said, "At least we know that the person who was behind Edwin's house was the perp."

"So, that means it isn't him," Harutyun said.

"Unless," Dance pointed out, "Edwin himself was the source of the bone dust and he left the trace when he walked back to see who'd been spying on him."

"Exactly, Kathryn," Rhyme said.

Harutyun muttered, "That's the way this case's been going—he's guilty, he's innocent, guilty, innocent."

Rhyme wheeled back to the microscope. "Hm, still a few things I want to look at. Ammonium oxalate . . . Scotch?"

Crystal Stanning broke her vow of silence. "You . . . you found some traces of liquor?"

"No, no, I *want* some scotch."

"Oh, well, we don't actually have any in the sheriff's office."

"Really?" Rhyme sounded surprised.

"Lincoln," Thom said.

"I was simply asking." He returned to the microscope.

Dance and O'Neil looked over the chart, on which Sachs had highlighted Rhyme's deductions.

• Sunday. Robert Prescott homicide, convention center stage/orchestra pit/scaffolding
  —strip lamp
    —no matching friction ridge prints
    —no matching tool marks (unit removed by wing nuts)
  —fifty-foot power cord
    —no matching fingerprints
  —smoke detectors in pit, disabled
    —no matching fingerprints
    —smudges determined to be produced by latex gloves, brand unknown, not associated with gloves in Edwin Sharp's possession

—cardboard cartons moved from projected path of victim
  —no matching fingerprints
  —smudges determined to be produced by latex gloves, brand
    unknown, not associated with gloves in Edwin Sharp's
    possession
—unique trace from stage/orchestra pit/scaffolding
  —triglyceride fat (lard)
    —2700K color temperature (yellowish)
    —melting point: 40–55 degrees F
    —specific gravity: 0.91 at 40.0 C
    —**Determined likely to be neatsfoot oil, treatment for leather sports
      equipment, tack and gun slings**
—no footprints/vehicle tread marks

• Monday. Frederick Blanton homicide, gas station, near San
Joaquin River
  —two 9 mm shell casings
    —weapon possibly Det. Gabriel Fuentes's, no casings for
      comparison
      —Determined likely to be his weapon
    —no friction ridge prints
    —extractor marks match those found at Sheri Towne scene
  —one 9 mm slug recovered
    —lands and grooves match slugs from Sheri Towne scene
  —accelerant
    —Shell gasoline, 89 octane
    —gasoline container destroyed
    —no footprints/vehicle tread marks

• Monday. Frederick Blanton's residence, Fresno
  —no relevant friction ridge prints, footprints, vehicle tread marks

• Monday. Public phone in classroom building at Fresno College
  —No relevant friction ridge prints
  —unique trace collected
    —calcium powder
      —**Determined likely to be human bone dust**
    —chemicals: limonite, goethite and calcite.
      —**Determined likely to be gangue, ore collection and processing
        byproduct**
  —no footprints/vehicle tread marks

• Tuesday. Sheri Towne crime scene
  —cigarette ash
    —**Determined likely to be Marlboro**
  —twenty-three 9 mm shell casings
    —weapon possibly Gabriel Fuentes's, no casings for
      comparison
      —**Determined likely to be his weapon**
    —no friction ridge prints
    —extractor marks match those at gas station scene
  —seven 9 mm slugs recovered
    —lands and grooves match those at Frederick Blanton scene

—no friction ridge prints
—no footprints/vehicle tread marks

- Tuesday. Emerson High School stadium, PA system facility
  —no friction ridge prints
  —no footprints/vehicle tread marks
  —unique trace recovered
    —calcium powder
      —**Determined likely to be human bone dust**

- Tuesday. Park across from Mountain View Motel
  —Marlboro cigarette. DNA analysis requested
  —fishing line trip wire, generic brand
  —no friction ridge prints
  —no footprints/vehicle tread marks

- Wednesday. Edwin Sharp's house
  —outside:
    —boot print probably cowboy-style, unable to determine size,
      male or female
    —no vehicle tread marks
    —unique trace materials
      —triglyceride fat (lard)
        —2700K color temperature (yellowish)
        —melting point: 40–55 degrees F
        —specific gravity: 0.91 at 40.0 C
        —**Determined likely to be neatsfoot oil, treatment for leather
          sports equipment, tack and gun slings**
      —fungus
        —**Determined likely to be used in place of chemical-based fertil-
          izers**
      —chemicals: limonite, goethite and calcite
        —**Determined likely to be gangue, ore collection and processing
          by-product**
      —mineral oil, with lime sulfur
        —**Determined likely to be organic pesticide**
      —calcium powder
        —**Determined likely to be human bone dust**
      —ammonium oxalate
  —inside:
    —latex gloves, not associated with those at Prescott homicide
    —household cleaning materials (to eliminate trace?)
    —no cigarettes, matches or lighters, odor of cigarettes

It was then that Dance's mobile buzzed. She regarded the text with a frown. "I'll be right back," she told
the others.

She walked outside and into the parking lot of the
sheriff's office. She nearly laughed to see P. K. Madigan
undercover—he was now in khakis, a plaid shirt and tan

vest, the fishing cap and mirrored aviator sunglasses.

Dance smiled. "Hi, I—"

But Madigan interrupted and said urgently, "We've got a situation. I mean, *you*'ve got a situation."

"Go on."

"I've spent the last sixteen or so hours online, look-ing up everything I could find about Edwin, Kayleigh, fans . . . everything."

This was the assignment Dance had given P. K. Madigan, the job she'd described as "unpleasant," since it involved sitting at a desk, not the greatest job in the world for an active law enforcer like the chief detec-tive, who seemed to enjoy fieldwork, unlike a lot of his counterparts. But Dance believed it was important to continue to monitor Edwin's online activity, and to find any new posts and sites he visited. With their limited manpower, she'd enlisted Madigan.

"Where's Edwin now? He under surveillance?"

"He was. I'll check," Dance replied and placed a call. She posed the question to Dennis Harutyun, who was probably a bit mystified by Dance's disappearance. But he didn't query her; he just said, "Hold on." A moment later he came back on the line. She heard frustration in his voice. "This is odd. Edwin went to the mall—Fashion Fair on Shaw. Parked in the lot near East Santa Ana. The depu-ty thought Edwin'd lose him in the stores so he stayed with the car. That was two hours ago. He hasn't been back."

"He knew he was being tailed and he jumped."

"Probably."

"Okay. I'll be back in a few minutes."

After she disconnected she told this information to Madigan, who grimaced hard. "Hell." Then he asked, "You had any evidence suggesting he'd become violent?"

"No." Dance explained that she'd interviewed him, then added, "But people like that keep a tight lid on their emotions. Something can push them over the edge real fast."

"Well," Madigan said urgently, "I'm pretty worried about something. A half hour ago there were some postings on some of Kayleigh's fan sites. Anonymous, but they were sites where Edwin has posted in the past. The posts were the same, saying something to the effect of, 'Watch the news, Kayleigh. Maybe you'll finally understand how much I love you.'"

"John Hinckley."

"Yep. I remember what you told us in the first briefing."

That occasionally a stalker had a total break with reality and when he gave up hope that he'd be with his love, he'd kill someone to cement himself in her thoughts forever.

"Here's the URLs of those sites." Madigan handed her a sheet of yellow-lined paper. "Have Computer Crimes track 'em down and see where they were made from."

"Thanks, Chief."

"No," he said, offering a wan smile, "thank *you*, Deputy."

She returned to the office and handed Dennis Harutyun the sheet of paper. "What's this?" he asked.

Dance explained, without mentioning Madigan's name, about the threatening posts. "We need to trace them. Edwin's name doesn't appear but these're blogs and sites he posts to regularly."

"Where'd you get the sites?" Amelia Sachs asked.

"Just some outside research."

But Harutyun looked at the handwriting and frowned, perhaps recognizing it and deducing the source was his ousted boss. Still, he said nothing and called the office's computer crimes operation and ordered them to locate the posts and try to trace them.

Crystal Stanning went online and reviewed the posts. O'Neil said, "It may not be him. Kayleigh has to have other obsessive fans. We can't forget that."

But a moment later Harutyun's phone hummed. He looked down. "It's Computer Crimes." He took the call and listened for a moment. "Okay. Thanks." He disconnected and slipped the phone away. "The posting was from Java Hut."

Harutyun said, "At Fashion Fair. That's where Edwin is right now."

"Maybe he's still there," Amelia Sachs said and Harutyun called Dispatch to order deputies to the shopping center to find Edwin. He reminded them that he could be armed.

Stanning asked, "He's thinking of a mass shooting at the mall?"

Sachs said, "That could be it but the typical stalker killing profile is more one-on-one. An assassination."

"True," Dance said. "And it's usually somebody famous. So that he'll get the attention of his object."

"But who's the planned victim?" Harutyun wondered aloud.

O'Neil continued to read the posts. "They don't mention anybody in particular."

Dance joined him, arm against arm, and they stared at the posts.

"There, that one," Dance muttered, pointing. She read it aloud. " 'I've seen all your postings, about Kayleigh. You claim you like her, you claim you love her music. But you use her like everybody does, you stole Leaving Home to keep the hispanics happy. Your a fucking hypocrit.' "

Lincoln Rhyme asked, "You have any idea who he's talking about?"

"I know exactly who he means," Dance replied.

Chapter 55

"IT'LL BE ALL right, Congressman," Peter Simesky said.

Davis didn't need reassurance. He needed his family taken care of. He called Suze again and left another message for her to stay in the house with the kids. There was possibly a little security problem. Stay put, lock the door. Call me. Love you.

"Please have Jessie find my wife, Peter."

"I'll do that, sir. But there's no indication that this Sharp wants to hurt anybody but you. Besides, I don't think there's any way he could get to L.A. He was at a mall here in Fresno this morning, according to the police. And everybody's looking for him."

"He actually thinks I'm exploiting Kayleigh?"

"Using her—well, and that song, 'Leaving Home'—just to increase your Latino voter base."

"That's bullshit! I've been a huge supporter of hers all along. I've been posting on her site and the blogs for a couple of years. Before she even wrote the song."

Simesky reminded, "Oh, he's a psycho, Bill. Agent Dance said he has no sense of reality."

"She said he could be like Hinckley?"

"Could be."

"Jesus. They've got to find him. If he can't kill me maybe he'll just go on a rampage."

The men were in the Coronado, one of the nicer hotels in Fresno, and to Davis it seemed plenty secure, if you stayed away from the windows. But Davis's aides, Simesky and Myra Babbage, and the police thought he should move to a more secure location.

If it wasn't for his family's safety Davis would have been amused. He was extremely unpopular in certain circles and had been threatened a number of times for his positions on various issues. Just mention relaxing immigration laws at a cocktail party and see what happens; imagine the consequences when it's a campaign position of a potential presidential candidate. And yet here he was being threatened not by any rabid right-wingers but by a crazy guy who probably didn't even know what the word "immigration" meant.

A knock on the door. Davis stepped forward but the aide waved him back and called, "Yes?"

"Kathryn Dance and Deputy Harutyun are here," the campaign staff security man traveling with them, a massive fellow named Tim Raymond, called from outside.

Simesky opened the door and the two entered. The aide gave Dance a smile.

Davis had been amused at Simesky's flirting earlier with Dance, at Kayleigh Towne's house; there was no reason why a single man who was witty and charming shouldn't turn his attentions toward an attractive single woman about his same age. But at this meeting, they were both pure business.

"Congressman, Peter," Dance said.

Her green eyes quickly but calmly took in all the rooms, presumably for security threats, lingering briefly on the windows. Davis noted that she was now armed; she hadn't been before. This made him a bit more uneasy.

Simesky asked, "Where are we with all this? What do we know?"

Dance said, "We're still trying to find Edwin. Michael O'Neil—a deputy from Monterey—and the others are back at the sheriff's office working on that. He's vanished from the mall where he sent the website post. His car's still there but he could have other wheels. Until we have a better idea where he is, we want to get you to that safe house as soon as possible. Are you ready to leave now?"

"Sure. Where is it?"

Harutyun said, "A place we use about a half hour north of here, in the woods."

"Yes, all right." He grimaced. "I just don't want to be seen as running from this guy."

Simesky said, "We go through this a lot, Bill. People aren't going to care. They'd rather have a live candidate than a dead martyr."

"I suppose." Davis thought of something. Kathryn Dance was with a statewide agency so he said to her, "Could you get police to my house in L.A.? I'm worried about my family."

"Of course. I'll call our office and have a CBI team there, with tactical LAPD. We work with them a lot."

"Thank you," he said, feeling some relief, tepid though it was. He gave her the address and Susan's phone number.

Dance made the call and then disconnected. Officers, she said, were en route. Davis was all the more impressed with her for her cool efficiency and decided that, as Peter had suggested, she'd be perfect in his administration.

Then, thank you, Lord, his wife called. "Honey?" the woman blurted. "Jess came to the school. What's going on? Are you all right?"

"Yes, yes . . ." Davis explained the situation, adding that there would be some police or troopers at the house in just a minute or two. "There's a little security thing. Probably nothing. Don't open the door for anybody but the police. They'll be from the LAPD and the California Bureau of Investigation."

"What is it? Another threat from those isolationist idiots?"

"No, this is just a crazy guy, looks like. We're ninety-nine percent sure he's not down there but I just want to make sure you and the kids are all right."

"You're sounding too calm, Bill," Susan said. "I hate it when you sound that way. It means you're not calm at all."

He laughed. But she was right. He was too calm.

Dance tapped her wristwatch.

"I'm fine. I've got police here too. I have to go. I'll call you in a bit. Love you."

"Oh, honey."

He reluctantly disconnected.

Simesky called Davis's other aide, Myra Babbage, who was at the local campaign headquarters, and told her to join them at the safe house.

Then, with Dance and Harutyun leading and Tim Raymond in the rear, Davis and Simesky moved quickly through the hotel corridor and down into the garage, where they climbed into a sheriff's office Tahoe SUV.

Dance said to Harutyun, who was driving, "I'd say lights, no sirens for two or three miles. Bust it, really move . . . and use side streets and alleys. Then flashers off and normal stream of traffic to the safe house."

"Sure thing."

"You think he's nearby?" Simesky asked, looking out the windows uneasily.

"He's invisible," Dance said cryptically. "We just don't know."

As the big vehicle accelerated fast, the CBI agent

gripped the hand rest and looked queasy. Davis reflected that if she did join his administration she would not
do well on one of his speedboat outings.

On the other hand, he sensed she and Susan could
become good friends.

Ten minutes later, when it seemed clear that Edwin
was not following, they slowed and entered a highway.
After a half hour of driving, the deputy turned down a
deserted road, drove for another mile or so and, passing
no houses along the way, finally approached a fancy log
cabin. The one-story rambling brown structure was in
the middle of a large cleared area—good visibility of the
grounds, should anyone try to assault the house.

And there were also, Davis could see, only a few
windows and all of them shuttered or shaded. Although
he was perhaps more of a target than some politicians
anyone who's run for office instinctively considers security, particularly lines of fire and sniper's vantage points.
Everywhere. All the time.

Thank you, Second Amendment.

Chapter 56

KATHRYN DANCE GRATEFULLY climbed out of the SUV and inhaled the pleasant, astringent smell of pine.

The nausea from the rocky drive persisted but was fading.

She watched Harutyun approach the house and punch keys on a number pad and a green light came on. He stepped inside and deactivated another security system. Then he turned some switches and lights clicked on, revealing a functional interior, with no personality whatsoever: brown shag carpet that smelled of old automobile interiors, stained photographs in cheap plastic frames, Mediterranean-style lamps and furniture with excessive scrolls. A ski resort rental. The ancient Dodge smell was supplemented by that of musty upholstery, mold and cooking fuel.

All that was needed to complete the kitsch was a mounted bear or elk head.

The place was big. It appeared to have four or five bedrooms and several offices behind the living room and kitchen.

Dance exchanged mobile numbers with Tim Raymond, the security man, who remained outside. Harutyun shut the door and locked it. Then the mustachioed detective walked through the house to make sure it was secure. Simesky accompanied him.

A few minutes later Raymond called Dance and told her that everything seemed fine along the perimeter.

Dance looked around the austere facility and then at Davis, who now that his wife was protected seemed simply irritated that a security issue was taking time from his campaign and his congressional duties. He confirmed this a moment later when he muttered that he was due to meet workers at another farm soon but that clearly wasn't going to happen. He'd have Peter or Myra cancel for him. "Pisses me off, I have to say." He sat and rubbed his eyes with his knuckles, then scrolled through his iPhone.

Simesky and Harutyun returned. "All clear, windows and doors secure and armed," the deputy told them and passed out bottled water.

"Thanks." Davis drank one down.

Dance's phone hummed with an incoming email. Rather than read it on the small screen, she opened her computer and went online. She smiled at the header: *Bird Shit.*

The message was from Lincoln Rhyme and had to do with some additional analysis of the trace outside Edwin's house.

> Finally managed to isolate the other trace in the ammonium oxalate. They were phosphates and residue of animal matter. It's bird shit. Exactly what kind it is, I can't say. I didn't bring my bird shit recognition kit with me. Nor have I been able to gin up support for a bird shit genome project. But I can say the excreting birds were most likely resident in a coastal region. Fish had been the mainstay of their diet. For what it's worth. Here's the whole list. Don't understand why nobody drinks in this department.

He included the entire evidence chart and Dance read through it again, amused to note that when someone—Amelia Sachs, presumably—had added the recent discovery, she'd been a bit more delicate in her description.

- Wednesday. Edwin Sharp's house
  —outside:
    —boot print probably cowboy-style, unable to determine size, male or female
    —no vehicle tread marks
    —unique trace materials
      —triglyceride fat (lard)
        —2700K color temperature (yellowish)
        —melting point: 40–55 degrees F
        —specific gravity: 0.91 at 40.0C
        —**Determined likely to be neatsfoot oil, treatment for leather sports equipment, tack and gunslings**
      —fungus
        —**Determined likely to be used in place of chemical-based fertilizers**
      —chemicals: limonite, goethite and calcite
        —**Determined likely to be gangue, ore collection and processing by-product**
      —mineral oil, with lime sulfur
        —**Determined likely to be organic pesticide**
      —calcium powder
        —**Determined likely to be human bone dust**
      —ammonium oxalate
        —**Determined likely to be bird excrement, probably from coastal area**

She read through the list several times more.

And then:

A to B to Z . . .

Dance closed her eyes and let her mind wander where it would. Then she went to the website they'd looked at earlier, containing the threat to Davis. She scrolled through the posts.

Harutyun asked, "Anything helpful about where Edwin might be?"

"Maybe," she answered absently, lost in thought.

Simesky sighed. "Doesn't this guy know that if he killed the congressman, he'd get arrested and, in this state, probably end up on death row?"

Eyes still on her computer screen, Dance explained, "That doesn't matter to him. Not at all." A glance at Davis. "By killing you, he's honoring her."

The congressman laughed sourly. "So basically, I'm a sacrificial goat he's offering up to his goddess."

Which described the situation pretty well, Dance reflected and returned to the browser.

Chapter 57

PLAN YOUR ACTS and act your plan.

Peter Simesky's analytical mind continued to measure the actual milestones of his plan against the projected ones, and he found it proceeding apace. In general, the events were in harmony with what he and Myra Babbage had been working on for the past ten months.

He now stood in a den behind the living room, reviewing text messages on one of his many anonymous and untraceable accounts. He peeked out into the living room where the irritatingly smart Kathryn Dance, Congressman Davis and Deputy Dennis Harutyun sat, looking at—though probably not really watching—an old TV. Some game was on. Davis wasn't happy to be here but he didn't look particularly scared.

Simesky turned and walked into the kitchen in the back of the safe house.

The plan . . .

Whose goal was quite simple: to eliminate the traitor to America, Congressman William Garrett Davis, the politician who would sell the country out to people who didn't belong here, who used it for their own gain, who despised the red, white and blue but were happy to rob this glorious nation blind. How difficult it had been for Simesky to feign admiration and undying devotion to Davis and get a job on the staff, then work his way into the man's inner circle. He had, however, done a damn good job of it, spending more hours than virtually anyone else on Davis's team. He'd done whatever was necessary to ingratiate himself into the man's inner circle and gather as much information as he needed so they could stop the traitor, who—if elected president, as might very well happen—would ruin our great nation.

A little over a year ago, when Davis's popularity began to surge, Simesky was with a think tank based in Texas, with offices in Washington, New York, Chicago and L.A. It was part of an informal association of wealthy businessmen in the Midwest and South, who ran companies and nonprofits and even a few universities. This group of men—and yes, they were exclusively men and, by the way, white—had no official name but informally, and with some wry humor, they'd adopted one, which had been bestowed by some demonic liberal media blogger. The journalist had referred to the cabal contemptuously as the Keyholders, because, he reported, the senior leaders believed they held the key to curing all of the nation's woes.

The group loved it.

The Keyholders funneled huge sums to candidates they thought would best uphold proper ideals to keep America strong: reduced federal government, limited taxation, minimal participation in world geopolitics and, most important, the elimination of virtually all immigration. Curiously, the Keyholders had little patience for what they considered, in their opinion, unfocused and often simpleminded movements like the Tea Party, the religious right and those railing against abortion and homosexuality.

No, the main issues that mattered to the Keyholders were the death of American self-reliance through socialism and the dilution of the purity of the nation through immigration. Leaders like Bill Davis would drive the country straight to bankruptcy and moral corruption.

Generally, the Keyholders' efforts involved financial support for candidates, publicity, misinformation campaigns against traitorous politicos and reporters, personality smears and stings.

But sometimes more was needed.

And that's when Peter Simesky's obscure think tank would receive a call, asking him to handle a particularly critical matter.

However he thought best.

However extreme the solution.

The Keyholders knew that whatever the mission, Simesky would create an effective and careful plan, so it was obvious that the death of this muckraking liberal journalist had to be an accident, or of that environment activist was a suicide, or of that reformer congressman was an assassination spawned by a stalker's love for a famous singer.

And those clever plans often involved a fall guy.

Hello, Edwin.

Using the stalker came to mind last winter after he and Myra Babbage—his business partner and occasional lover—had infiltrated Davis's ranks. Doing his typically exhaustive research, Peter Simesky had learned that Davis was a huge fan of Kayleigh Towne. The congressman had used the bitch's pro-immigration song "Leaving Home" at rallies and in campaign ads.

Simesky reviewed Kayleigh's websites and learned of a fanatical fan named Edwin Sharp, who posted hundreds of comments about the singer and was described by other fans as a "weirdo."

Perfect.

The Keyholders had quite some significant resources and it took only a day to get into the Internet service providers handling Kayleigh Towne's and Edwin's email accounts. Unfortunately there didn't seem to be anything particularly threatening about Edwin's letters and posts. But he was clearly unhinged and troublingly persistent and that would be enough for Simesky's plan. He and Myra sent Edwin emails and letters posing as Kayleigh, reporting that she was flattered by his attention and even suggesting that she'd like to get together with him. But she had to be careful, put on a facade of indifference, or her father would cause terrible problems.

Delete all the emails, burn my letters. You have to, Edwin. I'm totally afraid of my father!

The notes suggested that, whatever she said in public, she'd enjoy seeing him at the concert on Friday. If possible she'd see him later too. In private.

Edwin, I was thinking about you last night. You know girls have those kinds of thoughts too. . . .

Myra Babbage had come up with those lines.

And Edwin had done just what they'd wanted, descended on Fresno in all his psychotic glory, far more of a nut job than they'd hoped.

He and Myra Babbage had conducted surveillance at Edwin's rental in Fresno to learn his routine and steal some evidence that could be planted at the site of Davis's assassination to implicate the stalker. Then, today, it was time to act. Myra had called Edwin, pretending to work for Kayleigh. She explained the singer had decided she wanted to see him but they had to be very careful. He should go to the Fashion Fair shopping mall and lose the police, then wait at Macy's loading dock.

Myra had cruised past and waved. The poor fool had jumped into the stolen SUV, grinning in anticipation. When he turned to put his seat belt on she'd hit him with the stun gun, injected a sedative and taped him up. She'd then gone into the mall and uploaded the announcement from Java Hut that someone was about to do something that would make Kayleigh remember him forever. The context made clear that Bill Davis was to be the victim.

And now, Myra and a barely conscious Edwin Sharp were en route to the safe house.

In a few minutes the plan would be completed: Myra would arrive, smile at the security man, Tim Raymond, and then blow him away with her pistol. At the same time Simesky would step into the living room and shoot the congressman and the others. Then he and Myra would drag Edwin into the room, shoot him in the head with Harutyun's gun and dust the stalker's hand with gunshot residue.

Simesky would make a panicked call begging for help and an ambulance, explaining that he'd gotten the gun away from the stalker and shot the psycho himself.

Plan your acts and act your plans . . .

But sometimes there were variations.

Kathryn Dance.

Her appearance could help smooth over one matter he'd been worried about—that there might be some suspicion if only he and Myra were left alive. If Dance survived too the scene would seem a bit more legitimate. Though he'd have to orchestrate it so that, of course, she couldn't see him as the shooter.

Simesky would shoot Dance in the back, paralyzing but not killing her, then he'd murder Davis and Harutyun. After they were dead, Simesky would call out something like, "Edwin, no! What are you doing?"

Ideally Dance would be conscious and she'd hear his cry. She'd later report the story to the police, confirming that Edwin was the sole shooter. If not, and she died, well, no huge loss.

After all, Simesky thought angrily, you could've gone out to dinner with me, bitch. What would it've hurt?

Chapter 58

SIMESKY GLANCED AT his Rolex.

Three minutes to go.

Myra Babbage would be heading toward the safe house now, moving up the drive. Easing closer to the living room, Simesky couldn't detect the sound of the tires because of the thick walls, but, over the noise of the game on TV, he could hear Dance saying, "What's that? You hear something? A car?"

"I think so. Wait, no, I'm not sure." The voice was Davis's.

Two shots in Kathryn's spine. Two in Harutyun's head. Two in Davis's.

What should Simesky shout? "My God, it's him! That stalker!" Was that credible? Maybe: "Edwin, Jesus, no!"

In the living room Davis's phone trilled. "Hello . . . Hi. Yeah, we're inside." Then, to the others: "It's Myra. She just got here."

Harutyun said, "You know, we didn't tell her to make sure she wasn't being followed."

Simesky thought he heard Dance say something to the effect that Edwin did a lot of research but it would be pretty unlikely that he even knew who Myra was, let alone been able to find and follow her.

Ah, if you only knew . . .

One minute, according to the Rolex.

Dance was saying, "No, Congressman, please stay back from the window."

"We know who it is."

"Still, let's just be on the safe side."

Out of sight in the den Simesky pulled on latex gloves, opened his computer bag and removed the pistol, a cold one—stolen. That was one thing about this great country; if you wanted an untraceable gun you could get one, real easy. He knew it was loaded and he knew exactly how it worked. And he'd already fired it a dozen times to extract some GSR, gunshot residue, now in a Baggie, which he'd plant on Edwin's hands. But he checked the weapon again.

Two shots, then two, then two.

"Peter?" the congressman called from the living room.

Simesky replied, "Be there in a sec. Anybody want coffee?"

"No thanks," Davis said absently. "Myra's here."

"Good."

"Kathryn, Dennis? Coffee?"

They both declined.

Simesky slipped closer to the doorway to the living room, pressing his back against the adjoining wall, staying well out of sight, waiting for Myra's gunshots, killing Raymond.

Harutyun said, "We had a real president stay here once. He'd come for a conference with the governor. Had to sign something so I wouldn't tell who it was."

"Can we play Twenty Questions to find out?" Dance asked.

The detective laughed.

Davis said, "I was at Camp David last week. It's not as fancy as you'd think."

Would those be his last words?

And what was Edwin Sharp thinking as he was enduring, though probably not enjoying, his final moments on earth?

"Hey, look, the game," Davis said. "Triple play!" The volume on the TV went up. Spectators roared.

A glance at the Rolex. Right about now Myra would shoot.

Simesky would step into the doorway and do the same.

Two.

Then two and two more.

Edwin, no! My God! . . .

He wiped his hand on his slacks and took the pistol again.

Now!

But no shots sounded.

Another minute passed, silence except for the televised crowd and baseball game announcer on the TV.

What was going on? Sweat on Simesky's brow.

And then at last: gunfire from outside.

A half dozen shots. The snapping clatter of a firefight, small arms.

Shit, Simesky thought. What's this about? He considered his plan and how the rattle of weapons might fit into it. Had there been another deputy on the scene who'd gotten here earlier? Or had a local cop happened by and noticed a woman with a weapon or a hog-tied Edwin Sharp?

Now, all was silent.

Act your plan . . .

Simesky, thinking: Sometimes you *couldn't,* though. Sometimes you needed to improvise. But to do that, you needed facts.

Only there were no facts.

He decided to go ahead anyway. The three in the

room would be focused on what was happening outside the windows, staying down, staying silent.

Two, two and two . . . Kill Raymond when he walked inside, if he was still alive. Then clean up as best he could. Too bad about Myra; he assumed she was gone.

But there were larger issues at stake.

Simesky gripped the gun firmly, slipped the safety lever forward and took a deep breath. He turned fast and stepped through the arched doorway into the living room, aiming at where Harutyun and Dance had been—the most immediate threats. He was adding poundage to the trigger, when he froze.

The room was empty.

The alarm pad was blinking green. Someone had disarmed the system so Davis, Dance and Harutyun could leave silently. What the hell was this? He walked further into the room. And then he saw the side window was up. That's how they'd escaped.

Simesky noticed too in the middle of the floor a pad of yellow paper. On it was scrawled a message: *Plot against your life Simesky involved Myra too Maybe others We leave NOW Side window NOW*

Oh, no . . .

Who? he thought.

But then realized: Why even ask? Kathryn Dance, of course.

A fucking liberal soccer mom from a small town had outthought him and the Keyholders.

How she'd done this was beyond a mystery to him. But she had. She'd probably texted for backup and alerted Raymond, who'd fired on Myra when she got out of the car and presented a threat.

And could—

He heard a man's voice from behind him, Dennis

Harutyun's. "Simesky, drop the weapon and raise your hands over your head."

The deputy would have snuck through the back door. Dance probably was covering the front.

Simesky assessed the situation. He reflected that Harutyun was a true rube; he'd probably never fired his weapon in the line of duty. Simesky, on the other hand, had killed eight people in his life and gone to bed each night afterward with a clear conscience.

He glanced back. "What are you talking about? I'm just trying to protect the congressman from that killer. I heard gunshots. I haven't done anything! Are you crazy?"

"I'm not going to tell you again. Drop the weapon."

Simesky was thinking, I have my Cayman Islands account. I have any one of the Keyholders' private jets at my disposal.

Just fight your way out. Turn and shoot. He'll be totally freaked out, he'll panic. Fucking small-town cop.

Simesky started to turn, keeping the gun low, unthreatening. "I just—"

He heard a stunning bang, felt a burn in his chest.

The sensations were repeated a moment later. But both the sound of the second explosion and the tap on his skin were much softer than the first.

Chapter 59

"BOTH DEAD?"

"That's right," Harutyun told Sheriff Anita Gonzalez.

Ten people were in her office at the FMCSO, which made it pretty cramped.

P. K. Madigan was back, though still unofficially, because it had, after all, been his information that had led to uncovering the plot.

Also present was a public affairs officer from the county. Dance noted that Harutyun seemed infinitely pleased at this—somebody else to handle the press conference. Which was going to be big. Very big.

Lincoln Rhyme, Thom Reston and Amelia Sachs were here too, along with Michael O'Neil and Tim Raymond, the congressman's own security man. In the interest of safety Congressman Davis was onboard his private jet, heading back to Los Angeles.

Anita Gonzalez asked, "Any other perps working with Simesky and Babbage?"

Dance replied, "I'm sure there are. But they are—well, *were*—the only active participants on the scene so far. Our office and Amy Grabe, the FBI's agent in charge in San Francisco, are tracing associates and connections."

Michael O'Neil said, "There seems to be some affiliation with that outfit they call the Keyholders. Some political action group."

"Political action? Hell, they're assholes," Madigan muttered, digging into his ice cream. "Wackos."

Lincoln Rhyme said, "But rich and well-connected wackos."

"Did either of them say anything before they died?" Gonzalez asked.

Tim Raymond said, "No. Myra was walking toward me when I got the text from Agent Dance to treat her like a hostile." He shrugged matter-of-factly. "I lifted my weapon when she was about thirty feet away. She was hiding a forty-five under her coat and she engaged. Afraid I couldn't take any chances." He was shaken but not, Dance assessed, from the shootout; rather by the fact that he'd missed the threat posed by the assassins— who had also been masquerading as his friends and co-workers.

Harutyun said, "And Simesky didn't seem to believe me when I said, 'I'm not telling you again.'" He was as calm as ever, displaying no effects whatsoever from killing the congressman's aide.

"And Edwin?" the sheriff asked.

"We found him in the back of the SUV Myra stole. The stun gun that she used was pretty powerful and he's doped up. But the medics said he's fine."

"How'd you figure it out, Kathryn?" Madigan asked.

"It wasn't just me." She nodded toward Lincoln Rhyme and Amelia Sachs.

The criminalist said offhandedly, "Combination of things. Your man Charlie, by the way, is pretty good. Don't let him come visit me in New York. I might steal him away."

"He's done that before," Thom Reston said, earning a raised eyebrow from Rhyme, which told Dance that he was quite serious about offering Shean a job.

Since the criminalist wasn't explaining his contribution further, Dance did. "There were some questions raised about what Charlie's crime scene people found at the convention center and behind Edwin's house, where he claimed somebody'd been spying on him."

"Yeah, Edwin told me," Madigan said with a grim visage. "And I didn't believe him."

Dance continued, "One was bird droppings from seagulls."

Rhyme corrected, "The actual phrase was shit from, quote, 'birds most likely resident in a coastal region.' Not indigenous, mind you. I had no idea where they came from or where they were going. My only point was that the birds in question probably spent time recently on the coast dining on oceanic fish. And then we also identified some oil and fungus used in organic farming." A nod toward Sachs. "She has a pretty decent garden, by the way. I don't get the point of flowers myself but the tomatoes she grows are quite good."

Dance elaborated, "I remembered that Congressman Davis, Simesky and Babbage had been in Monterey campaigning, which is on the coast, where they might've picked up the bird-do trace. And they'd been stumping in ecofriendly organic farms from Watsonville to the Valley here."

"But why'd you get suspicious enough to consider that maybe Edwin wasn't the killer in the first place?" Madigan asked.

Dance laughed. "Bird shit again, in a way. See, in the header, Lincoln wrote just that. 'Bird shit.' But in the evidence chart he sent me he used the word 'excrement.'"

"That was Sachs," Rhyme grumbled.

"Well, that made me think of the website post threatening the congressman. I realized it just didn't sound like Edwin."

"The kinesics of language," O'Neil said.

"Exactly."

She showed them the post that had raised some alarms.

I've seen all your postings, about Kayleigh. You claim you like her, you claim you love her music. But you use her like everybody does, you stole Leaving Home to keep the hispanics happy. Your a fucking hypocrit. . . .

"That's not Edwin's tone. I've never heard him say or write an expletive. And there're grammatical mistakes: commas that weren't necessary and the misspelling of 'hypocrite' and 'you're,' which he never did in his emails to Kayleigh. Oh, and in his emails when he referred to one of her songs, he put the title in quotation marks. In the post that threatened Congressman Davis, the title wasn't set off at all. It struck me that it could have been written by somebody who *thought* that's what a crazy stalker would post.

"Then there were some questions that came up during my interview with Edwin." She explained about using content-based analysis in looking at what Edwin had said, rather than kinesics and body language. "Since I couldn't use traditional kinesic analysis I looked at the facts he was telling me. And some of them were inconsistent. Like the number of letters and emails Edwin received from Kayleigh. She and her lawyers said Edwin was sent a half dozen replies—all form emails or snail-mail letters. But in the interview Edwin told me he'd received more than that . . . and he suggested to Pike that he'd found them very encouraging.

"I thought at first that was a product of his problems with reality awareness. But then I realized this was different. See, stalkers may misinterpret the *implications* of facts but they'll know what those facts *are*. However Edwin misconstrued Kayleigh's message in the letters, he'd know for certain exactly how many letters he received. Did that mean somebody else, posing as Kayleigh, had been sending him emails and letters?

"And then"—she delivered this with a wry smile at Michael O'Neil—"I wondered why was Peter Simesky so interested in me? He said the congressman wanted to bring me on board and maybe he did. But I think Simesky put that in Davis's head. It gave Simesky a chance to see how we were coming with the investigation and what we knew. Myra also seemed very interested in who I worked for. And the two of them, and Davis, had flown into San Francisco the other day; they might've bought the prepaid mobiles in Burlingame then. It's near the airport."

Madigan muttered, "So they killed Bobby and the file sharer to establish the pattern of Edwin's guilt."

"As tough as it is to consider that," Dance said, "yeah. I think that's the only reason they died." She glanced Rhyme's way. "After I got your text in the safe house about the bird excrement, I got suspicious about people close to Davis. I emailed my associate, TJ Scanlon, to run deep background checks on everyone on Davis's staff. Everybody was clean—but Simesky and Myra were too clean. They were perfect models of political aides, textbook. And they'd joined the campaign on the same day. And it was impossible to find out anything about them before they joined. TJ thought that was odd and kept digging and found some connection with the Keyholders group—who were on record as condemning many of Davis's positions but were especially vehement about his stand on easier immigration.

"I decided to play it safe and we got out through the side window of the safe house just as Myra arrived and engaged Tim." A nod toward Raymond. "We know what happened next."

P. K. Madigan pointed his spoon at the man in the wheelchair. "You sure you don't want any ice cream?"

"Not my vice of choice," the criminalist said.

Crystal Stanning walked into the sheriff's office. "We just found the good Samaritan."

"Who?" Madigan asked in blunt impatience. Apparently forgetting he was a civilian.

"The woman who gave Edwin directions when he got lost."

Ah, Alibi Woman.

"Edwin was right. It was at the same time Sheri Towne was attacked. And she positively identified him."

Madigan sighed. "Well, we got this one wrong, boys and girls. Get Sharp in here. I for one am going to apologize."

A moment later Edwin was escorted into the office and he looked around a little bewildered. His hair was askew. He seemed a bit dizzy, though he was fascinated with Rhyme and the wheelchair.

Gonzalez explained what had happened—which included the revelation that most of the emails he'd received from Kayleigh were fake, not from her at all.

Dance noted his face fall. "She didn't send them?"

Thick silence for a moment and Dance said, "She sent a few but, I'm sorry, Edwin, the ones actually from her were just form letters. Like she sent to everybody."

Edwin slipped his hands into his jeans pockets. "I never would've gotten so . . . you know, funny about her, if I knew. Think about it, somebody as pretty and talented and famous as her tells you she's interested in you, that you mean a lot to her . . . what was I supposed to think?"

"I understand, Edwin," Dance said kindly.

Madigan said, "I'm sorry too, son."

Edwin said nothing for a moment, eyes again on the wheelchair. "So, I'm not a suspect or anything?"

"Nope," Harutyun said.

He nodded and then focused on Madigan. "Well, then, I don't have much interest in that complaint I made against you, Detective. And Deputy Lopez. I was just doing what I needed to. It was like self-defense, you understand."

"I do, and that's good of you, Edwin. Fact is, when it comes to Kayleigh, we all get a little overly enthusiastic."

"I'd kind of like to leave now. Is that okay?"

"Sure is, son. We'll get a statement from you later or tomorrow about what happened with Simesky and the woman—the kidnapping. I'll have somebody get you home now. You're in no shape to drive. You can pick up your car tomorrow."

"Thanks, Detective." Shoulders down, chest collapsed, he headed out the door. Despite the fact he was hard to read kinesically, Dance could see genuine sorrow in his posture.

Chapter 60

IN THE SERVICE area of the sheriff's office Lincoln Rhyme aimed for the ramp leading outside. He was accompanied by his New York companions, as well as Kathryn Dance and Michael O'Neil. "Time for a drink, I'd say, then back to San Jose."

"Time for coffee in the van," Thom corrected, his boss.

"*I'm* not driving," Rhyme replied acerbically. "*I* can drink."

"But," his aide countered fast, "I'm sure it's illegal to have open containers of liquor in a moving vehicle, even if you're not driving."

"It's not open," Rhyme snapped. "My tumbler has a lid on it."

The aide said thoughtfully, "We could of course stay here talking but that just means we'll get to the bar in San Jose that much later."

Rhyme scoffed but the expression vanished as he said good-bye to the law enforcers and, with a smooth gesture, lifted his working right arm to Dance and gripped her hand. She kissed his cheek, then embraced Sachs.

O'Neil added, "I'll see you both Sunday. I'm bringing the kids over." He glanced at Sachs. "You're interested, we just got the new H&K MP7."

"The little bullet."

"Right. Smaller than a BB, seventeen-caliber. You want to come out to the range and put some holes in paper on Monday?"

"You bet I do," Sachs said enthusiastically.

"Kathryn?" O'Neil asked.

"I'll pass, I think. I'll hang out with Lincoln and Thom."

And with Jon Boling too? she wondered, then stepped on that thought.

The trio from New York headed out the door.

O'Neil too said good-bye to the locals, and Dance walked with him outside into the sultry air.

"You in a hurry to get back?" she found herself asking. Hadn't planned it. She was thinking they might have dinner, just the two of them.

A pause. She could tell he too wanted to stay. But then he shook his head. "Thing is, Anne's driving down from San Francisco, picking up some things. I ought to be there." He looked away. "And the papers'll be ready tomorrow, the settlement agreement."

"So soon?"

"She didn't want much."

Also, a woman who cheats on her husband and abandons her children probably isn't in much of a position to demand much, Dance reflected. "You doing okay?" One of those pointless questions that's usually more about the asker than the askee.

"Relieved, sad, pissed off, worried about the kids." As lengthy a discussion of his emotional health as she'd ever heard from Michael O'Neil.

Silence for a moment.

Then he gave a smile. "Okay, better go."

But before he turned Dance found herself impulsively reaching up, one hand behind his neck, her arm around his back, and pulling him close. She kissed him hard on the mouth.

She thought, No, no, what the hell are you doing? Step back.

Yet by then his arms were enveloping her completely and he was kissing her back, just as firmly.

Then finally, he eased away. Came in for one more kiss and she gripped him even harder and then stood back.

She expected an oblique glance—his waiting state—but O'Neil stared easily into her eyes and she looked back just as comfortably. Their smiles matched.

Brother, what have I done now?

Kissed the man I truly love, she thought. And that unexpected thought was more stunning than the contact itself.

Then he was in the car. "I'll call you when I get back. See you on Sunday."

"Drive carefully," she said. A phrase that had set her on edge when her parents would tell teenage Kathryn the same. As if, oh, right, I was going to drive off the road until you reminded me.

But as a woman who'd lost one husband to the highway, it was a sentence she could not stop herself from uttering occasionally. He closed the door, glanced at her again and lifted his left palm to the inside windshield and she pressed her right to the glass outside.

He put the car in gear and pulled out of the lot.

"IF THAT DON'T beat all," Bishop Towne said, sipping his milk.

"Right," Dance said to him and his daughter, on the front porch of his house. "Edwin was innocent. Didn't kill a soul. Totally set up."

"He's still a shit."

"Daddy."

"He's a little fucking shit and I wouldn't mind if he went to jail for something. But it's good to know he's not going to be a problem anymore." The grizzled musician squinted at Dance. "He's *not,* is he?"

"I don't think so. He's mostly sad that Kayleigh didn't send him those personal emails and letters, the ones Simesky made up."

"We should sue those bastards," Bishop said. "The Keyholders? The fuck are they about?"

"Daddy, really. Come on." Kayleigh nodded toward the kitchen, where Suellyn and Mary-Gordon were helping Sheri bake something fragrant with vanilla. But the man's raspy voice probably hadn't carried inside.

Kayleigh said, "I'm not going to sue anybody, Daddy. We don't need that kind of publicity."

"Well, we're going to get publicity whether we want it or not. I'll talk to Sher about spinning it." Then he patted his daughter on the shoulder. "Hey, lookit the good news, KT. The bad guys're dead and Edwin's out of the picture. So, no more talk about canceling any concerts. Speaking of that, I've been working on the song order again and I think we've got to move 'Leaving Home.' Everybody wants it. Encore'd be best. And I'd get the kids' choir to sing the last part in Spanish."

Dance was aware that Kayleigh's shoulders had risen in tension at these comments. Clearly she herself still wasn't so sure about the concert. Just because the killers had been stopped and Edwin absolved didn't mean she was in the mental state necessary to put on a show in the shadow of the recent crimes.

And then Dance noticed the young woman's posture collapse subtly. Which meant surrender.

"Sure, Daddy. Sure."

The tone of the evening had changed quickly but,

oblivious to it, Bishop Towne rose like a buffalo climbing out of a stream he'd just forded and ambled inside. "Hey, M-G, whatcha baking?"

Kayleigh looked after him, grim-faced. Dance used the opportunity to fish into her purse and hand her the sealed envelope that contained Bobby's in-the-event-of letter and a copy of the adoption papers. The singer weighed it in her hand. Dance said softly, "That turned up in the investigation. I'm the only one who knows. You handle it however you want."

"What—?"

"You'll see."

The woman stared down at the slim envelope, clutching it as if it weighed ten pounds. Dance realized that she knew what it contained. "You have to understand. I just . . ."

Dance hugged her. "It's not my business," she whispered. "Now, I'm going to get back to the motel. I've got a report to dictate."

Kayleigh slipped the envelope into her pocket, thanked Dance for all she'd done and went into the house.

Dance walked down to her SUV. She happened to glance back into the house and could see a bit of the kitchen, Suellyn and Sheri at the island, looking at a cookbook. Kayleigh scooted up onto a stool nearby, lifted Mary-Gordon to her lap. No kinesic analysis was necessary to tell from the girl's amused squirming that the embrace was particularly strong.

Driving down the lengthy, dim driveway, Dance was thinking not of the Towne clan but of the potential train wreck her personal life might be headed for. She thought back to kissing O'Neil and felt a twisting in her belly—radiating a perfect balance of joy and alarm.

She scrolled through her iPod playlist on the SUV's

entertainment screen to find the song that had just come to mind, one of Kayleigh's, not surprisingly. "Is It Love, Is It Less?" The lyrics rolled out through the Pathfinder's resonant sound system.

> *Is it left, is it right? Is it east, is it west?*
> *Is it day, is it night? Is it good or the best?*
> *I'm looking for answers, I'm looking for clues.*
> *There has to be something to tell me the truth.*
> *I'm trying to know, but I can just guess,*
> *Is it love between us?*
> *Is it love, is it less?*

Thursday

Chapter 61

"GRACIAS, SEÑORA DANCE."

"De nada."

In the garage of Jose Villalobos, Dance clicked off the digital recorder and began to pack away the cables and the microphones. She'd spent the day not as a law enforcement agent but as a recording engineer and producer, and Los Trabajadores had just finished the last tune—a *son huasteco,* in the traditional style of music from northeastern Mexico, featuring a resonant eight-stringed instrument like a guitar, a *jarana,* and a fiddle. The violinist, a wiry forty-year-old originally from Juarez, had played up a storm, even slipping into Sté-phane Grappelli Hot Club de France improvs.

Dance had been delighted at the bizarre, captivating journey of the music and had to force herself to keep from clapping time to the speedy, infectious tunes.

Now, just after 5:00 P.M., she shared Tecates with the band and then wandered back to the Pathfinder. Her phone hummed and she saw Madigan's text, asking if she would come in and review the transcript of her report about the Peter Simesky–Myra Babbage case, which she'd dictated last night.

She debated a moment—she was exhausted—but decided to get it over with. Scrolling through her iPhone she saw a missed call too.

Jon Boling.

She debated again about the "San Diego Situation," as she'd taken to calling it. And the first thing in her thoughts was the kiss with Michael O'Neil.

I can't call Jon, her mind told her.

As her finger hit REDIAL.

A trill of numbers. Then . . . voicemail.

Disappointed, angry and relieved, she disconnected without leaving a message, thinking that would be a good title for a Kayleigh Towne song: "Straight to Voicemail."

A half hour later she arrived at the sheriff's office. She was now an official honorary deputy and she strode past the desk sergeant and security without any challenges. Several law enforcers she hadn't met waved friendly greetings to her.

She stepped into Madigan's office. The chief detective had been officially reinstated; Edwin had dropped the charges.

"Don't you ever do sprinkles?" she asked, sitting down on the battered couch, eyeing the cardboard cup he was enthusiastically excavating.

"What?" Madigan asked.

"On your ice cream? Or whipped cream or syrup?"

"Naw, it's a waste of taste. Calories too. Like cones. I'll give you my theory of ice cream sometime. It's philosophical. You ever make it?"

"Make ice cream?"

"Right."

She said, "The world is divided into people who make ice cream and yogurt and pasta and bread. And those who buy it. I'm a buyer."

"I'm with you there. This's yours."

He produced another cup. Chocolate chip. A metal spoon too.

"No, I—"

"You say no too quick, Deputy," Madigan grumbled. "You want some ice cream. I know you do."

True. She took it and ate several big mouthfuls. It was nice and melty. "Good."

"Course it's good. It's ice cream. There's the state-ment, you want to take a look-see and let me know what you think." He slid the papers toward her and she read.

Crystal Stanning had transcribed it from Dance's tape and it was pretty accurate. She expanded on a thought or two. Then slid it back.

Even at this hour the San Joaquin Valley heat per-meated the building. *Hell, I'm going to Macy's, pick up a one-piece and float in the Mountain View pool until I wrinkle.* Dance stretched and stood up, about to say good night to the detective when his desk phone rang and he hit SPEAKER. "Yeah?"

Dance finished the ice cream. Thought about asking for some more, but decided against it.

Course it's good. It's ice cream. . . .

"Hey, Chief, it's Miguel. Lopez."

"You worked for me for four years. I know your voice," the man snapped, examining the volcano core of his own cup, maybe tallying up how many bites he had left. "What?"

"Something kind of funny."

"You gonna tell me what or just let that hang?"

"You listen to KDHT?"

"The radio? Sometimes. Get to the point. What's your point?"

The deputy said, "Well, okay. I was listening on my way home and there's a call-in show. 'Bevo in the Eve-ning.'"

"Lopez!"

"Okay, so he's the DJ and they do requests. What

happens about five minutes ago is some listener requests a song. I mean, *part* of a song. One of Kayleigh's."

Dance froze. She sat down. Madigan barked, "And?"

"The request was in an email. Signed, 'A Kayleigh fan.' It was for 'Your Shadow.' The last verse only. The DJ thought it was kind of funny, just the one verse, and played the whole song. But I got to thinking—"

"Oh, Christ," Dance whispered. "Nobody ever played the fourth verse—to announce Congressman Davis's killing!" She thought of Lincoln Rhyme's comment: *And he's smart, right? He started with phones to keep you busy, then switched to other ways to play the song, like radio call-in requests?* . . .

"Shit." Madigan was nodding. He asked Lopez if the email had said anything else.

"No. Just that."

Madigan disconnected without saying good-bye. He immediately called the station and got put through to the studio, told Bevo it was police business and asked that the email be forwarded to him. As they waited, he muttered, "And, hell, you know, we're still looking for the connection between Simesky and Myra Babbage and the other killings—Bobby and Blanton, that file sharer, the attack on Sheri Towne. But nobody's found anything yet."

A moment later a flag popped up on his computer screen. The email request to the studio from a cryptic account, of random letters and numbers, was nothing more than what Lopez had already told them. Madigan called the Computer Crimes Division and forwarded it. A few minutes later they learned that it was an anonymous free email account and had been sent from a hotel in the Tower District.

"Let's get the list of guests staying there," Madigan said.

But Dance frowned. "Won't do us any good. He won't be a guest. He would've just picked up the wireless signal in the lobby, or even from the parking lot. Probably he's got some connection with the area. But not the hotel."

"You think that the assassination plot was just a coincidence? And there really *is* a stalker?"

"Well, we know it can't be Edwin. He has an alibi. And it doesn't need to be a stalker. It could be *anybody*, trying to frame Edwin to cover up the attacks—of Bobby, the file sharer or Sheri Towne. . . ." She shook her head. "Or maybe those were just to establish a pattern . . . and the real intended victim's *next* on his list."

"Shit. How'd we miss this? . . . But who's the new vic? What's the fourth verse?"

Dance recited,

> You can't keep down smiles; happiness floats.
> But trouble can find us in the heart of our homes.
> Life never seems to go quite right,
> You can't watch your back from morning to night.

Madigan sighed. "Kill somebody in their home. That's like the other verse, about the road—not very fucking helpful."

"There's the reference to 'floating.' Another river, pool, some other body of water?"

"I don't have a clue. We've got a dozen lakes around here, nothing big close to town, though. Hundreds of miles of riverbanks. And must be a thousand pools. More."

"Okay, maybe there's some connection with the Tower District. But we've got to narrow it down more." Dance thought for a moment. "You know, there was some physical evidence that Charlie's people found that we never really looked at, because we had enough to figure out what Simesky and Myra were up to."

Madigan called Charlie Shean, at CSU, had a conversation with him and jotted notes. After hanging up he said, "What wasn't accounted for was gangue . . . industrial by-product stuff, or whatever it is. Never heard of that before. Human bone dust too. And Marlboros. Did Simesky or Myra smoke?"

"I never saw them."

The chief glanced at his notes. "Also the boot print, with the really sharp toe. And some neatsfoot oil—leather treatment for baseball gloves. Maybe the dearly departed Peter Simesky played on a fascist softball league."

A to B to Z . . .

Dance cocked her head. "That's not all it's used for."

Chapter 62

FINALLY, KAYLEIGH TOWNE was back in her own house, her sanctuary.

If only for a few hours. Alicia had texted that she wanted to see her about some matters having to do with the concert but she didn't want to meet her at Bishop's house.

I hear you there, sister. And when Alicia suggested they meet at Kayleigh's she readily agreed. Darthur Morgan had driven her back here and then he'd collected his own car and said good-bye.

"Tell you, ma'am: been real good working with you."

"Still 'ma'am,' after all we've been through?"

"That's right, Kayleigh ma'am." And he'd cracked what she believed was his first smile.

She laughed and hugged him, which he responded to stiffly but with good humor.

Then he'd driven away and Kayleigh was alone. But the relief she felt because Edwin wasn't really a dangerous stalker was fading and ill ease seeped in to replace it—which had nothing to do with the events of the past few days and those horrible people using her as an excuse to kill the congressman.

No, it was a discomfort that struck closer to home.

Hey, lookit the good news, KT. The bad guys're dead and Edwin's out of the picture. So, no more talk about canceling any concerts. . . .

Why hadn't she said no to her father? Just *insisted* that they cancel? Didn't he get that danger wasn't the reason she didn't want to go ahead with the concert? It wasn't even that Bobby was dead, that Sheri'd nearly died. . . . She just plain and simple didn't want to get up onstage.

I'm not Superwoman, Daddy.

Your goals aren't my goals.

Why was he so oblivious to that? The whole Industry was a huge bulldozer, pushing forward, forward, and if somebody got crushed—Bobby's life, Kayleigh's joy—so what? It was unstoppable.

No, of course Bishop Towne didn't get that. All he got was that Kayleigh had to make money, had to feed her staff and family, had to feed the voracious fans, had to keep the record label and promoters happy.

And, she suspected, keep the memory of Bishop Towne alive—even among younger people who'd never heard him sing, hell, never heard of him at all.

And screw his daughter's own peace of mind.

Screw what mattered most to her, just having a simple life.

Hm, she reflected. "A Simple Life." Not a bad song title. She wrote it down, a few other phrases. Then she glanced at her watch. Alicia wasn't due for another half hour. Kayleigh walked upstairs to her bedroom.

Through her mind went a verse from the now infamous "Your Shadow."

> You sit by the river, wondering what you got
> wrong,
> How many chances you've missed all along.
> Like your troubles had somehow turned you to
> stone
> And the water was whispering, why don't you come
> home?

Oh, what a time that had been, just sixteen, missing her mother so terribly, missing her baby, her father, just out of jail for the car accident, pressuring her to appear at some of his shows and launch her own career, which she wasn't even sure she wanted. Overwhelmed, depressed. She'd driven to Yosemite by herself, gone hiking. And suddenly everything was too much for her. She'd looked down at the clear river and walked into it, on impulse. No plans, not really intending to hurt herself—or maybe she had been. Kayleigh didn't know then and she didn't know now. A minute later another hiker had plucked her out and sped her to the hospital. She was in danger more of hypothermia than drowning but not even much threat of that.

Now Kayleigh sat on the bed and read once more the copy of Bobby's letter, which expressed his desire that most everything he had go to Mary-Gordon, a few things to Kayleigh. She didn't know if this was legal as a will but if she took it to a lawyer she supposed the news would become public about Mary-Gordon's parentage.

Bishop would explode. And the fans? Would they desert her? Kayleigh could honestly say that she didn't much care about either of those happening, not in her present frame of mind.

But there was also a chance that the girl herself would find out. She'd have to learn at some point, of course. But not now, at this age. Suellyn was her mother and Roberto her father. Kayleigh would never think about disrupting the girl's life. She slipped the envelope away in her top dresser drawer. She'd work out something to make sure the girl received what her biological father wanted her to have.

Yes, it was too late for Kayleigh when it came to Bobby and Mary-Gordon. But it wasn't too late for the life she dreamed of. Find a man, get married, have lots of other babies, play music on the front porch—a few concerts now and then.

Of course there was that little part about "finding a man."

Since Bobby, there'd been no one she felt really intense about. She'd been only sixteen then but she decided that the yardstick of love at that age was the best standard you could have, the purest, the most honest, the least complicated.

A single note in her mind's ear. A C sharp followed by five other notes, and they carried a phrase, "How I Felt at Sixteen."

She sang it.

Good meter and there was a lot that rhymed with "sixteen." That was a key consideration in writing music. What rhymed with what. "Orange," for instance, was not a word you ended lyric lines with. "Silver" was tricky too, though Kayleigh'd managed to work it into one of the songs on her recent album.

She sat down at the dressing table she used for her desk here in the bedroom. She pulled out a yellow pad and a few sheets of music staff paper. In three minutes she'd written the melody and a number of phrases and portions of the song.

I still recall how I felt at sixteen.
You were a king and I was your queen
Love was so simple, way back when,
I wish life could be like that again. . . .
When I was sixteen . . .

Oh, Bobby . . .

Kayleigh cried for a full five minutes. Then grabbed some more tissues and dried her face; she'd used nearly two whole boxes this week.

Okay, enough of that. . . .

She cranked up the Bose iPod player, tapped the Lo-retta Lynn playlist.

In the bathroom, she filled the bathtub, pinned her hair up and stripped, then sank into the deep water, listening to the album.

It felt wonderful.

Chapter 63

THEY HAD THEIR answer.

Dance, Dennis Harutyun and Pike Madigan were in the tiny apartment of Alicia Sessions, and they were surveying the evidence they'd just uncovered. Cowboy boots, with needle-sharp toes, like those that made the prints behind Edwin's house. And in the kitchen was neatsfoot oil for treating Alicia's equestrian tack; Dance recalled her quarter horse bumper sticker and her love of riding. They found cartons of Marlboros in her apartment. The dwelling also was in the Tower District, near the hotel from which the email request for the fourth song had been sent.

But far more incriminating were the two garbage bags full of Edwin Sharp's trash stolen from his house in Fresno, including receipts and some mail addressed to him in Seattle—to plant at Kayleigh's, to convince the police and jury that Edwin was the one behind the attacks and that he had killed Kayleigh. And hidden under Alicia's bed was Deputy Gabriel Fuentes's pistol case—without the weapon—stolen from near the theater when the cop was tailing Edwin.

"Alicia knew where Gabriel was," Dance had reminded them. "She was in the briefing at headquarters."

At first they'd been unable to come up with a motive for setting up Edwin Sharp. But a moment ago Dance had learned the answer. To Madigan and Harutyun, she was displaying two dozen sheets of paper, all pretty much the same—attempts to forge Kayleigh's handwriting on a note that read:

> *To who it may concern*
> *Just want to say a few things to the people close to me if anything happens to me on the road . . . Can't help but thinking about Patsy Cline in that airplane. . . . Well, if anything does, I'd like Alicia to take over as front for the band. She knows the songs as good as me and can hit those high notes better. And one more thing, I want you to have one hell of a party and make sure she sings "I'm in the Mood (for Rock 'n' Roll)," which she inspired me to write.*
> *I see you in heaven, luv you all!*
> *Kayleigh*

"Jesus," Madigan muttered, "Kayleigh's the fourth victim. The last verse. 'Trouble can find us in the heart of our homes.' Alicia's going to kill her in her house."

Dance ripped her phone from the holster and punched in the singer's number.

I SHOULD WRITE a song about things like this, Kayleigh thought, thoroughly enjoying the bath, the soundtrack of Loretta Lynn, the violet scent of the candle she'd lit.

"The small pleasures," she sang. No. "The little pleasures." Scans better. The extra syllable helped.

It would be about how the tragedies in life, the

things we can't control, are often diminished, if not can-
celed, by the small things.

"An antidote to pain."

Nice line, she thought. Nobody'd ever used "antidote" in a song that she knew of. Good. But then . . .
wait. Hold on. You don't have to write a song every five
minutes.

But she didn't actually *write* them. She never did.
That was the secret. They wrote themselves.

In the other room she heard her phone ringing. Kayleigh debated. Ignore it. Four rings, then voicemail.

"I love the summer rain . . . It's an antidote to
pain. . . ." Hm, she thought wryly. Awful! Just because
some lines come fast doesn't mean they're any good.
But part of being a pro is knowing what sucks and what
doesn't. She'd work on it.

Then, hearing the mobile trill again, she thought
of Mary-Gordon. Was Suellyn calling because she was
sick, did she want Kayleigh to bring a special toy from
the house? Concern for the little girl was what prodded Kayleigh out of the tub. She dried off and dressed
fast in jeans and a blouse. Pulled on socks. And her
glasses.

Maybe it was Alicia calling back. What exactly did
she want to talk to her about, out of Bishop's hearing?

Could be anything, she decided. The assistant and
Bishop had never really gotten along. Her father liked
women who fawned. Alicia did what she was supposed
to for him—he was the head of the company—but there
was always some tension between them because she
would not kowtow to the big man.

She picked up the phone. Ah, Kathryn's number.
She hit the CALL-BACK button.

As it rang, she glanced out the window. It was dark
now but she made out Alicia's blue pickup truck sitting

in the drive. Kayleigh hadn't heard her arrive but she could let herself in. She had a key.

Dance's phone clicked.

Kayleigh started to say, "Hey, how're—?"

But the agent said urgently, "Kayleigh, listen to me. I don't have time to go into the details. Alicia Session's on her way there. She's going to kill you. Get out of the house. Now!"

"What?"

"Just get out!"

Downstairs, the kitchen door opened and Alicia called out, "Hey, Kayleigh. It's me. You decent?"

THROUGH HER PHONE Kathryn Dance heard Kayleigh's voice catch. Then she whispered, "She's here! She's downstairs. Alicia!"

Oh, no. How to handle it?

Dance, Harutyun and Madigan were in the FMC-SO cruiser speeding away from Alicia's apartment in the Tower District. Dance told the men that Alicia was already at Kayleigh's house and then said into the phone, "Is Darthur there?"

"No, he's gone. We thought it was all over with, with Simesky dead."

"Get out. Can you run into the woods?"

"I . . . No. I'm upstairs. I don't think I can jump. And I'd have to go past her if I went downstairs. Can I talk to her? Why does she—"

"No, you have to hide, stay away. She has a gun. We'll have troopers there as soon as we can but it'll be twenty minutes. Are you in a room with a lock?"

"My bedroom. Yes. But it's not much."

"What about a weapon?"

"My gun's downstairs, locked up."

"Just barricade yourself in the room. And stall."

"Oh, Jesus, Kathryn. What's going on?"

"Barricade yourself as best you can. We'll be there soon."

The siren spread outward on the hot, dry air and the urgent blue and white lights ricocheted off cars and signs and windows as they raced through the evening.

"KAYLEIGH?" ALICIA CALLED again from downstairs.

Where was she? Kayleigh wondered. Still in the kitchen? The den?

"Down in a minute." She stared at the door.

Close it, girl! What's the matter with you. Buy time. Lock it, barricade it.

At the door she called, "Just out of the shower. I'll be down in five." She closed and locked the door. But the chair she tried to wedge under the knob was too low. Her dresser was too heavy to move. The vanity table wouldn't stop Mary-Gordon.

Find a weapon. Anything.

A nail file? A lamp?

Don't be an idiot, jump!

She ran to the window. Below her was not only concrete but a wrought-iron fence. If she didn't break her back she'd be impaled.

Listening at the door again, ear against the wood.

"Kayleigh?"

"Be down soon! Have a beer or make some coffee!"

Jump out the window. It's your only chance.

Then Kayleigh thought suddenly: no fucking way.

I'm fighting.

She grabbed the vanity stool and ripped off the Laura Ashley padded covering. The furniture was five pounds of hard wood. Not much but it would have to do. I'll lure her up here and bash her head in.

Kayleigh moved to the door, listening. She took a firm stance, gripping the stool like a baseball bat.

Then her phone rang.

Squinting at the screen. The number was vaguely familiar. Wait. . . . It was Edwin Sharp's! She recalled the number from the label of the redwood tree toy he'd helped Mary-Gordon pick out.

"Hello, Edwin?"

He said tentatively, "Hey, Kayleigh, listen. I'm almost there. Alicia asked me not to call you, just to come over. But, I don't know, what's this all about? Is it some kind of settlement thing? I don't want anything from you. It wasn't your fault what that guy with the congressman did."

And with a heart-shaking jolt, Kayleigh understood. For whatever reason Alicia had set up Edwin. She'd asked *him* here too and was going to make it look like *he* killed her.

"Oh, Edwin, there's a problem."

"You sound funny. What's the matter? I mean—"

"Stay away! Alicia's here. She's going to kill me. She wants to—"

A pause. "You're not, like, serious?"

"She's setting you up. She's here now."

"I'll call the police."

She said, "I did. They're on their way."

"I'm five minutes away."

"No, Edwin, don't come here! Go to Bradley Road, the minimart. Stay there, stay with people. That way nobody can blame you for whatever happens."

It was then that Kayleigh smelled smoke.

Edwin was saying something. She ignored him and turned her ear toward the door. Yes, the crackle of flames was coming from downstairs.

No, no! My house, my guitars! She's burning them!

Like Bobby and the file sharer and Sheri, she's going to burn me too.

"Kayleigh, Kayleigh?" Edwin's voice rose from her phone.

"There's a fire, Edwin. Call the fire department too. But don't come here. Whatever you do."

"I—"

She disconnected.

And the bitter, stinging smoke began to seep under the bedroom door.

Chapter 64

THE SMOKE AND flames were growing.

Love is fire, love is flame. . . .

My house, my house, Kayleigh thought as tears of sorrow, of pain from the smoke, of fear rolled down her cheeks. My guitars, my pictures. . . . Oh, this can't be happening!

The door was hot to the touch now and outside the window, reflections of the flames from downstairs flickered across trees and the lawn.

Kayleigh debated. Where was Alicia? She couldn't stay downstairs in the flames, of course. She'd probably left.

Well, fuck her. I'm saving my house!

Kayleigh ran into the bathroom and grabbed a fire extinguisher, years old but, according to the gauge, still charged. She unlocked the bedroom door and eased it open. The fire was concentrated in the hallway on the ground floor and on the stairs themselves, the carpeting. It gave off thick clouds of astringent smoke from the flaming nylon. Sparks zipped through the air. Kayleigh caught a full breath of the foul stench and retched. She lowered her head and got a breath of more or less clean air, another. She stood. The fire wasn't out of control yet. If Alicia had left she could put out enough of it to get to the kitchen, where there was a much bigger extinguisher. And the hose in the garden.

She eased out.

Just then a huge bang from downstairs resounded through the house, a flash in the smoke. A bullet plowed into the door near her head. Two more.

Screaming, she dove back into her room and slammed the door, locked it. Kayleigh decided she had no choice but to risk a twenty-five-foot jump to the ground. Would she break her legs and just lie there in agony until Alicia shot her? Would she get speared on the fence and bleed out?

But she wouldn't burn to death, at least. Running to the window, she flung it open and looked out toward the road. Not a single flashing light yet. Then she gazed down, trying to judge angles and distances.

She found a place she might land, just past the fence. But then she saw, at the exact spot she'd land, Alicia's shadow, moving back and forth, almost leisurely. She was at the front door and probably anticipating Kayleigh's jump and aiming at that very spot.

Shadows . . .

Kayleigh sat down on the bed, grabbed a picture she had of Mary-Gordon and hugged it to her chest.

So, this was it.

Mama, Bobby, I'll be with you soon.

Oh, Bobby . . .

She thought of the song she'd written for him years ago. "The Only One for Me."

More tears.

But just then another gunshot resounded from downstairs. . . . Then two or three more. Kayleigh gasped. Could the police be here after all?

She ran to the window and looked out. No, no one was here. The driveway was empty, except for Alicia's truck. And there were no flashing lights on the horizon.

Two more shots.

And from downstairs, a voice calling her name.

A man's voice.

"Kayleigh, come on, hurry!"

She opened the door cautiously and peered down.

Jesus! Through the smoke she could just make out the form of Edwin Sharp, beating down the flames on the stairs with his jacket. Alicia lay on her back, on the marble of the hallway, eyes gazing up, unseeing. Her face was bloody. She'd fallen onto a patch of burning wood floor and her clothes were on fire.

Kayleigh understood: Edwin had ignored her warning and continued to the house anyway.

"Hurry!" he cried. "Come on! I called the fire department but I don't know when they'll be here. You have to get out!"

His slapping at the flames wasn't doing much to stop the spread, though he'd beat out a narrow path down the stairs to the ground floor.

She made her way along this now. He was pointing into the den. "We can get out that way, through the window!"

But she said, "You go! I'm going to fight it."

"No, we can't!"

"Go!" she shouted and turned the small extinguisher on the flames.

Edwin hesitated, coughing hard, and returned to flailing away with his jacket. "I'll help you."

She gave him a smile and called, "In the kitchen, there's another extinguisher. Beside the stove!"

Choking, Edwin staggered through the arched doorway and returned a moment later with the extinguisher, much bigger than Kayleigh's, and started to douse the flames too.

With a horrified glance at Alicia's burning body, Kayleigh ran out the back door and returned a moment later with her garden hose. She began attacking the stubborn fire as Edwin, next to her, blew bursts of foam from the big extinguisher. They both retched and coughed and tried to blink away tears from the smoke.

The singer and her stalker held their own but only for a time. Soon Edwin's extinguisher ran out and an outrider of fire melted her garden hose.

Too late . . . no! My house.

But then sirens sounded and outside the evening darkness filled with flashing lights as the first fire trucks arrived. Men and women in their thick yellow outfits hurried into the house with hoses and began battling the flames. One fireman bent over Alicia's body, no longer burning but smoldering badly, and felt for a pulse. He looked up and shook his head.

Another ushered Kayleigh and Edwin toward the front door and they staggered outside. Kayleigh made her way down the stairs into the yard, coughing and spitting the terrible bits of soot and ash from her mouth. She paused on the lawn and vomited painfully. Then she looked back, realizing that Edwin was lagging behind.

She saw him on his knees on the porch. His hand was at his throat. He lifted his fingers away and looked at them. Kayleigh saw the digits were dark but not stained with soot, as she'd thought. Blood was flowing from a wound in his neck.

Alicia had shot him before he wrestled the gun away from her.

He blinked and looked at Kayleigh. "I think . . . I think she . . ." His eyes closed and he collapsed backward on the wooden deck.

Chapter 65

KATHRYN DANCE WAS sitting next to Kayleigh Towne on the steps of her house. They were bathed in a sweep of colored lights, blue and red, with flashes of white. Beautiful and troubling.

The young woman was diminished, her posture collapsed—chin tucked, shoulders slumped. She was smeared with Edwin Sharp's blood, from trying to staunch the bleeding. In kinesic analysis Kayleigh's carriage could be read as defeat and acceptance, the goal of every interrogator. But the pose was also an indication of exhaustion or disbelief.

P. K. Madigan was directing the FMCSO's crime scene team in their search of the house, and the fire department was making sure there was no chance of the flames sprouting up again.

"I don't understand any of this," Kayleigh whispered.

Dance explained what they'd learned about Alicia and found in her apartment. "And in her truck? There was a Baggie filled with things she stole from Edwin's rental. She was going to plant them here." Dance then explained the why. "There was a note too. She'd forged your handwriting and did a pretty good job of it. If anything happened to you, you wanted her to take over the band."

"She asked Edwin here tonight too so it'd look like

he'd killed me. He gets arrested and nobody believes him when he claims he's innocent."

"Exactly."

Kayleigh rubbed her face; her jaw tightened. "Alicia wanted to be me. She wanted fame and money and power. That's what this fucking business does to people. It twists them, seduces them. I'm sick of it! I'm so sick of it." She looked toward the medics. "I told him not to come. I knew he'd get blamed if anything happened. But he came anyway."

As some EMTs got Edwin into one of the two ambulances, another approached them. "Agent Dance. Ms. Towne . . . Mr. Sharp's lost a lot of blood. We've stabilized him as best we can but, I'm sorry to say, it's not looking good. We have to get him to the hospital for surgery as soon as we can."

"Is he going to live?" Kayleigh asked.

"We don't know at this time. Was he a friend?"

Kayleigh said softly, "In a way. He's a fan of mine."

Chapter 66

TWO HOURS LATER, a tired-looking surgeon, a South Asian man in green scrubs, walked slowly down the bleached-lit hallway of Fresno Community Hospital toward the waiting area.

Dance looked at Kayleigh and together they rose.

The man didn't seem to know whom to deliver the news to: the famous Fresno singer or the tall woman with the gun on her hip. He spoke between them as he said Edwin Sharp would survive. The blood loss was bad but he would ultimately recover fully. "The bullet missed the carotid and his spine." Edwin would be coming out of the anesthesia now. They could see him for a few minutes if they wanted.

They found the recovery room and stepped inside to find Edwin staring groggily at the ceiling.

"Hey," he mumbled. "Hey." Blinking. "Feels like it did when I had my tonsils out." His voice didn't seem to be affected; he spoke softly, though, and a bit garbled. And he seemed completely drained.

Kayleigh said, "You look pretty good, all things considered."

Though the bullet hole would be fairly small—about nine millimeters, of course—the eggplant-colored bruise extended well beyond the thick bandage covering the wound.

"Doesn't, uhm, you know, hurt much yet." He studied an IV drip, probably morphine. He added, "And I'm getting some pretty nice pills after I'm out, the, uhm, doctor tells me. The doctor, you know.

"I'm getting discharged tomorrow." He had a loopy grin on his face and for once the smile wasn't the least bit weird. "I thought I'd be here, you know, for a week. Maybe more than a week." His eyelids dipped and Dance wondered if he was slipping off to sleep. They then opened once more. "A week," he repeated drunkenly.

"I'm glad you're feeling better," Kayleigh said. "I was pretty worried."

He frowned. Speaking slowly: "Didn't bring me flowers, I notice. No flowers. Afraid I'd misinterpret it?" Then he laughed. "Joking."

Kayleigh smiled too.

Edwin's face grew somber. "Alicia . . . what was that all about? Did she go crazy? I mean, Alicia. What happened?"

Dance said, "She was going to kill Kayleigh and plant some things she got from your house so you'd get blamed for it. She forged a note saying that Kayleigh wanted Alicia to front the band."

"She did *that*? Killed Bobby Prescott too? And attacked your stepmother?" Edwin asked.

Kayleigh nodded.

Then, echoing the singer's comments of a few hours earlier, he added, "She did it . . ." Focusing again. "She did it to be famous. Everybody wants that, I guess. It's like a drug. Like writing Harry Potter, being Daniel Craig. They want to be famous."

Her eyes damp, Kayleigh whispered, "I don't know what to say, Edwin. . . . What a mess this's all been."

He tried to shrug but winced from the pain.

"You didn't need to come to the house, Edwin. I told you it was dangerous."

"Yeah," he said, maybe being sardonic, maybe not quite grasping what she'd said. He was really drugged.

"What happened back there?" Dance asked.

He tried to focus. "Back there?"

"At Kayleigh's?"

"Oh, at Kayleigh's . . . Well, she told me about Alicia and the fire so I called the fire department but I couldn't stop. You told me to stop, right?"

"I did."

"But I couldn't. I kept going to the house. When I got there I parked on the shoulder, so Alicia wouldn't see me. I went through the trees and got to the house. The kitchen door was open and I saw Alicia by the stairs. She didn't see me. I tackled her. She was really strong. I mean, you know, *really.* I didn't expect that. The gun went off before I got it away from her. She jumped at me and I shot her. I didn't think. I just pulled the trigger. I didn't even know *I* got shot. All I remember is we were trying to put the fire out, you and me . . . and then I woke up here."

His eyes closed slowly then leveraged open and he looked at Kayleigh. "I was going to mail you something before I left. There's a card. I was going to send you a card. There's a present inside too. My jacket. Look in the pocket. Where's my jacket?"

Dance found the garment in the closet. Kayleigh fished through the pocket. She extracted a stamped envelope, addressed to her.

"Open it."

She did. Looking over her shoulder, Dance noted the silly drugstore card with a mournful-looking dog on the front, the balloon above its head reporting, "I'm 'Dog-gone' sorry."

Kayleigh smiled. "And I'm sorry too, Edwin."

"Look in the tissue."

She opened the square of thin paper; inside were three small guitar picks. "Oh, Edwin."

"I got a deer antler in this pawn shop in Seattle. I made them out of that."

"They're beautiful." She showed them to Dance, who agreed.

"I . . ." His eyes floated in an arc around the room and he remembered what he was going to say. "I sent them to you before but you sent them back. I mean, somebody sent them back. But if you want, you can have them now."

"Of course I want them. Thank you so much. I'll use them at the concert. In fact, I'll thank you in person for them there."

"Oh, no. I'm headed back to Seattle. I was packing up when Alicia called." A wan smile.

"Leaving?"

"Better for you, I think." He laughed. "Better for me too, you know. You think a famous star kind of likes you, then next thing some crazy people want to use you to assassinate a politician and some psycho's stolen your trash to frame you for murder. Never thought being a fan could be so dangerous."

Both Dance and Kayleigh smiled.

"Think I'm . . . think I'm . . . better off in Seattle." His head eased toward his chest and he muttered, "It's not as hot either. It's really hot in . . . it's hot here."

Kayleigh smiled but said earnestly, "Edwin, you can't drive like this. Wait a couple of days. Please. Come to the concert if you're feeling up for it. I'll get you a ticket front row center."

He was fading fast. "No. Better. It's better if I . . ."

Then he was sound asleep. Kayleigh looked over the picks and seemed genuinely moved by the gift.

She and Dance then left the hospital. They were in the parking lot when Kayleigh gave a laugh.

The agent lifted an eyebrow.

"Hey, you hear the one about the blond country singer?"

"Tell me."

"She was so dumb she got dumped by her stalker."

Friday

Chapter 67

THE DAY OF the show.

The band had arrived from Nashville at nine A.M. and come straight here, the convention center, where Kayleigh and the crew were waiting. They got right to work.

After a couple of hours Kayleigh had called a break. Backstage she had a tea and called Suellyn, then spoke to Mary-Gordon; she was going to take the girl shopping that afternoon for a new dress to wear to the concert.

After she disconnected she picked up her old Martin again and practiced a bit more with the picks that Edwin had given her.

She liked them a lot. Top flat-pickers, like Doc Watson, Norman Blake, Tony Rice and Bishop Towne, would never use big flexible triangles; the real virtuosos used small, hard picks like these. Kayleigh was more a strummer, but she still liked the control that—

A voice startled her. "How's the action?" Tye Slocum asked, appearing silently from nowhere, despite his size. His eyes were on the instrument.

Kayleigh smiled. The guitar tech was referring to the height of the strings above the fret board. Some guitars had a bolt or nut that could be turned to easily alter the action. Martins didn't; to make that adjustment required more effort and skill.

"Little low. I was getting some buzz on the D."

"I've got a saddle I can swap," he said. "I just found some bone ones. Real old. They're pretty sweet." The saddle, vital to a guitar's tone, was the white bar on the bridge that transmitted the sound from the strings to the body. Acoustically the best material was hard ivory, from forest elephant tusks; soft ivory was the next best—from large African elephants. Bone was the third best material. Both types of ivory were available—some legally and some not—but Kayleigh refused to use ivory and wouldn't let anyone in her band do so either. Tye, though, had good sources for vintage bone, which produced a sound nearly as good.

A pause. "Just wondering: Is he going to be mixing tonight?" A glance toward the control platform in the back, where Barry Zeigler sat with hard-shell earphones on, hands dancing over the console.

"Yeah."

Tye grunted. "Okay. Sure. He's good."

Bobby Prescott had not only been the chief roadie but handled the demanding job of sound mixing, his father's profession, at the live shows. Anyone on the crew could do a decent job on the massive, complex Midas XL8 mixing console—Tye was pretty good himself—but she had decided to ask Zeigler, as long as he happened to be in town. Her producer had started in the business as a board man when his own dreams of being a rock star hadn't come to pass. Nobody was better than Barry at getting right both the FOH—front of house—audio, along with the foldback: the sound the band heard through their monitors.

Slocum wandered off to his workstation of tuners, strings, amps and tools. Kayleigh walked out onstage and the rehearsal resumed.

Her band was made up of artists whose whole professional lives had been devoted to music. There are a lot of talented people out there, of course, but Kayleigh had worked hard to assemble folks who understood her and her songs and the tone she strived for. Folks who could work silkenly together; oh, that was important, vital. There are few professions as intimate as making ensemble music, and without complete synchronicity among the performers the best songs in the world and the most talented front person will be wasted.

Kevin Peebles was the lead guitarist, a lean, laid-back man in his thirties whose mahogany scalp glistened with sweat under the lights. He'd been a rocker for a few years before turning to his real love—country, a genre in which his race had not been traditionally well represented.

Bass player and backup singer Emma Sue Granger was one of the most beautiful women Kayleigh'd ever seen. With shoulder-length raven-black hair, decked out with occasional microbraids and a flower or two, Granger wore tight sweaters she knitted herself and leather pants. Kayleigh's audience was 60 percent female, but for the sake of the other forty, Emma Sue got a lot of front-stage time.

In a battered straw cowboy hat, brims rolled into a near tube, plaid shirt and ancient blue jeans, Buddy Delmore manned the band's pedal steel guitar, the smooth, seductive instrument that Kayleigh, for all her talent, had never been able to play. She thought anybody who could master one well was a genius. He also would play the distinctive-sounding Dobro and National steel guitars, with their pie-plate resonators. The sixty-five-year-old was from West Virginia and played music to support his true love: chicken farming. He had eight children, the youngest of whom was two.

The drummer was new to the group. Alonzo Santiago had come out of the barrio in Bakersfield and could make rhythm with anything he could pick up or touch. This too was magical to Kayleigh, who could perfectly follow a beat but relied on others to create and sustain it. Santiago was one of those crazy parents who'd actually given his young children drum sets, only to be disappointed to learn his daughter dreamed of being a NASCAR driver and his son a comic book artist.

The other band member, a sturdy, round-faced redhead in her forties, was the "orchestra." Sharon Bascowitz was one of those people who could pick up an instrument, even one she'd never seen, and play it like a virtuoso. Sousaphone, cello, harpsichord, marimba, Native American flute . . . anything. Sharon could get it to sing. Always decked out in three or four colorful layers of tie-dye and lace, and dangling with glittering fake jewels, the woman was as brash as Emma Sue was shy.

The rehearsal was informal; they'd performed most of the material so often, it probably wasn't even necessary, but there was a new song order and Kayleigh had added Patsy Cline and Alison Krauss/Robert Plant covers and had written two new songs, which she'd faxed to the band last night. One was dedicated to Bobby; Alicia would not be mentioned, Kayleigh had decided.

They finished the raucous and fun "I'm in the Mood (for Rock 'n' Roll)" and she looked toward Barry at the mixing board. He gave her a thumbs-up. He was satisfied. She was satisfied. Kayleigh announced to the band and crew, "Okay, I think that's it for now; reconvene at six for the final sound check."

According to the God of Performances, Bishop Towne, you could never rehearse too frequently but you *could* rehearse too much. They needed a break now, to let the new ideas bake.

She handed off her Martin to Tye Slocum to fit with the new saddle, slugged down another iced tea and picked up her phone. Debating a moment, then a moment longer. Finally she did something she couldn't have imagined until today.

Kayleigh Towne called Edwin Sharp.

"Hello?" He still sounded a bit groggy.

"Hey, it's Kayleigh."

"Well, hi."

"Are you in the hospital still?"

He laughed. "Didn't think I'd really hear from you. No. I got sprung."

"How you feeling?"

"Sore, sore, sore."

"Well, I hope you're well enough to come to the show," she said firmly. "I got you a ticket."

There was silence and she wondered if he was going to refuse. But he said, "Okay. Thanks."

"I've got it now. Meet you for lunch?"

She could have left it at the will-call window but that seemed petty, considering what he'd done for her. She'd reconciled with Sheri; she could do the same with Edwin.

He said, "I'm supposed to go see Deputy Madigan to give them a statement, but that's not till two. I guess. Sure."

He suggested a diner he'd been to. She agreed and they disconnected. Kayleigh headed for the stage door, glancing at Tye Slocum, who had already destrung her Martin and was filing away on the new bone saddle, as lost in his task as a sculptor completing his masterwork.

Her eyes then rose and looked into the murky heaven of the convention center. Kayleigh had wakened that morning at her father's house, thinking that the concert was the last thing she wanted. She'd even considered

using the smoke from the fire at her house as an excuse to cancel, reporting that her throat still stung, even
though it was fine. But once she'd arrived here, greeted
the band members, tuned up and walked out onstage,
her attitude changed completely.

Now she couldn't wait for the concert. Nothing was
going to stop her from giving the audience the best
show they'd ever seen.

Chapter 68

THE CASE WAS over.

But one consequence of that resolution for Kathryn Dance was that a greater problem loomed.

One she'd have to face soon and she'd decided today was the day.

She'd had a decadent brunch of huevos rancheros and was now back in her Mountain View Motel room, on the phone with her website partner, Martine, discussing the songs she'd recorded of Los Trabajadores. She'd emailed them to the woman and they'd spent hours deciding which of the two dozen they'd make available on their site.

The decisions were hard; they were all so good.

But from time to time, as the women spoke, that Greater Problem intruded, the one Dance was now resolved to deal with: the question about the men in her life. No, that's not correct, she reminded herself. There was only *one* man in her life—in *that* way. Jon Boling. That he was close to ending the relationship was irrelevant. She had to keep Michael O'Neil out of the equation for the time being. This was between her and Boling.

So what'm I going to do?

"Hey, you there?" Martine's voice nudged her from her thoughts.

"Sorry." They returned to the task and finished the

Los Trabajadores song list. Then she disconnected the call, flopped down on the bed and told herself: Call Jon. Have it out.

Dance stared out the window, eyes on what might have been a true mountain view had the day been exceedingly clear, which it definitely wasn't, not in this dead end of summer.

She then scrutinized her mobile, which she turned over and over in her hand.

The photo skin on the back depicted two children with giddy smiles, and two dogs in the oblivious joy of dogness.

The other side was her phone's address book window, Jon Boling's number highlighted and ready to be dialed.

Back to the pictures.

Eyes on a bad painting on the wall, of a harbor. Did the interior designer think all Californians owned sailboats, even those three hours from the coast?

Flip . . . the phone's address book. Her French braid tickled her left ear. She absently flicked the strands aside.

Call or not, call or not?

Her intent was to ask bluntly why he was moving to San Diego without talking to her first. Odd, she reflected, she had no problem slipping on her predator specs, sitting down across from snarling Salinas gangbanger Manuel Martinez to learn where he'd buried a portion of the remains of Hector Alonzo, specifically the head. But asking a simple question about her lover's intentions was paralyzing.

Then a wind shear of anger. What the hell was he thinking? Becoming friendly with the children, easing into their lives, making himself a part of the family, fitting in so seamlessly.

She grew analytical. Maybe this was the answer: on the surface Jon Boling had been perfect for her, fit, funny, kind, sexy. They'd had no harsh words, no fights, no fundamental collisions of any kind—unlike, for instance, as with Michael O'Neil. . . . Wait, she reminded herself. O'Neil did not exist for the purposes of this equation.

With Boling did the absence of friction mean the gears of love weren't truly engaging?

Could there be more love in sweat than in laughter?

That just didn't seem right.

Clutching the phone, turning it over, over, over . . .

Call, not call?

Children screen children screen children screen . . .

Maybe I'll flip it like a coin on the bed and let fate take charge.

Children screen children screen . . .

Chapter 69

KAYLEIGH MET A slow-moving Edwin Sharp in the front of the diner.

She liked the choice of restaurant; it was in a quiet part of town and she suspected she wouldn't have to deal with autograph hounds. That was something even minor celebrities like her always had to consider.

He greeted her at the door with a smile and let her precede him into the air-conditioned, brightly lit restaurant, which was nearly empty. The waitress grinned, noting their famous patron, but Kayleigh was an expert at categorizing fans. She knew the woman would be efficient and cheerful but far too nervous to utter a word beyond order taking and comments about the heat.

They sat at a booth and ordered iced teas and, for Kayleigh, a burger. Edwin got a milkshake; the wound in his neck made chewing painful, he explained. "I love 'em. But I haven't had one for months. Hey, if nothing else, you got me to lose that weight I'd been trying to for years."

"Wow, that bruise is something."

He lifted the chrome napkin holder and used it as a mirror. "I think it's getting worse."

"Hurts a lot?"

"Yeah. But the big problem is I have to sleep on my back, which is something I've never been able to do."

Their meals came and they ate and sipped. He asked, "How's your house?"

"I'll need new carpets, have to replace a lot of floor and a wall. The big problem is the smoke damage. It got into everything. They're talking about a hundred thousand dollars. Half my clothes have to go too. They stink."

"Sorry."

Then an awkward silence arose and it was clear Edwin didn't want to talk about the terrible events of the past few days. Fine with her. He started chatting about music and some of the founding women of the country scene. He talked about the records in his collection—he still listened to a lot of music on LPs and had invested in an expensive turntable. Kayleigh too thought that vinyl—analog recordings—produced the purest sound, better than the highest-quality digital.

Edwin mentioned he'd just found some Kitty Wells singles in a used record shop in Seattle.

"You like her?" Kayleigh asked, surprised. "She's one of my favorites."

"Have almost all of her records. You know she had a *Billboard* hit when she was sixty?"

"I did, yeah."

Wells, who started singing in the 1950s, was one of the first women inductees into the Country Music Hall of Fame.

They talked about country music back then—Nashville versus Texas versus Bakersfield. She laughed when Edwin quoted Loretta Lynn, who fought her way up through the male-dominated recording Industry: "A woman's two cents' worth is worth about two cents in the country music world."

In Edwin's opinion country represented the best of commercial music, much better than pop and hip-hop. It was well crafted, used appealing tunes and incorporated themes about important issues in everybody's lives like family, love, work, even politics. And the musicians were top craftspeople, unlike many folk, alternative, hip-hop and rock artists.

On the broader issue of the music world, he wasn't happy about the decline of the recording Industry and thought that illegal downloads would continue to be a problem and erode the quality of performances. "If artists don't get paid for what they do, then what's the incentive to keep writing and making good music?"

"I'll drink to that." Kayleigh tapped her iced tea glass to his milkshake.

When they were through with lunch, Kayleigh gave Edwin his ticket. "Front and center. I'll wave to you. Oh, and those picks are the best."

"Glad you liked them."

Her phone buzzed. A text from Tye Slocum: *the Martin's ready to go, how you doing?*

Curious. He rarely texted, much less about something as mundane as the status of an instrument.

"Everything okay?"

"Yeah, just . . ." She didn't finish and put her phone away. She'd respond later.

The bill came and Edwin insisted on paying. "Well, this is a real treat. I never thought I'd be in the front row at a Kayleigh Towne concert."

They walked into the parking lot. As they approached her Suburban, Edwin gave a laugh and pointed to his old red car, a few spaces down from hers. "'Buick' would be pretty tough to rhyme with. Good thing you picked 'Cadillac.'"

"'Toyota' would've been worse," Kayleigh joked.

"Hey, now that you know I'm not the crazy person you thought I was, how about dinner sometime? Maybe after the concert?"

"I usually go out with the band."

"Oh, that's right. Well, sometime, maybe . . . How 'bout Sunday? You don't leave again for two weeks. The Vancouver show."

"Well . . . weren't you leaving?"

He pointed to his throat. "Taking those pain pills. You were right—they're pretty heavy duty. Probably better if I don't do any long-distance driving. I'm back in the rental for a few days."

"Oh, sure, you have to be careful." They were at her SUV. "Okay, thank you again, Edwin. For everything you did. I'm sorry for what you've been through."

She nearly hugged him and kissed his cheek but decided not to.

XO . . .

"'I'd Do It All Again,'" he said, smiling. The title of one of her first hits. Kayleigh laughed. After a moment he said, "Hey, here's a thought: I could drive up to Canada. Vancouver's not that far from Seattle. I know some great places. There's this beautiful garden in the mountains, where—"

She smiled. "You know, Edwin, it's probably best if we don't get together. Just . . . I think it's best."

A grin crossed his face. "Sure. Only . . . well, after everything, I just thought . . ."

"It's probably best," she repeated. "Good-bye, Edwin." She extended her hand.

He didn't take it.

"So . . . you're breaking up with me?" he asked.

She started to laugh, thinking he was joking—like his reference to the flowers in the hospital last night. But his eyes narrowed, focusing on hers. And the smile morphed into the one she recognized from before. The faint twisting of his lip, fake. "After everything," he repeated in a whisper.

"Okay, you take care," she said quickly. And gripped her key fob, unlocking the door.

"Don't go," he said in a breathy whisper.

Kayleigh looked around. The parking lot was deserted. "Edwin."

He said quickly, "Wait. I'm sorry. Look, let's just take a drive and talk. We can just talk. Nothing more than that for now."

For now. What did he mean?

"I think I should go."

"Just talk," he said stridently. "That's all I'm asking."

She turned fast but Edwin stepped quickly forward, boxing her in. "Please, I'm sorry. Just a little drive." He looked at his watch. "You don't have to be at the concert hall for six hours and thirty minutes."

"No, Edwin. Stop it! Get out of my way."

"You like men who talk, remember your song, 'You Never Say a Word'? That's not me. Come on. You liked talking to me at the restaurant just now." He gripped her arm. "That was so much fun. The best lunch I've ever had!"

"Let go of me!" She tried to push him away. It was like trying to move a sack of concrete.

He said ominously, "You understand I was almost killed." He pointed to his neck. "I was almost killed saving you! Did you forget that?"

Oh, Jesus Lord. He shot himself. Alicia was innocent. He set her up. Edwin killed Bobby, he killed Alicia! I don't know how but he did it.

"Please, Edwin. . . ."

He released her, relaxed and looked contrite. "I'm so sorry! Look, this isn't going well. Here's the thing, you need a place to stay. The fire at your house. You could stay with me until it's fixed."

Was he serious?

She spun around and tried to bolt. But his massive hand went around her face and pinched hard. An arm gripped her chest and squeezed as he dragged her to the back of his Buick and opened the trunk. The struggle for air became more and more hopeless. As her vision crumbled to black, she heard—she *believed* she heard—a voice, singing in a whisper, "Always with you, always with you, your shadow. . . ."

Chapter 70

KATHRYN DANCE DIDN'T play coin toss with the phone.

She decided to be an adult about the whole San Diego Situation. She rose and hit CALL as she pitched out her Starbucks carton.

Her eyes were on the motel room trash can as Boling's phone rang once.

Twice.

Three times.

She disconnected fast.

Not because she'd lost her nerve about talking to him; no, another thought surfaced.

A to B to Z . . .

How did Edwin Sharp know that Alicia Sessions had stolen his trash?

That's what he'd said in the hospital. Yet she'd never mentioned the fact. Dance had said only that Alicia had taken some things of his. That she had garbage bags in her apartment was never mentioned.

Slow down, she told herself. Think.

Could he have learned about it some other way? She decided no. At Kayleigh's house last night he was unconscious for most of the time and only the medics spoke to him, not Madigan or Harutyun, the only others who knew about the trash. And Kayleigh and

Dance were the first ones to visit him in the hospital.

A logical deduction on his part? If Alicia was going to plant something of his it made sense for her to have taken his trash.

Surely possible.

But another explanation was that *Edwin* had put the two bags of his trash in Alicia's apartment, along with the notes supposedly forged by the assistant, but that he himself had produced. He'd then planted the evidence outside his own house, like the neatsfoot oil trace and the boot print, to implicate Alicia, suggesting she'd been spying on him last Saturday.

No, no, this was absurd. The shooting incident at Kayleigh's house? That surely had been Alicia.

Or had it?

Rethink the scenario, Dance told herself. What had Kayleigh told her, Madigan and Harutyun about the attack last night?

Was there any possible way Edwin had orchestrated it? Think.

A to B to Z . . .

Come on, you get into the minds of killers plenty. Do it now. How would *you* have set it up?

And the ideas began to form.

Edwin goes to Alicia's, ties her up. He plants his own trash, Gabriel Fuentes's gun case and the forgeries of Kayleigh's note there. Uses her phone to send texts to Kayleigh and to his own phone about meeting at Kayleigh's house, and he goes to the hotel near Alicia's and uses her computer to send the request for the fourth verse to the radio station.

But there were two cars at Kayleigh's. His own and Alicia's. Well, maybe he pays a teenager or field picker to drive his car to the shoulder in front of Kayleigh's house and leave it there, then vanish. Then he drives to Kayleigh's in Alicia's pickup, with her tied up in the back. Or maybe she was already dead at that point—the time of death, with a badly burned body, would be close enough.

But Kayleigh heard Alicia calling her name in the house.

A tape recorder!

Edwin could have threatened her back at the apartment to say Kayleigh's name into a high-def digital recorder—the same one used to play "Your Shadow" to announce the impending murder.

With your eyes closed, you couldn't tell the difference between someone really singing or the digital replay. Only a pro would have a recorder like that.

Dance recalled her reply to Kayleigh:

Or a fanatical fan.

He'd probably planned out several scenarios for the "rescue" of Kayleigh Towne—depending on where the singer was in the house when he arrived. If she was downstairs or on the porch, maybe the fight with Alicia would have occurred in the driveway or out by the road. But when he'd gotten to the house he would have seen her in the bedroom. That gave him the chance to get inside and masquerade as Alicia—all thanks to Dance herself, of course, who'd called Kayleigh and told her to barricade herself upstairs.

And Edwin's wound? Well, if he was mobile now, the gunshot may have been dramatic but obviously it wasn't that serious.

The bullet missed the carotid and his spine. . . .

Dance pulled a portion of her own skin away from her neck. Yes, he could easily have shot himself and missed anything vital.

She tried to consider any other items of evidence that were unaccounted for.

The bone dust was the first thing that came to mind.

Human bone dust.

The guitar picks! Made not from a deer antler but from the hand of Frederick Blanton, the file sharer—the body part hadn't been burned away; Edwin had cut it off before he set the fire. He'd lied about sending the picks to her earlier; how would Kayleigh know? Her assistant returned everything he'd sent, probably unopened.

Grim justice for a singer; using picks made out of the bone of a man who'd stolen her music.

It's a wild theory. But . . .

Close enough for me, Dance decided and called Kayleigh. No answer. She left a message, telling her what she suspected, then called Bishop Towne and told him the same.

"Oh, fuck," the man growled. "She's having lunch with him right now! Sheri was at the convention center for the rehearsal. She left an hour ago to meet him."

"Where?"

"Well, I'm not sure. Hold on."

After an excruciatingly long time, he came back on. "The San Joaquin Diner, on Third. Do you—"

"If she calls you have her get in touch with me right away." Dance hung up and debated calling 911 or the sheriff's office. Which would be the shorter explanation?

She dialed.

"Madigan," came the voice.

"Chief, it's Kathryn. No time now but I think Edwin's our perp after all."

"What?" She heard a tap, an ice cream cup being set down. "But . . . Alicia?"

"Later. Listen. He and Kayleigh're at the San Joaquin Diner. On Third. We need a car there now."

"Know it, sure. He armed?"

"All the firearms we know about're accounted for but it's pretty easy to buy a piece in this state."

"Gotcha. I'll get back to you."

Dance paced along the carpet, then hurried to the room's desk, where her notes from the case sat. There were dozens and dozens of pages. If she'd been working one of her own cases, especially a task-forced operation, she would have organized and indexed them by now. But since it seemed that the case had been resolved and others would be handling the prosecution, she hadn't yet bothered. Now, she spread the pages out on the bed—her conversation with the witnesses, the evidence Lincoln Rhyme and Amelia Sachs had analyzed, the notes from the interview with Edwin.

But as it turned out, Kathryn Dance didn't need to parse her handiwork to determine if Edwin was or was not the perp.

P. K. Madigan called back and, in a voice uncharacteristically rattled, blurted, "She and Edwin left the diner a half hour ago. But her SUV's still in the lot. And her keys were on the ground nearby."

"She dropped them, to let us know he'd snatched her. Her phone?"

"Battery's out or it's been crushed. No signal to trace. I sent Lopez to Edwin's house and the Buick's there. But the place is empty, looks like he's moved out."

"He's got new wheels."

"Yep. But I checked. Either stolen or bought private. Nothing at DMV in his name, no rentals at any of the companies in our database. He could be driving anything. And going anywhere."

Chapter 71

ALIBI WOMAN HAD lied.

When Dance had spoken with her on the phone, twenty minutes before, seventy-two-year-old Mrs. Rachel Webber had once again—and very quickly—verified Edwin's story about the time he'd been at her house on Tuesday.

But it took the agent only three minutes of trim questioning to learn what really happened: Edwin had found her in the garden early that morning. He'd forced her inside with a gun and gotten the names of her children and grandchildren and said that when the police came to ask her, she was to say he was there at twelve-thirty.

Now Dance and Dennis Harutyun were listening to Madigan having a conversation with the Crime Scene Unit boss. Finally he grunted and slammed the receiver down. "Backyard of Edwin's, Charlie's folks found some human bones and some tools. Buried deep, so CSU wouldn't find them when they searched the other day. You were right, Kathryn; he made those guitar picks himself, outa that file sharer's hand."

Dance rocked back and forth in a cheap swivel chair in Madigan's office. A cup of ice cream soup sat coagulating beside his phone. And she thought again, How did I miss? What'd gone wrong? She hadn't been able to read his deception but she'd known that body language analysis of someone like Edwin Sharp would be difficult if not impossible.

So she'd looked at the facts he'd mentioned, tried to analyze not his kinesics but his verbal content. Well, think about it. Was there anything that might help them find where Edwin would go with his love?

And what would happen when they got there?

Dance believed she knew the answer to *that* question and she did not want to consider it.

Harutyun asked, "Why didn't he just snatch her a few days ago?"

Dance gave her thoughts. "Oh, he didn't *want* to snatch her at all. It's why he set up Alicia as the killer. So he could rescue Kayleigh and win her over with his heroism. Like some arsonists—they set fires and then rescue people, to be heroes. Which is exactly what he did.

"He probably pitched his case to her at lunch, reminding her that he'd saved her life, why didn't they go out on a date, or something like that. She said no. That was his last chance to be close to her in private so he did what he had to, kidnapped her. But it's not impulsive. Believe me, he's known this was a possibility and he'd had it all planned out as a last resort."

Something was eating away at her. Something elusive. Facts again . . . verbal content. Facts were not meshing.

What is it?

She sighed. The thought vanished before it solidified. Then:

Wait . . . Yes! That's it!

She grabbed the phone and placed a call to her friend and colleague, Amy Grabe, FBI Special Agent in Charge, San Francisco.

The woman's low, sultry voice said, "Kathryn, saw the wire—kidnapping and possible interstate flight."

"That's why I'm calling."

"It's really the singer Kayleigh Towne?"

"I'm afraid so. A stalker."

"Well, what can we do? You think he's headed this way?"

"That's not why I'm calling. What I need are a couple of field agents in the Seattle area. I have to conduct an interview with a witness and I don't have time to get up there. It's got to happen now."

"Can't you do it over the phone?" the SAC asked.

"I tried that. It didn't work."

Chapter 72

WELL, THOUGHT KATHRYN Dance, staring at the computer screen. Look at this.

The woman she was gazing at, presently in Seattle and connected via Skype, could have been Kayleigh Towne's sister.

Not an identical twin but real close. Straight, blond hair, a petite frame, a long, pretty face.

Edwin's former girlfriend, Sally Docking, stared nervously at the computer screen. Her voice broke as she said, "These people, I don't understand. I didn't do anything wrong." There were two FBI agents behind her in the living room of her Seattle apartment.

Dance smiled. "I just needed them to bring one of their computers so you and I could have another chat."

Actually they were there because she didn't think Sally would voluntarily go onto Skype for a second conversation.

Dance's voice was casual, despite the urgency she felt. "You'll be all right. Provided you tell me the truth."

Not "tell me the truth *this time*." That was too confrontational.

"Sure."

A discrepancy had occurred to Kathryn Dance—certain facts were not lining up. Now that Edwin Sharp had been revealed to be the perp, his behavior with

Sally Docking didn't ring true. Her earlier account of life with Edwin had been more or less credible over the phone but a kinesic expert needs to *see* her subject, not just hear, to spot deception.

And so Amy Grabe had called the Seattle field office of the Bureau and sent two agents to Sally Docking's apartment in a working-class section of the city. They brought with them a very expensive laptop, which incorporated a high-definition webcam.

Dance was in a conference room in the sheriff's office, the overhead lights off but a desk lamp not far from her face. She'd adjusted the illumination carefully; she needed Sally to see her very clearly—and under ominous lighting. Sally was lit by ambient rays but the lens and software rendered the image perfectly.

"It looks like a nice apartment, Sally." Dance wore her pink-rimmed glasses, the nonthreatening ones, unlike the steel- or black-rimmed predator specs she put on when she wanted to present an aggressive image.

"It's okay, I guess. I like it. Rent's cheap."

Dance asked a number of other questions about the girl, her family, her job, as she drew a baseline of the woman's behavior. She caught only one microburst of stress, when Sally said she didn't mind the commute to her job at a mall fifteen miles from where she lived.

Good, she was getting a feel for the woman, who tended to appear nervous and uncertain even when she was being asked simple questions and answering truthfully.

After ten minutes of this, Dance said, "Now, I'd like to talk to you about Edwin some more."

"Everything I told you was true!" Her eyes bored into the camera.

This was awkward: a blunt denial quickly delivered. Dance couldn't over- or underreact; it might tip her hand. "It's just routine. We often follow up to get more information when there's been a change in developments."

"Oh."

"We need your help, Sally. See, the situation down in Fresno's . . . difficult. Edwin may have been more involved in a crime than it originally seemed. I'm worried that he might be going through a bad phase and could hurt somebody. Or hurt himself."

"No!"

"That's right." Dance had made certain that not a single soul leaked to the public the news that Edwin had snatched Kayleigh. Sally Docking wouldn't know. "And we need to find him. We need to know where he might go, places that are important to him, other residences he might have."

"Oh, I don't know anywhere like that." Her eyes whipped to the computer screen.

A baseline variation. It confirmed that she did have some ideas. But dislodging this nugget would take some work.

"Well, you might know more than you think, Sally."

"But I haven't heard from him for a long time."

Nonresponsive. And the vague adjective didn't mask the fact that this was probably a lie but Dance let it go for now. "Well, not necessarily someplace he wanted to move to. Just someplace he mentioned when you were together."

"No."

"No?"

Sally was thinking quickly. "I mean, he was pretty much into Seattle. He didn't travel much. He was, like, a homebody kind of guy."

"Never mentioned anything, really?" A glance at the sheet in front of her.

Sally caught the glance.

As long as you tell the truth . . .

"I mean, he talked about going on vacations some. You know. But I didn't think that's what you meant."

"Where did he want to go?"

"Nashville was one place. The Grand Ole Opry. And then maybe New York, so he could go to some concerts."

Edwin Sharp probably did say that but he was not going to run off to Nashville or Manhattan with Kayleigh Towne and set up housekeeping, however skewed his sense of reality.

But Dance said, "Good, Sally. That's just the sort of thing we're looking for. Can you think of any other places? Maybe you were watching a TV show and he said, 'Hey, that looks neat.' Something like that?"

"No, really." Eyes on the web camera.

Lie.

Dance grimaced. "Well, I appreciate you trying. I don't know what I'm going to do. You were really the only person we can turn to."

"Me? I broke up with him a while ago. Uhm, nine months. About that."

"I just mean you had a very different relationship with Edwin than some people. You won't believe it but he can be very abusive and obsessive."

"No, really?"

Dance's heart tapped faster. She was on the trail of her prey and closing in. Still, easy as could be, she continued, "That's right. When people reject him, that pushes a button. Edwin has issues about abandonment and rejection. He clings to people. Since *he* broke up with *you,* you're not a negative in his life. In fact, he told me he still feels bad about the breakup."

"You were talking about me with Edwin? Like, recently?" Delivered fast, like spilled water.

"That's right. Funny, you could get the impression, from what he said, that he kind of misses you." Dance crafted her sentences very carefully. She never intentionally deceived her subjects but sometimes let them do it for her. "I wouldn't be surprised if he was curious what you're up to."

Sally swallowed and, with tentative fingers tipped in blue polish, she brushed at her long hair—an echo of Kayleigh's, though not as long, not as fine. When she tilted her head Dance noticed the roots; she was not a natural blonde. The young woman asked in a slightly higher pitch—a stress tone: "What did he want to know?"

"Just general things." Intentionally evasive.

She swallowed again.

Dance glanced down at a blank sheet of paper then up once more. She noted a faint glistening of sweat on Sally's forehead as she strained to see it.

The FBI has some really good equipment.

Dance again glanced down at the sheet and Sally's eyes dropped toward the desk in front of her as if the paper were two feet from her. Dance asked, "Your brother in Spokane? And your mother in Tacoma?"

"I just . . . my brother, my mother?"

"Edwin was close to them?"

The stalker had not said more than one or two sentences about Sally Docking and nothing at all about her family. Dance had looked up the details through Washington state and federal records, after she suspected the true relationship between the two.

"Did he say anything about *them*?" Sally asked.

"They were friendly, weren't they? Close?"

"I . . ."

"What, Sally? Would you be concerned if Edwin showed some interest in your family?"

Ah, the power of the hypothetical.

Some interest in . . .

"What did he *say*?" she blurted. "Please tell me!"

"What's the matter, Sally?" Dance tried to appear perplexed.

"I . . ." The tears began. "What did he *say*?" Behind her, one FBI agent shifted, perhaps sensing the edge of hysteria, as was Dance. "Edwin? What did he say about my family?"

Dance said evenly, "Why are you troubled? Tell me." Her brow furrowed.

"He's going to hurt them! He won't understand that I did what he wanted. If he mentioned them to you it means he's going to hurt them to get back at me. Please, you have to do something!"

"Wait." Dance looked troubled. "I hope you're not telling me that *you're* the one who wanted to break up."

"I—"

"Oh, no. That changes everything. . . . I mean, what I told Edwin . . ." She stopped speaking and peered at Sally uneasily.

"Please! No! What did you tell him? Where is he? Is Edwin going to Tacoma, Spokane?"

"We don't know where he is, Sally, I told you that. . . . Let me think. Okay, this is a problem."

"Don't let him hurt my mama!" She was sobbing now. "Please! And my brother's got two babies!"

The scenario was playing out just as Kathryn Dance had planned. The agent had needed to plant the seeds of fear within the woman to get her to open up and had formed her questions to give the impression that Edwin was practically en route to kill her family . . . and possibly then her.

Breathless with tears: "I did what he wanted. Why is he going to hurt us?"

Dance said sympathetically, "We can help you, Sally. But we can't do anything for you or your mother or brother if you're not honest."

In fact, she'd already talked to the local authorities and made sure that both Sally's mother's and brother's houses were being guarded, though the family members didn't know it at this point.

Sally struggled for breath. "Please. I'm sorry. I lied. He told me I had to. He told me if anybody asked, I was supposed to tell them that he was the greatest guy and never stalked me or anybody and *he* broke up with *me*, not the other way around. I'm sorry but I was scared. Send the police to my mother's. And my brother. He's got the babies! Please! I'll give you the addresses."

"First, tell me the truth, Sally. Then we'll see about the police. What's the real story between Edwin and you?"

"Okay," the woman said, wiping her face with tissues one of the agents behind her provided. "Last year Edwin was a security guard in the mall where I was working and he saw me and it was like, bang, he got totally obsessed with me."

Because she looked like Kayleigh Towne.

"He started this campaign to win me over. And one thing led to another and we started going out. Only he got weird. I wasn't allowed to do this, couldn't do that. . . . Sometimes he just wanted to sit and look at me. He'd just stare or lie in bed and stroke my hair. It was so fucking creepy! He'd tell me how beautiful I was, over and over. The fact is he thought I looked like this singer—the one he liked. I think I mentioned her before. Kayleigh Towne."

Sally scoffed, "We had to play her music all the time. He talked about her every day. Mostly it was 'poor Kayleigh this, poor Kayleigh that.' Nobody understood her, her father sold the family house she loved, her mother died, the fans don't treat her right, the label doesn't record her right. He went on and on. I couldn't take it. I just left one night. It was sort of okay for a month. He stalked me, yeah, but it wasn't terrible. But then his mother died and he freaked out. I mean totally."

The stressor event that had pushed him over the edge.

"He came over, crying and acting all weird, like his life was over with. I felt bad for him—and I was scared—so we got back together. But he just got stranger and stranger. He wouldn't go out at all, he made me drop all my friends, he got jealous of men at work. He thought I was sleeping with every one of them there. As *if* . . . All he wanted was for me to be at home with him. Look at me and watch TV and have sex. He'd play her music when we did that. It was horrible! Finally . . ." Sally debated and pulled her sleeve up and displayed a scar on her wrist. "It was the only way I could get free. But he found me and got me to the emergency room. I think that convinced him to back off."

"When was this?"

"December, last year."

The second stressor event, the one that had initiated his stalking Kayleigh.

Dance made a decision. "He's kidnapped her, Sally."

"Who, Kayleigh Towne?" she whispered. And yet she didn't seem too shocked.

"We'll protect you and your family, Sally. I promise. And we'll get him and put him in jail for the rest of his life—he's also killed some people."

"Oh, no. My God, no."

"But we can only do that if you help us. Do you have any idea where he might go?"

Another debate raged within her.

She knows something. Come on, Dance thought. Come on. . . .

"I . . ."

"We'll get the police to your family, Sally. But you have to meet us halfway."

"Well, he said he had this, like, religious experience, seeing Kayleigh sing for the first time. An outdoor concert, a couple years ago. He said if he could live anywhere, that's where it would be. In a cabin in the woods near there."

"Where?" Dance asked.

"Some town in California, on the ocean. Monterey. I don't know exactly where it is."

Dance finally looked away from the screen and caught Madigan's eye. She looked back at the tearstained face of her subject. "That's all right, Sally. I do."

Chapter 73

AS THEY DROVE along, Edwin Sharp was singing, loud and more or less in key.

> She gets gallons to the mile, not the other way
>   round,
> And the tailpipe, it really makes a pretty nasty
>   sound,
> The heater hardly works at all and forget about the
>   air.
> Duct tape's been involved in most of her repairs.
> But she's big and fast and solid and I know I can
>   depend
> On her to always be there . . . unlike a lot of men.
>
> She's my red Cadillac . . . my red Cadillac.
> She gets me where I'm going, and she always gets
>   me back.
> I love her like a sister, she's my red Cadillac.

"We had to say good-bye to her," he called into the back of the van. "My red Buick. Sorry."

Kayleigh was concentrating on not crying. This was a survival, not an emotional, issue. Her nose was already perilously stuffed up and she was sure if she started sobbing she'd suffocate. The tape on her mouth was a tight seal. She wasn't blindfolded but she was in the far back of the windowless van, on the floor. He'd pulled her boots off. Lovingly smelled the leather. Sick.

They were about an hour from Fresno, though she didn't know which direction, probably in the foothills toward Yosemite or the Sierras because the road seemed to be at an incline. West or south, the landscape was flat. They stopped once, after Edwin had glanced into the rearview mirror at her and he'd frowned. He pulled off the road and climbed into the back; she'd shied away. He'd said, "No, no, made a mistake there." A thick strand of her hair had been imprisoned by the duct tape and Edwin had carefully loosened it and worked the hair free from the adhesive. "Can't have that." And he recited again how long it had been since she'd cut it. "Ten years, four months . . . You could write a song. That'd be a good title."

Then to her horror he'd pulled a brush from his pocket and run it through her hair gently, meticulously. "You're so beautiful," he'd whispered.

Then the drive had resumed.

He now sang, " 'She gets me where I'm going and she always gets me back. She's my red Cadillac.' Love it, just positively love it."

Kayleigh's hands were cuffed in front of her. She'd hoped she could grab one of the rear door levers, open it and tumble out, taking her chances on the road and traffic.

But there were no door levers. He'd removed them. Edwin Sharp had planned this carefully.

As he continued to sing, she felt the van turn off the main road and drive for a time along a smaller highway, one in bad condition. Definitely going up. Ten minutes later the tires began to crunch over dirt and gravel. Then the surface got even rougher and the vehicle strained uphill for several miles. Finally the van leveled off and ten minutes later came to a stop.

Edwin climbed out. Then there was silence for a long moment.

This isn't fair, she thought. It just isn't goddamn fair.

You walk out onstage and sing folks your songs,
You make them all smile. What could go wrong?

"Hey there!" Edwin was opening the rear door, revealing a field surrounded by a pine forest. He helped her out and pulled the tape off her mouth—gently, though she was thoroughly repulsed once more by the touch of his skin on hers. She smelled his aftershave— yes, definitely her father's—and his sweat.

She inhaled hard, shivering with relief. She felt like she'd been half drowned.

Edwin stepped back and stared at her adoringly but there was no artistic admiration in his gaze now; his eyes lingered on her breasts and crotch.

"My boots," she said.

"Naw, I like you barefoot." A glance down. "We'll have to do something about that polish. It's a little too red, you know."

Then he was gesturing at a small single-wide trailer, covered with camouflage netting. It sat in the middle of the clearing. "Familiar?"

"Look, if you let me go, you can have a head start. Six hours, ten hours. And I'll arrange to get you money. A million dollars."

"Doesn't it look familiar?" he repeated, irritated that she wasn't understanding.

She gazed around. It did, yes. But what was— Oh, my God . . .

Kayleigh realized, stunned, where she was standing. This was the property she'd grown up on! That her grandfather had cleared and where he'd built the family house. Edwin had put the trailer pretty much where the manse had been. There'd been a lot of clearing over the years but she could easily recognize landmarks from her childhood. She remembered that Edwin had been aware that she'd been upset Bishop had sold the property—just as he'd lost his own childhood house. How had he found the land? A deed search, she supposed.

Kayleigh knew too that because the company that had bought up all of the private property here had gone bankrupt, there wasn't a soul around for twenty miles.

Edwin said with a sincere intensity, "I knew how much this meant. This property. I wanted to give it back to you. You'll have to show me where you rode your pony and walked your dogs when you were a little girl. We can go for the same walks. That'll be fun! Maybe we'll do that before supper tonight."

She supposed she should play along, pretend she was touched and then when his back was turned grab a rock and break his skull and run. But she couldn't feign. Revulsion and anger swirled within her. "How the hell can you say you love me and do this?"

He grinned and gently stroked her hair. She jerked her head away. He hardly noticed. "Kayleigh . . . from the first time I heard your opening number at that concert in Monterey, I knew we were soul mates. It'll take you a little longer but you'll figure it out too. I'll make you the happiest woman in the world. I'll worship you."

He covered the van with a camouflaged tarp, secured it with rocks and slipped his arm around her shoulders, very firmly. He guided her toward the trailer.

"I don't love you!"

He only laughed. But as they approached the trailer,

his gaze morphed from adoring to chill. "He fucked you, didn't he? Bobby. Don't say he didn't." He eyed her carefully as if asking tacitly if it was true. And wanting to hear that it wasn't.

"Edwin!"

"I have a right to know."

"We were just friends."

"Oh, I don't know where it's written friends don't ever fuck. Do you know where that's written?"

So, the sanitized language from earlier—in conversation and emails—had been phony, just another part of the innocent image he created. And she now knew that he *hadn't* been simply tapping his leg in time to the music the other day.

They were at the trailer door now. He calmed and smiled again. "Sorry. I get my hackles up, thinking about him."

"Edwin, look—"

"I should carry you over the threshold. The wedding night thing, you know."

"Don't touch me!"

He gazed at her with some pity, it seemed, then pushed the door open and swept her up into his arms like she weighed nothing at all. He carried her inside. Kayleigh didn't resist; one of his massive hands firmly cradled her throat.

Chapter 74

"WE'RE ON OUR way," Kathryn Dance said into her phone, speaking to Michael O'Neil.

She then gasped as Dennis Harutyun nearly demirrored his cruiser as the passenger side of the car came within inches of the truck he was passing. He skidded back into the lane and sped up.

"Are you okay?" O'Neil asked. "Are you there?"

"Yes. I'm . . . yes." She closed her eyes as Harutyun took on another tractor-trailer.

O'Neil was at his desk in his own sheriff's office. Dance opened her eyes briefly and asked, "What's in place?"

"Two helicopters around Point Lobos—that's where Edwin first saw Kayleigh at the concert two years ago. And another chopper's covering the area from Moss Landing up to Santa Cruz. Concentrating on the deserted areas. CHP's setting up roadblocks around Pacific Grove, Pebble Beach and Carmel. We've got about forty Monterey county and city uniforms involved."

"Good."

"And your boss is doing his thing."

The head of the Monterey branch of the California Bureau of Investigation, Charles Overby, the consummate artist at press conferences, was enlisting the aid of the public to be on the lookout for Edwin Sharp and Kayleigh Towne.

The many fan sites too were abuzz and included pictures of the suspect and his victim, though Dance supposed that anyone with a TV or iTunes subscription knew what Kayleigh Towne looked like.

"How're you doing?" O'Neil asked, echoing his earlier question.

A curious inquiry.

But not so curious in the context of where they'd left their personal lives just before he returned to Monterey.

But now was not the time for those considerations.

"Fine," she said. Which didn't mean fine at all but was like a fencer's parry. She hoped O'Neil got it.

He seemed to. He asked, "What's your ETA?"

She glanced at Harutyun and posed the question.

"Half hour," he said.

Dance relayed this to O'Neil and added, "Better go, Michael. We're doing about two hundred miles an hour here."

Drawing a rare smile from the mustachioed deputy.

They disconnected. She leaned back against the headrest.

"You want me to slow down?" Harutyun asked.

"No, I want you to go faster," Dance said.

He did and she closed her eyes once more.

"WHAT DO YOU think?" Edwin asked cheerfully. He waved his arm around the trailer, which was perfectly neat and scrubbed. It was also stiflingly hot.

Standing in the kitchenette, still cuffed, Kayleigh didn't answer.

"Look, a high-def TV and I've got about a hundred DVDs. And plenty of your favorite foods." He opened cabinets to show her. "Whole Foods. Organic, of course. And your favorite soap too."

Yes, it was, she noted. Her heart sank at this foresight on his part.

She also noticed several lengths of chain in the trailer, fixed to the walls, ending in shackles. Apparently Edwin's idea of thoughtfulness was to glue lamb's wool to the metal clamps that would fit around her ankles and wrists.

Mr. Today . . .

Then, once again, his smile faded. "If you'd gone out with me, like I asked," Edwin said, "we wouldn't've had to go through all of this. Just dinner. And stayed in my rental for a few days, while they fixed your house. What was the big deal?"

Kayleigh sensed he was shivering with anger.

Edwin has a reality problem. All stalkers do.

His voice grew cold again. "I know you're not a virgin. . . . I'm sure you didn't *want* to fuck anybody, it just sort of happened. You *did* fuck Bobby, didn't you? . . . No, I don't want to know." He reflected for a moment. "And I'm sure you didn't do anything weird—you know, disgusting. Sometimes the good girls—the ones in glasses and buttoned-up blouses—they can do really sick things. But you wouldn't." He looked at her closely. But then like a light switch clicking on, his face warmed and he was smiling. "Hey, it's okay. You're mine now. It's going to be okay."

He showed her the trailer more closely. The place was a shrine to her, of course. Posters and memorabilia, clothing and photos.

Kayleigh Towne everywhere.

But no weapons.

No sharp knives in the kitchen—the first thing she looked for. Also, no glass or ceramic. It was all metal and plastic. She noticed a pack of cigarettes and looked for a lighter. But there was none.

He followed her gaze. Edwin said quickly, "Don't worry. I don't smoke, not anymore. Just needed a few of those to point the finger at that bitchy Alicia. For you, Kayleigh, no cigarettes and no liquor. I'm clean. And I never did drugs—like that *friend* of yours Mr. Bobby Prescott."

Sweat poured, her skin crawled. "This is hopeless, Edwin. You don't think ten thousand people are going to be looking for me?"

"Maybe not. They might think you ran off with somebody you realized loved you and cared for you. They'll still be thinking Alicia was behind it all, killed Bobby and tried to kill you."

Was he that far removed from reality?

"But even if they *are* looking, they aren't going to find us. They think we're in Monterey, hiding out. Two hundred miles away. This bitch I went out with for a while told them that's where we'd be. I knew she'd turn me in. I set that up a long time ago. We're completely alone here. . . . On the drive? There wasn't a single helicopter or roadblock all the way from Fresno. If they thought we were headed here, they could've shut down Forty-one in a minute. No, Kayleigh, they'll never find us."

"You put this all together . . . to, what? Win me over?"

"To make you see reason. Who else would go to all this trouble, except somebody who loved you?"

"But . . . the congressman? I don't understand."

He laughed. "Oh, yeah, that was interesting. I learned a lesson there. I've stopped posting things on-line. That's how Simesky found out about you and me. You didn't believe me when I said the whole world was trying to exploit you."

You and me . . .

"But something good came out of that. I *did* see somebody outside my house on Saturday night. It was Simesky or that Babbage woman but at the time I thought it was just kids. But that got me thinking. I'd set it up so that it looked like Alicia had been spying on me. I planted some evidence that'd make the police think she was the stalker. Sometimes it's lucky how things work."

Then Edwin grew impatient. He looked at her hair, her breasts, her legs. "Well, come on. You know what it's time for." He glanced toward the rumpled bed, beside which was a Bose iPod player. "You see that? I've got fifty of your concerts I recorded. I have a nice recorder. I saved up to buy it. We'll play your concerts while we, you know. . . ." His face blossomed with concern. "Oh, don't worry. Yeah, I recorded them but I never sold the songs or shared them with anybody. It was just for me . . . and now for *us*."

"Please, no, Edwin. Please."

He stared at her hair, then leaned against the kitchen sink. "You shouldn't be so . . . you know, standoffish. I did you a favor. Fred Blanton was a shit who stole your music. And Alicia, well, she probably *did* want your career. And Sheri? Oh, please. You deserve a better stepmother than her. She's a store clerk who got lucky with Bishop. She's not worthy of you, Kayleigh. They deserved to die. And Bobby? All he wanted to do was fuck you." And once more he stared at her, awaiting confirmation of her infidelity.

Then he seemed to control himself.

She said, "At least, let me clean up? Just a shower please. I don't feel comfortable like this."

"I don't think so."

She snapped, "And you say you're Mr. Today?

Bullshit. I just want to take a fucking shower and you won't let me?"

He frowned. "All right. Only don't say words like that. Don't ever say words like that again."

"All right, I won't."

"You can take a shower. But you know I have the only keys and there're no weapons here. And all the windows are barred."

"I figured that. I really just want to clean up."

He undid the cuffs and she rubbed her wrists.

Shoulders slumped, she walked through the narrow space into the bathroom.

"Oh, Kayleigh. Wait."

She stopped and turned. He was awkward. Was his face reddening? "About that woman I was telling you about. The one in Seattle. You don't have to be jealous. It wasn't serious between us. I never slept with her. Really. Honest."

Kayleigh could see he was lying but what shocked her was that he seemed honestly to believe that his fidelity was important to her.

He smiled. "Hurry back, love." And he walked into the bedroom to wait.

Chapter 75

EDWIN COULDN'T DECIDE which of her songs was his favorite.

But then he realized that that debate was a clunker, another of his mother's terms. It was like you didn't have a favorite kind of food, you liked everything (well, *he* did, at any rate—he would have weighed three hundred pounds if Kayleigh hadn't been in his life to keep him trim).

He clicked the air conditioner on a little higher—with the camouflage tarp covering the trailer it was beastly hot inside. But he still kept the temperature warm. Kayleigh, he'd noticed before she headed to the shower, had been sweating. The beads on her skin had turned him on even more. He imagined licking her temples and scalp and grew even more aroused. It had been okay fucking Sally, with Kayleigh Towne's voice singing through the speakers, but this would be a thousand times better.

The real thing.

Hey, that was a pretty good title for a song. "The Real Thing." He'd mention it to her. He had this idea that they could write songs together. He'd come up with the words and she'd write the melodies.

Edwin was good with words.

He thought again: Wedding *afternoon*. Not wedding night. Afternoon.

That was pretty funny.

That got him wondering if she'd ever made out with

anybody when she and her family had lived here. There was that line in her song where she referred to "a little teenage lovin'," at the old house, which had made him absolutely furious when he'd first heard it. Then he remembered Bishop had sold the place when she was about twelve or thirteen. And because she was a good girl he doubted that she'd done anything more than kiss a boy and maybe do a little petting, which nonetheless also stabbed him with jealousy.

Bobby . . .

He hoped the fucking roadie had felt a lot of pain as he died. At the convention center he hadn't screamed as much as Edwin would have liked.

Edwin listened to the running water, pictured her naked inside the shower. He was growing hard. He remembered the article in *Rolling Stone* about her.

Good Girl Makes Good.

And he decided to relent.

He'd forgive her for fucking Bobby. He'd ask her again and insist she be honest. He had to know but whatever she said, he'd forgive her.

He stripped his shirt off and kneaded his belly. Still a bit of excess skin from where he lost all that weight. But he'd kept the fat off, at least.

Anything for Kayleigh.

Should *he* take a shower too? No. He'd taken one that morning. Besides, she'd have to get used to having him on top of, or behind, her whenever he was in the mood, whether he was clean or not.

She was his wife, after all.

He turned on the radio and caught the news. It seemed the police hadn't gone with the innocent interpretation of Kayleigh's disappearance. Pike Madigan's voice was explaining solemnly about the kidnapping and alerting people that it was likely that Edwin Sharp and

Kayleigh Towne were on their way west, heading toward the Monterey area.

"We don't know the vehicle they're in, but go to the website we've set up and you can find Sharp's picture."

Ah, I knew I could count on you, Sally, you lying little slut. He wondered momentarily who'd gotten her to talk. Kathryn Dance came to mind. Had to be her.

Of course, the diversion about Monterey would buy them only so much time. They'd have to move but this place would be safe for a month or so. Kayleigh had said she liked Austin. Maybe they'd go there next. It was Texas; there had to be wildernesses to hide out in. But then she also had commented in her "On the Road" blog that she liked Minnesota. That might be a better place, especially when she had the baby. The weather would be cooler. Tough to be pregnant in the heat, he imagined.

Babies . . .

Edwin had Googled that cycle thing about women's bodies. He wondered where Kayleigh was with that. Then decided it didn't matter. They'd make love at least every other night, if not more. He'd hit the target sooner or later.

He undid his jeans, slipping his hand into his Jockeys, though he didn't need any preparation there.

Then the shower water stopped. She'd be toweling off now. He pictured her body. He decided to establish a rule that they had to walk around the trailer naked. They'd only get dressed when they went outside.

Inhaling deeply, he smelled the sweet scent of shampoo fragrance on the humid air.

"Edwin," Kayleigh said, a playful tone. "I made myself ready for you. Come look."

Grinning, he walked to the doorway and found her in front of the bathroom door, fully clothed.

Edwin Sharp blinked. Then the smile vanished and he cried out in horror.

Chapter 76

"NO, NO, NO! What'd you do?"

She'd found tiny blunt-end fingernail scissors in the vanity kit he'd bought. TSA approved for air travel and therefore safe.

But they would still cut. And that's just what she'd done with them: she'd sheared off all her hair.

"No!" He stared in horror at the pile of glistening blond strands on the bathroom floor as if looking at the body of a loved one.

"Kayleigh!"

A two- to three-inch mop of ragged fringe covered her head. She hadn't showered at all, she'd spent the ten minutes destroying her beautiful hair.

In a mad singsong, she mocked, "What's the matter, Edwin? Don't you like me now? Don't you want to stalk me anymore? . . . It doesn't matter, does it? You love *me*, right? It doesn't matter what I look like."

"No, no, of course not. It's just . . ." He thought he'd be sick. He was thinking, how long does it take for hair to grow?

Ten years, four months . . .

She could wear a hat. No, he hated women in hats.

"I think it looks like you care a lot. In fact, you look real upset, Edwin."

"Why, Kayleigh? Why did you do it?"

"To show you the truth. You love the girl on the album covers, on CMT, on the videos and the posters. In *Entertainment Weekly*. You don't love me at all. Remember that day we were alone in the theater in Fresno? You said my voice and hair were the best things about me."

Maybe he could find somebody to take her hair and make a wig until it grew back. How could he do that, though? They'd recognize him, they'd report him. No, no, no, no, no! What was he going to do?

Kayleigh taunted, "You want to fuck me now? Now that I look like a boy?"

He walked forward slowly, staring at the pile of hair.

"Here!" she screamed and grabbed a handful, flung it at him. It flowed to the floor and Edwin dropped to his knees, desperately grabbing at the strands.

"I knew it," she muttered contemptuously, backing into the bathroom. "You don't know me. You don't have a clue who I am."

And then he got angry too. And the answer to her question was, Yes, I do know. You're the bitch I'm going to fuck in about sixty seconds.

He started to rise. Then saw something in her hand. What—? Oh, it was just a cup. It had to be plastic. There wasn't anything inside that could be broken or made into a knife.

He'd thought of that.

But one thing he hadn't thought of.

What the cup held:

Ammonia, from under the sink. She'd filled it to the brim.

The cut hair wasn't a message or a lesson. It was a distraction.

He tried to turn away but Kayleigh stepped forward fast and flung the chemical straight into his face; it spread up his nose, into his mouth. He managed to save his eyes by half a second, though the fumes slipped up under his lids and burned like red-hot steel. He cried at the pain, pain worse than any he'd ever felt. Pain as a creature, an entity, a *thing* within his body.

Screaming, falling backward, wiping frantically at his face. Anything to get away! Choking, gasping, coughing.

It hurts, it hurts, it hurts!

Then more pain as she hit him hard in the throat, the wound where he'd fired the bullet into his own neck.

He screamed again.

Doubling over, paralyzed, he felt her rip the keys from his pocket. He tried to grab her arm but she was quickly out of reach.

The bitter, biting chemical flowed deeper into his mouth and nose. He sneezed and spit and coughed and struggled to catch his breath. Edwin staggered to his feet and shoved his face under the faucet in the kitchen sink to rinse the terrible fire away.

But there was no water.

Kayleigh had run the supply dry.

Edwin stumbled to the refrigerator and yanked it open, feeling for a bottle of water. He found one and flushed his face, the cold liquid little by little dulling the sting. His vision, though fuzzy, returned. He stumbled to the front door, which she'd closed and locked. But he took a second key from his wallet and opened the door, then hurried outside, wiping his eyes.

He looked around. He spotted Kayleigh running down the road that led to the highway.

As the pain diminished, Edwin relaxed. He actually smiled.

The road was three miles long. Gravel. She was barefoot.

She wasn't going to get away.

Chapter 77

EDWIN STARTED AFTER her, jogging at first, then sprinting.

The terrible burn of the chemical had diminished his passion but not eliminated it. He was all the more driven to fling her to the ground, rip her jeans off. Then over onto her belly . . .

Make her cry, the way he was crying. Teach her who was in charge.

He saw her disappear around a curve in the road, only a hundred feet away. He was closing fast.

Seventy feet, fifty . . .

Teach her that she was his.

And then he turned the corner.

He ran for ten more steps, five, three, slowing, slowing. And then Edwin stopped. His shoulders sagging, coughing hard from the run and the ammonia.

And he laughed. He just had to.

Kayleigh stood with two people: a uniformed deputy and a woman, who had her arm around the singer.

Edwin laughed once more, a deep, hearty sound. The sound his mother made when she was happy and sober.

The man was a deputy he recognized from Fresno, the one with the thick black mustache.

And the woman, of course, was Kathryn Dance.

The deputy held a pistol, aimed squarely at Edwin's chest.

"Lie down," he called. "Lie down, on your belly, hands to your side."

Edwin debated. If I take one step I'll die.

If I lie down I'll go to jail.

Thinking, thinking . . .

In jail at least he'd have a chance to talk to Kayleigh, possibly to see her. She'd probably come visit him. Maybe she'd even sing for him. They could talk. He could help her understand how bad everybody else was for her. How he was the man for her. How he was Mr. Today.

Edwin Sharp lay down.

As Kathryn Dance covered him with her pistol, the deputy circled around, cuffed his hands and lifted him to his feet.

"Could I get some water for my eyes please? They're burning."

The officer got a bottle and poured it over Edwin's face.

"Thank you."

Other cars were arriving.

Edwin said, "The news. I heard on the news—you thought we were in Monterey. Why did you come here?" He was speaking to the dust and gravel but the person his words were intended for answered.

Dance holstered her pistol and replied, "We have teams in Monterey, true, but mostly for the press. So you'd think you'd fooled us if you listened to the radio or went online. To me, it didn't make sense for you to go there. Why would you tell Sally Docking anything about a location unless you figured she'd tell us eventually? That *is* a pattern of yours, you know. Misinformation and scaring witnesses into lying.

"As for here? CSU found trace evidence near your house that could have come from a mining operation. I remembered Kayleigh's song 'Near the Silver Mine.' You knew she was unhappy Bishop sold the place and it made sense you wanted to bring her back here. We looked at some satellite pictures of the place and saw the trailer. Camouflage netting doesn't really work."

Edwin reflected that Kathryn Dance was impressive but she quickly vanished from his thoughts entirely as he looked toward Kayleigh, standing defiant, feet apart, staring back coldly. Still, he had the impression that there was a spark of flirt in her eyes.

As soon as her hair grew back, she'd be beautiful again.

God, did he love her.

Chapter 78

AT SEVEN-THIRTY THAT night Kathryn Dance was backstage at the convention center.

There'd been talk about canceling the concert but, curiously, Kayleigh Towne was the one who insisted that it go on. The crowds were rapidly filling the venue and Dance sensed the same electricity that she remembered from her times on stage as a folksinger, years ago.

There really was nothing like that utter exhilaration, the power of voice and music in unison, streaming from the speakers, the audience yours, the connection consuming. Once you've been up in front of the lights it's easy to understand the addiction of having thousands of people in your spell. The power, the drug of attention, affection, need.

It's why performers like Kayleigh Towne continue to climb up onstage, despite the exhaustion, the toll on families . . . despite the risk from people like Edwin Stanton Sharp.

The singer was dressed for the concert—in her good-girl outfit, of course. The only difference was that tonight she was the good girl who'd just been playing softball with friends; on her head a Cal State Fresno Bulldogs' cap covered her shorn hair.

At the moment she was off to the side, "banging in" a new guitar. She wouldn't perform on her favorite Martin until it had been restrung and completely cleaned—because of the human bone picks Edwin had given her. Dance, as unsuperstitious as they came, couldn't blame her one bit; she herself might've thrown out the instrument and bought a new one.

"Well." P. K. Madigan wandered up, accompanied by a short, round woman of about forty. She had a pretty face, rooted forever in her high school years, with big cheerful eyes and freckles, framed by page-boy-cut brown hair. Dance found it charming that they held hands.

He introduced Dance to his wife.

"The CBI's welcome in Fresno anytime," Madigan told her, "provided *you're* the point person."

"It's a deal. Let's just hope you don't get any more cases like this one."

"We're gonna hear the concert," he added dubiously. "Or some of it. Long as it doesn't get too loud. Oh, here."

He thrust a box into her hand. Dance opened it and laughed. It was a Fresno Madera Consolidated Sheriff's Office badge.

"Tin star."

She thanked him and resisted the urge to pin it to her green silk blouse.

Madigan looked around grumpily and then said, "All righty then." He led his wife to their seats. It might have been Dance's imagination but he seemed to be looking for something in the back of the hall. Was it shadows or stalkers or ice cream vendors?

Dance turned her attention back to Kayleigh, who'd handed off the new guitar to Tye Slocum with some instructions. The singer then spoke to the band about some last-minute changes in the order of who would take instrumental solos and when. She'd changed a verse in one of her original songs, one that was meant for Bobby. Now, it included a few lines for Alicia. She'd told Dance that she was praying that she could get through the number without crying.

Tye Slocum shyly approached and told her the action had been adjusted as she wanted. She thanked him and the big man waited a moment. His generally evasive eyes snuck a glance or two at the singer's face and then he headed off. One might infer something suspicious from the expressions and kinesics, but to Dance all they revealed was a sheen of adoration. Which would forever remain unrequited.

But it was clear that he would never act on his secret hope—beyond microsecond glances and making sure her guitars were ready for battle.

Tye Slocum defined the difference between the normal and the mad.

It was then that a man in chinos and starched dress shirt, without tie, came up to Kayleigh and Dance. He was in his midthirties and had a boyish grin. Curly black hair was losing the war against a shiny scalp.

"Kayleigh, hi." Nothing more for a moment, other than a polite nod to Dance. "I'm Art Francesco." Both Dance and Kayleigh regarded him cautiously until his all-access badge dangled forward.

"Hi," Kayleigh said absently. Dance assumed he was a friend of Bishop's; she thought she'd seen them talking earlier that night in the parking lot.

"I'm so sorry about everything's that happened. Your dad told me. What a terrible time. But that guy's in jail, right?"

"Yes."

"Thank God. Well, just wanted to say how happy I am we're going to do business together."

"Uh-hum. And who are you again?"

He frowned. "Art. Art Francesco." A pause and when she gave no reaction the man added, "Your father mentioned I'd be coming tonight, didn't he?"

"Afraid he didn't."

He laughed. "Isn't that just like Bishop—a genius, you know. Sometimes details elude him."

A card appeared.

Dance didn't have to be a kinesics expert to note the shock that went through Kayleigh's body. The agent glanced at the singer's hand. The card was JBT Global Entertainment.

"What do you mean, doing business?"

Francesco licked the corner of his mouth. "Well, I'm sorry. But—"

"What is this?" Kayleigh snapped.

"Well, I thought your father. . . . He didn't say he hadn't told you. I just talked—"

"Tell me what?"

"Jesus Christ. Look, I'm sorry. He said he was going to tell you this morning, after we signed up everything. But with that crazy man, maybe he forgot or was distracted."

"Signed up *what*?"

"Well, you. Signed up *you*. He's . . . I'm sorry, Kayleigh. Oh, shit. I really thought you knew." Francesco looked miserable. "Look, why don't you talk to your father?"

The singer stepped forward. She'd just survived a homicidal stalker. She wasn't going to be put off by a suit from L.A. "*You* tell me. Now."

"He just signed you with Global. He's not renewing with Barry Zeigler and your label."

"What?"

"Can he do that?" Dance asked.

Jaw set in anger, Kayleigh muttered, "Yeah, he can.

It was set up that way when I was a minor. I never changed it. But he never did anything that I didn't agree with. Until now."

Francesco said, "Oh, but it's a great deal, Kayleigh. And the money! . . . You won't believe the money. You've got hundred-percent creative control. Bishop and his lawyers drove a really tough bargain. It's a three-sixty deal. We'll handle all your concert tours, your recordings, production, CDs, download platforms, marketing, advertising . . . everything. You'll go international, bigtime. We've already got commitments from CMT and MTV, and HBO is interested in a special. That all happened just today after he signed up. And Starbucks and Target both want exclusive albums. This is taking you to a whole new level. We'll get you into amphitheaters, Vegas, London. You'll never have to play little . . . places like this again."

"This little place happens to be my hometown."

He held up his hand. "I didn't mean it that way. It's just, this'll expand your career exponentially. I'm sorry it happened this way, Kayleigh. Let's start over." He extended his hand.

She ignored it.

Bishop Towne had seen the exchange and, with a disgusted look on his face, ambled over. He said, "Artie."

"I'm sorry, Bishop, I didn't know. I thought you'd told her."

"Yeah," he growled. "Stuff happened today. Didn't get around to it." As Dance expected, Bishop's eyes dipped to the stage and remained focused there. "Give us a minute, Artie."

"Sure. I'm sorry."

Kayleigh turned on her father. "How could you? I told Barry we weren't talking to Global. I told him that!"

"KT," he said in a soft rasp, "Barry's part of the past.

That world is gone now, record companies. It's the past."

"He was loyal. He was always there. He made me platinum."

"And in a few years, there won't be any platinum, not like there used to be. It's going to be downloads and TV and concerts and deals with retailers and airlines and ad agencies. The Industry's always been changing. That's the way it works. We're in a new era."

"That's a nice speech. Sounds like you've rehearsed it plenty." Her eyes narrowed and Dance saw within them an anger and defiance that had never been present when speaking with her father. She laughed coldly. "You think I don't see what's going on here? This isn't about me. It's all about you, isn't it?"

"Me?"

"You fucked up your career. You let your voice go to hell and now you can't sing or write your way out of a paper bag. So what do you do? You become the great impresario. What's Global's tagline going to be? 'Now Appearing . . . Bishop Towne's Daughter'?"

"KT, of course not. That's—"

"What's Barry going to do?"

"Barry?" As if Bishop hadn't thought about it. "He'll change with the times or he'll get into a new line of work. Or we'll have Art find a place for him at Global. We still need producers."

"So that's how you treat your friends. It's sure how you treated me, isn't it? You made me give up my . . ." She tailed off. Dance knew what was in her mind but the young woman wasn't going there now. "You made me give up so much, just so you could stay in the Industry. It was the only way you could hang on."

She wheeled around and walked away.

He shouted, "KT!"

She paused.

"You wait just a minute there."

Kayleigh turned back defiantly and Bishop approached. He regarded her not as a child but as a peer. Oblivious to onlookers he muttered, "You're acting like a spoiled little girl. All right, you want the truth? Yeah, I asked your sister and Congressman Davis here to discourage you from canceling. And, yeah, I cut the deal with Global. But, why I did that, it's *not* about me. And it's not about *you* either. You want to know what it's about? Do you?"

"Yeah, tell me," she snapped.

Bishop pointed to the filling seats. "It's about *them*, KT. The audience. They are the only thing in the universe that matters."

"I don't know what the hell you're saying."

"What you've got comes along once or twice in a generation. Your voice, your music, your stage presence, your writing . . . Do you know how rare that is? You know how important?"

His voice softened. "Music's the truth nowadays, KT. We don't get answers from religion or politicians; we sure as hell don't get 'em from TV news. We get answers from *music*. The whole world walks around with those little earplugs feeding songs into their brains. Why? So they can learn the truth! They need people who can put into words and music the answers they need. People who take away their sadness, make 'em understand everybody goes through lousy times too, show 'em there's hope, make 'em laugh.

"And for you, doing that's easy as fallin' off a log. It wasn't for me. But it is for you. Tell me, KT, how many songs you think up in the last coupla days? Without even trying? How many? A dozen, I'll bet."

Kayleigh blinked and Dance saw that he was right.

"That's a gift, honey." A mournful smile. "Pushing

you was never about me. It was 'cause I knew you had that gift. . . . I knew you'd be everybody's shadow, KT. I'm sorry you don't like it but that's the hand you got dealt. You gotta play it." He pointed out to the audience. "They need you."

"Then they're gonna be pretty disappointed tonight. Because this concert's going on without me."

With that, she was gone.

The two dozen people backstage were now all staring silently at the old man. He'd screwed up, probably intentionally not telling her about the Global deal so she'd go ahead with the concert. But Dance's heart went out to him. He looked shattered.

But Dance's meditations on the Towne family vanished at that moment.

She heard a familiar voice behind her. "Hey there."

She turned.

Well . . .

Jon Boling's common greeting, just like his personality, was easy, friendly. And more than a little sexy, Dance had always felt.

Until now.

She stared blankly. He gave a surprised laugh, apparently assuming she was caught up in whatever drama was going on backstage at the moment—all the somber faces. And he stepped forward, wrapping his arms around her.

She returned the pressure anemically, feeling the weight of the blunt realization that he'd come all the way here—three hours—to tell her he was leaving her and moving to San Diego.

At least he's got the balls to tell me face-to-face. . . .

A line, Dance reflected wryly, that had a good country beat to it, though she guessed it wasn't the sort of phrase that would ever appear in a Kayleigh Towne song.

Chapter 79

"YOU LOOK MORE surprised than I thought you would," Boling said, stepping back from the embrace.

He looked around, an exaggerated frown on his face. "Your secret lover must be here somewhere. And, dammit, I *bought* a ticket. You probably got him comped."

Dance laughed, though the sound only made her feel worse, a reminder of the many good times they'd shared. They walked to a deserted part of the backstage area.

Boling looked around. "What's going on? Everybody okay?"

"Hard to say." She couldn't avoid the cryptic response.

He looked her over. "We've had the worst phone luck. I've been doing ten-hour days. And you, your mom said you were working on that kidnapping case. Some vacation you had, hm?"

My mother, my spy.

"And Lincoln and Amelia were here?"

"Couldn't've done it without them." She told Boling about the minute bits of trace that gave her the idea that Edwin had taken Kayleigh's song to heart, the one about growing up near a silver mine. "That's how we traced him."

Boling leaned forward and kissed her quickly, his lips firmly against hers.

Her phone vibrated. A glance downward. It was Michael O'Neil.

Well, how's that for some irony?

"You have to get that?"

"I'll let it go," Dance said.

"Good turnout," he said. "I listened to one of Kayleigh's CDs on the way here. I can't wait for the show."

"About that . . . there may be a rain check situation."

And she told him about the blowup between father and daughter.

"No! You mean cancel the whole show?"

"Looks like it."

The crew, Kayleigh's band, the local backup musicians, a children's choir . . . everybody was standing around awkwardly, heads and eyes pivoting, engaged in a radar search for the centerpiece of the evening. The sense of dread was evident. Kayleigh was the least temperamental performer on earth. If she stormed out it was not diva drama, with her in the trailer waiting to be coaxed back. Her absence probably reflected the sentiment in one of her early hits: "Gone for Good (and It's Good to Be Gone)."

Bishop Towne, alone, wiped his hands on his slacks. It was five minutes past showtime. The audience wasn't restless yet but they soon would be.

Dance found her shoulders in a terrible knot. She glanced back at Boling's handsome face, his thinning brown hair, his perfect lips.

But, she told herself, feeling the spring steel of her soul flex within her, she'd lost one man to tragedy and she would far rather lose one this way—everyone going forward in life, healthy and with some vestige of affection. Something might work out in the future. At least there wasn't—she assumed—somebody else in his life. She would make sure that Boling and the children stayed in touch. Thank God they hadn't actually moved in together.

"Here. Snuck this in."

He handed her a Starbucks cup and she smelled immediately that it contained red wine, and since Boling was the barista it would be a good one. Yes, a nice Malbec, she deduced from a sip—one of the varieties they'd been exploring lately at wine tastings in Monterey and Carmel. They'd had so much fun on those nights. . . .

Kathryn Dance told herself: No tears.

That was nonnegotiable.

"Everything okay?"

She explained, "Tough case."

"I was worried about you when we kept missing calls."

Quit doing that! she silently raged. Make me hate you.

He sensed her tension and backed off, let go of her hand, gave her space.

And that conscientiousness irritated her even more.

But then he decided it was time. She could easily tell from his stance. Yes, he probably wanted to wait before delivering the bad news but preferred to get it over with. Men did that. Either they never said anything personal and serious, or they blurted it all out at the wrong moment.

Boling said, "Hey, wanted to talk to you about something."

Oh, that tone.

God, how she hated that tone.

She shrugged, sipping some of the wine. A big sip.

"Okay, I know this is going to seem a little odd but . . ."

For God's sake, Jon, get on with it. I've got my children to get back to, my dogs, my guests from New

York . . . and a friend here who's about to become the nemesis of 35,000 people.

"Sorry, I'm a little nervous about this."

"Jon, it's okay," she said, finding her voice surprisingly warm. "Go on."

"I know we've had a, well, sort of policy of not traveling with the kids, not overnight. Well . . ." He seemed to realize he was stammering and now just blurted, "I'm thinking I'd like all of us to take a trip." He looked away. "For this consulting gig, they need me down in San Diego for two weeks—La Jolla. The company rented me a place near the beach. It's a month rental and they said I could keep it for a week or two after the job's done. So I was thinking we could all drive down, see Hearst's Castle, then go to Lego Land and Disneyland for the kids. Well, actually, *I* want to go there too. Not Lego Land particularly. But Disneyland. So, what do you think? A week in San Diego, all four of us?"

"A week?"

He grimaced. "Okay, I know it's hard for you to get off, especially after you took some time now. But if there's any way you could . . . See, it's a four-bedroom place. We'd have separate rooms, all of us. You and me too. But still, it's a good step forward, with the kids, I was thinking. Traveling together but not *together* together, you know what I mean?"

"A week?" Dance was stammering herself too.

He'd be thinking: I said that, didn't I?

Oh, God—the move was temporary. Her mother hadn't gotten all the information.

He sensed her hesitation. And said stoically, "No problem. If that's too much time, maybe you and the kids could fly down and we could spend a few days together. I mean, you could always come down alone but,

I don't know, I thought it might be nice to take a family vacation."

Those last two words were like lace trim: flimsy yet hopeful.

"I . . . hey." He stumbled back as she threw her arms around him, both euphoric and utterly ashamed of her assumption, which was based on the worst thing a law enforcer can be swayed by—faulty information.

She kissed him energetically. "Yes, yes, yes! We'll work it out. I'd love to." Then she frowned. "But a favor?"

"Sure, of course."

She whispered, "Can you and I get adjoining rooms? Sometimes the kids go to sleep early."

"That can be arranged."

She kissed him once more.

Just as her phone chirped. This time, O'Neil had sent a text: *Signed the divorce papers. Enjoy the concert. See you soon . . . I hope.*

Oh, brother, she thought.

Oh, brother.

Another *ding*. She looked down: *XO, Michael.*

She slipped the phone away and took Boling's hand.

"A problem?" he asked.

"No," she said. "No problems at all."

Then the hulking form of Bishop Towne was approaching. He paused and, ignoring Boling, grunted to Dance, "Guess this is it." He took a deep breath. "Times like these're when I really miss a drink. Guess I better go make a slew of people real unhappy."

He ambled out onstage.

There was, of course, a resounding thunderclap of applause and shouts; this was Mr. Country himself greeting them, about to introduce his even more talented daughter.

He waved.

Pandemonium.

Dance and Boling walked into the wings to see better. As the spotlight found Towne, he looked diminished and old and in pain. He squinted slightly, hesitated and continued to an active microphone.

He scanned the crowd and seemed surprised there were so many people there, though Dance suspected that the savvy businessman would know the exact head count and box office receipts.

He rasped, "Good evening, y'all. I—" His voice caught and he started again. "I surely do 'preciate you coming out tonight." Bishop, Dance had noted, had no Southern accent when he was engaged in regular conversation. Now, a twang of Appalachia tinted his words.

More whistles and shouts and applause.

"Listen up, listen up. Uhm, I have an announcement I'd like to make."

There was a beat as the crowd grew silent, expecting something was wrong, perhaps related to Kayleigh's kidnapping earlier in the day and the other events of the past week.

Collective dismay was starting to brew.

"Again, we 'preciate your being here and appreciate all the support you've shown to Kayleigh and the band and her family during this difficult time."

He cleared his throat once more.

As he said, "I gotta tell you—" The applause began again and kept going and kept going, swelling, swelling, and became a force of its own. Within two or three seconds, the entire crowd was on its feet, howling, clapping, whistling.

Bishop was confused. What was this about?

Dance too didn't have a clue, until she looked stage

left and saw Kayleigh Towne walking forward, carrying a guitar and waving to the crowd.

She paused and blew them a kiss.

More unearthly sounds filled the concert hall, glow sticks waved back and forth, flashes from the prohibited cameras exploded like sunlight on choppy water.

Dance noticed that Suellyn and Mary-Gordon were now standing with Sheri Towne in the wings opposite, watching Kayleigh stride up to her father. They weren't alone. Art Francesco, from Global Entertainment, was now with them and chatting warmly with Sheri and her stepdaughter.

Onstage, Bishop bent down, hugged his daughter and she kissed him on his cheek. Kayleigh lowered a second microphone to her mouth and waited until the crowd grew silent.

"Thank you all! Thank you! . . . My daddy was going to tell you we have a big surprise for you tonight. But I decided I couldn't let him get away with hogging the spotlight, like he usually does."

Huge laughter.

"Anyway, what we want to do tonight is open the show with something we haven't done for years. A father-daughter duet." A bit of South was in her own voice now.

More otherworldly applause.

She handed Bishop the guitar and said, "Y'all probably know my daddy's a better picker than me so I'm going to let him have the git-fiddle and sing and I'm going to do a bit of harmony. Now, this's a song that Daddy wrote and used to sing to me when I was a little girl. I think it was probably the first song I ever heard. It's called 'I Think You're Going to Be a Lot Like Me.'"

A glance his way and he nodded, the faintest of smiles curling into his weathered face.

As the surge of applause and hoots settled, Bishop Towne swung the guitar strap over his broad shoulders, strummed to test the tuning and he and Kayleigh adjusted the microphones.

Then he looked behind him toward the band, now in position, noted that they were ready and turned his attention back to the thousands of expectant fans, silent as thought. He started tapping his foot, leaned forward and counted out into the microphone, "One . . . two . . . three . . . four . . ."

Your Shadow

1. You walk out onstage and sing folks your songs.
You make them all smile. What could go wrong?
But soon you discover the job takes its toll,
And everyone's wanting a piece of your soul.

Chorus:

When life is too much, just remember,
When you're down on your luck, just remember,
I'm as close as a shadow, wherever you go.
As bad as things get, you've got to know,
That I'm with you . . . always with you.
Your shadow.

2. You sit by the river, wondering what you got
   wrong,
How many chances you've missed all along.
Like your troubles had somehow turned you to
   stone
and the water was whispering, why don't you come
   home?

Chorus.

3. One night there's a call, and at first you don't
   know
What the troopers are saying from the side of the
   road,
Then you see in an instant that your whole life has
   changed.
Everything gone, all the plans rearranged.

Chorus.

4. *You can't keep down smiles; happiness floats.*
But trouble can find us in the heart of our homes.
Life never seems to go quite right,
You can't watch your back from morning to night.

Chorus.

Repeat Chorus.

Is It Love, Is It Less?

1. *A warm autumn night, the state fair in full swing,*
We walked back to my place and sure enough one
    thing
Led to another and at dawn you were there.
Your breath on my shoulder, your hand in my hair.

2. *Just a week later, it happened again,*
I was sure that we'd move to lovers from friends,
But that time I woke to a half empty bed,
And at least two months passed till I saw you again.

Chorus:
Is it left, is it right? Is it east, is it west?
Is it day, is it night? Is it good or the best?
I'm looking for answers, I'm looking for clues.
There has to be something to tell me the truth
I'm trying to know, but I can just guess,
Is it love between us?
Is it love, is it less?

3. *I saw you and some girl on the street one day.*
Oh, look, here's my friend, I heard you say.
But the "friend" that you meant wasn't her; it was me,
And you took her hand, pleased as could be.

4. *Then just a month later, we meet for a beer,*
We got to talking and then I hear,
you wonder out loud how life would be
if you got married to someone like me.

Chorus.

5. *I read blogs and the papers, I watch cable news.*
But the more that I hear, I get more confused.
Which reminds me of us, I simply can't tell
If I'm immune or I'm under your spell.

Chorus.

Near the Silver Mine

1. *I've lived in LA, I've lived in Maine,*
New York City and the Midwest Plains,
But there's only one place I consider home.
When I was a kid—the house we owned.
Life was perfect and all was fine,
In that big old house . . . near the silver mine.

Chorus:
The silver mine . . . the silver mine.
I can't remember a happier time,
In that big old house . . . near the silver mine.

2. *I remember autumn, pies in the oven,*
Sitting on the porch, a little teenage lovin',
Riding the pony and walking the dogs,
Helping daddy outside, splitting logs.
Life was simple and life was fine,
In that big old house, near the silver mine.

Chorus.

3. It stewed in the summer and froze in the winter,
The floors were sure to give you splinters.
A little wind and we'd lose the lights,
But nobody cared, it just seemed right.
Life was cozy and all was fine,
In that big old house, near the silver mine.

Chorus.

4. We'd go to the mine and sneak up close
To watch the train fill up with loads,
And wonder which nugget of shiny silver
Would become a ring for some girl's finger.
The future was bright and life was fine
In that big old house near the silver mine.

Chorus.

5. There was always kin and pickers too,
From daddy's band, playing country and blues,
They'd clear a table to be a stage,
And get me up to sing and play.
Life was good and all was fine
In the big old house near the silver mine.

Chorus.

6. My sis was born there and I was too.
And grandpa passed at eighty-two,
Asleep upstairs 'neath grandma's quilt.
in the house that he himself had built
To give his family a place real fine,
That big old house, near the silver mine.

Chorus.

The Truth About Men

1. Listen up, sonny boy, I've got some shocking news.

We girls, we got some problems, sure, we sometimes get the blues.

We get a little crazy, we fall head over heels.

We live to shop and drive for miles just for a good deal.

2. But one thing you can count on, we tell it to you straight.

I'm overdrawn, I'm leaving you, I'll be two hours late.

Maybe it's from playing cards, but you guys sure do bluff.

Don't you know that commandment: Thou shalt not make stuff up?

Chorus:

Men lie . . . [Clap hands five times] Men lie . . .

Last time that I looked, one and one do not make three,

If that's your kind of math, it's not good enough for me.

Men lie . . . [Clap hands five times] Men lie.

3. You'll call me in the morning, you'll be back home by eight.

You're gonna have just one more beer, my mom and dad are great.

You've never touched a single joint, you swear you sent that text.

You just need to cuddle, the last thing you want is sex.

Chorus.

4. *You boys're cute, you take us out, you can make*
   us laugh,
And nine times out of ten, you're just big pussy-
   cats.
No, I can't deny that most of you are fun.
You just got to work on, problem number one.

Chorus.

5. *I found a note from Stephanie. You said you*
   dated her.
But it was years and years ago, the time was just a
   blur.
So I called her up and chatted about you and her,
   of course,
When were you going to tell me, you never got
   divorced?

Chorus.

Then, fading out:

You fib . . . you prevaricate . . . you tell tall tales . . .
   you fabricate.
It must be something in your genes . . . or in your
   jeans.
Men lie . . .
[Clap hands five times]
Men lie . . .

Another Day Without You

1. *I see you on the street, holding someone else's*
   hand.
She's acting like she owns you—and that's more
   than I can stand.

I know that you're unhappy. I see it in your eyes.
It's clear that you don't love her, that you're living
in a lie.

Chorus:
And it's another day without you . . . Oh, such
lonely time.
But in just a little while . . . I'm going to make you
mine.

2. Ever since we met, I'm twice the girl I was.
Nothing keeps me going the way your smile does.
We have our time together but it's really not the same.
The thought you share a bed with her is driving me
insane. . . .

Chorus.

3. I'll steal you away, I will steal you for good.
I'll never have to share you; we'll live the way we
should.
It won't be too much longer until I set you free.
Then I'll never let you go, I'll keep you close to me.

Chorus.

Repeat Chorus.

My Red Cadillac

1. One Saturday a while ago, I went out for the
night.
The music, it was playing loud, everything seemed
right.
You smiled my way across the room and moved up
really near.
We talked and laughed and then you said, "Hey,
let's get out of here."

2. We walked outside and found my car. I sped into
   the street.
The night was really perfect, till I saw you weren't
   too pleased.
"What's wrong?" I asked, slowing down, before we
   got too far.
You said, "Just wondering if you ever thought 'bout
   getting a new car?"

Chorus:
She gets gallons to the mile, not the other way
   round,
And the tailpipe, it really makes a pretty nasty sound,
The heater hardly works at all and forget about the
   air.
Duct tape's been involved in most of her repairs.
But she's big and fast and solid and I know I can
   depend
On her to always be there . . . unlike a lot of men.

She's my red Cadillac . . . my red Cadillac.
She gets me where I'm going, and she always gets
   me back.
I love her like a sister, she's my red Cadillac.

3. This Caddie's got a history that goes back lots of
   years.
My daddy gave her to me as soon as I could steer.
She's the one who's moved me to a half a dozen
   states
And come with me to weddings and funerals and
   dates.

4. She hasn't got a GPS, the windshield's none too
   clear.
There's no pine tree freshener hanging from the
   mirror.

I don't reserve my Sundays to polish, wax and
   clean.
She's a wash and wear gal—an awful lot like me.

Chorus.

5. This Caddie is America, made for fast and far,
I feel a patriotic spirit when I'm driving in this car.
We've been from north to south, from sea to shining
   sea.
She's part of that tradition that made this country
   free.

6. That Saturday a while ago, if you're wondering
   how it went,
I pulled up to the curb, turned to that boy and said,
"So long, friend, I think you better hitch a ride on
   back.
There's no better judge of men than this here Cadillac."

Chorus.

Fire and Flame

1. I'm drawn to you, like a moth to flame.
Once we met, I was never the same.
To reach that light, moths fly for miles,
That's what I'd do, just to see your smile.

Chorus:
Love is fire, love is flame
It warms your heart, it lights the way.
It burns forever just like the sun.
It welds two souls and makes them one.
Love is fire, love is flame.

2. *I know some boys as smooth as ice,*
I can't deny some look real nice.
But I don't care if they're slick and cool,
They don't ignite me like you do.

Chorus.

3. *Some folks hook up not to be alone.*
Or they want babies and to make a home.
Nothing wrong with that, for them it's fine.
But I like my furnace turned up high.

Chorus.

4. *You can keep those days in early spring.*
A gentle autumn's not my thing.
No, I want sun and blaring heat—
Sweaty love, just you and me.

Chorus.

The Puzzle Of Your Heart

1. *A quiet Sunday, the rain comes down.*
Hey, you want to play a game?
I look around.
There's a jigsaw puzzle on the shelf.
A country scene, some old-time art
Of farms and fields and stacks of hay.
We pour some wine, curl up and start.

Chorus:
One piece there, and one piece here.
Some fall in place and some won't fit.
It's just not clear
How I can take these mismatched parts
And put together the puzzle of your heart.

2. *You want to stay, you have to go,*
I think I love you but I'm confused.
I just don't know.
Sometimes you stay, sometimes you run.
The past is good, but the future looms.
Let's have a baby, or maybe not.
Let's buy this place, no, we should move.

Chorus.

3. *The hours pass, there's not much done.*
The middle's harder than we thought.
It's been fun.
But the rain's let up. Let's take a walk.
We've got an hour before it's night.
Oh, you'd rather watch the game?
I understand. No, it's all right.

Chorus.

4. *I get back home and in the hall*
I find a note. You're outside jogging
After all.
I try a jigsaw piece or two,
But finally I admit defeat.
I guess that's how it often goes,
Some puzzles we just can't complete.

Chorus.

Leaving Home

1. *Packing up the suitcase, filling boxes to the brim.*
Years and years of memories, trying to fit them in.
I never really thought that there might come a
time,

*When everything would change and I'd have to say
  good-bye.*

Chorus:
Now I'm starting over, starting over once again,
To try to make a new life, without family or friends.
*In all my years on earth, there's one thing that I
  know:*
*Nothing can be harder than to leave behind your
  home.*

*2. This room, it was my daughter's, who's grown
  and lives nearby.*
*She's got babies of her own, oh, I'll miss them till I
  cry.*
*This room is the one where my man and I would
  sleep.*
*Or sometimes never sleep at all, if you know what
  I mean.*

Chorus.

*3. And here's the porch we'd sit on, after dinner
  every night.*
*My husband talked about his job and I'd tell him
  'bout mine.*
*Then dishes and some cleaning, some homework
  and to bed.*
*And the joy of seeing sunrise as the day would start
  again.*

Chorus.

*4. Oh, we had quite some parties, to mark those
  special times.*
Christmases and Easters and the Fourth of July.
Any cause for celebration, but the best, at least for me,

Was my daughter's graduation when she got her degree.

Chorus.

5. We worked hard at our jobs and bought ourselves this home.
We gave back what we got and never hurt a soul.
But I guess I was just naïve and I didn't see the truth:
Why judge people by their hearts? It's simpler to use rules.

6. Now the bus drives through the gate, at the border line,
And drops me off in Juarez, deported for the crime
Of loving the great USA as if she were my own.
I turn and say good-bye to what's been my only home.

Chorus.

Then in Spanish:
"America the Beautiful"

O beautiful for spacious skies,
For amber waves of grain,
For purple mountain majesties
Above the fruited plain!

America! America!
God shed His grace on thee,
And crown thy good with brotherhood
From sea to shining sea!

O beautiful for pilgrim feet
Whose stern impassion'd stress

A thoroughfare for freedom beat
Across the wilderness.

America! America!
God shed His grace on thee,
And crown thy good with brotherhood
From sea to shining sea!

Mr. Tomorrow

1. You know me by now, you've got to believe
You're the number-one girl in the world for me.
I've sent her the papers and she's promised to sign
It'll just be a while, these things take some time . . .

Chorus:
And his words are so smooth and his eyes look so
    sad.
Can't she be patient, it won't be so bad?
But sometimes she thinks, falling under his sway,
She got Mr. Tomorrow; she wants Mr. Today.

2. Love that new dress, you're looking real hot.
Let's go out dancing. Oh, wait, I forgot.
Me and my buddy, we got something to do.
But next week, I promise, it's just me and you.

Chorus.

3. Hey, I hardly know her, she's only a friend.
We've had lunch once or twice and that was the
    end.
I wouldn't have left that receipt in my pants
With something to hide. Why would I take that
    chance?

Chorus.

4. What happened last night, I was a fool.
I didn't mean it, I was in a bad mood.
I won't drink again, I promise, you'll see.
To think that I hit you—you know that's not me.

Chorus.

5. Sure, I want babies, I swear that it's true:
Pretty girls growing up to look just like you.
But waiting a while—that's what I'd prefer
Until we're both ready, what can it hurt?

Chorus.

I'm in the Mood (for Rock 'n' Roll)

(Slow tempo)
1. We've got a night together, we're sitting on the
     couch,
This doesn't happen often, alone inside our house.
You open up a real nice wine, the candle light is low.
We're both thinking of romance and where the
     night might go.

Chorus:
Now, baby, baby, baby—you better know it's true
I'm in the mood . . .
In the mood . . .
In the mood . . . for rock 'n' roll!

(Tempo and volume way up)

Sometimes it's the only way only way to fix your
     achin' soul:
Ditch the soft, crank up the loud and go with rock
     'n' roll.

Rock 'n' roll,
rock 'n' roll.
When you're down and when you're out and just
*   can't be consoled.*
Get yourself in the mood, the mood for rock 'n' roll.

2. You know that I'm a good girl . . . I don't do too
*   much wrong.*
I treat folks right, work real hard, playing tunes
*   and writing songs.*
But there's another side to me, that you don't see a
*   lot.*
I like to kick my shoes off and get crazy and get hot.

Chorus.

3. My iPod's filled with pop and jazz and Motown
*   and with blues*
And soul and folk and hip-hop, not to mention
*   country tunes.*
But there's times I just can't help it, I need a concert
*   hall*
filled with glam and spotlights and speakers twelve
*   feet tall.*

Chorus.

4. Way up high in heaven, the choir sits on clouds,
And plays their harps and trumpets, and makes
*   angelic sounds.*
But I just have this feeling that once or twice a year,
St. Pete digs out his Fender for all paradise to hear.

Ending Chorus:
Now, baby, baby, listen up—you better know it's
*   true*
He's in the mood . . .

In the mood . . .
In the mood . . . for rock 'n' roll!

Sometimes it's the only way to fix on achin' soul:
Ditch the soft, crank up the loud and go with rock
    'n' roll.
Rock 'n' roll,
rock 'n' roll.
When you're down and when you're out and just
    can't be consoled.
Get yourself in the mood, the mood for rock 'n' roll.

The Crew

Bobby Prescott	Traynor Davis
Tye Slocum	Sandy ("Scoop") Miller
Hector Garcia	Carole Ng
Sue Stevens	

The Band

Kevin Peebles, *lead guitar*
Emma Sue Granger, *guitar,*
    bass
guitar and vocals
Buddy Delmore, *National*
guitar, Dobro and pedal
    steel

Alonzo Santiago, *drums*
    and
    percussion
Sharon Bascowitz, *key-*
    board,
saxophone, oboe, cello and
    vocals
Kayleigh Towne, *guitar,*
    vocals

Produced by Barry Zeigler, BHMC Records.
With thanks to Alicia Sessions and Bishop Towne—Love
you, Daddy!

This album is dedicated to my niece,
Mary-Gordon Sanchez,
the cutest six-year-old on the planet!

Afterword

I'd like to express my appreciation to Ken Landers and Clay Stafford, American Blackguard Film and Television and the supremely talented musicians who made this project possible, especially our wonderful singer, Treva Blomquist. For details on all the personnel, go to my website or www.americanblackguard.com. Treva's website is www.trevamusic.com. A wonderful organization in North Carolina, Music Maker, also provided great assistance. Check out their website, www.musicmaker.org.

Thanks to my regular crew, Deborah, Cathy, Victoria, Vivienne, Betsy, Carolyn, Jamie, Francesca, Julie, Jane, Will, Tina . . . and, of course, Madelyn.

Finally, special thanks and all my best wishes to my friends at Simon & Schuster: Jessica Abell, Louise Burke, Amy Cormier, Jon Karp, Sarah Knight, Molly Lindley, Irene Lipsky, Phil Metcalf, Carolyn Reidy, Kelly Welsh and everyone else.

The lyrics to all the songs in this novel are © 2011 Jeffery W. Deaver.

CARTE BLANCHE

JEFFERY DEAVER

Available from Pocket Books

His hand on the dead-man throttle, the driver of the Serbian Rail diesel felt the thrill he always did on this particular stretch of railway, heading north from Belgrade and approaching Novi Sad.

This was the route of the famed Arlberg Orient Express, which ran from Greece through Belgrade and points north from the 1930s until the 1960s. Of course, he was not piloting a glistening Pacific 231 steam locomotive towing elegant mahogany-and-brass dining cars, suites and sleepers, where passengers floated upon vapors of luxury and anticipation. He commanded a battered old thing from America that tugged behind it a string of more or less dependable rolling stock packed snugly with mundane cargo.

But still he felt the thrill of history in every vista that the journey offered, especially as they approached the river, *his* river.

And yet he was ill at ease.

Among the wagons bound for Budapest, containing coal, scrap metal, consumer products and timber, there was one that worried him greatly. It was loaded with drums of MIC—methyl isocyanate—to be used in Hungary in the manufacture of rubber.

The driver—a round, balding man in a well-worn cap and stained overalls—had been briefed at length about this deadly chemical by his supervisor and some idiot from the Serbian Safety and Well-being Transportation

Oversight Ministry. Some years ago this substance had killed eight thousand people in Bhopal, India, within a few days of leaking from a manufacturing plant there.

He'd acknowledged the danger his cargo presented but, a veteran railway man and union member, he'd asked, "What does that mean for the journey to Budapest . . . specifically?"

The boss and the bureaucrat had regarded each other with the eyes of officialdom and, after a pause, settled for "Just be very careful."

The lights of Novi Sad, Serbia's second-largest city, began to coalesce in the distance, and ahead in the encroaching evening the Danube appeared as a pale stripe. In history and in music the river was celebrated. In reality it was brown, undramatic and home to barges and tankers, not candlelit vessels filled with lovers and Viennese orchestras—or not here, at least. Still, it *was* the Danube, an icon of Balkan pride, and the railway man's chest always swelled as he took his train over the bridge.

His river . . .

He peered through the speckled windscreen and inspected the track before him in the headlight of the General Electric diesel. Nothing to be concerned about.

There were eight notch positions on the throttle, number one being the lowest. He was presently at five and he eased back to three to slow the train as it entered a series of turns. The 4,000-horsepower engine grew softer as it cut back the voltage to the traction motors.

As the cars entered the straight section to the bridge the driver shifted up to notch five again and then six. The engine pulsed louder and faster and there came a series of sharp clangs from behind. The sound was, the driver knew, simply the couplings between wagons protesting at the change in speed, a minor cacophony he'd heard a thousand times in his job. But his imagination told him the noise was the metal containers of the deadly chemical in car number three, jostling against one another, at risk of spewing forth their poison.

Nonsense, he told himself and concentrated on keeping the speed steady. Then, for no reason at all, except that it made him feel better, he tugged at the air horn.

Lying at the top of a hill, surrounded by obscuring grass, a man of serious face and hunter's demeanor heard the wail of a horn in the distance, miles away. A glance told him that the sound had come from the train approaching from the south. It would arrive here in ten or fifteen minutes. He wondered how it might affect the precarious operation that was about to unfurl.

Shifting position slightly, he studied the diesel locomotive and the lengthy string of wagons behind it through his night-vision monocular.

Judging that the train was of no consequence to himself and his plans, James Bond turned the scope back to the restaurant of the spa and hotel and once again regarded his target through the window. The weathered building was large, yellow stucco with brown trim. Apparently it was a favorite with the locals, from the number of Zastava and Fiat saloons in the car park.

It was eight forty and the Sunday evening was clear here, near Novi Sad, where the Pannonian Plain rose to a landscape that the Serbs called "mountainous," though Bond guessed the adjective must have been chosen to attract tourists; the rises were mere hills to him, an avid skier. The May air was dry and cool, the surroundings as quiet as an undertaker's chapel of rest. Bond shifted position again. In his thirties, he was six feet tall and weighed 170 pounds. His black hair was parted on one side and a comma of loose strands fell over one eye. A three-inch scar ran down his right cheek.

This evening he'd taken some care with his outfit. He was wearing a dark green jacket and rainproof trousers from the American company 5.11, which made the best tactical clothing on the market. On his feet were well-worn leather boots that had been made for pursuit and sure footing in a fight.

As night descended, the lights to the north glowed more intensely: the old city of Novi Sad. As lively and charming as it was now, Bond knew the place had a dark past. After the Hungarians had slaughtered thousands of its citizens in January 1942 and flung the bodies into the icy Danube, Novi Sad had become a crucible for partisan resistance. Bond was here tonight to prevent another horror, different in nature but of equal or worse magnitude.

Yesterday, Saturday, an alert had rippled through the British intelligence community. GCHQ, in Cheltenham, had decrypted an electronic whisper about an attack later in the week.

> meeting at noah's office, confirm
> incident friday night, 20th, estimated
> initial casualties in the thousands, british
> interests adversely affected, funds
> transfers as discussed.

Not long after, the government eavesdroppers had also cracked part of a second text message, sent from the same phone, same encryption algorithm, but to a different number.

> meet me sunday at restaurant rostilj
> outside novi sad, 20:00. i am 6+ feet tall,
> irish accent.

Then the Irishman—who'd courteously, if inadvertently, supplied his own nickname—had destroyed the phone or flicked out the batteries, as had the other text recipients.

In London the Joint Intelligence Committee and

members of COBRA, the crisis management body, met into the night to assess the risk of Incident 20, so called because of Friday's date.

There was no solid information on the origin or nature of the threat but MI6 was of the opinion that it was coming out of the tribal regions in Afghanistan, where al-Qaeda and its affiliates had taken to hiring Western operatives in European countries. Six's agents in Kabul began a major effort to learn more. The Serbian connection had to be pursued, too. And so at ten o'clock last night the rangy tentacles of these events had reached out and clutched Bond, who'd been sitting in an exclusive restaurant off Charing Cross Road with a beautiful woman, whose lengthy description of her life as an underappreciated painter had grown tiresome. The message on Bond's mobile had read, NIACT, Call COS.

The Night Action alert meant an immediate response was required, at whatever time it was received. The call to his chief of staff had blessedly cut the date short and soon he had been en route to Serbia, under a Level 2 project order, authorizing him to identify the Irishman, plant trackers and other surveillance devices and follow him. If that proved impossible, the order authorized Bond to conduct an extraordinary rendition of the Irishman and spirit him back to England or to a black site on the Continent for interrogation.

So now Bond lay among white narcissi, taking care to avoid the leaves of that beautiful but poisonous spring flower. He concentrated on peering through the Restoran Roštilj's front window, on the other side of which the Irishman was sitting over an almost untouched plate and talking to his partner, as yet unidentified but Slavic in appearance. Perhaps because he was nervous, the local contact had parked elsewhere and walked here, providing no number-plate to scan.

The Irishman had not been so timid. His low-end Mercedes had arrived forty minutes ago. Its plate had revealed that the vehicle had been hired today for cash under a false name, with a fake British driving license and passport. The man was about Bond's age, perhaps a bit older, six foot two and lean. He'd walked into the restaurant in an ungainly way, his feet turned out. An odd line of blond fringe dipped over a high forehead and his cheekbones angled down to a square-cut chin.

Bond was satisfied that this man was the target. Two hours ago he had gone into the restaurant for a cup of coffee and stuck a listening device inside the front door. A man had arrived at the appointed time and spoken to the headwaiter in English—slowly and loudly, as foreigners often do when talking to locals. To Bond, listening through an app on his phone from thirty yards away, the accent was clearly mid-Ulster—most likely Belfast or the surrounding area. Unfortunately the meeting between the Irishman and his local contact was taking place out of the bug's range.

Through the tunnel of his monocular, Bond now studied his adversary, taking note of every detail—"Small clues save you. Small errors kill," as the instructors at Fort Monckton were wont to remind. He noted that the Irishman's manner was precise and that he made no unnecessary gestures. When the partner drew a diagram the Irishman moved it closer with the rubber of a propelling pencil so that he left no fingerprints. He sat with his back to the window and in front of his partner; the surveillance apps on Bond's mobile could not read either set of lips. Once, the Irishman turned quickly, looking outside, as if triggered by a sixth sense. The pale eyes were devoid of expression. After some time he turned back to the food that apparently didn't interest him.

The meal now seemed to be winding down. Bond

eased off the hillock and made his way through widely spaced spruce and pine trees and anemic undergrowth, with clusters of the ubiquitous white flowers. He passed a faded sign in Serbian, French and English that had amused him when he'd arrived:

SPA AND RESTAURANT ROŠTILJ

LOCATED IN A DECLARED THERAPEUTIC REGION, AND IS RECOMMENDED BY ALL FOR CONVALESCENCES AFTER SURGERIES, ESPECIALLY HELPING FOR ACUTE AND CHRONIC DISEASES OF RESPIRATION ORGANS, AND ANEMIA. FULL BAR.

He returned to the staging area, behind a decrepit garden shed that smelled of engine oil, petrol and piss, near the driveway to the restaurant. His two "comrades," as he thought of them, were waiting here.

James Bond preferred to operate alone but the plan he'd devised required two local agents. They were with the BIA, the Serbian Security Information Agency, as benign a name for a spy outfit as one could imagine. The men, however, were undercover in the uniform of local police from Novi Sad, sporting the golden badge of the Ministry of Internal Affairs.

Faces squat, heads round, perpetually unsmiling, they wore their hair close-cropped beneath navy-blue brimmed caps. Their woolen uniforms were the same shade. One was around forty, the other twenty-five. Despite their cover roles as rural officers, they'd come girded for battle. They carried heavy Beretta pistols and swaths of ammunition. In the backseat of their borrowed police car, a Volkswagen Jetta, there were two green-camouflaged Kalashnikov machine guns, an Uzi and a canvas bag of fragmentation hand grenades—serious ones, Swiss HG 85s.

Bond turned to the older agent but before he spoke he heard a fierce slapping from behind. His hand moving to his Walther PPS, he whirled round—to see the younger Serb ramming a pack of cigarettes into his palm, a ritual that Bond, a former smoker, had always found absurdly self-conscious and unnecessary.

What was the man *thinking*?

"Quiet," he whispered coldly. "And put those away. No smoking."

Perplexity sidled into the dark eyes. "My brother, he smokes all time he is out on operations. Looks more normal than *not* smoking in Serbia." On the drive here the young man had prattled on and on about his brother, a senior agent with the infamous JSO, technically a unit of the state secret service, though Bond knew it was really a black-ops paramilitary group. The young agent had let slip—probably intentionally, for he had said it with pride—that big brother had fought with Arkan's Tigers, a ruthless gang that had committed some of the worst atrocities in the fighting in Croatia, Bosnia and Kosovo.

"Maybe on the streets of Belgrade a cigarette won't be noticed," Bond muttered, "but this is a tactical operation. Put them away."

The agent slowly complied. He seemed about to say something to his partner, then thought better of it, perhaps recalling that Bond had a working knowledge of Serbo-Croatian.

Bond looked again into the restaurant and saw that the Irishman was laying some dinars on the metal tray— no traceable credit card, of course. The partner was pulling on a jacket.

"All right. It's time." Bond reiterated the plan. In the police car they would follow the Irishman's Mercedes out of the drive and along the road until he was a mile or so from the restaurant. The Serbian agents would then pull the car over, telling him it matched a vehicle used in a drug crime in Novi Sad. The Irishman would be asked politely to get out and would be handcuffed. His mobile phone, wallet and identity papers would be placed on the boot of the Mercedes and he'd be led aside and made to sit facing away from the car.

Meanwhile Bond would slip out of the backseat, photograph the documents, download what he could from the phone, look through laptops and luggage, then plant tracking devices.

By then the Irishman would have caught on that this was a shakedown and offered a suitable bribe. He'd be freed to go on his way.

If the local partner left the restaurant with him, they'd execute essentially the same plan with both men.

"Now, I'm ninety percent sure he'll believe you," Bond said. "But if not, and he engages, remember that under no circumstances is he to be killed. I need him alive. Aim to wound in the arm he favors, near the elbow, not the shoulder." Despite what one saw in the movies, a shoulder wound was usually as fatal as one to the abdomen or chest.

The Irishman now stepped outside, feet splayed. He looked around, pausing to study the area. Was anything different? he'd be thinking. New cars had arrived since they'd entered; was there anything significant about them? He apparently decided there was no threat and both men climbed into the Mercedes.

"It's the pair of them," Bond said. "Same plan."

"*Da.*"

The Irishman started the engine. The lights flashed on.

Bond oriented his hand on his Walther, snug in the D. M. Bullard leather pancake holster, and climbed into the backseat of the police car, noticing an empty tin on the floor. One of his comrades had enjoyed a Jelen Pivo, a Deer Beer, while Bond had been conducting surveillance. The insubordination bothered him less than the carelessness. The Irishman might grow suspicious when stopped by a cop with beer on his breath. Another man's ego and greed can be helpful, Bond believed, but incompetence is simply a useless and inexcusable danger.

The Serbs got into the front. The engine hummed to life. Bond tapped the earpiece of his SRAC, the short-range agent communication device used for cloaked radio transmissions on tactical operations. "Channel two," he reminded them.

"*Da, da.*" The older man sounded bored. They both plugged in earpieces.

And James Bond asked himself yet again: Had he planned this properly? Despite the speed with which the operation had been put together, he'd spent hours formulating the tactics. He believed he'd anticipated every possible variation.

Except one, it appeared.

The Irishman did not do what he absolutely had to.

He didn't leave.

The Mercedes turned *away* from the drive and rolled out of the car park on to the lawn beside the restaurant, on the other side of a tall hedge, unseen by the staff and diners. It was heading for a weed-riddled field to the east.

The younger agent snapped, "*Govno!* What he is doing?" The three men stepped out to get a better view. The older one drew his gun and started after the car.

Bond waved him to a halt. "No! Wait."

"He's escaping. He knows about us!"

"No—it's something else." The Irishman wasn't driving as if he were being pursued. He was moving slowly, the Mercedes easing forward, like a boat in a gentle morning swell. Besides, there was no place to escape *to*. He was hemmed in by cliffs overlooking the Danube, the railway embankment and the forest on the Fruška Gora rise.

Bond watched as the Mercedes arrived at the rail track, a hundred yards from where they stood. It slowed, made a U-turn and parked, the bonnet facing back toward the restaurant. It was close to a railway work shed and switch rails, where a second track peeled off from the main line. Both men climbed out and the Irishman collected something from the boot.

Your enemy's purpose will dictate your response—Bond silently recited another maxim from the lectures at Fort Monckton's Specialist Training Center in Gosport. You must find the adversary's intention.

But what *was* his purpose?

Bond pulled out the monocular again, clicked on the night vision and focused. The partner opened a panel mounted on a signal beside the switch rails and began fiddling with the components inside. Bond saw that the second track, leading off to the right, was a rusting, disused spur, ending in a barrier at the top of a hill.

So it was sabotage. They were going to derail the train by shunting it on to the spur. The cars would tumble down the hill into a stream that flowed into the Danube.

But why?

Bond turned the monocular toward the diesel engine and the wagons behind it and saw the answer. The first two cars contained only scrap metal, but behind them a canvas-covered flatbed was marked OPASNOST–DANGER! He saw, too, a hazardous-materials diamond, the universal warning sign that told emergency rescuers the risks of a particular shipment. Alarmingly, this diamond had high numbers for all three categories: health, instability and inflammability. The W at the bottom meant that the substance would react dangerously with water. Whatever was being carried in that car was in the deadliest category, short of nuclear materials.

The train was now three-quarters of a mile away from the switch rails, picking up speed to make the gradient to the bridge.

Your enemy's purpose will dictate your response. . . .

He didn't know how the sabotage related to Incident 20, if at all, but their immediate goal was clear—as was the response Bond now instinctively formulated. He said to the comrades, "If they try to leave, block them at the drive and take them. No lethal force."

He leaped into the driver's seat of the Jetta. He pointed the car toward the fields where he'd been conducting surveillance and jammed down the accelerator as he released the clutch. The light car shot forward, engine and gearbox crying out at the rough treatment, as it crashed over brush, saplings, narcissi and the raspberry bushes that grew everywhere in Serbia. Dogs fled and lights in the tiny cottages nearby flicked on. Residents in their gardens waved their arms angrily in protest.

Bond ignored them and concentrated on maintaining his speed as he drove toward his destination, guided only by scant illumination: a partial moon above and the doomed train's headlight, far brighter and rounder than the lamp of heaven.